SIMON SCARROW

BROTHERS IN BLOOD

headline

First published in Great Britain in 2014
by HEADLINE PUBLISHING GROUP

1

Cataloguing in Publication Data is available from the British Library

ISBN 978 0 7553 9393 0 (Hardback)
ISBN 978 0 7553 9394 7 (Trade Paperback)

Typeset in Bembo by Avon DataSet Ltd, Bidford-on-Avon, Warwickshire

Printed and bound in Great Britain by
Clays Ltd, St Ives plc

Papers used by Headline are from well-managed forests
and other responsible sources.

HEADLINE PUBLISHING GROUP
An Hachette UK Company
338 Euston Road
London NW1 3BH

www.headline.co.uk
www.hachette.co.uk

For my son Joseph,
who has become a man.

THE ROMAN ARMY
CHAIN OF COMMAND

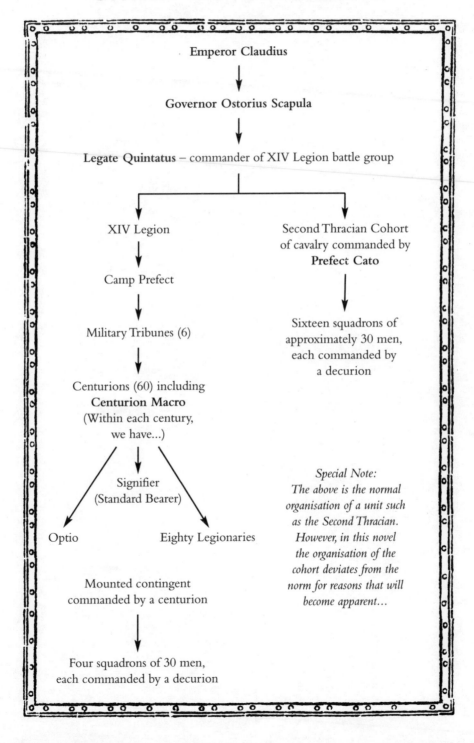

Emperor Claudius

↓

Governor Ostorius Scapula

↓

Legate Quintatus – commander of XIV Legion battle group

XIV Legion

↓

Camp Prefect

↓

Military Tribunes (6)

↓

Centurions (60) including
Centurion Macro
(Within each century,
we have...)

Signifier
(Standard Bearer)

Optio   Eighty Legionaries

Mounted contingent
commanded by a centurion

↓

Four squadrons of 30 men,
each commanded by a decurion

Second Thracian Cohort
of cavalry commanded by
Prefect Cato

↓

Sixteen squadrons of
approximately 30 men,
each commanded by
a decurion

Special Note:
The above is the normal
organisation of a unit such
as the Second Thracian.
However, in this novel
the organisation of the
cohort deviates from the
norm for reasons that will
become apparent...

THE ROMAN PROVINCE OF
BRITANNIA AD 52

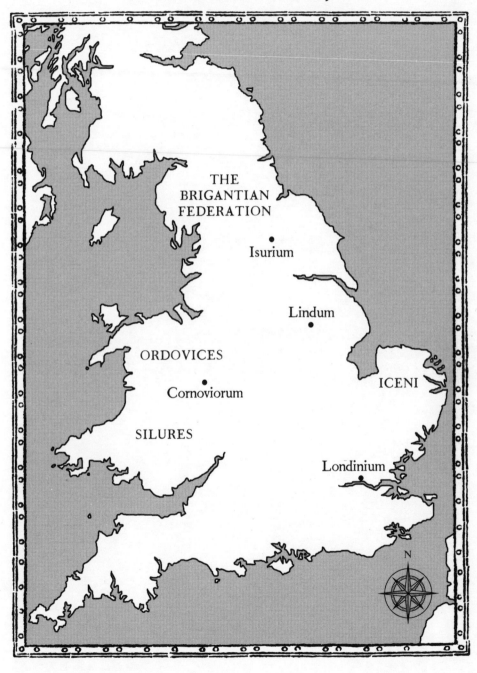

CHAPTER ONE

Rome, February AD *52*

The streets of the capital were filled with people enjoying the unseasonal warm sunshine. It was shortly after midday and the sun shone from a clear sky. Musa sensed that he was being followed even before he first caught sight of his pursuer. That was the instinct that had first drawn the attention of his master: the innate ability to sniff out danger. A priceless quality in his line of work. The small fortune that had been spent on training him since he had been plucked from the streets off the Aventine had honed his quick wits and swift reflexes.

He was as skilled as any agent working out of the imperial palace. He knew how to stalk and kill in silence. How to disfigure and dispose of a body so that there would be very little danger of any of his victims being found, let alone identified. He knew how to code and decode messages, which poisons worked most effectively and left no telltale traces. Musa knew how to tail a man through crowds and down almost deserted alleys without ever giving away his presence.

He had also been taught to spot when he in turn was being stalked. A moment earlier when he had stopped at a baker's stall on the edge of the Forum, appearing to all about him as just another customer eyeing up the arrangements of small loaves and pastries covering the stall, he had picked out the man: thin, dark-haired, in a plain brown tunic, who had also stopped, at a fruit stall fifteen paces back, and casually picked up a pear to scrutinise.

Musa kept him in view out of the corner of his eye, taking in every detail of his carefully anonymous appearance. After a moment he recalled seeing him in the street outside the house he had been sent to by his master earlier that morning, to convey a message. One that was too important to commit to paper, and that he had been required to memorise before setting out. His tail had been part of a group of men huddled round a dice game and he had stood up, stretched and sauntered down the street in the same direction as Musa, threading himself through the crowd. It was a detail he had observed and discounted at the time. But not any more. It was too much of a coincidence.

He smiled grimly to himself. Well then, the game was on. There were plenty of tricks he knew to lose the man. If he was any good he would see through most of them quickly enough. But Musa possessed one advantage that would give him the edge in the coming battle of wits: he had been born in these streets, had grown up in the gutter and spent most of his youth as a ragged orphan running with the street gangs. He knew every twist and turn of the streets and alleys of the vast city that sprawled across the seven hills crowding upon the fast currents of the River Tiber.

From the dark features of the man in the brown tunic Musa guessed that he was not a native of the city, but from somewhere in the eastern empire, or beyond. He could not hope to follow Musa through the maze of dark, stinking alleys of the Subura, the slum that stretched out beyond the Forum. He would lose his tail in there, and the gods help the man if he got lost while trying to follow his prey. The inhabitants of the Subura were a close-knit bunch and could smell an outsider a mile off, if only because they did not stink as much. He would be easy pickings for the first gang that decided to fall on him.

A flicker of pity crossed Musa's mind, and he banished it at once. There was no room for sentiment in this game. The other man's master was doubtless as ruthless as his own and he would just as willingly cut Musa's throat for no better reason than he had been ordered to. Musa's hand slipped down to his belt and his fingertips gently caressed the slight bulge of the knife concealed beneath the broad band of leather. He felt reassured and abruptly turned away from the baker's stall and made off at a swift pace towards the arch leading out of the Forum. He did not have to glance back to know that the man was following him. He had turned to look the moment Musa began to move.

As he pressed through the crowd, drawing sharp comments and vicious looks from some of those he brushed past, Musa felt his heart begin to beat more quickly. A queer mixture of excitement, fear and exhilaration filled his stomach. He passed under the arch, its curved ceiling echoing back the shuffle of sandals and brief exchanges of those beneath more distinctly than the hubbub of the city on either side. He turned to his left and trotted across to the opening of an alley leading towards the Subura. A short distance ahead of him a boy in a grubby tunic and a worn pair of sandals tied together with rags was squatting against a grimy wall festooned with crude graffiti, watching those passing by. A thief, Musa decided. He knew the type well enough and he reached into his purse for a bronze coin.

'Lad, there's a man in a brown tunic following me. If he comes this way tell him I took a different route, that alley over there.' Musa pointed across towards a steep lane heading in a different direction. He flipped the coin towards the boy who snatched it out of the air and nodded. Then Musa ducked into the alley leading towards the Subura. The gloomy thoroughfare was narrow and rubbish lay in small heaps along each side. There were far fewer people here and he broke into a run, keen to put as much distance between himself and his pursuer as soon as possible.

With luck he would have lost him at the arch. If his opponent was any good then he would suspect that Musa would try and escape him in the winding alleys of the Subura, and might well question the boy who had been watching those passing by. He might believe the lad's lie, and even if he didn't the moment's hesitation would delay his pursuit long enough for the trail to grow cold by the time he reached the slum district. Musa ran on for several hundred paces, turning to the right and left as he entered the crumbling tenement blocks that stretched high above, almost seeming intent on crushing the narrow sliver of sky that ran unevenly above the dark alleyways. Then he slowed to a walk and breathed deeply, wrinkling his nose in disgust at the foul odour of rotting food, shit, piss and sweat that he had once taken for granted.

Musa wondered how he could ever have stomached the squalor amid which he had grown up. Since then he had become used to the scented worlds of the rich and powerful, even if he only lived on its periphery, working in the shadows. Still, he remembered these narrow streets and alleys well enough to know exactly where he was and how he could work his way round the slum before resuming his way to the house on the Quirinal hill where his master was waiting for him. Here, in the Subura, there were other dangers to be aware of and Musa proceeded cautiously, watching each man, or group of men, who approached him along a street, weighing up any threat they might pose to him. But aside from a few hostile glances, they left him alone and he eventually reached the small square in the heart of the Subura where a large fountain supplied the locals with water from a spur leading off the Julian aqueduct.

As usual the square was crowded with women and children burdened with heavy jars sent to collect water for their families. Many had stopped to gossip. Among them were small groups of youths and men, sharing wineskins as they talked or played dice. Musa was wearing a plain black tunic and, aside from the neat trim of his hair and beard, did not stand out from the rest. He felt some of the tension ease from his body and approached the fountain. He leaned over the edge of the stonework and cupped his hands in the water and drank enough to slake the thirst he had worked up eluding his pursuer. Then he splashed some water over his face and stood up and stretched his shoulders with a sense of satisfaction that his skills had served him well again.

He turned away from the fountain, and froze.

The man in the brown tunic was standing no more than fifty feet away, beyond the press of people around the fountain. He was no longer attempting to blend in, but met Musa's gaze directly and smiled. The expression on the man's face chilled Musa's blood even as questions raced through his mind. How was this possible? How had the man kept up with him? How did he know where to find him? Perhaps he was a native of the city after all. Musa cursed himself for underestimating his opponent so completely.

Once again his hand slipped to his belt as he sought the reassurance of his blade now that the stakes had risen. This was no longer a matter of eluding the man. Now there was likely to be a confrontation, a far more dangerous prospect. Musa knew there was a lane that led from the square directly towards the street that climbed the Quirinal hill and he began to edge towards it, steeling himself for a sudden sprint. If he had not enough guile to escape his pursuer, then he would simply have to outrun him.

The man kept level with him as he worked his way out of the

crowd and then, as Musa's intentions became obvious, he smiled again and wagged a finger at him. For the first time Musa felt a feeling of dread, a chill that knotted itself into the back of his neck. The man nodded towards the lane and Musa glanced across the square and saw two burly figures emerge from the shadows and block his way.

'Fuck . . .' he muttered to himself. Three of them. Perhaps more. He could not fight his way out of the trap. Everything depended on his speed now. He moved back into the crowd where he hoped he would be safer for a moment and glanced round the square. There were four other routes open to him. He chose an alley opposite the two men and furthest from the first man. He recalled that it ran parallel to the road leading to the Quirinal. If he followed it far enough he could cut up towards the safety of his master's house. Musa steeled himself and took a deep breath before he burst into a run, thrusting people out of his way. The air behind him filled with the angry curses of those he had knocked aside but he paid them no heed. He emerged from the crowd and dashed across the grimy flagstones towards the opening to the alley. He heard another shout above the din behind.

'Go! Get after him!'

Musa reached the entrance to the alley and plunged into the gloom. For a moment the contrast with the brighter light of the square made it difficult to see the way, but he ran on regardless, hoping that he would not trip, or blunder into someone, or his boots lose their grip on the filth-encrusted paving stones. Then his eyes began to adjust and he picked out the details ahead of him. The small arched doorways, the entrances to tiny businesses struggling to survive on what profits were left to them after the gangs of the Subura had taken their dues. A handful of raddled women and men draped in rags held out their hands and mumbled requests for food or money and he dodged round them as the sound of his pursuers chased him along the alley. Musa gritted his teeth and urged his legs on with a growing sense of desperation.

Fifty paces ahead a shaft of light penetrated the gloom as the sun shone down the wider street that led towards the Quirinal and Musa felt a flicker of hope in his heart. If he could stay ahead of the men for another quarter of a mile he would reach safety. The junction neared and he welcomed the bright glow of the sunlight piercing the dark world of the slum. He was only ten paces from the corner when he felt a sharp blow to his shin and then he was hurtling through the air. He threw his hands out and landed heavily in the narrow channel running down the centre of the alley where foul puddles of waste lay. The impact drove the air from his lungs and for an instant Musa lay gasping for breath as his ribs burned with pain. He knew he must move and forced himself on to his knees. The thud of boots filled the air and he reached for his knife as he struggled to stand, straining to breathe. The blade came out and he began to turn, determined to strike at his enemy.

Instead a boot lashed out, smashing into his hand, and the knife dropped from his numbed fingers. Another boot struck him in the side, knocking him over and driving what little air was left in his lungs out with an agonising grunt. Musa lay doubled up, mouth open, straining to breathe as he looked up. There was the man in the brown tunic, with one of his thugs on each flank in a half crouch, fists bunched. Musa could not see what had caused him to fall and the look of pained confusion on his face made the man smile.

'Too bad, Musa, me old cock. You put on a decent effort. But it's over now, nay?' He looked up, over Musa's shoulder and grinned. 'Good work, Petulus. Out you come, lad.'

A shadow separated from a doorway to the side of the street and moved into the light and Musa saw a small ragged urchin clutching a length of wood. He recognised him at once. The boy he had tipped a coin to misdirect his pursuer. He had been part of the pursuit all along. Not only that, but Musa now realised that he had been steered into this precise alley where the boy had lain in wait. It was a well-worked trap. As good as anything he could have arranged. Better even. He shook his head and rolled on to his back.

'Get him up, boys.'

Rough hands grasped Musa's limbs and hauled him on to his feet. A hand reached out and lifted his chin sharply. He saw the man in the brown tunic standing squarely in front of him. 'Someone wants a little word with you, Musa.'

Musa stared back, teeth gritted. Then, without warning, he spat in the man's face. 'Fuck you,' he gasped. 'And fuck that Greek piece of shit you work for!'

A glint of anger flared in the man's face before he smiled coldly. 'The same piece of shit your master is carved from, my friend.'

Then he nodded and a dark piece of sacking dropped over Musa's head. He smelled olives briefly before there was a dazzling white explosion of light and sharp pain and then everything went dark.

CHAPTER TWO

'That's a nasty blow.' A voice penetrated his dazed mind. 'You better not have scrambled the bastard's brains.'

Musa groaned and rolled his head to the side. He opened his eyes a crack and saw that he was in a stone cell, lit by the pale yellow glow of oil lamps. His head was pounding and the movement sent a wave of nausea sweeping through his guts. He was lying on his back; a wooden table from the touch of his fingers. He tried to move his hand but felt the tug of restraints. It was the same with his other hand and feet and he lay still, feigning half-consciousness as his mind struggled to think coherently through the shattering pain in his head. His shin also throbbed and he recalled the boy with a sense of betrayal mixed with self-contempt for having been taken in by him.

'Just a tap on the head, that's all we gave him,' a voice growled and Musa recognised it as belonging to the man leading the party who had caught him. 'He'll be right as rain when he fully comes round.'

'He's moving. Musa's awake.'

Musa heard footsteps approaching and a pair of hands grasped the neck hem of his tunic and gave him a shake.

'Eyes open, Musa. Time to talk.'

He fought the urge to respond and played dead. The man shook him again and then slapped the side of his head.

Musa blinked his eyes open and squinted slightly. He saw the man leaning over him nod with satisfaction.

'He's good.'

'Then let's not waste any time. Go and fetch Ancus.'

'Right, chief.' The man went away and Musa heard footsteps, then a door opening and the sound of sandals climbing steps. He turned his head and saw the full extent of the room for the first time. It was a low-ceilinged chamber, below ground, he assumed, from the dankness of the air, the lack of natural light and the quiet. Two lamp-holders were suspended from the ceiling, each bearing two brass oil lamps that provided the dull illumination. Besides the table, there appeared to be only one other item of furniture: a small bench upon which lay a set of tools, glinting in the lamplight. Beside the table, his head hidden in shadow, stood a thin man in a clean white tunic and calfskin boots that stretched halfway up his shins. The man stood silently for a moment before speaking in a soft, dry tone, too quietly for Musa to identify his voice.

'Before you even think about it, I should say that any shout or cry that you may make will never be heard by a soul outside of this room. We are in a cellar of a safe house.'

Musa felt a tremor of fear ripple down his spine. There was only one reason why someone would want to have access to such a place. He glanced at the bench again and understood what the tools were for.

'Good,' said the other man. 'You realise what's coming. I won't insult your undoubted intelligence by saying that you will tell us what we want to know in the end. If your master has trained you as well as I have trained my men, you will present something of a challenge. I should warn you that there is no better man than Ancus in his field. Given enough time he could make a rock talk. And you, Musa, are no rock. Just a thing of flesh and blood. A weak thing. You have vulnerabilities, like every man. Ancus will discover them in the end, just as surely as day follows night. You will tell us what we want to know. The only question that matters is how long you can hold out. We have plenty of time to find out the answer to that. Or you could talk now and save us all from an unpleasant experience.'

Musa let his mouth open a fraction to curse the man, then clamped his lips shut again. One of the first things he had been taught about such situations was that it was vital not to utter a single word. The moment you spoke, you opened the door to further exchanges and aside from the danger of letting slip snippets of information, it provided the interrogator with the opportunity to establish a relationship and a means of working his way into your thoughts to play on your weaknesses. Better to say nothing at all.

9

'I see,' the other man said. 'Then we must proceed.'

In the tense silence that fell between them the only sound that intruded was the steady drip of water on the other side of the chamber. All the time the other man did not move, but stood still, his face concealed. Eventually Musa heard the distant approach of footsteps, then the steady slap of sandals on the steps outside. The door opened and two men entered, the one he already knew, and a squat, powerfully built man with closely cropped hair and scarred features. At first Musa thought that he must have been a gladiator but then he saw the mark of Mithras on the man's brow and put him down as a soldier.

'He's all yours, Ancus,' the man in the shadows said.

Ancus cuffed his nose and looked Musa over. 'What do you want from him, master?'

'I want to know why he was visiting the house of Vespasian. And I want to know what designs our good friend Pallas has on the campaign in Britannia. I want the names of any agents Pallas has in that province and what their precise orders are.'

Ancus nodded. 'Anything else?'

'That will do for now.'

Ancus nodded, approached the table and leaned over Musa. 'I expect you know the form. I'm a stickler for following procedure so we'll start with the horrors, eh?'

He crossed to the bench and considered the tools of his trade before making a few selections and returning to the table where he laid them down beside Musa.

'Here we go. Thought we'd start with the feet and work up.' He held up a pair of iron pincers and winked. 'For the toes. After that I'll flay the skin back to your ankles.' He held up a surgeon's knife and a pair of slender meat hooks. 'Then I'll break your legs and break your knees with this.' He showed Musa an iron bar. 'If that don't loosen yer tongue then it's off with your cock and balls, my friend. Trust me, you'll want to speak before I do that.'

Musa forced himself to control his expression and stare back impassively. A bead of sweat broke free from his hairline and ran across his forehead. The interrogator reached a stubby finger out and delicately lifted the drop from Musa's skin.

'Not so brave as we make out, eh?' He chuckled and licked the drop of sweat from his finger before he picked up the pincers and moved down towards Musa's feet. Musa gritted his teeth and strained every muscle in his body as he fought to control his terror over what was to come. Then he felt a hand seize his foot and hold it tightly. Musa squirmed, twisting his foot as violently as he could one way, then the other, trying to loosen the grip.

'Hey, Septimus, make yourself useful. Hold that still.'

The man in the brown tunic stepped up and grasped Musa's foot and wrestled it to stillness. Musa felt the metal close round his big toe, pressing on the flesh and bone. Ancus took a sharp intake of breath and pressed on the arms of the pincers. A loud cracking snap cut through the grunts of Septimus and Musa's face twisted up into an expression of torment.

'Let me know when he's ready to talk,' said the man in the shadows. 'I'll be upstairs.'

He moved out of the alcove and Musa blinked away the tears in his eyes so that he might see the man better, and his heart sank as he caught sight of the thin, dark features of the imperial secretary of Emperor Claudius. Narcissus, so long the real power behind the throne, but now challenged by his rival, Pallas. The latter was Musa's employer. He aimed to eliminate Narcissus the moment the Emperor died and power passed to his adopted son, Nero. Pallas had already wormed his way into the bed of Nero's mother. It was only a matter of time before he controlled Agrippina as thoroughly as Narcissus had once controlled Claudius. The men were the most bitter of rivals, Musa knew, and that meant that he would be spared no agony until he told Narcissus what he wanted to hear. He felt the pincers shift to the next toe and saw Narcissus glance back with a look of disgust as he left the chamber, just as a second toe bone snapped between the iron jaws of Ancus's pincers.

The sun had set by the time Septimus climbed the steps to find his master. He was rubbing his hands clean on a strip of Musa's tunic as he entered the small kitchen above the chamber. Narcissus was alone, sitting on a simple stool by a table, an empty platter and clay beaker beside him, bearing the remains of a meal he had bought from a nearby market when the screams from below had become too irritating.

'He's ready to talk.'

'About time, nay? I was beginning to lose faith in Ancus.'

'No call for that, Father. He was doing his best. The truth is Musa was a hard man to break.'

Narcissus nodded. 'That's good. If we can turn him, then he might be a useful asset in time.'

'If not?'

'Then he'll be another casualty of the conflict between myself and that bastard, Pallas. Let's hope we can persuade Musa to pick the right side. Come on.'

Narcissus led his son down into the system of cellars beneath the safe house and descended the steps into the chamber where Ancus was waiting with his victim. Narcissus averted his gaze from the bloodied ruin of Musa's legs and snapped. 'Cover that mess up!'

Ancus pursed his lips but did as he was told and reached for the torn remains of Musa's tunic and arranged it over the man's legs as best he could. When he was done, Narcissus approached the table, trying not to notice the blood spattered across it and dripping on to the floor, nor the gobbets of flesh and strips of skin. Narcissus struggled to contain his frustration. Musa was in a pitiful state, staring wide-eyed at the ceiling as his body trembled. He was beyond saving. Any thought of turning him was pointless. Musa was muttering a prayer as Narcissus leaned over him.

'They tell me you are ready to talk.'

Musa did not seem to notice him and Narcissus leaned a little closer and took the man gently by the jaw and turned his face so that their eyes met.

'Musa, I want the answers to my questions. Are you ready?'

There was a blank look in the man's eyes and then recognition and a struggle to concentrate before he nodded, swallowed, and replied, 'Yes.'

Narcissus smiled. 'That's better. Now then, this morning you set out from the palace at first light to visit a house on the Aventine.'

'Was it only . . . this morning?'

'Yes,' Narcissus replied patiently. 'You were followed by Septimus here, who managed to stay with you without being spotted. This time.' He glanced at his agent son and Septimus had the good grace to

look embarrassed. 'Although you took the usual precautions, changing pace, doubling back and so on, Septimus stayed with you and saw you enter the house of Senator Vespasian. Now, I know that the good senator has been spending the last few months at his villa at Stabiae. There are rumours that all is not well between him and his wife, sadly. So I assume that the reason for your visit was to see his wife Flavia, nay?'

Musa stared at him a moment and nodded.

'Then please tell me that it isn't because you've taken a leaf out of your master's book and decided to screw someone above your social station.'

Ancus chuckled until the imperial secretary shot him an angry look and he fell silent and turned his attention to rinsing his instruments clean in a small bowl of stained water. Narcissus turned his attention back to the man lying on the table.

'So what was your business with Flavia?'

'A . . . message, from Pallas.'

'I see, and what was this message?'

'My master asks her for her support . . . when Nero comes to the throne.'

'More *if* than *when*, my friend. Your master is fooling himself if he thinks he can draw on the support of Flavia and her circle of associates. Contrary to the face she so carefully presents to the public, the woman is a fervent republican. She'd sooner devour her children than support your scheming snake of a master. The lovely Flavia has been most useful in drawing traitors out of the shadows to join her conspiracy against the Emperor, never suspecting that I watch her every move.' He paused and stroked his cheek. 'Tell me, what did Pallas promise Flavia in return for her support?'

'Preferment . . . for her husband. When Nero comes to . . . power.'

'The poet emperor and the professional soldier. I doubt there would be much in the way of small talk there. Besides, Vespasian seems to make his own fortune in this world. An admirable man in many ways, but there's more than a spark of ambition there as well. He will need to be watched, and I have just the agent for the job. There's not a man born who can resist the charms of young Caenis. My dear Musa, I fear your visit to Vespasian's house has been a waste of time. Your master,

13

Pallas, has put you at great risk for nothing. He has caused you this torment on little more than a speculative whim. All that you have endured here today can be blamed on him. On his poor judgement. Surely you can see that?'

Narcissus scrutinised Musa's expression, looking for any sign of the doubt he was trying to plant. The business with Flavia was no more than a ploy, the chink in his opponent's armour that he wanted to prise open to reveal the secrets he was really after.

Musa's expression suddenly screwed up and he clenched his teeth as he struggled to contain a fresh wave of agony. The imperial secretary indulged him, waiting patiently for the pain to subside before he pressed him again.

'Musa, you are being used by Pallas. He regards you as nothing more than a worthless tool to be thrown away on the chance of securing the goodwill of Flavia. Think on that. How little regard he has for you. You are a good man, I can see that. Every bit as skilful as the best of my agents. There would be a place for you at my side, when you recover. I swear it. Serve me and you will be treated with respect and rewarded well.' He cupped Musa's cheek in his hand. 'Do you understand?'

Musa stared up at him, and a tear rolled from the corner of one eye. He swallowed and nodded weakly.

'There,' Narcissus said soothingly. 'I'm glad you've seen sense. It pains me to see what has been done to you. After we've spoken I'll have you moved to a comfortable room in my house, and your wounds will be treated. When you've fully recovered we'll talk about finding you a position in my organisation.'

Musa closed his eyes and nodded weakly.

'There's one other thing, before we leave this place,' Narcissus continued. 'I need to know what Pallas is up to in Britannia. Has he spoken of his plans for the new province?'

'Yes . . .'

'I think you should tell me about it,' Narcissus coaxed gently. 'If you are to work for me there must be no secrets between us, my friend. Tell me.'

Musa was silent for a moment, steeling himself to control his pain before he spoke. He did not open his eyes as he spoke, breathing

14

shallow breaths as he kept his body as still as possible in order to prevent the pain worsening.

'Pallas wants the campaign to fail . . . He wants Rome to withdraw from Britannia.'

'Why?' Septimus intervened.

'Shhh!' Narcissus silenced him. 'Stay back and keep your mouth shut.' He turned back to Musa. 'Continue, my friend. Why would Pallas want us to leave the island?'

'He seeks to undermine Claudius . . . If the legions withdraw then it will embarrass the Emperor, and his legitimate son, Britannicus.'

'And it will undermine me, of course.'

'Yes.'

Narcissus smiled. That was the real reason for Pallas's scheme. It had little to do with the Emperor, who was old and would die within a matter of years, if not months, in any case. It had everything to do with eliminating any rivals for the position of closest adviser to the Emperor when Nero took the throne. Since Narcissus had supported the invasion and worked hard to win round the senators who had doubted the wisdom of the conquest of Britannia, any withdrawal from the island would destroy his reputation and influence at the imperial court. It would also damage Prince Britannicus who had been named for the conquest of the island. Who would support the cause of an emperor named after an island that had effectively defied the will of Rome?

Narcissus drew a deep breath before he pressed on with his interrogation. 'How does Pallas intend to achieve his aim?'

'He has sent an agent . . . to conspire with Caratacus . . . and a powerful noble of the northern tribes . . . If Caratacus can unite them . . . then our legions cannot win . . . The province must fall.'

'The name of the agent? What is his name? Speak.'

Musa shook his head and winced. 'I do not know. Pallas did not say.'

Narcissus hissed and stood up with an exasperated expression.

'There's more . . . Something more you should know,' Musa muttered.

'What?'

'The agent has another purpose . . . To eliminate two of your men.'

15

'My men?' Narcissus cocked an eyebrow. 'I have no agents in Britannia.'

'Pallas thinks otherwise . . . He means to kill two officers he knows are linked to you.'

'Who?'

Musa struggled to concentrate before he spoke again. 'Quintus Licinius Cato . . . and Lucius Cornelius Macro.'

'Those two?' Narcissus could not repress a chuckle. 'They don't work for me. Not any more. Pallas is wasting his time if he thinks their deaths will harm me. Besides, I pity any of his agents that decide to cross swords with those two. Is that it? Is there anything else to tell me?'

Musa licked his lips and shook his head slightly. 'No, that is all.'

'You've done well, my friend.' Narcissus patted his hand. 'Now it's time to rest. Time to recover.'

The corners of Musa's lips twitched in a brief smile of relief and his body relaxed. Narcissus released his hand and moved away, over towards the door, and he gestured to Septimus to join him.

'So now we know.'

'What are you going to do about it?' his son asked quietly. 'We have to warn General Ostorius.'

'I think not. Better he is not aware of it. The matter needs to be dealt with quietly. We need to send our own man after Pallas's agent. Track him down and put an end to his scheme. At the same time he can get a warning to Cato and Macro.' He gave a wry smile. 'I rather think they will be unhappy to receive any news from me, but it's only fair to warn them. Besides, I may have some need of their services again at some point. We shall see.'

Septimus shrugged, then asked, 'Who will you send?'

Narcissus turned to him and looked his agent up and down. 'I suggest you buy some warm clothes, my boy. From what I hear, the climate in Britannia is inclement at the best of times.'

'Me? You can't be serious.'

'Who else can I trust?' Narcissus spoke in an urgent undertone. 'I'm hanging on to my position at the Emperor's side by my fingernails. I'm no fool, my son. I know that some of my agents have already gone over to Pallas, and others are thinking about it. You are the best of my men, and the only one I can fully trust, if only because you are my son. It has to be you. If I could send someone else, I would, believe me. Do you understand?'

He stared intently into Septimus's eyes, almost pleading, and the young man nodded reluctantly.

'Yes, Father.'

Narcissus squeezed his shoulder affectionately. 'Good. Now I have to return to the palace. The Emperor will expect to see me at dinner. You take charge here. Get this place cleaned up and pay Ancus off.'

Septimus jerked his thumb towards the table. 'What about him?'

Narcissus glanced at the mangled agent of his enemy. 'He's no further use to us. Nor anyone else. Cut his throat, make his face unrecognisable and dump the body in the Tiber. It's likely that Pallas is already aware that he has gone missing. I'd rather Musa disappeared. That should discomfort that preening bastard, Pallas. See to it.'

CHAPTER THREE

Britannia, July

'Dear me, I can see that this one's had a lot of wear and tear,' the Syrian tutted as he examined Cato's cuirass, running his fingers across the dents and rust gathering in the grooves between the muscled design. He turned the cuirass round to look at the backplate. 'That's in better shape. As you would expect from one of the Emperor's most fearless officers. The exploits of Prefect Quintus Licinius Cato are legend.'

Cato exchanged a sardonic glance with his companion, Centurion Macro, before he responded. 'At least amongst the ranks of armour merchants.'

The Syrian bowed his head modestly and set the cuirass down and turned to face Cato with an apologetic expression. 'Sadly, sir, I think it would cost more to recondition this armour than it is worth. Of course, I would be pleased to give you a fair price if you were to trade it in against a new set of armour.'

'A fair price, I bet,' Macro chipped in from the comfort of his chair where he stretched out his legs in front of him and folded his thick arms. 'Don't listen to him, Cato. I'm sure I can get one of the lads down the armourer's forge to knock it into shape for a fraction of the price this scoundrel will charge for a replacement.'

'Of course you could, noble Centurion,' the Syrian responded smoothly. 'But every knock, as you put it, that is added to this cuirass weakens the whole. It makes the armour brittle in places.' He turned to Cato with a solicitous look. 'My dear sir, I could not sleep easily knowing that you had gone to war against the savage warriors of these lands wearing armour that might imperil your life and rob Rome of the services of one of its finest officers.'

Macro gave a cynical guffaw from the other side of Cato's tent. 'Don't let the rascal sweet-talk you, there's nothing wrong with the armour that a little bit of work won't put right. Might not look the best on parade but it's good enough to do its job.'

Cato nodded, but as he looked at the cuirass lying on the table, it was obvious it had seen better days. He had bought it, together with the rest of his armour and weapons, from the stores of the London garrison when they had returned to Britannia earlier in the year. It had been a cheap, hurried purchase and the quartermaster had explained that there had only been one previous, careful owner, a tribune of the Ninth Legion, who had only worn the armour for ceremonial occasions, favouring a mail vest when on duty. It was only when the lacquer and polish had begun to wear away that the lie had been exposed. As Macro had commented, it was more than likely that the cuirass had seen service back in Julius Caesar's time.

Cato sucked in a deep breath as he came to a decision. 'What's it worth?'

A slight smile flickered across the merchant's lips and he folded his hands together as if considering the prospect. 'I think it might be best to consider what you would replace the armour with before we agree on a trade-in price, noble sir.'

He turned to the chest his slaves had carried into the prefect's tent. With a deft flick of his wrists he undid the catches and raised the lid. Inside there were a number of bundles of thick wool. The merchant turned a few flaps back before he selected two and placed them on the table, beside Cato's cuirass. Then he folded the cloth back to reveal a mail vest and a gleaming fish-scale vest. Stepping aside so that his customer could see the pieces, he waved his hand over his offerings.

'Sir, I give you the finest armour you can buy anywhere in the empire, and at the most reasonable prices you will find. On that you have the word of Cyrus of Palmyra.' He touched his heart.

Macro nodded. 'That's set my mind at rest, then. Bound to get yourself a fine bargain here, Cato.'

The merchant ignored his customer's cynical friend and beckoned the prefect towards the table. Cato stared down at the sets of armour for a moment and then reached down and picked up a corner of the mail shirt, feeling its weight.

'Lighter than you thought, eh?' The merchant ran his fingers over the metal rings. 'Most mail armour is made out of cheap iron, but not this. The manufacturer is a cousin of mine, Patolomus of Damascus. You have heard of his work, I am sure.'

'Who hasn't?' Macro asked drily.

'My cousin has perfected a new metal, with a higher copper content to make it lighter without sacrificing its integrity. Why not try it on and see for yourself, noble Prefect? No obligation to purchase at all.'

Cato traced the tips of his fingers over the armour and then nodded. 'Why not?'

'Allow me, sir.' The Syrian swept up the mail vest and expertly bundled the fall and clenched his fingers round the heavy mass as he held it up. Cato stooped to get his head through the neck opening and then tucked his thumbs in as he eased his hands into the short arms of the vest. The merchant worked the mail down and gave it a final brush with his hand as if to ease out an imaginary crease and then stood back and folded his hands under his thin, pointed beard. 'Even though it is a humble mail vest it fits you like the finest goatskin glove, sir! Elegant! So elegant.'

Cato turned to a small camp table where he kept his mirror, brushes, strigils and the Samian-ware pot containing the scented oil he used for his ablutions. Holding the polished brass mirror out at arm's length he inspected himself critically. The mail was fringed with a serrated tip pattern and hung well on his slight frame. The metal was of a lighter hue than normal mail and gleamed dully in the daylight streaming in through the tent flaps.

'Comfortable, is it not?' the Syrian purred. 'You could march in that all day and fight a battle at the end of it and be only half as tired as you would be wearing your old cuirass. And it does not hamper your movements as much. A warrior needs to flow in his movements, no? This armour will give you the freedom of an Achilles, noble sir.'

Cato twisted on his hips and tried a few movements with his arms. It was true that the mail felt a little less cumbersome than mail vests he had worn in the past. He turned to his friend. 'What do you think?'

Macro cocked his head slightly to the side and looked Cato up and down. 'It looks like a good fit, my lad, but what matters is how good it is at keeping out the weapons of your enemies. Mail is good enough for the slash of a sword, even though a decent blow will break the bones beneath. The real danger is from the point. A decent javelin or arrowhead will pierce mail easily enough.'

'Not this vest,' the merchant intervened, and pinched a fold of the mail. 'If I may explain, sir? See here, the links are riveted. That gives added strength and will keep the barbarous points of your enemy at bay. Your learned companion, the formidable Centurion Macro, will surely know that a riveted vest is far, far better than those whose rings are merely butted up, or overlapped. Moreover, as you can see, the rings are smaller, making it harder still to pierce this superb example of my cousin's fine workmanship.'

Cato tilted his head to look at the mail on his shoulder. It was as the merchant said: each ring sealed with a tiny rivet, a time-consuming process that meant that it took far longer to produce this vest than those worn by the majority of soldiers in the legions and auxiliary units. That would be reflected in the cost of it, he reflected as he chewed his lip. He had recently received his first pay since landing in Britannia nearly four months before. It had been six months since he had officially been appointed to the rank of prefect, with an annual wage of twenty thousand denarii. He had drawn five thousand in advance to cover the modest wedding feast following his marriage to Julia, and to pay for his kit and travel to take up his command. The dowry paid by her father, Senator Sempronius, had been left with Julia so that she could buy them a small house in Rome, furnish and staff it and have enough on deposit to live off the interest until Cato returned, or sent for her. Meanwhile he had received the second quarterly payment of his salary and could afford to buy some new kit.

Not having the benefit of coming from a wealthy family, like many men of his rank in the army, Cato was growing conscious of the simpleness of his small wardrobe and his armour. He was not unaware of the haughty glances cast at him by some of the other officers every time General Ostorius summoned his subordinates to the daily briefings at his command tent. Despite his fine military record, there had been no mistaking the disdain in the voices of those who placed more value on aristocratic lineage than raw ability and proven achievements. Even the general himself had made little secret of his disapproval of the youngest auxiliary cohort commander in his army.

That, Cato was certain, lay behind the general's decision to put him in charge of guarding the army's baggage train. The baggage escort comprised the survivors of the garrison of the fort at Bruccium, a wing of Thracian cavalry, brigaded with Macro's cohort of legionaries from the Fourteenth Legion. Both units had suffered heavy losses during the siege of the fort and there was little chance of being assigned to other duties before the end of the campaign season when the army went into winter quarters. Until then, Cato, Macro and their men would trudge along with the carts, wagons and the camp followers towards the end of General Ostorius's column which was wending its way into the heart of the mountainous lands of the Silurian tribe.

They were pursuing the enemy commander, Caratacus, and his army comprised of Silurian and Ordovician warriors, together with small bands of fighters from other tribes who had chosen to continue fighting the Romans. It was the general's intention to run Caratacus to ground and force him to give battle. When that happened, the natives would be no match for the professionals of the Roman army. The enemy would be crushed, their leader killed or captured, and the new province of Britannia could finally be regarded as pacified, nearly nine years after Claudius's legions had first landed on the island.

'Well, noble sir?' The Syrian merchant broke into his thoughts. 'Is the mail to your liking?'

'It fits well enough,' Cato conceded. 'What does it cost?'

'I would normally ask no less than three thousand sestertians for such a piece of equipment, sir. But, in view of your fame, and the honour you do me in serving you, I would accept two thousand, eight hundred.'

That was far more than Cato had expected. Over three years' pay for a legionary. However, his existing armour was no longer suitable for battle and there were only a handful of armour dealers amongst the camp followers, and with little competition they were bound to charge a premium.

Macro choked. 'Two thousand eight hundred? Fuck off!'

The merchant raised his hands placatingly. 'It is the finest mail armour in the province, sir. Worth twice the modest price I am asking.'

Macro turned to his friend. 'Don't listen to the greedy little bastard. The mail's not worth half that.'

Cato cleared his throat. 'I'll deal with it, if you don't mind, Centurion.'

Macro opened his mouth to protest before his ingrained sense of discipline took control of him and he nodded curtly. 'As you wish, sir.'

Cato eased the chain mail back over his head, with the help of the merchant, and set it down beside the scale armour. 'What about that?'

'Ah, your discerning eye has no doubt observed that this, too, is the work of my cousin.' Cyrus hefted the scale armour and held it up for his customer to see as he continued. 'For the same modest price as the mail, this will give you even better protection, sir, with the added lustre of the impression you will create on the battlefield as your foes are dazzled by the gleam of your silvered magnificence.' The light gleamed off the polished scales which reminded Cato of the skin of a freshly caught fish. He could well imagine himself in battle, standing out amid the throng, where his men could see him clearly. Therein lay the problem, since he would stand out equally well to any enemy determined to strike down a Roman officer. All the same, Cato mused, it would give him a certain dash when he put in his appearance amongst the ranks of the senior officers.

'Ahem.' Macro cleared his throat. 'Could you use some advice, sir?'

Cato tore his eyes from the scale vest. 'Well?'

Macro stepped towards the merchant who was still holding the scale vest up to the sunlight to show it to best advantage. Lifting the hem, Macro tapped a finger on the thick leather jerkin to which the scales had been sewn. 'There's your problem. A scale vest is a good piece of kit in a dry climate. As our Syrian friend says, it offers better protection, but what happens when it rains, eh? This leather will soak up the water and add as much again to the weight of the vest. You'll be clapped out before you know it.'

'But summer is on us,' said Cato.

'And that means it won't rain, I suppose.' Macro shook his head. 'You know what the weather's like on this bloody island. It's wetter than the cunny of a Suburan whore at the games.'

Cato smiled. 'Sounds like you've been reading Ovidius again.'

Macro shook his head. 'No need for the theory when you know the practice. Same as anything in life.'

'Spoken like a soldier.'

Macro bowed his head. 'I thank you.'

Cato turned his attention back to the scale armour. He was very tempted to buy it, largely because it would give him a distinguished appearance in the eyes of those officers who scorned him. And yet that might be the cause of even more disdain, he feared. His fine new armour would merely give them fresh cause to sneer at the common soldier who had risen so far above his station in life. Reluctantly he gestured towards the mail.

'I'll have that.'

The merchant smiled and placed the scale shirt back into its blanket and hurriedly returned it to the chest. 'Two thousand eight hundred then, my dear Prefect.'

'Two thousand five hundred.'

Cyrus looked pained and his dark brows knitted together in a brief frown. 'Come, sir, you jest with me. I am an honest businessman. I have a family to feed and a reputation to uphold. There is no armour you could buy for that price that would match the quality of my cousin's work. Sir, think on it. If I accepted such a price, it would only be because I knew that all the claims that I have made for its quality were not true. And you would know it too, my dear sir. The fact that I would not sell it for less than, say, two thousand seven hundred, is eloquent proof of my belief in the highest standards of my wares.'

Cato fixed his features into an implacable expression as he responded. 'Two thousand six hundred.'

The Syrian sighed. 'My heart grows heavy that you should treat me so . . .' He paused as if in an agony of indecision, then continued in a long-suffering tone. 'However, I would not see you go into battle poorly protected, honoured Prefect. For that reason alone, I would accept two thousand six hundred and seventy-five.'

'Two thousand six hundred and fifty, and not a sestertian more.'

The merchant smiled. 'We have a deal. For that price, and your old breastplate, which has no value, as we have already decided.'

Cato shook his head. 'Just the coin. And I'll want a mail shoulder cape and fastenings as well.'

Cyrus paused and held out his hand. 'You strike a hard bargain, Prefect. You have the advantage of me. But I will accept your offer.'

Cato took his hand and there was the briefest pressure of flesh on flesh before the merchant withdrew and bent over the chest to fish out a small mail cape whose rings were made of cheaper iron, but still riveted, Cato noticed with relief. He considered whether it was worth insisting on having the cape match the mail of the vest, but then decided not to. He was never comfortable when haggling over a purchase and was now keen to conclude his business with the merchant.

He crossed the tent to the iron-bound chest beneath his camp bed and took the key from round his neck and unlocked it. He had been paid in a mixture of gold, silver and bronze coins and counted out the payment into a leather pouch. In the meantime the merchant called for his slaves to come and remove his trading chest from the tent. Having checked the coins and totalled their value, the merchant bowed deeply and backed out of the tent flaps.

'An esteemed honour to have done business with you, sir. Should any of your brother officers be in need of armour, be sure to inform them of Cyrus of Palmyra, proud purveyor of the finest protection to the heroes of the empire. The gods save you.'

With a last bow he disappeared and Macro puffed out his cheeks as he stared down at the mail vest.

'Hope it's worth it.'

'Time will tell.' Cato drew a breath and called out, 'Thraxis! In here!'

A moment later a short, broad-shouldered auxiliary trooper hurried into the tent and saluted. Though he had joined a Thracian unit, Cato's new manservant was from Macedonia and had the dark features and narrow eyes of his race. Cato had picked him out to replace his previous servant who had died in the fort at Bruccium. Despite his lack of experience as a servant, the man had a clean record and his decurion vouched for his honesty and his command of Latin. He would do for the present, Cato decided, but once the campaign season was over he intended to buy himself a good-quality slave from the market in Londinium to take on the necessary duties and allow Thraxis to return to his squadron.

Cato pointed to his breastplate. 'I'll be saving that for ceremonial use only. Get down to the camp-followers' market and find some

25

lacquer. I want it cleaned up, painted and polished so that it gleams like new.'

'Yes, Prefect.'

'And while you're there, is there anything we need for my personal stores?'

Thraxis lowered his gaze and thought briefly. 'Wine and cheese, Prefect. The stock is running low.' He flashed a glance in Macro's direction. 'Due to recent consumption.'

'Is there enough coin in my mess kitty?' asked Cato.

'Yes, Prefect. Though it will require fresh funds by the end of the month.'

'Very well, see if you can buy some decent wine this time. The last two jars tasted like piss.'

'Really?' Macro looked up. 'I didn't notice.'

Cato sighed, and continued addressing his servant. 'Good wine, understand?'

'Yes, Prefect. A wine merchant joined the camp yesterday. He has fresh stock. I'll try him.'

'You do that. Dismissed.'

His servant bowed smartly and left the tent. Macro waited until he was out of earshot and then scratched his cheek. 'Not sure what to make of that one.'

'Thraxis? He's working out well. Good soldier too.'

'That's just it. Don't sound like no auxiliary soldier to me. More like one of those smart-arsed Greeks.'

'I think you're referring to philosophers.'

Macro shrugged. 'I think my description does 'em more justice. Anyway, you know what I mean.'

Cato sighed. 'It takes all kinds, Macro.'

'Not in the army, lad. Our business is killing people. It's not a talking shop. And speaking of talking . . .' Macro fished into his haversack and brought out a large waxed tablet. He opened it and glanced over the notes he had scratched into the waxed surface before he automatically adjusted his composure to a more businesslike manner. His voice altered subtly, Cato noted. Gone was the easy tone of a comrade as Macro became the senior centurion of the Fourth Cohort of the Fourteenth Legion.

'Daily report for yesterday, sir. Strength returns. First Century: sixty-two fit, eight sick, one detached to headquarters duty.'

'And what would that be?'

'Interrogation, sir. Legionary Pullonius's skills are required for questioning the latest batch of prisoners.'

'Very well. Carry on.'

Macro glanced at his notes again. 'Second Century: fifty-eight fit, ten sick. Surgeon says he doesn't think one of them will live out the day.'

Cato nodded as he did some quick mental arithmetic. Macro's cohort had suffered heavy losses at the fort and rather than field six sparsely manned centuries, Cato had ordered that the survivors be formed into two units with a more acceptable level of manpower so that they could operate as effective tactical units. The same was true of his own cohort, the Second Thracian Cavalry. There were just enough troopers left to fill the saddles of three squadrons, barely ninety men in all. So his command, the escort of the baggage train and camp followers, amounted to two hundred and ten men. If Caratacus managed to slip a raiding force in between General Ostorius's main column and the rearguard they could play havoc before a sufficient force could be marshalled to drive them off again. And if that calamity did come about, it was certain that the general would hold Cato to account, despite the lack of men available to him. Such were the iniquities of an officer's life, Cato reflected with weary bitterness.

'What else?'

'The grain supplies are running low. Four days of full ration left. Also the armourer has complained about the leather he's been having to use for repairs to the men's segmented armour.'

'What's wrong?'

'Damp's got to it. Most of our stock is useless. Replacement straps keep breaking.'

'Then have him draw more from stores.'

Macro clicked his tongue. 'That's just it. He can't draw them from the Fourteenth's stores because the quartermaster refuses to let him.'

Cato closed his eyes. 'Why?'

'Because he reckons my cohort is on detached duty, in which case we are to draw on the escort column's stores.'

27

'But we don't have any leather.'

'That's not his problem, he says.'

Cato hissed and opened his eyes. 'You spoke to him then?'

'Oh, yes. Nothing doing. He suggested I take it up with my commanding officer, and so here I am.'

'Thanks.'

Macro grinned. 'Goes with the rank, sir.'

'I'll see what can be done about it at headquarters, after the general's briefing is over.' Cato folded his arms. 'Is that all?'

'For now, sir.'

'Then we're done. Thank you, Centurion.'

Macro saluted and left the tent, leaving Cato to give vent to his frustrations. He raised his eyes and briefly prayed to Jupiter, best and greatest, that he would not be burdened with escorting the baggage train for much longer. It was bad enough that his two units were woefully under-strength, low on supplies and their needs were largely ignored. What was worse was the nature of the duty itself, constantly having to cajole and bully the contracted mule drivers to get the supply wagons moving, herding the merchants, wine sellers, prostitutes and slave dealers along in the wake of the main body of the army. Frequently having to resolve disputes between them and cracking a few heads together whenever any arguments broke out that threatened to stop their advance along the muddy track churned up the boots of the legionaries marching at the head of the column.

Cato stepped out of the tent and surveyed the scene before him. Dusk was closing in over the Silurian mountains, painting the sky with a faint lilac hue. The army had halted during the afternoon to make camp and now that the last defences had been prepared, it was settling down for the night. Due to the narrowness of the valley floor the soldiers had been obliged to construct a long thin rampart rather than the usual regular rectangle. As a result, the baggage train and the haphazard sprawl of tents and shelters of the camp followers stretched out on either side, beyond the regular lines of the tents belonging to the men of the escort detachment. The horses of the Thracians were contentedly chewing on their evening feed in a roped-off enclosure.

To his right, two hundred paces away, were more ordered lines of tents where the two cohorts of the rearguard were camped. A similar distance to the left were the long rows of tents belonging to the main body of the army, as neatly ordered as the ground allowed, and arranged about their commanding officer's tent. The largest tent that Cato could see was on a small rise, over half a mile away: the headquarters of General Ostorius. Scores of fires had been lit, and the glow of the flames pricked out of the gathering veil of darkness. Looking up, beyond the staked parapet running along the rampart, Cato could see small parties of horsemen from another cavalry unit on the slopes surrounding the camp, some starkly outlined against the fading glow of the setting sun. And beyond them, out there in the wilderness of these mountains, lay the army of Caratacus that the Romans were pursuing – for the moment anyway, Cato thought. He had fought the Catuvellaunian king before and had learned to respect him. Caratacus might yet spring a surprise on them. Cato smiled grimly. In fact, it would be a surprise if he didn't.

The thin brassy notes of a cornu cut through the hubbub of shouted orders, muted conversation and braying. Cato listened attentively and recognised the signal summoning unit commanders to headquarters. He turned back into his tent and pulled on and laced up a leather jerkin with its protective strips that covered his shoulders and dropped from his waist to his thighs. He slung his sword strap over his shoulder and snatched up his woollen cape. It would be dark by the time he returned to his tent and he knew these valleys well enough to know how cold they became at night, even in what passed for a summer in Britannia. Stepping out of his tent, Cato fastened the pin at his shoulder and adjusted his cloak as he waited for Macro to stride up from his tent line. Then the two of them set off through the camp towards headquarters.

CHAPTER FOUR

'Now that we're all here, I can begin.' General Ostorius glanced at Cato and Macro pointedly before he looked over the faces of the officers seated on camp stools and benches in front of him. The last to arrive, Cato and Macro sat at the back, on the end of a bench, amongst the other auxiliary unit commanders. Cato was the youngest by some years and most of the other prefects had hair flecked with grey, or had already lost much of it. Some were scarred, like Cato, whose face was bisected by a jagged white line from a sword cut he had received in Egypt. In front of them sat the senior officers of the two legions in Ostorius's column, the Fourteenth and Twentieth: the centurions commanding the cohorts, the junior tribunes and the broad-stripers who were destined to lead their own legions provided they showed the necessary potential, and lastly the two legates, veterans who had each been entrusted with command of one of the empire's elite fighting formations.

General Ostorius stood facing his officers, a thin, wiry aristocrat of advanced years, his face deeply creased and fringed with cropped white hair. He had a reputation as a tough and experienced officer with a sound grasp of strategy, but to Cato he looked frail and worn-down. His judgement was questionable too. Before Cato and Macro had returned to the province, the general had provoked an uprising by the tribesmen of the Iceni. He had been preparing for a campaign against the Silures and the Ordovices and to ensure the security of the rest of the province he had ordered the Iceni to lay down their arms.

It had been a tactless move, causing grave offence to the warrior caste of the tribe who had been prepared to fight rather than give up their weapons. The ensuing revolt had been easily crushed, but it had

30

delayed the campaign and bought Caratacus much needed time to organise his new allies. It had also humiliated the Iceni and their allies, and those tribes now regarded the Romans with thinly veiled hostility. That was the kind of wound to the pride that would fester in the hearts of the native tribesmen, Cato reflected. He doubted that it would be the last time the Iceni defied Rome. The final battle of the brief revolt had been won by tribal levies commanded by Roman officers. The divisions between the British tribes did far more to undermine the cause of those who opposed Rome than the swords of the legions. As long as the largest tribes continued to nurture their age-old rivalries, Rome would win the day. But if they ever united, then Cato feared that the Emperor's soldiers would be swept from the island amid a tide of carnage and humiliation.

Ostorius raised a hand and addressed his officers.

'Gentlemen, as you know, we have been pursuing Caratacus through these wretched mountains for over a month now. Our cavalrymen have been doing their best to keep in contact with the enemy, but the terrain favours him rather than us. Too many choke points where the Silurian rearguard can turn and hold us off while the main body of their army escapes. So far we have remained in touch with the enemy. But the mists of the last few days have enabled Caratacus to give us the slip.'

There was no concealing the disappointment in his voice and Ostorius ran his gnarled fingers through his hair as he continued. 'The scouts report that there are two routes that the enemy could have taken. Tribune Petillius, the map, if you please.'

One of the junior tribunes hurried forward with a roll of leather and set it up over a wooden easel beside the general's desk. Night had fallen outside and the map was illuminated by the oil lamp stands in the tent, so Cato had to squint to make out the details. The features of the map betrayed one of the main difficulties of the campaign. While the coastline was delineated in detail, thanks to the work of the naval squadron operating from Abona, the inland sections of the map were sparsely marked, and only then as the advance of the army uncovered the landscape it passed through. Such was the loyalty of the local people to their cause that none was willing to serve as a guide for the Roman forces, even for a small fortune in silver.

Ostorius approached the map and tapped his finger on the soft parchment. 'This valley is where we are camped. Some ten miles ahead it divides . . . Here. One branch appears to head deep into Silurian territory. The other leads north, towards the Ordovices. If we turn south on the assumption that Caratacus is headed that way then he will continue to lead us a merry old chase through the mountains. That said, the longer it continues, the more strain he places on his food supplies. The Silurians have already suffered enough hardship feeding his troops and enduring the raids that we have mounted on their settlements. We can keep up the pursuit until the end of the campaign season but the chances are that Caratacus will elude us and then we will have to begin a new hunt for him next year.'

There were a few mutters from some of the officers and Ostorius pursed his lips irritably. 'Quiet, gentlemen! I know how you feel about spending any more time in these wretched mountains. But grumbling will not get us the result we desire. We must force the enemy to battle. Only then can we be sure of destroying him once and for all. That is why I hope that Caratacus has turned north. If, as I suspect, he intends to keep his army intact rather than risk exhausting it and losing most of his strength to straggling, then he will retreat to his strongholds in Ordovician territory and draw on the plentiful supplies he has there. He knows that he risks being forced to defend those lands if we pursue him, but at the same time he can keep open his lines of communication to the Brigantes.' Ostorius turned to the map, which did not extend as far as the tribe he was referring to so he waved a hand in the air above and to the right of the map. 'Up that way.'

Cato and some of the other officers smiled indulgently before the general lowered his arm and continued. 'As you may know, there are elements amongst the Brigantes who are more than sympathetic to Caratacus. We've already had to intervene once to keep Queen Cartimandua in power. Her decision to ally herself with Rome has not played well with many of her nobles but, according to the latest intelligence, she has the matter in hand. It's some gratification to see that she is proving her loyalty to the Emperor. Mind you, so she should, given the amount of gold the Emperor has paid for her loyalty. Thank the gods that other women can be bought more cheaply, though from what I hear, the further we venture into the mountains, the more our ladies of easy virtue in the civilian camp are upping their prices. We'd better catch Caratacus soon or they'll bankrupt my army.'

There was laughter at the general's comment this time, and even Cato chuckled.

'True enough,' Macro grumbled under his breath. 'Grasping little cows.'

The mood in the tent had become less formal and, watching the general's expression, Cato caught the intelligent gleam in the old man's eye and realised that the moment of levity was a little trick to draw his officers closer to him. A useful device, Cato decided, making a mental note to use it when he addressed his own subordinates.

'So, gentleman, if our soldiers are to avoid financial ruin, we must track down and complete the destruction of Caratacus. The man has been a blade in our side from the first moment we set foot in these lands.' Ostorius's expression became serious. 'He is a noble foe. The best enemy I have had the honour of fighting, and there is much that can be learned from a leader of his calibre. Therefore I would ask that he be taken alive when the time comes. His death would be a great pity. If the man can be tamed then I am certain he would be a powerful ally. But I digress.' He turned back to the map. 'I have sent scouts down both valleys with orders to locate the enemy. We will advance once we know which direction Caratacus has taken. Until then the army can rest in camp. Use the time wisely. Have the men clean their kit, see to their blisters and get some sleep. For the officers I have arranged a different form of entertainment.' He pointed to the map again, a short distance from where the army was in camp. 'We passed this vale this morning. A dead end according to the patrol that explored it. However, there's plenty of game there. Deer and some wild pigs. It would be a shame to pass up the opportunity while we await news of Caratacus. So I invite you all to a hunt there. Find a good horse, a sturdy spear and join me at the posterior gate at dawn tomorrow . . . Who is with me?'

Macro stood up at once. 'Me, sir!'

At once the rest followed suit, Cato amongst them, all eager to escape the duties in the camp and lose themselves in the thrill of the hunt. The cheering quickly died down as Ostorius cracked a smile and waved his hands to calm their spirits.

'Good! Good. Before I dismiss you, some will have noted the arrival of a new face to our happy little brotherhood. Marcus, stand if you will.'

A tribune seated at the front of the tent rose to his feet and turned to face his comrades. Cato saw that he was a tall, broad-shouldered officer of about twenty. He wore a polished breastplate with a simple design and his cloak and body were spattered with mud, indicating that he had only recently reached the camp. His fair hair was thinning and lay in neatly oiled curls on his scalp. He nodded a greeting and smiled pleasantly as he glanced round the faces before him. The general patted him on the shoulder.

'This is Senior Tribune Marcus Sylvanus Otho, of the Ninth Legion. He is in command of a detachment I have ordered up from Lindum. He rode ahead to announce their arrival on the morrow. Four more cohorts to add to our strength, more than enough to ensure that we crush the enemy when they finally find the courage to turn and face us. I take it you will be joining the hunt tomorrow, Tribune Otho?'

The young man's smile faded for a moment. 'Nothing would give me greater pleasure, sir. However, I feel it is my duty to be here when the men reach camp.'

'Stuff and nonsense!' Ostorius barked. 'The camp prefect will show them to their tent lines, as he will be in command during my absence. Isn't that right, Marcellus?' The general gestured towards a weathered veteran sitting in the front row.

The officer shrugged. 'As you say, sir.'

'There, your men are taken care of.'

The tribune bowed his head wearily. 'I thank you, sir.'

Ostorius beamed at him and clapped the officer on the shoulder before waving him back to his seat. He turned to the others.

'It is the tradition, before a hunt, to celebrate with a feast. Alas, the poor rations available to us on the march are barely adequate to the task, but my cook has tried his best . . .' The general clapped his hands and the flaps at the back of the tent parted as two soldiers beyond drew them aside to reveal a tented extension to the general's command post. Several trestle tables had been set up side by side to create a long dining table, lined with benches. Jars of wine and oil-lamp stands were

34

arranged at intervals and the surface was laden with silver cups, platters and trays heaped with small loaves. A waft of warm air carried the faint scent of roasting meat to the officers in the adjoining tent and Macro smacked his lips.

'Pork, if I'm not mistaken. Please gods, let it be pork!'

Despite feeling that he should show a measure of the aloofness due his rank, Cato could not help his stomach giving a little growl at the imminent prospect of good food and wine. Meanwhile, the general was smiling at the expressions of his officers and he briefly milked the moment before turning towards the table and beckoning them to follow him. 'To your places, gentlemen.'

The officers rose and eagerly followed their commander. Each man was familiar with the strict precedence of the seating and once Ostorius had taken his place at the head of the table, the legates of the two legions sat on either side, then the senior tribunes, the camp prefects, before the prefects of the auxiliary units, in order of seniority. This left Cato nearly halfway down the table, next to the centurions commanding the legionary cohorts. Macro sat opposite and instantly reached for the nearest jug, peered inside to make sure it was wine, and filled his cup to the brim. Then he shot a guilty look across at Cato and raised the jug as he cocked an enquiring eyebrow.

'Thank you.' Cato picked up his cup and reached over for Macro to pour.

'Mind moving up a place?

Cato glanced round to see Horatius, prefect of a cohort from Hispania, a mixed unit of infantry and cavalry. Like Cato, he had only recently been appointed to his command and had joined Ostorius's army a few months before. He was a scarred veteran who had earned his command the hard way after reaching the exalted post of First Spear centurion of the Twentieth Legion. In the normal run of things Cato's command of a mounted unit would mean that he held the superior rank, but at present the command of the baggage train conferred the lowest status amongst the prefects. He rose to his feet and the centurions to his right shuffled down to make space for him. Horatius nodded his thanks as he took the spot Cato had given up. He settled himself and turned to Cato with a curious expression.

'Your Thracian lads aren't quite the ticket, are they?'

'Sir?'

'They look like a bunch of ruffians with those beards, black tunics and cloaks and so on. Not quite what I'd expect from a regular army unit. You should insist on higher standards, Cato.'

'They fight well enough.'

'That's as maybe, but they create something of a bad impression.'

Cato smiled. 'That's the effect my predecessor was going for. It's also the reason why they have their own banner. The enemy fear them and know their name.'

'Yes, I've heard. The Blood Crows.'

Cato nodded.

'I think scarecrows would be more appropriate . . .' Horatius nodded at Macro and gestured to his cup. 'If you don't mind.'

Macro frowned slightly but did as he was bid then set the jug down heavily before picking up his own cup. He took a healthy swig and smiled.

'That's good stuff. Nice to see the general looks after his officers.'

Horatius smiled thinly. 'I wouldn't jump to any conclusions. This is the first time he's put on a feed for months. The old boy's scenting the kill. Maybe that's what minded him to lay on the hunt. Venison tomorrow, Caratacus the day after, eh?'

'I'll drink to that!' Macro raised his cup and took another swig.

Cato lifted his wine and took a sip, conscious that his friend would drink to pretty much anything. The wine's refinement surprised him. A rich, smooth, musty flavour, quite unlike the sharp tang of most of the cheap wine imported into the island where it could be sold for a substantial profit, regardless of its quality. His thoughts shifted back to the other prefect's comment.

'Let's not cook the deer before we catch it. I doubt the enemy's going to let us run them down as easily as tomorrow's prey.'

Horatius scratched his jaw. 'I hope you're wrong. Not just because I've had enough of chasing those bloody barbarians around these mountains. It's Ostorius I'm worried about.' He lowered his voice as he glanced quickly towards the head of the table. Cato followed his gaze and saw the general staring into a silver goblet as he listened to the conversation of the two legates. The verve of the man who had delivered the briefing shortly before had evaporated. Now the general looked tired and his lined face inclined forward as if his head was a burden on his thin shoulders. Horatius let out a sigh. 'Poor bastard's just about done in. This will be his last campaign, I'm thinking. And he knows it. That's why he's so determined to catch Caratacus before it's too late. His military career is going to end here in the mountains. Victory or defeat, or the humiliation of sitting in Rome while his replacement finishes the job and reaps the rewards . . .' He sipped his wine. 'Be a shame, that, after all the groundwork that Ostorius has put in.' The prefect smiled at Macro and Cato. 'Still, there's every chance we'll corner the enemy soon, eh?'

'I hope so.' Cato made himself smile encouragingly. 'Even if we only get to watch proceedings from the rear of our lines.'

Horatius made a sympathetic noise. 'You have to pay your dues, my boy. Command of the baggage train escort ain't likely to win you any medals but it's a necessary job. Do it well and you'll get your chance to win a name for yourself in due course.'

Cato stifled the urge to tell the other officer that he had seen his share of action across the years of his service in the army. Along with Macro he had faced, and overcome, more danger than most of Rome's soldiers would ever face in their careers. He had most definitely paid his dues. But his experience had taught him that life seldom bestows its rewards in proportion to the efforts men have taken to earn them. It had also taught him never to underestimate his enemy. Even now, with the might of the Roman army breathing down his neck, Caratacus might yet cheat Ostorius of the final triumph of his long and glorious career.

His thoughts were interrupted as two of the general's servants entered the tent with a sizzling, glazed roast pig. It was skewered on a stout wooden shaft, the ends of which were supported by the servants' shoulders. They struggled to a small side table and laid their burden down. The tent filled with the rich aroma of the cooked meat and the officers eyed the main course of the feast appreciatively. One of the servants looked to the general for permission to continue and Ostorius flicked his hand in curt assent. Taking out a sharp knife from his belt, the servant began to hack off chunks of pork on to a platter for his companion to distribute to the officers, starting at the head of the table. While the rest of the most senior officers ate hungrily, Ostorius simply picked at his meal, Cato noticed.

Once he had been served, Cato drew his dagger and cut his chunk of pork into more manageable pieces. Opposite, Macro tore at his meat, jaws working furiously. He caught Cato's eye and grinned, juice dribbling from the corner of his mouth. Cato returned the smile before turning back to his neighbour.

'What do you know about the new arrival?'

Horatius pointed the tip of his knife up towards the head of the table. 'Tribune Otho?' He paused briefly to think. 'Not much. Only what I've heard from a mate who was reporting from Lindum a few days ago. Our lad arrived from Rome less than two months ago, the ink still wet on his letter of appointment. Popular enough, though he's still got plenty to learn about the army. Like most of them broad-stripers. Give 'em a couple of years and they'll do us no harm. Best we can hope for really.'

He paused to eat another mouthful and then, when he did not continue, Cato cleared his throat. 'Nothing else? Is that all your friend had to say about Otho?'

'Near enough. There was something else.' Horatius lowered his voice and leaned closer. 'There was a rumour about the reason behind his fetching up here on this miserable island.'

'Oh?'

'You know how it is, Cato. One servant mutters something to the next and before you know it they're saying two and two make five. In this case, it seems that our friend Otho was sent here on the orders of the Emperor, as a punishment. If you're going to punish someone, that's the way to do it, sure enough – send 'em to Britannia.'

Cato's curiosity was piqued and he swallowed hurriedly in order to urge his comrade to say more. 'What was the punishment for?'

Horatius winked. 'Something to do with his wife. She insisted on coming with him from Rome. Read into that what you will. According to my mate, she's quite a looker.'

Cato sucked in air between his teeth. He had wondered about bringing his own wife, Julia, with him, but had decided against it due to the danger posed by an unsettled province, swarming with the enemies of Emperor Claudius. If Otho had chosen to permit his wife to accompany him then it was possible that he felt she would be in greater danger if she remained in Rome. That, or perhaps the tribune was obsessively jealous and dare not leave his wife to her own devices in the capital.

The thought sparked off a stab of jealousy in Cato's gut and unbidden images and anxieties about Julia's fidelity rushed into his thoughts. She was part of the social world of the aristocrats; there were plenty of wealthy, powerful, well-groomed men to catch her eye, and with her beauty she could have the pick of them if she wished. He forced such fears from his mind, furious and ashamed with himself for doubting her. After all, was he not availed of the same opportunities to indulge himself in the towns and tents of the camp followers, albeit that the company was somewhat less select and self-regarding? And Cato had not broken faith. He must trust that Julia had similarly honoured him. What else could he do? Cato asked himself. If he tormented himself with such fears it would be a dangerous distraction – for him and, more importantly, for his men.

He tried to clear his mind as he ate some more meat and washed it down with another sip of wine. 'Is that all you know about the tribune?'

Horatius looked at him sharply. 'That's all. I ain't the town gossip, Cato. And frankly that's the limit of my fucking interest in the new lad and his wife.'

'Fair enough.'

But the other prefect was not done with Cato yet and turned to look across the table. 'Hey, Centurion Macro!'

Macro looked up.

'You've served with Cato for a while, right? Is he always so nosy?'

'Sir?'

'You know, asking questions all the time?'

Macro chuckled, the wine working its effect on him as he responded with a slurred edge of his words. 'You don't know the half of it. If something happens, the prefect wants to know the reason why. I keep telling him, it's the will of the gods. That's all a man has to know. But not him. He has the mind of a Greek.'

'Really?' Horatius shuffled on the bench. 'Just as long as that's as far as his taste for Greek ways takes him.'

Macro roared with laughter. 'Oh, in that respect he's as straight as a

39

javelin. And with good reason. You should see his wife. Prettiest girl in Rome.'

Cato frowned and gritted his teeth as he pointed a finger at Macro. 'That's enough, Centurion. Understand?'

His friend's sharp tone cut through the fog in Macro's mind and he lowered his gaze guiltily. 'Apologies, sir. I spoke out of turn.'

Cato nodded. 'Quite. And I'll thank you to remember that.'

A difficult silence fell over the other officers in earshot of the sharp exchange, but the hubbub in the rest of the tent continued and a moment later the men on either side of Cato and Macro had returned to their good-humoured banter. But the mood between the two friends remained soured for the rest of the feast.

As the last of the dishes were cleared away and the officers began to rise and take their leave, Cato made his way over to the junior tribune responsible for supplies on the general's staff.

'Gaius Portius, a word.'

A short, round-faced young officer with a mop of dark curly hair turned from his companions and smiled blearily at Cato. 'Yes? P-prefect Cato, isn't it?'

Cato stared at him coldly. He himself had only drunk the one cup of wine, as he disliked the feeling of being drunk, or more particularly the consequences of the feeling, and was quite sober.

'I wish to speak to you about the supply situation.'

'Of course, sir. First thing in the m-morning. Oh, hang on. The hunt. After that then, sir. S-soon as possible.'

'I wish to speak now, Portius.'

The younger officer hesitated a moment, as if he might protest, but Cato's stern expression brooked no defiance and the tribune turned to his friends. 'You fellows carry on. I'll s-see you in the mess.'

His comrades exchanged sympathetic looks with Portius and he clapped a couple of them on the shoulder as they stumbled out of the tent. Portius turned back to Cato and tried to focus his mind. 'I'm all yours, sir.'

'Good. Since you seem to have some trouble remembering my name, I'll remind you. Quintus Licinius Cato, Prefect of the Third Thracian Cavalry and, for now, the commander of the baggage train escort. Mind you, you should already be aware of that, given how many requests I've sent to headquarters over the last month chasing up our rations and the kit my two units require, urgently. But I've had no response. It's not an acceptable state of affairs, is it, Tribune Portius?'

The tribune raised a hand in protest. 'Sir, I understand your situation. However, yours is not a front-line command. Supplies are limited and there are other units with a higher pr-priority.'

'Bollocks,' Cato snapped. 'The auxiliaries and legionaries under my command are front-line troops. We don't need to prove our worth. In any case, the general has entrusted us with guarding the baggage train. There wouldn't be any bloody supplies if we failed in our job. If my horses and men go without adequate feed and rations then they're not going to be on top form should the enemy decide to strike at the wagons and people I'm protecting. My men are going to be even less effective if they can't get their kit repaired due to lack of the materials needed to fix them. We're short-handed as it is. If we are attacked and the enemy manage to break through, it will be in no small part your responsibility, Tribune Portius. I will make sure that everyone knows it, from the common soldier right up to the general, and the Emperor back in Rome.' He leaned forward so that their faces were no more than a foot apart and tapped the tribune firmly on the chest. 'Think what that will do to your prospects. You'll be lucky if your next post is supervising the sewers in some desert shithole on the edge of the known world.'

Portius edged back and shook his head. 'You don't understand, sir. If I could give you everything you wanted I would. But I have to d-decide which commander's requests are justified.'

'And I've just told you why mine are. From now on you are going to see to it that my Thracians and Centurion Macro's legionaries are given what are they are due and what they need. If you don't then I am going to hunt you down at headquarters, or wherever you drink with your friends, and I'm going to give you a bollocking in front of them that neither you nor they are going to forget anytime soon. Is that clear?'

Portius nodded nervously. 'Quite c-clear, sir.'

'Good. Then see to it that our rations are issued on time, and in the right amount, first thing tomorrow. Same goes for the leather and other kit I've asked for.'

'Yes, sir.'

Cato stared at the tribune for a moment longer, to make the most of the young officer's discomfort. Then he continued in a menacing tone, 'Don't let me have any cause to repeat this ever again . . .'

'No, sir. Never again. I swear, by the gods.'

'The gods will be the least of your worries. If you fail me, and I fail the army, then some enemy warrior is going to carve you up. And if he doesn't then *I* will.'

'Are you threatening me, sir?'

'No, I'm promising you.' Cato narrowed his eyes and spoke softly. 'Now, get out my sight before I forget the legal niceties and just wring your wretched neck myself.'

Portius backed away a few steps before he dared to turn and hurry from the tent as Cato glared after him. Once the tribune had gone, Cato relaxed and allowed himself a small smile. It had felt good to unnerve the younger officer. And it had been good for the other man as well. Hopefully from now on he would do his job properly. At the same time, the fact that he had bullied another person and felt pleasure from it troubled Cato. He had seen enough bullying in the army in his time to know that while it worked to get a job done in the short term, it undermined the recipients in the longer term. That aside, he had had a glimpse of himself being the cause of and enjoying the discomfort of another person. It was not an edifying experience and he felt the burden of shame settle on his shoulders as he made to leave the tent.

'Bravo, Prefect Cato.'

He turned quickly and saw that he was not the last officer remaining in the tent as he had thought. A figure detached itself from the shadows at the side and moved into the glow of the oil lamps. It was the legate of the Fourteenth, Quintatus, the man who Cato had suspected of having a hand in sending him to take command of the fort at Bruccium, a task that had nearly cost him and Macro their lives.

Quintatus smiled. 'Nice piece of beasting there. The pathetic little whelp deserved it. Too many of the junior tribunes fetch up in the army thinking it's some kind of a game. A chance to get away from their families and still carry on behaving like the other drunken rakes in Rome. Discipline is what they need and discipline is what the army gives them.'

Cato took a deep breath. 'I was simply reminding him of his duties, sir.'

'Of course you were, and you did a good job of it.'

The legate regarded him for a moment, his cold eyes twinkling as he sized Cato up. 'You think that being given the command of the baggage train escort is some kind of a punishment, don't you?'

'Someone has to do it,' Cato replied flatly.

'True. But why you? That's what you're wondering.'

'What I think is my own business, sir.'

'Maybe. But perhaps you are right to think there's a reason behind it, Cato. You're marked as one of Narcissus's men, no matter what you do. Narcissus is not the only man to have a private organisation of agents working for him. Pallas is the same. Another bloody imperial freedman with grand ambitions. And just as crafty and dangerous as his rival, Narcissus. If there's one thing you can be sure of, it's that Pallas will have agents on the staff of General Ostorius. And they won't shirk from doing you down.'

'So I've seen,' Cato replied, watching Quintatus closely. 'Are you one of Pallas's men?'

'Me?' Quintatus laughed. 'Fortunately not. I'm too high-born for that. Those Greek freedmen prefer not to work with public figures if they can avoid it. Better to use the kind of people who can't achieve the highest offices in the empire and therefore do not constitute a threat to the likes of Pallas and Narcissus. So rest easy on that account.'

'Nevertheless, you are aware of Pallas's plans with respect to me.'

'I was told to make your life difficult.'

'I think it was more than that. I think you were told to make it difficult for me to survive my last command.'

Quintatus shrugged. 'It might have come to that. Fortunately it didn't. You came through your experiences at Bruccium and learned that you were too good an officer to be thrown away on the whim of some freedman in Rome. You have nothing to fear from me, Cato.'

Cato gave a wry smile. 'You say that now . . .'

The other man frowned. 'Please yourself. I merely wished to put your mind at ease on my account. The danger comes from another direction.'

Cato felt a tiny trickle of icy fear work its way down the nape of his neck. 'Who? The general?'

'Ostorius? Hardly. He's a straight as they come. You think that's the reason for your being posted to the baggage escort?'

'It had crossed my mind,' Cato admitted.

'You were chosen for other reasons,' Quintatus said wearily. 'In fact it was my suggestion. Both units of the Bruccium garrison had suffered grievously. There aren't enough of your men left to take their place in the battle line. I have no doubt about their fighting quality, and sought to put your men where they could do the most good. That's the reason. I'm not trying to undermine you.'

Cato thought it through and saw that there was sense to it. He was even slightly flattered by the thought that he and his men were well regarded by the legate. But he still could not bring himself to trust Quintatus.

'Thank you, sir.' He said wearily.

'Think nothing of it. I just wanted you to know that your quality is known by your superiors. I, for one, would sooner have you fighting at my side than stick a knife in your back.'

'That's gratifying to hear.'

The legate cocked an eyebrow. 'Don't push your luck . . . We'd better get a good night's sleep before the hunt.'

Without waiting for a reply Quintatus turned away and strode out of the tent. Cato closed his eyes and rubbed his brow. His heart was heavy with foreboding. The very reason that Narcissus had pulled some strings to get a posting for Macro and him in Britannia was to get them far away from the scheming of the imperial freedmen. Especially as Macro had witnessed an intimate encounter between Pallas and the Emperor's new wife, Agrippina. Now it seemed that the reach of Pallas comfortably extended to the very wildest frontier in the empire.

A nasty thought struck Cato. It was just possible that Narcissus had sent them here for reasons other than their safety. It would be typical of the man. In which case they faced danger on two fronts: the enemy warriors to their front, and the agents of Pallas at their backs.

His heart felt heavy and a terrible tiredness seemed to settle on his shoulders. Was there no escaping the machinations of those who played their deadly game of self-advancement in the shadow of the

Emperor? One thing was certain, he must be careful and watch for signs of danger. If the agents of Pallas were already in Britannia, and if they believed that he and Macro were still acting on the orders of Narcissus then they would take every opportunity to remove them from the game, as they saw it.

'Fuck ...' Cato muttered to himself bitterly as he trudged out of the tent and began to make his way back to the tents of the escort units. 'Why me? Why Macro?'

He smiled at himself. He knew exactly what Macro would say to that. The same thing he habitually said when faced with such questions: 'Because we're here, Cato, my lad. Because we're here.'

CHAPTER FIVE

'Fine morning for it!' Cato stretched his back and looked up into the clear heavens. Not a cloud was in sight and there was no wind. The air was still damp and cool and he breathed deeply. He had tried his best to dismiss his concerns the previous night when he returned to his tent. Instead he forced himself to think of Julia and the house he planned to build in Campania one day, once he had amassed a fortune from booty earned during his duty. There had been precious little of that so far, but if the campaign in Britannia came to a successful conclusion there would be riches to be made from selling prisoners to the slave dealers. That, and a share of any gold and silver taken. More than enough to buy a slice of the peace and quiet of Campania, where he and Julia could raise a family, and he could take his place amongst the magistrates of the nearest town. Perhaps Macro might choose to live nearby and they could drink and recall the old days. On such wistful thoughts he had easily drifted off to sleep.

'What's that?' Macro growled, his head in his hands. He was sitting on the other stool warming himself by the freshly lit fire in front of Cato's tent. 'Fine morning? What's fine about it?'

Cato could not help smiling at his friend's discomfort. Macro never drank with any thought of the consequences.

'Clear skies, clean air and the prospect of a day's hunt. Cause enough to feel in a fine mood.'

'So you say.'

'Ah, here's Thraxis.' Cato sat down as his servant walked up with a heavy iron pot, a thick rag wrapped round the handle to protect his hand. He placed it close to the fire before removing the lid. In his other hand he carried two mess tins and a wooden ladle.

'What do you have for us?' asked Cato with a quick wink as he craned his neck to peer into the pot.

'Thought you could use something hearty to fill your stomachs for the day, Prefect.' The servant dipped the ladle in and stirred the thick grey contents of the pot.

'It's gruel with bacon, fat and some honey I bought in the traders' market last night.' He leaned forward and sniffed. 'Ah! That's good.'

Thraxis hefted a dollop out of the pot and flicked it into one of the mess tins with a dull splat. He handed it to Cato along with a spoon. 'There you are, Prefect.'

Cato nodded his thanks and raised the mess tin. He took a small spoonful and blew across it before tentatively taking his first taste. It was hot and flavoursome and he eagerly helped himself to another, while his servant filled the next mess tin for Macro and offered it to the centurion.

'Sir?'

Macro looked up, bleary-eyed and with a thick growth of stubble on his cheeks. He reluctantly took the mess tin.

'Thraxis,' Cato intervened. 'Have our boots, cloaks and canteens ready for us once we've eaten.'

'Yes, Prefect.'

Cato turned his attention back to his friend. It was several days since Macro had been to the barber for his last shave and he was starting to look more untamed than the wildest of Celts, Cato mused. His friend's hair was beginning to go grey at the temples and, if Cato was not imagining it, receding a fraction from his forehead. Hardly surprising as Macro was in his fortieth year and had spent twenty-four years in the army, having lied about his age to join at sixteen. Cato paused before eating his next spoon of gruel and cleared his throat.

'Any thoughts about what you're going to do when we get to the end of the year?'

Macro had been staring at the mess tin in his lap, wondering if he dare try to eat some of the concoction Thraxis had produced, suspicious that Cato's servant had deliberately gone for a meal that was guaranteed to turn the stomach of even the hardest old soak in the legions. He looked up at Cato. 'Mmmm?'

'This is your demob year. You're on the short enlistment. So?'

Macro worked his spoon round the gruel. The legions discharged time-served men every other year, which meant that soldiers served a twenty-four or twenty-six year enlistment. He braced himself and took a spoon and chewed it slowly, forcing himself to swallow before he replied.

'Had a letter from my mum in Londinium. The inn she bought is making a packet and she wants me to join her and expand the business.'

'Oh?'

This was the first Cato had heard of the letter, and he felt a twinge of anxiety as he regarded his friend, the man he had served with ever since joining the Second Legion as a pasty-faced recruit ten years ago. Life in the army without Macro was unthinkable, but he had to accept that his friend was reaching the end of his enlistment and might well choose to take his discharge bounty and retire.

Macro considered a second spoonful and decided against it for the moment. He looked up at Cato. 'I don't know, lad. Sometimes I think I'm getting a bit long in the tooth for soldiering. Can't deny the prospect of running a drinking hole for the rest of my days isn't tempting.'

'And you handle your drink so well,' Cato smiled.

'I don't get as much practice as I'd like.'

'I think regular practice would kill you, on the evidence of this morning.'

'If anything is going to kill me, it's this bloody poison your servant has mixed. Might as well cut out the middle man.' Macro turned and flicked the contents of the mess tin into the fire where the gruel steamed, bubbled, spat and hissed for a moment. He scratched his chin in thought. 'I don't know, Cato. My limbs are getting a bit stiff. I ain't as strong or as quick as I used to be, and in this trade that isn't good. I've been in plenty of fights. Good times, eh? Up until this year I've fought well enough. But lately? I get the feeling that I've already been as good a soldier as I am ever going to be. From here, it's downhill. At some point, I'm bound to run into an enemy I can't beat. When that day comes the chances are I'll be cut to pieces. It might be for the best if I quit before that happens.'

Cato had been listening with a sinking heart. When Macro finished he looked at him to see how he would respond.

Cato shook his head slowly. 'Well, I have to say, I'm surprised. I'd never have thought you'd be the one to jack in soldiering to run an inn. There's still plenty of fight left in you as far as I'm concerned, and of course it'd be a sad loss for the army . . .' The string of platitudes dried up and Cato sat in awkward silence, not quite certain how to voice his real reasons for not wanting Macro to take his discharge.

His friend was watching his downcast expression closely and suddenly he could contain his mirth no longer and let out a roar of laughter.

'If you could see your face! It's a bloody picture!'

Cato was startled by the sudden transformation. 'What are you talking about?'

Macro shook his head. 'Just fucking about with you, lad! Paying you back for that shit you had Thraxis put together. Think I didn't see that wink?'

'You mean . . . You aren't thinking of leaving the army?'

'What? Are you mad? What else can I do? I'd be bloody useless on civvy street.'

It was hard not to show his relief, even though he was annoyed by the petty trick. Cato wagged a finger at him.

'Next time, I'll give orders for your discharge myself. Just to make certain.'

'Oh sure. Anyway, you'll not get your chance. I've already handed in my request to extend my enlistment. Just waiting to hear back from the legate, and then I'm signed up for another ten years.' He leaned forward and clapped Cato on the shoulder. 'You don't get rid of me that easily!'

'Glad to hear it,' Cato said with feeling and hurriedly turned his attention back to his breakfast, determined not to let his relief show.

The grizzled veteran smiled to himself, touched by the sentiment of his younger friend. His gaze returned to the pot by the fire. A thin trail of steam curled up from the gruel and he felt his stomach lurch in disgust at the very idea of trying to eat.

'You should try some,' Cato urged. 'Or you'll be hungry later on.'

'Eat that? No fucking chance. I'd sooner lick a turd off a stinging nettle.'

'Interesting notion.' Cato stroked his chin thoughtfully. 'I'll see if Thraxis has the recipe.'

It was mid-morning before the hunting party had gathered at the entrance to the vale General Ostorious had chosen for the site of the day's entertainment. There were over a hundred officers, with their mounts, and twice as many soldiers and servants, together with several carts carrying the necessary equipment and provisions. A table had been set up beside a brazier and as the officers arrived they were given a cup of heated wine. Macro downed his with an appreciative smack of his lips as if the previous night had never happened. The soldiers assigned to act as beaters began to quietly file up the vale and work their way around the sides to the far end. Other men set to work erecting the wicker screens that would funnel the deer and boar into the killing zone. Once that was done they began to take out the hunting bows and arrow-filled quivers from one of the carts and lay them out on a leather groundsheet to keep them off the dew-dampened grass.

The general was the last to arrive, riding up accompanied by the two legates and his personal bodyguard of eight hand-picked legionaries. He wore a thick cloak about his body, even though the sun shone and bathed the mountainous landscape in its warm glow. Despite his cheery demeanour Cato realised that he was putting on a performance of hearty good health and humour for his subordinates.

Ostorius dismounted and took some wine, cupping his gnarled fingers tightly round the goblet. Cato watched him as he moved through the gathering, greeting his officers. Then the prefect's eye caught a movement down the valley in the direction of a camp. A horseman was galloping up on a sleek black mount. As he got closer, Cato saw that it was the tribune who had arrived the previous day. He reined in a short distance from the other officers and wagons, spraying clods of earth on to one of the general's servants. Dropping from the saddle, he thrust the reins into the man's hands and swiftly joined the others, breathing heavily from his ride. The sudden arrival had caused a moment's lull in the conversation and Ostorius rounded on the tribune with a frown.

'Young man, I don't know what passes for good manners in Rome these days, but I'll thank you to ensure that you never arrive late to any meeting or gathering where your commanding officer is already present.'

Tribune Otho bowed his head. 'My apologies, sir.'

'And what reason explains your tardiness?'

Otho looked up and hesitated a moment before he replied. 'There is no excuse, sir. I woke late.'

'I see. Then clearly you need training in the art of wakefulness. Five days' command of the night watch should suffice.'

'Yes, sir.'

Cato and Macro exchanged a quick look. The general had just condemned the young tribune to five days with almost no chance to sleep. The officer in charge of the night watch was obliged to distribute the password to each sentry and then do the rounds of the camp between changes of watch to ensure that every man was alert and gave the right challenge. It was a tiresome business, all the more so after a day's march. That was why the duty was shared amongst the tribunes of an army.

'That's a bit harsh,' Cato muttered.

Macro shrugged. 'It'll teach the young pup a lesson he won't forget in a hurry. It'll be good for him.'

'Good for him? He'll be on his knees by the end of it.'

'It'll be the making of him.'

'Or the breaking of him.'

Macro looked at him. 'Cato, you know how it is with training. You have to push a man further than he thinks he can go. That's how it works. That's why you've turned out as well as you have.'

It was true, Cato admitted to himself. Youngsters like Otho needed to be tamed and become inured to the hard conditions of the army as soon as possible, for their own good, and for the good of the men they commanded.

Ostorius dismissed the tribune with a curt wave of his hand and turned to the centurion from the Twentieth who had been appointed the day's master of the hunt.

'Are we ready?'

The centurion saluted and gestured into the vale. 'Nearly, sir. The beaters are getting into position.'

Cato looked up and saw the tiny figures extending into a line amid the mottled green and brown of the distant bracken. Already he could pick out other movement as large animals scurried away from the beaters. There was a small forest growing either side of a stream that flowed into the main valley. A small group of deer were visible in the shadows of the treeline. Plenty of game, then, just as the general had said.

The centurion turned to the men working on the wicker screens. Already the makings of a large funnel angled into the mouth of the vale with pens at the end. There were gaps between each panel to provide shooting positions for the hunters. The lines were set at a right angle so that the arrows would provide a crossfire without endangering any of the officers in the party. 'Just finishing that off, sir, and we're ready for you to give the signal to begin.'

Ostorius nodded approvingly and then addressed his officers. 'Pick your weapons, men. We'll start with the shoot.'

Cato, Macro and the others moved across to the bows and quivers filled with broad-pointed hunting arrows that lay on the leather goatskin covers. They chose their weapons and bracers and some of the more experienced officers tested the draw weights to get a feeling for the power of their chosen bow. Cato and Macro had never trained as archers and took what came to hand before making their way over to the wicker screens and taking their places at the gaps left between the screens. As Cato slipped the small iron hooks of the quiver over his sword belt, Tribune Otho approached and took the adjacent shooting position. They exchanged a nod before Cato held out a hand.

'Haven't had the chance to make your acquaintance yet. Prefect Quintus Licinius Cato of the Second Thracian Cavalry.'

The younger man grasped Cato's forearm and smiled cheerfully. 'Tribune Marcus Silvius Otho.' He glanced past Cato with an enquiring expression. 'And this is?'

Macro leaned his bow against the screen and stepped forward. 'Centurion Lucius Cornelius Macro, commanding the Fourth Cohort of the Fourteenth Legion, sir. Though at the moment my cohort is attached to the prefect's command, escorting the baggage train.'

'Oh, that sounds like quite a responsibility.'

'Not as much as we'd like, sir.' Macro smiled faintly.

Otho pursed his full lips briefly, unsure how he should phrase his next words. 'Pardon me, Prefect, but I'm still somewhat new to this game and there weren't any auxiliary units at Lindum. Do I call you sir? Or do you call me sir?'

Cato was taken aback. Any tribune, broad-stripe or otherwise, should have taken the effort to learn such basic facts of military life. He cleared his throat and made to explain. 'You are second-in-command to your legate, Hosidius Geta. Technically. In practice the camp prefect takes command if Geta falls or is absent. In the normal course of things I would call you sir. But as you command a detachment from the Ninth Legion, you are a minor formation commander and therefore an equal. In which case I call you Tribune and you call me Prefect. In formal situations. Today, I am simply Cato.'

Otho's eyes bulged as he struggled to take it all in. Then he nodded. 'Cato it is. And Centurion Macro calls me sir. Is that right?'

Macro nodded. 'And that ain't going to change unless the world gets turned upside down and some lunatic makes me a senator. Or you foul up spectacularly and get broken down to legionary, sir.'

The tribune glanced over his shoulder in the direction of General Ostorius. 'I trust it won't come to that. Not before I serve my time out and return to Rome.'

Cato recalled the comment of Horatius the night before. 'I take it you are keen to get your military service over with.'

'Rather!' Otho replied with feeling. 'Much as I like the fresh air and earthy companionship, there's no place like Rome, nay?'

'Thankfully,' Macro added, burdened by bad memories of the capital.

'I could stand to return there soon,' said Cato. 'I was married recently and had to leave my wife behind. Though, as I understand it, your wife has accompanied you on campaign.'

'That's right. Poppaea and I can't be parted from each other.'

'Although you are now.'

'Not at all. Her carriage is with the cohorts marching to join Ostorius. To be honest, that's why I reached the hunt late. I was hanging on just in case the column made the camp this morning. No such luck. And now I am in bad odour with the general as a result.'

Cato puffed his cheeks as he appraised the younger officer. He appeared to be the most unsoldierly tribune Cato had ever encountered. And the presence of his wife here on the frontier either spoke volumes for their mutual feeling, or there was something more to it, as Horatius had hinted. Cato decided to probe a little further. 'It's quite unusual for an officer to bring his wife. I certainly wouldn't want mine enduring the hardships of camp life, regardless of how much I miss her.'

Otho lowered his gaze and turned his attention to positioning his quiver comfortably. 'It's not as simple as all that, actually.'

'Oh? How so?'

The tribune clicked his tongue. 'We left under a bit of a cloud. The thing is, Poppaea was married to another chap. Dreadful, dour fellow with large ears and precious little of interest between them, or indeed anywhere else on his body. Rufus Crispitus.' He looked sharply at Cato. 'You know of him?'

'No.'

'Not surprised. He makes an art of being invisible at social gatherings. The sort of fellow who could stand as a model for those tiresomely dull sculptures of provincial magistrates, if you know what I mean.'

Macro looked at Cato with a puzzled expression and shook his head.

'Anyway,' Otho continued. 'To cut a long story somewhat less so, I seduced Poppaea.' He smiled. 'As it happens, she seduced me. She's a bit of a game girl in that respect.'

'I like her already, sir,' Macro chipped in with a grin.

The tribune shot him a cross look, before he continued. 'Before you know it we're quite madly in love. Our joy was unbounded.'

'And I'm willing to bet Rufus Crispitus did not approve,' said Cato.

'Not half! The chap was furious. First time in his life he ever showed any kind of emotion. So he makes a beeline to the imperial palace and demands that the Emperor punish us both. As he was still married to Poppaea he was fully within his rights to give her a good hiding. However, Crispitus — ever the fool — made rather too much of his demands and annoyed the Emperor. Claudius still had to do something for appearances' sake. So he demanded that Crispitus divorce Poppaea and we were offered a choice. Exile to Tomus, or I join the army and take Poppaea for my wife and we both disappear from Rome for a year or two until the scandal was forgotten. Well, I've read enough Ovidius to know that Tomus is the last place in the world to spend any amount of time. Or at least that's what I thought until we came here.' He shrugged. 'So there you have it. My tale of love and woe, to coin a phrase.'

They were interrupted by the sound of a horn and Cato looked round to see that the other officers were all in position, with Ostorius and the legates at the mouth of the wicker funnel.

'Here we go,' said Macro, drawing his first arrow and notching it to the bowstring. All along the line of the panels the other officers were similarly making ready and Cato watched as Otho drew a shaft and fitted the knock in one swift and clean motion.

'You've done this before.'

The tribune nodded. 'Brought up on an estate in Umbria. Started hunting as soon as I could walk.'

The sound of horns answered from the far end of the vale as the beaters began their advance, some thrashing at the heather with sticks while others beat mess tins together and paused every so often to blow on the horns. Ahead of them Cato could see the heather come alive with flurries of motion and then he saw the first of the deer spring up and appear to bounce down the slope towards the seeming safety of the trees. The game was still some distance off and Cato held his bow down, arrowhead pointing safely towards the grass between his feet.

'By the gods,' said Macro. 'There'll be plenty of meat on the table tonight. The old boy was right about this place. It's alive with game.'

The sound of the beaters' horns grew steadily louder and now Cato could hear the rattle of their mess tins and the faint swishing of their sticks. He felt his heart quicken and half raised his bow, fingertips of his right hand closing on the drawstring. The edge of the forest was no more than two hundred paces away and abruptly a doe burst from under the branches and bounded into the open. Two more followed and then a stag, tossing his antlers as he came into view. Cato made to raise his bow.

'Not yet, Prefect!'

He lowered his arms a little and turned towards Otho. 'What?'

The tribune's bow was grounded and he gestured towards the general close to the open end of the funnel. 'Don't know where you learned to hunt, but the protocol back home is to let the host shoot first.'

Cato flushed, cross with himself for not realising that would be the case. He had only ever hunted boars before in the army, from horseback, and though it was a different pursuit, the basic formalities were the same. The subordinates rode patiently behind their leader until the first beast was spiked, then it was free for all.

'Of course,' he said quietly. 'Thank you for reminding me.'

Otho looked surprised. 'Didn't your people take you out shooting game when you were young?'

Macro shook his head in amusement and muttered, '*Your people?* By the gods, it's a different world in Rome.'

Cato's embarrassment deepened. His origins were far from aristocratic. It was easy to understand the tribune's assumption about his origins. The auxiliary prefects of younger years tended to be appointed from the ranks of the senatorial families. His pain over being reminded of his humble past quickly turned his shame into bitterness. He turned on Otho.

'No. They didn't.'

'Too bad. Then you would have known what to do.'

'I suppose.'

'Anyway, here they come!' The tribune's voice rose in pitch as he pointed towards the first deer to approach the funnel.

Cato turned and saw the stag and its three does skittering from side to side as they were driven towards the waiting hunters. At the end of the far line of panels General Ostorius raised his bow and drew back his arm, trembling slightly with the effort. He sighted along the arrow shaft and picked his target. Cato, once more caught up by the excitement of the atmosphere, held his breath as he watched. The first of the does entered the funnel, but Ostorius still held back, waiting for the stag. Then, just as it approached the opening of the panels, Cato saw the arms of the general's bow snap forward and the arrow flew in a shallow arc towards the stag. It flashed past the animal's rump and disappeared into the grass.

'Oh, bad luck!' Otho muttered. 'Should have led the target more.'

Ostorius quickly notched another arrow as the stag quickly drew closer. He took aim and loosed the string, and there was no mistake this time. The shaft struck the animal in the shoulder and the sharp thwack of the impact was heard by all. The officers and men cheered their commander as the stag let out a wrenching bleat of pain and staggered to the side. Blood, red and glistening, streamed down its hide from the large wound torn in its flesh by the hunting arrow. The general had already strung another arrow and took aim again. The stag was a difficult target now as it kicked and bucked, trying to dislodge the shaft. The second arrow struck it in the rump and it stumbled into the grass before struggling back on to its legs just as a third arrow pierced its neck. Now the blood was flowing freely and every movement sprayed flecks of crimson through the air. The does kept their distance, fearful of the stag's violent movements. Cato regarded the spectacle with spellbound fascination. Though he knew he would be mocked for admitting it, he felt pity for the noble creature. The parallel with Caratacus was easily suggested to his restless mind. Both stag and enemy driven to their destruction. It felt like an omen. Another Roman triumph tinged with regret at the loss of a noble spirit.

But the stag had not given up yet. Bleeding heavily, it lowered its antlers and half ran, half stumbled towards the wicker panels extending either side of Cato. Then, with a shock, Cato realised that he stood directly in the line of the beast's charge. He froze.

'Cato!' Macro called out close by. 'Shoot it!'

CHAPTER SIX

The spell broke and he raised his left arm. The arrow was still notched, but slipped loose as his arm came level.

'Shit!' Cato hissed, frantically fumbling to refit the shaft. He was aware of the blur of movement a short distance away and the bellowing breath of the stag. When he looked up it was no more than ten feet from him. There was a flicker of movement from his left and a sharp thud as an arrow struck the stag in the chest and the iron barb tore through its heart. The stag fell forwards and rolled on the ground before crashing into the panel in front of Cato, flattening it and knocking him back on to the ground. An instant later Macro grabbed his arm and pulled him up, struggling to suppress a grin.

'All right, lad?'

'Fine, thanks.'

'Don't thank me. Thank the tribune there. If he hadn't acted you'd be all over that stag's horns right now.'

Cato looked round and saw Otho watching him, bow in hand, and another arrow already plucked from his quiver. 'I'm grateful.'

Otho shook his head. 'An easy shot. Think nothing of it.'

'LOOSE ARROWS!' the hunt master bellowed from the neck of the funnel. The tribune turned back to the funnel and prepared his next shot. By the time Cato had picked up his bow and retaken his place, the open ground in front of the funnel was thick with flying arrows. The does went down in quick succession, shafts protruding from their hides, and then there was a brief pause before more game came rushing forward, driven on by the beaters. Cato saw several more deer, and the first of the boars, head down as it launched into a charge. There were hares as well, bounding through the heather and into the expanse of grass in front of the hunters. He took a calming breath and securely fitted his arrow and raised the bow. Choosing the boar as his target, Cato lined up the tip of the arrow, drawing his hand back until he felt the back of his thumb come up against his cheek. He led the boar, aiming a short distance in front of its snout, then tracking it as it angled towards the opening of the funnel thirty paces away. Holding his breath, Cato closed his left eye and narrowed the right . . . then released his string with a flick of his fingers. The bow lurched in his hand and the arrow sped towards its target, striking it high on the shoulder behind the head.

'A hit!' Cato shouted, his heart leaping with surprised pride. He glanced at Macro. 'I hit it. Did you see?'

Macro was drawing a bead on his own target and answered through clenched teeth. 'Beginner's luck!' The centurion released his first arrow, and swore as it went wide of the mark. Cato turned to Otho, but the tribune's concentration was fixed on the game rushing towards him. For a moment Cato watched in admiration as the young man loosed arrow after arrow in quick succession, never pausing to celebrate a hit or curse a near miss. It was as if he was born to be an archer, thought Cato.

'Stand to, Cato,' Macro urged him. 'You're missing the fun!'

He focused his mind on his bow once again, bringing it up as his fingers scrabbled for a fresh arrow. There was only time for three more shots before the hunt master shouted the order to cease. The sudden stillness after the frantic action was shocking and for an instant the officers stared over the open ground littered with the feathered arrows and the bodies of stricken animals, some still writhing as they bled out.

Then an officer let out a shrill whoop and punched his fist into the air. The cry broke the tense silence and others joined in or turned to their comrades to boast about their fine shooting.

'What did you get?' asked Macro.

'Just one shot on the boar. The rest were misses.' Cato clicked his tongue.

'That big fellow must have unsettled your aim.'

Macro pointed to the stag, now lying still, head twisted to one side and tongue lolling from its open jaws.

'Nice thought, Macro. But the misses came after the boar, and that came after the stag. No need to make excuses for me. I'll have better luck with a spear against the boars later on.'

Macro leaned round Cato. 'What about you, sir?'

Tribune Otho tapped his empty quiver. 'Ran out. Shame, since I was starting to warm up nicely.'

'Good on you. So, how many hits?'

'How many?' Otho cocked an eyebrow. 'Why, all of them, of course.'

The hunt master called to his men and they entered the killing ground. The beaters headed back to their starting positions to prepare for the next shoot. Those animals that had survived the funnel were driven into the pens, with the deer and boars kept apart. Their escape was only temporary. While some men collected up the arrows that had missed and dug out the rest, others began to haul the carcasses to a spot a short distance from the carts to begin the messy work of gutting them. Servants replenished the officers' quivers ready for the next round.

Throughout the rest of the morning Cato continued to miss most of his targets no matter how hard he tried to make use of the advice offered to him by Tribune Otho. It was deeply frustrating to make little, if any, progress and by the end he was starting to develop a wholly irrational hatred of the bow which seemed to defy his attempts at mastering it. Macro had much better fortune and his cheerful banter grated on Cato's nerves as they made their way to the refreshment cart at midday.

The deer were hanging from wooden frames, limbs splayed with a dark slash across their stomachs. Their entrails were heaped a short distance away, a pile of glistening grey and purple that had already attracted crows who picked savagely at the unexpected bounty. Three boars lay on their sides beside the deer. A number of hares had been killed and these were thrown to the hunting dogs brought up from the camp for the afternoon's sport. They snarled as they fought over the bloody scraps of fur and meat.

Baskets of bread and cheese were set on the ground for the officers and wineskins passed round as they talked over the morning's shoot. Cato did his best to join in with the conversation of Macro and some of the other officers but his deplorable performance made him feel a bit of a fraud and he had to content himself with the odd nod and laugh as he stood on the fringe of the discussion. At the same time, he watched his comrades with an analytical eye and noted those who boasted freely, or seemed eager to please, and those who contributed to the conversation with the diffidence of professional soldiers. It would be useful to know more of the quality of the men he fought alongside.

A sudden commotion at the neck of the funnel drew Cato's attention and he saw two soldiers dragging what, at first, looked like another animal carcass from the killing zone. Then it moved and Cato saw a face fringed with matted hair looking up from the folds of a fur cloak.

'What's this?' Macro remarked. 'Looks like the lads have found themselves a prisoner.'

The officers fell silent as the native was manhandled over to the feet of the general and thrown to the ground. The man rolled on to his side and groaned as Ostorius demanded a report from the soldiers.

'We found him hiding up near the ridge, sir. There at the end of the vale. Lying in the heather.'

'He didn't try to escape?'

'No point, sir. We were all round him. Didn't have a chance.'

'And he didn't try to resist?'

'He couldn't, sir. He's been wounded. Look there.' The legionary leaned over the prisoner and grasped his arm and pulled it up for the general to see. There was a dark, crusted mouth of a large stab wound on his bicep. Ostorius examined it briefly before he spoke.

'Looks like it was caused by one of our weapons. Most likely as a result of a skirmish with some of our scouts. He's one of Caratacus's men.'

Otho edged towards Cato and muttered, 'How can he tell if it was a Roman weapon?'

'The Silurians fight like the rest of the tribes in Britannia: they like a long sword. That tends to lead to slashing wounds. Not a pretty sight. A lot of blood and a large gash. Whereas our men are trained to use the point, so you end up with wounds that look like that. Not so spectacular, but the blade goes in deeper than a cut and tends to cause more damage.'

'I see,' said the tribune.

'What shall I do with him, sir?' asked the legionary. 'Take him back to the camp? If we can sort the wound out, he could fetch a decent price.'

Ostorius stroked his chin as he considered the fate of the man lying before him. The Silurian was muttering away in his tongue in between groans caused by his wound and the rough handling he had received from the legionaries who had discovered him.

'Does anyone understand this uncouth wretch?' He looked round at his officers and men. 'Well?'

No one replied and the general stared down haughtily at the native. 'Then I have no use for another prisoner. We have enough already, and soon we'll have many more of them to sell to the slave dealers. Once we've dealt with Caratacus. But this one can add to the day's entertainment. It's time my hounds were given some exercise.'

Cato felt the hairs on his neck rise in foreboding as the general turned to the hunt master.

'We'll use this fellow. Get him up and take him into the funnel. We'll let him have a head start and then set the dogs on him.'

Cato took a step forward. 'Sir, wait.'

Ostorius turned to him with a scowl. 'What is it, Prefect Cato?'

'We have native scouts back at the camp. They can help with the interrogation of the prisoner.'

'There isn't going to be any interrogation.'

'But he might give us information about Caratacus, sir. At least he might have some idea where the enemy is heading.'

Ostorius shrugged. 'The scouts will discover that soon enough. We don't need this scum.' He prodded the Silurian with his boot. The man had grasped that his fate was in the balance and that it was Cato who was trying to save him. He shuffled closer to the prefect and raised his hands imploringly as he continued muttering.

'Why wait for the scouts to report, sir, if this man might give us the answer today?'

'Because this devil could just as easily lie as tell us the truth.' He crossed his arms and continued with a slight sneer, 'Now, if you have done with it, Cato, I'd like to continue with proceedings.'

Cato had no wish to see the prisoner torn apart by dogs but realised that he had already tested the general's temper as far as it was sensible to. He took one last glance down at the pathetic individual huddled by his boots and tore his gaze away as he saw the man's limbs trembling. Before he could protest any further Ostorius clicked his fingers at the legionaries and the soldiers grasped the man, pulling him to his feet and shoving him towards the wicker screens. The officers followed them and filed out to each side to get a good view of what was to come.

Macro fell into step with his friend and muttered, 'What do you think you're doing?'

'Trying to save that prisoner's life.'

'Well, you ain't achieved nothing except to piss the old man off. Ye gods! I thought I was the one who needed to watch his tongue around the quality.'

The legionaries held the man by his arms, causing him to grimace as his wound was squeezed. Fresh blood began to ooze from under the scabs.

'Bring up the hounds!' Ostorius ordered.

The hunt master gestured to two of his men and they unchained the dogs. There were six of them, large, shaggy hunting dogs bred by the natives. They brought them forward on leashes, fists bunched round the leather as the dogs strained against them.

'Give 'em a scent of the prey!'

The hunt master approached the prisoner, drew his dagger and cut a large strip off his cloak. He sheathed the blade and returned to the dogs, holding the strip beneath their muzzles as they sniffed eagerly. The Silurian now fully understood what was going to happen and he stared over his shoulder at the general as he begged for his life.

'Release him,' Ostorius said coldly.

The legionaries did as they were ordered and stepped away. The Silurian glanced at the faces on either side, vainly looking for any sign of help. The general raised a hand and pointed to the far end of the vale. 'Run . . . RUN!'

The prisoner did not move, until one of the legionaries drew his sword and brandished it in his face.

Cato drew a deep breath and muttered, 'You heard the general, you stupid bastard. Run!'

He took a few faltering steps into the funnel and then increased his pace and suddenly broke into a sprint, racing through the bloodstained grass. The hunt master brought the hounds forward and looked at the general questioningly. 'Now, sir?'

'Not yet. Let's give the man a chance. Or at least, let him think he has a chance,' he added cruelly.

The Silurian had almost reached the mouth of the funnel when Ostorius gave the nod. At once the leashes were slipped from the hounds' collars and they bounded forward into the funnel and after the Silurian. Cato could see that they would catch him long before he could even reach the edge of the forest. The Silurian looked back, saw the dogs, and tumbled over, causing most of the spectators to laugh. The laughter died in their throats as the leading hound suddenly stopped and lowered its head into the grass and came up with a bloodied maw. The other dogs broke off the chase to join in and Cato realised they must have come across the remains of one of the animals killed earlier.

Meanwhile the Silurian was back on his feet and making good his escape.

'The bastard's getting away!' someone shouted.

But Cato knew that the man was wrong. The first of the hounds was already resuming the chase. Then Cato's attention was drawn to one of the officers close by. It was Otho and Cato saw him snatch up a bow. It happened almost before Cato was aware of it. An arrow flew across the grass and struck the Silurian squarely in the back, over the heart. He collapsed to his knees, one hand feebly clawing at the shaft before it fell limply to his side and he toppled face first into the grass and lay still.

'By the gods!' Macro shook his head in admiration. 'Fifty, sixty paces, and he shot him through the heart.'

Cato could not share his friend's admiration. He turned to the tribune and regarded him closely before he spoke in a flat tone. 'A mercy killing?'

Otho stared back. 'There are some deaths from which a man should be spared, even an enemy.'

Not to be put off by his disappointment over the fate of the prisoner, the general gave orders for the boar hunt to begin. The horses were brought forward and the officers took up their hunting spears and mounted. There were only four boars that had survived the funnel earlier in the day and they were released one at a time to eke out the entertainment. Nervous and worn out, the beasts put on a poor show and were quickly run down and piked, with no injuries to any of the horses or riders.

By mid-afternoon the panels had been packed up, the victims of the day's hunt piled on to the bed of a wagon and the column left the vale and made its way back to the army. As they came in sight of the nearest gate Cato saw the rear of a column of legionaries entering the camp, their kit hanging from the marching yokes resting on their shoulders.

'Looks like the boys from the Ninth,' said Macro and at Cato's side the young tribune straightened up in his saddle, his eyes bright with excitement.

'So it is!'

Without further ado, Otho grasped his reins tightly and swerved his horse out of the column, spurring it into a gallop.

'Bit keen, isn't he?' said Macro.

'Yes, and I dare say it's not to rejoin his first independent command so much as his first dependent.'

Macro gave him a long-suffering look. 'The boy's not thinking,' he commented. 'The general's not going to like this.'

Sure enough, at the sound of pounding hoofs Ostorius had turned in his saddle, just in time to see the tribune galloping past.

'TRIBUNE OTHO!' Ostorius roared.

For a moment Cato was sure that the tribune would keep going, but sense prevailed and he reined in and turned his horse.

'Where do you think you are going?' the general demanded.

'If you please, sir. Those are my men, and my wife is with them.'

'That's no reason to behave like an excited schoolboy! I will not have my officers tearing around like dogs. What kind of impression does that give the men? Get back in line, Tribune Otho. I warn you. Do not give me any further cause to upbraid you or there will be severe consequences. Do I make myself clear?'

Otho bowed his head and muttered an apology. With a last look towards the rear of the column entering the camp he trotted his horse back along the column and rejoined Cato and Macro. No one spoke until they reached the camp and passed through the gate. The reinforcements from the Ninth Legion were resting on either side of the main route stretching through the camp to headquarters. They had downed their yokes and stood stretching their backs, or sat where the ground had not been too badly churned up. The four centurions in command of the cohorts were waiting beside a covered wagon halfway along the column and saluted Ostorius as he rode up to them. The general waved the rest of the hunting party on, and gestured to Otho to join him before he turned his attention back to the nearest of the centurions.

'I was expecting you to reach camp earlier than this.'

'Begging your pardon, sir, but we had to keep pace with the wagon.' He jerked his thumb over his shoulder. Cato saw there were two vehicles besides the standard supply wagons. One had a large wine jar painted on its cover, together with the legend, 'Hipparchus, wine supplier to the gods!' The other was a carriage covered with goatskin, with a laced flap over the opening at the rear. As he watched he could make out a delicate-looking hand unplucking the laces.

Ostorius sucked in a deep breath and addressed the centurions. 'Has the camp prefect assigned you tent lines yet?'

'Just doing it, sir. He's shifting some of the camp followers.'

Cato shared a weary glance with Macro and sighed. There would be complaints from the civilians to deal with later on.

'Very well. Tribune Otho!'

'Sir?'

'Take command of your men. Get the tents up and then report to headquarters to draw rations from the quartermaster.'

'Yes, sir.'

Ostorius flicked his reins and trotted back to the head of the hunting party, while Otho slipped from his saddle and landed with a squelch in the muddy track. Cato and Macro were passing the wagon when the flap opened and a head and shoulders emerged from the dim interior.

'Poppaea, my love.' Otho grinned in delight.

A servant hurried round from behind the wagon and lowered a set of wooden steps for his mistress to descend. As she came fully into view, Macro sucked in a breath.

'Now I understand why our boy was so keen.'

Cato nodded as he ran his eyes over the woman. She was tall and slender, with tawny blond hair plaited back behind her delicate ears. Her cheekbones were high and her features finely proportioned with sculptural precision. But he was surprised. Poppaea was beautiful, all right, but she was clearly several years older than her new husband. As she set eyes on him she smiled and it transformed her face completely so that she became radiant against the backdrop of mud and tents. Before Cato could pass any comment to Macro, he heard shouts from ahead and saw one of the headquarters clerks running towards the general. He stopped at the general's side and spoke hurriedly. The general snapped a few questions at the man before he dismissed him and turned to the hunting party that had stopped behind him.

'Officers! On me!'

Cato and Macro joined the others, urging their mounts forward until they clustered about the general. All trace of Ostorius's weariness had vanished from his face as he looked over their expressions eagerly.

'The scouts have found Caratacus! He's gone to ground on a hill not two days' march from here. We have him, gentlemen! At last we have him.'

CHAPTER SEVEN

The general dismounted on the gentle slope a hundred paces from the bank of the river that separated them from Caratacus's army. The current ran swiftly for some distance in either direction, violent swirls revealing where large rocks lurked beneath the surface. At its narrowest the river was fifty yards wide, with steep banks on either side that presented a difficult obstacle to any heavily armed soldier attempting to get across. Further difficulties were presented by the stakes that the Silurians had driven into the bed of the river at every point where it was possible to ford the river.

Prefect Horatius chewed his lip. 'It's going to be a bugger to get across.'

'True enough,' Macro agreed. 'But that's the least of our worries. It's what's waiting for us on the other side that gives me the terrors.'

The officers closest to him who had heard the remark shifted their gaze to the mass of the hill that rose steeply from the opposite bank. In places sheer cliffs dropped down to the water. Where it was possible to scale the slopes of the hill the enemy had piled boulders to create crude defence works. A second line of obstacles ran along the top of the slope where it began to level out at the summit, some four or five hundred feet above the river, Cato estimated. Enemy warriors lined the defences, in their thousands, glaring at the Roman army setting up camp on the gently rolling ground a quarter of a mile beyond the river. A green standard with what looked like some kind of red winged beast flapped in the breeze blowing at the crest of the hill. Beneath stood a party of men in ruddy brown cloaks and the patterned trousers favoured by the native warriors, watching the Roman officers below.

'There's Caratacus.' Cato pointed the group out.

Macro squinted at the men beneath the banner. 'No doubt gloating over the challenge he's set us. We'll soon wipe the smile off the face of that bastard.'

Horatius cleared his throat and leaned to the side to spit on the ground. 'Don't be too sure of that, Macro. He's picked good ground to make his stand. He's turned the hill into a bloody fortress.'

'It's still a hill, sir,' Macro maintained. 'Which means there must be a way to outflank his defences.'

'You think so? Look again.'

Macro surveyed the landscape before him. The hill extended at least a mile and a half before dropping away sharply at each end, and the river followed the contours, providing a natural moat for the makeshift fortress. 'What's on the far side of the hill?'

Cato shrugged. 'That's anyone's guess.' He indicated the squadron of auxiliary horsemen picking their way along the bank of the river. They were being shadowed on the far bank by a party of lightly armed natives who easily kept pace with the Romans. 'We won't know until the scouts report to the general.'

Tribune Otho had been standing a short distance away, scrutinising the enemy position, and came to join Cato and the others. He was wearing a silvered breastplate with an elaborate design of rearing horses etched into the surface. The polished strips of his leather jerkin gleamed in the sunshine and his cloak was clean and showed none of the fraying or small tears that marred the cloaks of the other officers. The rest of his armour and equipment was equally new and to cap it all he wore closed leather boots dyed red that laced up to the top of his shins.

'As bright as a newly minted denarius,' Macro muttered with a disapproving shake of his head. 'He's going to stand out like a swinging dick at a eunuch massage parlour. Every Silurian warrior worth his salt is going to be after his head.'

Cato had to agree. Soon after first setting foot on British soil he had discovered the natives' fondness for collecting the heads of those they defeated in battle. The head of a Roman officer was a most desirable trophy to display in their crude wattle and daub huts. With his good looks and his gleaming helmet with its bright red crest, Otho would draw the attention of every Silurian warrior that caught sight of him.

'Hello, chaps!' Otho waved a greeting as he strode up to them.

'Must say, those natives have a good eye for ground. But they'll be no match for the men of the Ninth, or even the other legions, I'll wager. Soon as the general gives the order we'll clear Caratacus and his mob off that hill.'

'Is that so?' Horatius sucked a breath in through his teeth. Cato saw the look of irritation flash across his expression before he smiled coolly at the tribune. 'Well, I'd be more than happy for you and your men to show us all how the job's done. Why don't you ask the general for the honour of leading the attack? I'm sure he would be impressed.'

Otho considered the idea briefly. 'Why not? About time I had a chance to do my duty.'

'Why not?' Macro frowned. 'Because you don't just go ploughing into the enemy, sir. There's a right way to go about this. And a wrong way.' He turned to Cato. 'Ain't that right, sir?'

Cato quickly understood the implied meaning of his comrade's remark. He nodded and addressed the prefect in a gentle tone. 'This is your first battle, I take it.'

'Well, yes. As it happens.'

'Then take the chance to watch and learn. You can prove yourself another time. Good soldiers learn from experience. Or they pay the price.'

Otho stared at him earnestly and turned back to scrutinise the enemy position. 'I understand.'

A moment later General Ostorius decided he had seen enough. He issued curt orders for pickets to be posted along the riverbank before mounting his horse and riding back into the camp. His staff officers scrambled to follow him and the others were left to ponder the formidable obstacles before them a while longer before they, too, turned away and returned to their units. The men toiled to construct the ditch and rampart that surrounded the vast area required for the two legions, the detachment from the Ninth, eight cohorts of auxiliary troops, the baggage train and the camp followers. It was more like a modest town than a camp, Cato mused as he approached the site of the main gate. The tower supports had already been driven into the earth and men were busy easing the crosspieces into position. As they reached the tent lines of the cohorts from the Ninth, Otho waved a hand and spurred his horse into a trot as he made for his headquarters

70

tent, the first to be erected by the men before they turned to their own, far more modest section tents where eight men slept cheek by jowl.

'The boy's keen to get back to his wife,' Macro chuckled. 'Not that I'm the marrying kind, but I can see the advantages of having your wife with you on campaign. Saves a fortune,' he added with a sly wink.

'I don't know about that,' said Cato. 'She looks like the kind of woman who is expensive to keep.'

'Your good lady excepted, name one aristocratic bit who isn't.'

Cato smiled. 'And that, my friend, is just one reason why I married her. As for the other reasons – don't ask.'

'As if.' Macro rode a short distance in silence before he added, 'Had any news lately?'

'Not since we landed.'

'That was nearly five months ago.'

Cato shrugged. 'We're fighting a war on the very fringes of the known world. It could take several months for a letter to reach me from Rome.'

'True. But I'm sure she's fine. Julia's a healthy girl. And loyal as veteran. Not that I'm suggesting there's any question . . .'

'Well, yes. Quite,' Cato responded tersely. 'But I can't be thinking about that. Not now. Not until we've defeated Caratacus.'

Macro nodded but glanced sidelong at his friend, not fooled for an instant by Cato's dismissive response. The lad had found his love, and it was typical of life in the army that he should be forced to leave her behind a mere month or so after their marriage. It was likely to be some years before Cato saw her again. Anything could happen in that time, Macro mused sadly as they reached the tent lines of the baggage escort detachment.

As the light faded in the evening and there was no sign of any imminent assault, most of the enemy warriors began to filter away from their barricades, climbing the slope to their encampment at the top of the hill. Fires were lit as the sun set and the glow of the flames lined the ridge. The Roman soldiers along the riverbank could just make out their opposite numbers on the far side. While most held their tongues,

71

every now and then insults were traded across the water until an optio, without any irony, bellowed to his men to keep watch in silence. Faint snatches of singing and laughter carried down the slope as Caratacus and his warriors worked themselves up into drunken fervour ahead of the battle they expected the next day.

In the Roman camp the mood was more subdued, more purposeful, as the soldiers went through the daily routines of military life. Once the tents were erected, they prepared their simple evening meals before those assigned to the first watch put on armour, took up weapons and marched to their posts. Their comrades sat around cooking fires, cleaning kit and sharpening weapons for the coming fight. In the main they talked quietly and those soldiers who had not yet put their hard training into bloody practice sat in silence, nurturing their courage and trying to put aside their fears: fear of death, fear of a crippling wound, fear of the terrible cold thrust of an enemy spear, sword or arrow, or the crushing blow of slingshot; and worst of all, fear of not being able to hide their terror in front of their comrades. Others sat with the veterans, earnestly seeking advice and guidance about how best to face what was to come. The advice was always the same. To trust their training, put their faith in the gods and kill every living thing that stood in their path.

In the headquarters tent the mood was equally sombre as General Ostorius and his senior officers also contemplated the morrow's events. His subordinates were sitting on stools and benches around the edge of the tent. The pale light of oil lamps added to the sense of gloom as the general addressed them.

'The cavalry patrols followed the river for ten miles in either direction. There seem to be no viable crossing places for the army. If we break camp and follow the river until we can turn Caratacus's position then he will of course be forced to abandon the hill and continue retreating. However, while he is retreating on his lines of supply into Ordovician territory we are extending ours, so the logistical advantage now belongs to the enemy. We've already seen how easily he has managed to elude us in previous campaigns.' Ostorius paused, before continuing with feeling, 'I do not want to spend another year in these wretched mountains chasing shadows. I do not want to see our legions and auxiliary cohorts slowly bleed to death in endless skirmishes and raids. The gods have placed Caratacus in front of us and we will fight him here. I will not give him any excuse to break contact and escape. He has offered us battle on his terms, and like it or not, that is what we must accept, gentlemen.'

He looked round the tent to make sure that his intent was understood. 'Since that is the situation, we are obliged to make a frontal attack across the river. I have decided that the first wave will go forward at noon tomorrow. That will give us time to site our artillery to bombard their barricades. Once we have opened some breaches we will be able to break through and take the hill . . . Any questions?'

'Plenty,' Macro whispered to Cato. 'But I know better than to ask.'

'Then I'll have to,' Cato said quietly. He leaned forward on his stool and raised a hand to draw the general's attention.

Ostorius faced him and clasped his hands behind his back. 'Prefect Cato, what do you have to say?'

'Sir, the first line of barricades are just about in range of our artillery. But not the second line. We will not be able to batter those down.'

'I realise that. Our men will have to fight their way over the defences.'

'But in order to do that, they are going to have to cross the river, find a way through the stakes in the river bed, climb on to the far bank, and up the hill in full armour. Then fight their way through the breaches in the first line and climb the rest of the way up the slope to the second line. No doubt they will be subjected to the enemy's missiles as they climb. Sir, I'd wager that by the time they reach the second line they will be too exhausted to fight.'

'Nevertheless, they will fight. And they will break through and win the day.'

'But the casualties are bound to be heavy, sir. Very heavy.'

'That may be so. If that is the price of finally defeating Caratacus then it is a price worth paying. But that need not concern you unduly, Prefect Cato. After all, you and your men will be guarding the baggage train and will not be playing any part in the battle. You will come to no harm.'

Some of the officers could not help smiling at the comment and Cato felt a surge of anger pulse through his veins. They might take offence at his swift promotion through the ranks but they had no right

73

to sneer at his courage. He had to force himself to speak calmly. 'In view of the challenge facing the army tomorrow, I respectfully submit that my men join in the attack, sir. They have already proved themselves against the enemy.'

'That will not be necessary. I think you overestimate the difficulties we face. Besides, your men are needed here. It would put my mind at rest knowing that the camp is being protected by men who are used to facing their enemy with a wall and rampart between them, as you proved so adeptly at Bruccium.'

This time the general had gone too far and for all his good judgement Cato's pride would not let the slur pass unanswered. He made to reply but Macro nudged him sharply and hissed under his breath, 'Leave it, Cato.'

For an instant Cato was on the verge of open confrontation with his commanding officer. Then he bit down on his injured pride and anger and eased himself back on to his stool. Ostorius regarded him haughtily, then shifted his gaze round the tent. 'Anyone else?'

It was a challenge as much as a question and every man in the tent understood that and did not wish to share in the dismissive scorn directed at Cato. There was silence. Ostorius nodded.

'Very well. Then the attack will be carried out by our legionaries. It's too tough a job for auxiliary cohorts. Instead, the auxiliaries will be leaving the camp under cover of darkness and marching round the hill to cut off the enemy's retreat.'

That caused murmurs to ripple amongst the officers seated around the tent. Night manoeuvres were difficult to carry out at the best of times. The Romans knew little of the ground they had to cover and would be vulnerable to any ambush that the enemy might have set. Equally, units might lose their way and not reach their assigned positions on time. It was a risky enterprise.

'I understand your concerns,' said Ostorius. 'But I will not give Caratacus and his men any excuse to abandon their position and escape. If that happens due to the negligence of any officer then be sure that they will be answerable to me, and to the Emperor. Every man will do his duty. You will be given your orders as soon as my clerks have them ready for distribution. You are dismissed, gentlemen.'

He returned to his desk at the far end of the tent and sat heavily on his cushioned chair. His officers rose and shuffled towards the open tent flaps. Cato hung back, even now ready to try and dissuade his superior, until Macro muttered, 'Don't do it, sir.'

Cato rounded on him and spoke quietly. 'Why did you stop me?'

'Jupiter have mercy . . . He was goading you. Surely you can see that? If you had answered back, you would only have been playing into his hands and made yourself look foolish in front of the others.'

Cato thought briefly and nodded. 'You're right . . . Thank you, Macro.'

As they left the tent, one of the general's clerks saw them and respectfully eased his way through the officers. 'Prefect Cato, sir.'

'What is it?'

'A package of letters arrived with the reinforcements from the Ninth, sir. This one is for you.'

He held out a slim, folded leather case, fastened by the wax seal of the Sempronius family. Cato's name, rank and the provincial headquarters of Camulodonum were written in a neat hand beside the seal. He recognised the writing at once as that of his wife, Julia, and he felt his heart give a lurch.

'Thank you.' He smiled at the clerk, who bowed and turned to find the next recipient of letters from the package.

'From Julia?' asked Macro.

Cato nodded.

'Then I'll leave you to read it. I'll be in the officers' mess.'

Outside the general's tent was an open area bounded by the other tents that made up the army's headquarters. The area was lit by the flames rising from iron braziers. It was a warm night and the only clouds in the sky were away to the west, leaving the stars to shine down unobstructed. It felt peaceful, and Cato was reminded of the last night he had spent with Julia in Rome, up on the roof terrace of her father's house. Even though it was winter, they too had been warmed by a fire, and each other, as they lay and gazed up at the heavens. He smiled fondly at the memory, before the familiar ache for her returned.

Moving close to the glow of the nearest brazier, Cato held the letter up and touched the smooth wax around the impression of the Sempronius motif, a dolphin. Then he tugged the leather cover and broke the seal, carefully opening the cover to expose the sheets of

75

papyrus inside. He angled them towards the flames and began to read. The letter was dated barely two months after he had left Rome and had taken another two months to reach him.

My dearest husband, Cato,

I take this chance to write to you as an acquaintance of my father who is leaving for Britannia and knows of you has asked if he might carry a message from me to you. Time is short so I fear I cannot express the emptiness in my heart that your absence causes. You are my all, Cato. So I pray daily for your safety and your swift return to me once you have completed your service in the army of Ostorius Scapula. I know that it may be years before we can be in each other's arms again, and I know I must be strong and constant in my affections, and I will be. And I would have you know that, with all my heart.

The news in Rome is that Ostorius is seeking an end to the campaign in Britannia to coincide with the end of his generalship. Father says that the Emperor has let it be known that such a victory is worthy of an Ovation. Inevitably the senators will vote accordingly. If so, then you are sure to be amongst those officers honoured alongside Ostorius in Rome. I pray so. It is no more than you deserve for your service to the Emperor.

Meanwhile, the Emperor grows old and the city is rife with rumour over who will succeed him. Though Britannicus is his natural child, it seems that the Emperor's new wife is doing all in her power to push the interests of her son, Nero. I cannot say I care for him. He lavishes praise and affection on his adoptive father way beyond the bounds of sincerity. And behind the scenes, Father says, the real struggle is between Claudius's closest advisers, Pallas and your old acquaintance, Narcissus. When there is a new Emperor one of them is not likely to survive the event.

But I grow weary of politics. Especially as I have been writing this while steeling myself to give you news of more import to the two of us. Father and I have found a house on the Quirinal that will suit us. No palace to be sure, but large and airy, with a small garden courtyard. A fine home for my dearest husband to return to, who, by the time he does, will be more than a husband. My darling Cato, I am with child. I am certain of it. Our child. The seed of you grows within me and it makes me feel closer to you, though you be on the far side of the empire. I must

finish this message now, the merchant is ready to depart. I send this,
with all my heart, your loving wife, Julia.

Cato felt a surge of ardour and affection swell in his heart. A child. Their child. It would be born in the autumn. Cato felt a sense of loss. He would not be there with Julia when the child came. In fact it was likely that he would not see the child for some years. The moment passed and the prospect of being a father lifted his spirits beyond all measure and banished all thought of weariness and the coming battle. He re-read the letter, this time savouring every phrase, every word, hearing Julia speak them in his mind. At length he refolded the letter and replaced it in its cover before carefully tucking it into his belt. He must tell Macro. He had to share his joy and they must celebrate.

The tent set up for the army's officers was a short distance from headquarters and as Cato strode towards it he could hear the sounds of laughter and the hubbub of lively conversation. He was surprised, given the dour mood in the general's tent shortly before. Perhaps the officers were drowning their anxieties in wine and the sweet beer brewed by the natives that had become popular with the soldiers serving in Britannia.

Ducking through the tent flaps, Cato was enveloped in the warm fug inside. The smell of drink mingled with the men's sweat and the acrid odour of woodsmoke. The sound of men's voices was deafening, but Cato's attention was instantly drawn to the individual who dominated the scene. In the middle of the tent stood the wife of Tribune Otho. She was surrounded by younger officers and a handful of older veterans, somewhat sheepishly enjoying the rare charm of a woman's company. She had just finished some remark and the men around her roared with laughter. At her side, his arm lightly about her waist, stood Otho, beaming with pleasure.

'And who is this dashing character?'

Cato's gaze flicked back to Poppaea and he saw that she was smiling at him. He hesitated, anxious to find Macro and share his news, but at the same time mindful of social niceties. He approached the woman, and the officers parted before him until he took her hand and bowed his head. Her skin was soft and white and just before she released her formal grip on his hand she gave it a quick squeeze.

77

'Prefect Cato, my lady. Commander of the Second Thracian Cavalry.'

'And guardian of the army's column of whores!' a voice called out from the crowd.

There was a quick chorus of laughter from some of the officers before Otho spoke. 'And this is my wife, Poppaea Sabrina.'

'A pleasure to meet you, Prefect. As it is to meet any of my new husband's comrades.'

Cato fumbled for an appropriate reply and gushed, 'The pleasure is mine, my lady.'

'Spoken like a happily married man,' she replied with a mischievous smile. 'Well, don't let me keep you.'

Cato bowed his head and backed away and she turned her attention back to the other officers. He glanced round and saw Macro over at the wine counter buying a small flask from the trader who had won the contract to supply the mess. Macro was reaching for his purse as Cato joined him.

'Put that away. This one is on me.' Cato turned to the merchant. 'What is your best wine?'

'Sir?' The merchant was a dark-skinned easterner, wrapped in thick tunic and cap, despite the heat inside the tent.

'Your best wine. What have you got?'

'There's the Arretian, but it's five denarians a flask.'

Cato rummaged in his purse and slapped down the silver coins. 'Fine. We'll have that.'

'A moment please.' The merchant ducked under the counter and stood again, holding a slipware amphora. He carefully extracted the stopper and filled a jug before replacing the amphora in its place of safety.

'What are we celebrating?' Macro asked with a puzzled expression.

Cato did not reply but filled them each a cup before handing one to Macro. 'There.'

Macro shook his head. 'What's this about, lad?'

'It seems that I am going to be a father … Cheers!'

Macro's eyebrows rose in surprise before a delighted expression creased his face.

Cato raised his cup and drank deeply, swigging down the fine wine as if it was water. As the last dreg dripped into his mouth he set it down on the counter with a sharp rap. 'Ahhhh!'

Macro grinned widely, revealing his uneven stained teeth. He downed his drink in half the time it had taken his friend and then threw his arms round Cato in a quick, crushing embrace.

'Why, that's bloody marvellous, lad! Bloody marvellous news!' He released Cato and stood back, still grinning. 'When?'

'I-I don't know. Julia just says that she is with child.'

'That's wonderful . . . I suppose that makes me a kind of uncle figure.'

'No chance!' Cato joked. 'Julia won't want our child swearing like a veteran before it can even walk.'

Macro growled and punched his friend lightly on the chest.

'Gentlemen!' a voice called from the entrance to the mess tent. All eyes turned towards the clerk holding a basket of waxed tablets. 'Unit commanders! Your orders!'

The cheerful mood died instantly as the senior officers clustered round the clerk and waited their turn to receive their tablet.

Cato's smile faded.

'Never mind, lad. We'll celebrate properly tomorrow night.'

'Yes.' Cato nodded. 'Tomorrow.'

He took a deep breath and left Macro to pour another cup of wine as he crossed the tent and joined the others waiting to discover their role in the coming battle. A battle he would experience as a mere spectator.

CHAPTER EIGHT

As Cato and Macro reached the headquarters tent of the baggage train escort, Thraxis ducked out of the tent flaps, the nearest campfire illuminating the concerned expression in his face.

'Prefect, thank the gods you are here.'

'What is it?'

'There's a man inside. He refuses to leave.'

Macro frowned. 'What man?'

'A wine merchant, sir.'

'Wine merchant?' Cato exchanged a puzzled look with his friend. 'What is a wine merchant doing in my tent at this hour?'

Thraxis chewed his lip. 'He says I cheated him, Prefect. I swear it's not true.'

'Cheated him? How?'

'He says I paid him in counterfeit coin, and that he's come to demand that you have me condemned.'

Cato paused. Using counterfeit coins was a capital offence. The Emperor did not take kindly to criminals debasing the money on which his face had been struck. The coins he had given Thraxis were genuine. Freshly minted denarians. There was no question of them being forged. Now he must deal with the accusation laid at the door of his servant before he could get some sleep. He toyed briefly with the idea of throwing the merchant out but knew that would only mean that the man would take his complaint to the general's head-quarters instead.

'Oh, very well,' he grumbled. 'Macro, I'll need you in on this.'

'Me? Why?'

Cato looked at him knowingly. 'Because you still have some of the same batch of coins that I do. You can vouch that they are genuine.'

Thraxis smiled gratefully and stepped aside to open the tent flaps for the two officers. Inside Cato's headquarters tent there was only one person sitting on a stool. The two clerks in charge of the cohort's records had gone off duty and the waxed slates and sheets of papyrus had been left in neat piles for them to resume the next day. There was only one lamp burning and the wine merchant's face was barely visible in the gloom.

Cato regarded their visitor irritably. 'My servant tells me that you wish to complain about the silver I gave him to pay you.'

The man rose to his feet and bowed. 'Noble Prefect, I apologise profusely that I must intrude upon your evening, but I come here on a matter of utmost importance.'

'Money.' Macro sniffed. 'That's all that your kind value.'

The merchant raised his hands and shrugged. 'Sir, it is the means by which we live. Who would not value it? But as I said, I must speak with the prefect. It would be best to send that Thracian dog away first.'

'Why?' asked Cato. 'If you mean to accuse him, then do it to his face and let him answer your accusations.'

Thraxis stood silently at the threshold of the tent, his face strained. Cato was not sure if the man was grateful to be given the chance to defend himself or would rather let his commander do it for him. The prospect of the situation degenerating into a slanging match between the merchant and his servant was more than Cato could bear at this hour. He sighed and jerked his thumb towards the tent flaps.

'Go and find some firewood. I want you to light the brazier in my sleeping quarters.'

'Yes, Prefect.' Thraxis bowed his head, and shooting a hateful glare at the wine merchant he ducked out of the tent and disappeared.

Cato slumped down on one of the clerks' benches and scratched his head. Macro stood, arms folded, watching the visitor.

'So,' Cato began. 'What's the story?'

The wine merchant slowly stepped forward, closer to the oil lamp, and by its light Cato and Macro could make out his features. He wore a plain brown tunic and breeches beneath his green cloak and thick-soled boots. His hair was dark and his face thin and bony. Cato recognised him with a look of surprise.

81

'Septimus . . .'

'What?' Macro's eyebrows rose. 'Septimus? By the gods, you're right. What in Jupiter's name are you doing here?'

The imperial agent smiled faintly and dropped the singsong tone he had used when posing as the wine merchant. 'And it's delightful to see you again, Centurion Macro. Aren't you going to ask me how my trip was?'

Macro's mouth was slack with surprise as he stared at the man. It was Cato who recovered first and fixed his eyes firmly on Septimus. 'Like Macro says, what are you doing here? Why the disguise?'

'I can avoid drawing any unwanted attention to myself as Hipparchus the wine merchant,' Septimus explained. 'I bought the business off the real Hipparchus back in Londinium, as well as some useless oaf that the Greek was using to help him. Anyway, come, my friends.' Septimus affected a hurt expression. 'Is this any way to greet an old comrade in arms? Have you so quickly forgotten that we fought side by side against the Emperor's enemies on the streets of Rome?'

'Bollocks to that,' Macro growled. 'Any son of Narcissus is no comrade of mine.'

'You're breaking my heart, Centurion.'

'Enough of this!' Cato snapped. 'Just explain what you are doing here. I don't suppose for a moment that you've come to investigate minor outbreaks of counterfeiting on the outer reaches of the empire.'

Septimus's mask of hurt pride disappeared. 'Very well, let's dispense with the pleasantries.'

'Let's!' Macro said brusquely.

'I've been sent here by my father.'

Macro held his head in his hands. 'Tell me it isn't true. Tell me that oily bastard doesn't want to get us involved in some wretched scheme of his.'

'Why did he send you?' Cato demanded. 'What does he want this time?'

Septimus looked offended. 'Narcissus has sent me to warn you of a threat to both your lives. You are in grave danger.'

'Really?' Macro raised his hands. 'Did you hear that, Cato? We're in danger. Here, in the heart of enemy territory, on the eve of a battle. In danger. Who'd have believed it?' He turned back towards Septimus.

'It is the imperial intelligence service you both work for, isn't it? Seems to me like you lot need to find yourselves a new title.'

'Ha . . . ha . . .' Septimus responded flatly. 'Much as I enjoy the sophisticated repartee of you soldiers, the hour is late and time is short. It would be best to discuss the matter at hand.'

Cato nodded, and crossed the tent to close the leather flaps and then did the same for the entrance to his personal tent. There was another entrance that Thraxis could use when he returned with the wood to build a fire in the brazier.

'Speak, then.'

Septimus settled on to a spare bench and collected his thoughts. 'Four months ago we took one of Pallas's agents off the street. We'd been following him for several days and noting that he had been to see a number of interesting characters in the city. Narcissus thought it was time to bring him in so we could have a quiet word.'

Cato did not have to imagine too hard the full meaning behind the euphemism and felt a chill in his spine as Septimus continued.

'In the course of our conversation with this man, Musa was his name—'

'Was?' Macro arched an eyebrow.

Septimus shot him a look. 'He is no longer relevant. Anyway, Musa revealed that Pallas had despatched an agent to Britannia to find and kill you two. As soon as Narcissus heard that he sent me here to warn you.'

'We're touched,' said Macro. 'How considerate of him.'

Cato stroked his chin and then shook his head. 'Four months ago, you said. Then it has taken you quite a time to reach us to pass on the warning.'

'It was a long journey. There were storms holding the ships back at Gesoriacum. It took me a while to track you down once I landed in Britannia.' Septimus shrugged. 'What can I say?'

Cato smiled slightly. 'The truth would be nice.'

'The truth is rarely nice. Trust me, I know.'

'Trust?' Cato shook his head. 'That's worth more than gold in this world, Septimus. It has to be earned. And Macro and I have done more than enough to earn it. So speak plainly. Why did it take so long for you to tell us about this threat?'

Septimus stared back, then took a deep breath before he spoke. 'Narcissus believes that Pallas's agents are here, and that they're plotting to undermine the establishment of a province in Britannia. I was to try and uncover the full extent of Pallas's plans. As well as passing on my father's warning to you.'

'That's more like it.' Macro patted Septimus on the back. 'See? Speaking the truth doesn't hurt.'

'Try telling that to Musa,' said Cato. 'Not that there's any chance of that now. Right?'

Septimus pursed his lips and gave a shrug.

'So what have you discovered?' Cato demanded.

'Precious little, actually. I don't know who the other side's agents are, nor how many of them are here. I do know that one of them arrived in Britannia recently. The one who has been sent to deal with you and Macro. I haven't yet discovered his identity. Meanwhile, be on your guard. The moment I discover who he is I will let you know, and you can deal with him.'

'Deal with him . . .' Cato repeated slowly. 'I see. This is the real purpose of your contacting us. Not to warn us, but to enlist our help. Narcissus wants this agent taken out of your little game and we're supposed to help you. Is that it?'

Septimus smiled. 'It wouldn't hurt for you to assist my father, even if only to save your own necks.'

Macro let out a deep sigh of frustration and anger. 'Let's throw this little snake out of here, Cato. We're done with Narcissus. We're back in the army now. All this bollocks about agents and threats is nothing to us. That's over.'

Cato shared the sentiment but as he scrutinised their visitor he grasped the essential reality of their situation and responded to his friend through gritted teeth. 'I would that it were so, Macro. With all my heart. But there's no escaping the consequences of what plays out back in Rome. It'll never be over for us. Not until Pallas or Narcissus falls from grace. And when that happens you can be sure that anyone even remotely connected with the loser is going to pay a heavy price. Isn't that right, Septimus?'

'I fear so, Prefect. That is why it is important to be on the winning side in the conflict between Pallas and my father.'

Cato narrowed his eyes shrewdly. 'And is your side winning at the moment?'

'My side?' Septimus looked surprised. 'You mean *our* side?'

'I mean what I say.'

'Prefect, whether you two like it or not, your fate is tied to that of my father, just as mine is. If Pallas wins the day, then we are all dead men. You may not even last that long. For whatever reason he may have, Pallas is especially keen to remove you now. My father thinks you know something that may endanger him. Any idea what that might be?'

Macro knew all too well. He had witnessed Pallas locked in a coital embrace with the Emperor's wife, Agrippina. If that was ever revealed then Claudius would be sure to have the imperial freedman executed. To be swiftly followed by the execution of Agrippina, or exile if she was lucky. Her son, Nero, the adopted heir of the Emperor, would also suffer, leaving the path open for Britannicus. But it was a dangerous secret to reveal. If Pallas and Agrippina bluffed their way out of the situation, a task made somewhat easier by the failing mind of the old Emperor, then their accusers would face the full wrath of Claudius instead.

'No,' Cato answered for them both. 'We don't know. We can't help you.'

'A pity. But it changes nothing. Pallas still wants you dead.'

'We can look after ourselves.'

'I'm sure you can. To a degree. But you are used to dangers that are out in the open. You will not see this one coming. Not until it is too late. Trust no one.'

Macro sniffed. 'Except you, and your father, of course.'

'Your enemy's enemy is your friend, Macro. You might not like it, but that's how it is. Our interests coincide. Narcissus needs whatever help you can give him. In return he does what he can to protect you.'

'That's the kind of protection I need like a sword in the guts.'

'As you will.' Septimus opened his hands in a brief gesture of helplessness. 'But if you won't help him for your own sakes, then do it out of a sense of duty to Rome.'

'Duty to Rome? You think Narcissus selflessly serves the interests of Rome?' Macro shook his head and gave a dry laugh. 'He's looking after himself, no matter how many of us he buries along the way.'

For the first time Septimus's composure appeared to slip. He rounded angrily on the centurion and stabbed his finger at him. 'My father has given his life to serving Rome! The emperors come and go but he has remained constant. He serves the empire and does all he can to protect it from enemies without and within.'

'I bet that's just what Pallas claims.'

'Pallas has no interest in Rome,' Septimus countered. 'He wants power and wealth for himself.'

Cato intervened. 'It hasn't escaped my attention that Narcissus has done pretty well out of serving Rome. Rumour has it that he's one of the wealthiest men in the city. In fact, I've heard that he has loaned considerable fortunes to some of the client kings here in Britannia. Is that true?'

Septimus looked down briefly and nodded. 'It's true. But then, so have many other wealthy men.'

'Including Pallas?'

'Not him. Not any more at least. He sold his loans to other parties at the end of last year. And there's a good reason behind that decision.' Septimus looked up at Cato. 'He's plotting against our interests here in Britannia. He's committing treason.'

'That's a serious accusation. You'd better explain yourself.'

Septimus folded his hands together before he continued in a quiet, earnest tone. 'You may have heard the story of how Claudius became Emperor. When his predecessor was butchered by Cassius Chaereas and his co-conspirators, that was supposed to be the end of the imperial line. Rome was to become a republic again. Only the Praetorian Guards realised that meant they would be out of a job. Without an emperor to protect they would be sent to join the legions. No more generous pay and perks. So they plucked Claudius out from the survivors of the imperial family and made him Emperor. And who were the Senate to argue with ten thousand Praetorians armed to the teeth? So he became Emperor Claudius.

'But it was hardly a popular choice. He needed to prove himself worthy of the title. He needed a great victory to ram down the throats of the Senate and to show the people of Rome that he could give them a victory. That's why he invaded Britannia. It gave legitimacy to his reign. Claudius had conquered the island that even Julius Caesar failed to humble. No one was going to argue with that. And that's why he has poured men and resources into Britannia ever since. The conquest must be completed. Britannia must become a settled province of the empire. If we fail here, then Claudius's regime is utterly discredited. His enemies will take heart and make ready to strike at him again. If they succeed, Rome will be plunged into strife again. Is that what you want?'

'If I recall,' said Cato, 'Narcissus was one of those who encouraged Claudius to invade Britannia.'

'So?'

'So this is as much about the safety of your father's position, and his finances, as it is about Claudius and the future of Rome.'

'What of it? It comes to the same thing in the end.'

'I'm glad we've established that. Saves you insulting us any further with appeals to our sense of duty,' Cato said harshly. 'What is it that you suspect Pallas is up to?'

Septimus took a deep breath and spoke calmly. 'It is my father's belief that Pallas wants nothing less than the collapse of this province. And he's prepared to do whatever it takes to ensure that end. He has agents on the island who seek to conspire with Caratacus to unite the most powerful tribes against Rome. If there is an alliance between the mountain tribes and the Brigantians or the Iceni, they will be strong enough to overwhelm our forces. Our legions will be driven back into the sea. Our towns and settlements will be burned to the ground and their inhabitants slaughtered. Rome will be utterly humiliated. Claudius will be shamed, and broken. He will be deposed, one way or another, and even if Rome is fortunate enough to escape the disaster of a new civil war, then Pallas will place Nero on the throne, with Agrippina at his side, and Pallas pulling the strings from the shadows.'

'Instead of Narcissus,' Macro said pointedly. 'A new emperor and a new imperial freedman running the show. That's the only difference.'

'You're wrong, Centurion. Even at the height of his powers my father was part of a council of advisers influencing the Emperor. Under Pallas there will be only one man. And his route to power will be paved with the corpses of the army here in Britannia. You, and all your comrades, and all those others who will die defending the empire once our enemies are encouraged to take up arms following our defeat in Britannia. Those are high stakes. Whatever you may think of my father, you cannot deny that Rome will face disaster if Pallas wins the day.'

Macro stood in thought for a moment, weighing up the imperial agent's explanation. Then he turned to his friend. 'What do you think, lad?'

'I think we have no choice.' Cato smiled weakly. 'Just for a change. It looks like Narcissus has manoeuvred us into another tight spot. Tell me, Septimus, and speak truthfully, did he know what he was sending us into when we were posted to Britannia? Was this part of his plan all along?'

'No. You have my word. My father knew that his influence over the Emperor was starting to wane. He wanted you sent here for your own safety.'

'That's what I understood, but now you'll have to forgive me if I am not as convinced as I was before. It's all a little too coincidental.'

'Damn right!' Macro nodded.

'Think what you like,' Septimus responded. 'It's the truth.'

The tent fell silent as the three men considered the situation. After some time Cato stirred and folded his hands together. 'The question is, what do we do now? You must have had a plan when you came here.'

'Of sorts.' Septimus sat back and ran his fingers through his hair. 'I've bribed a Brigantian nobleman to keep an eye on Queen Cartimandua's consort, Prince Venutius. He's said to be the one who is putting pressure on the queen to throw her lot in with Caratacus. For now, she's playing safe. She's got an alliance with Rome that gives her a ready supply of silver, and the promise of military support if she ever needs it. At the same time she's keeping the door open to Caratacus. A clever woman, but she's in a weak position. If she turns on Caratacus then half of her people will go over to the enemy, along with Venutius. If she turns on us then Venutius will lead her people to war, and when it's over, he'll want power for himself. Either way, she loses. Everything depends on keeping things as they are. If we lose

88

the Brigantians, we lose the province, and everything else. With luck, my spy at her court will warn me in enough time to alert General Ostorius to the danger.'

'How do you know you can trust the general?' asked Cato.

'Ostorius is an old-fashioned type. He wants glory for the family name. His ambition is to win a great victory and return to Rome and hang up his sword. It's some of the other officers I'm keeping an eye on.'

'Oh? Who? Legate Quintatus, for example?'

'Now you're fishing, Prefect. Yes, Quintatus is one. His family are followers of Agrippina's faction. Then there are a small number of senior officers who have arrived in Britannia recently. I know you've already met Tribune Otho and Prefect Horatius. What do you make of them?'

Cato considered his impressions of the two officers before he replied. 'Horatius seems like a reliable officer. Promoted from the ranks, far away from Rome.'

'Not far enough. He was a centurion in the Praetorian Guard at the time of Claudius's accession. He was one of the few who backed the Senate's call for a return to the Republic. Did he tell you that?'

'No. Why should he?'

'Then I guess you wouldn't know that he was reassigned to the Eleventh Legion soon afterwards.'

'Those arse-kissers?' Macro sneered. 'All ready to rise up against the new Emperor, until your father turns up with a hatful of gold and buys 'em off. What's the new title he's given them?' He concentrated for a moment and then clicked his fingers. 'Claudius's Faithful and Patriotic Eleventh Legion . . . Until they are paid off by the next man. Anyway, why send Horatius there if his loyalty is questionable?'

'Best to keep all your potential troublemakers in one spot.'

Macro pursed his lips. 'I see your point.'

'I'm not convinced he's our man,' Septimus resumed. 'But he's worth keeping an eye on. The more interesting character is Tribune Otho. His father was promoted to the Senate by Claudius, and has proved himself trustworthy. The son, however, has become a close friend of Prince Nero.'

'Sounds like our man,' said Macro.

Cato cleared his throat. 'Are you forgetting that I saved Nero's life? He said he would repay the debt one day. Perhaps I am not in so much danger as you imply, Septimus.'

'That was when you were serving undercover in the Praetorian Guard. Nero had no idea you were spying on behalf of Narcissus. I doubt he would even remember you now, Prefect. Besides, Nero is merely a figurehead. Pallas is the real danger. I doubt he will let some small obligation like that stand in the way of having you killed.'

They heard movement in Cato's tent as Thraxis returned with the firewood and started to build it up in the brazier. Septimus stood up.

'I have to go. I've a report to write to my father. I'll let him know I've appraised you of the situation. And that you're prepared to work with me to foil Pallas.'

'Now wait a minute!' Macro started.

'He's right,' Cato interrupted. 'We have to, Macro. For all our sakes.'

Macro opened his mouth to protest, then snapped it shut and shook his head.

'If you need to contact me,' Septimus spoke quietly, 'ask for Hipparchus the wine merchant. That's my cover. I'll be remaining with the army for a few days, and will send word to Rome of Caratacus's defeat. If he is taken, or killed, then Pallas's scheme will be dealt a grievous blow.'

'I hope you have the chance to report a defeat,' said Cato. 'Caratacus may defy us yet.'

'I shall pray for victory,' Septimus said simply. Then he clicked his fingers as if recalling something. 'One final thing I meant to ask. Senator Vespasian. You know him well?'

The two officers exchanged a glance.

'We have served under him,' said Cato.

'A damn fine officer,' Macro added. 'One of the best legates there is.'

Septimus smiled. 'So I gather. There's no doubting his soldierly qualities. I was more curious about the scale of his ambitions. Did he ever mention his plans for the future in front of you?'

'No,' Cato replied firmly. 'And he would be mad to. Why do you ask?'

The imperial agent pursed his lips. 'It's as well to keep an eye on the more promising military commanders. And their families in some cases. Take his wife, Flavia, for example.'

'What about her?' asked Macro.

'Your paths may have crossed at some point.' He turned to Cato 'And you certainly knew her in your youth, both at the palace and when you encountered her again when you joined Vespasian's legion in Germany.'

Cato nodded casually. 'That's right.'

'What do you make of her?'

'I've never given it any thought. She was the wife of the legate. That's all.'

Septimus stared at him and then shrugged. 'Fair enough. Just wondered. I'll leave you in peace now.' Bowing his head and speaking loudly he backed towards the tent flaps. 'A thousand apologies, Prefect! It was my mistake. I should never have accused your servant. I will send you a jar of my best wine to make amends. I bid you a good night and may your fortunes prosper in tomorrow's battle!'

He passed out between the tent flaps and disappeared. Macro looked at Cato in despair. 'You cannot be serious about working with—'

'Shh!' Cato warned him. A moment later the flap to his private quarters rustled aside and Thraxis poked his head through.

'Prefect, the fire is lit.'

'Thank you.'

Thraxis remained where he was and cleared his throat.

'Is there anything else?' asked Cato.

'I, er, overheard the wine merchant as he left, Prefect. I take it you have resolved the matter.'

'I did. A simple misunderstanding. He had mixed up your coins with those of another customer. You have nothing to be concerned about, Thraxis.'

The servant sighed with relief before he asked, 'Do you wish me to bring you anything to eat or drink, Prefect?'

'No. We're turning in. I shall wear my new mail vest in the morning. Be sure that it is laid out with the rest of my kit.'

'Yes, Prefect.'

'Then you may go.'

Thraxis saluted and ducked away. They waited a moment before Macro spoke in an undertone. 'As I was saying, we'd be mad to let ourselves get lured back into working for Narcissus.'

'Macro, we have little choice. Just because we don't want to be involved in the struggle between Narcissus and Pallas doesn't mean that they won't involve us. Now it seems they have. If Pallas is a threat to us we can't just ignore it. And if Septimus is telling the truth about the wider situation then we're in even bigger danger, and everyone else in the army along with us.'

'If he's telling the truth.'

'Can we take the risk that he isn't?'

Macro gritted his teeth. 'Fuck ... Fucking Narcissus. The bastard sticks to you like a dose of the clap. We ain't ever going to be free of him, are we?' he added miserably. 'Nor, it seems, is that poor sod Vespasian. Nor his wife. What was all that about Flavia?'

'I have no idea.' Cato shrugged. 'Chin up. We might finally get shot of Narcissus, depending on how tomorrow works out.'

'Oh great. Thank you for being such a cheery sod,' Macro grumbled as he turned towards the entrance to the tent. 'Just what I needed before I hit the sack.'

Cato watched him until he was out of sight. Then he stood up, closed his eyes and stretched out his arms and cracked his shoulders. Macro was right, there was much to think about. Much to worry about. But before that, there was a battle to fight.

CHAPTER NINE

'There we go,' Macro said as the headquarters' trumpets sounded, the flat notes echoing back off the cliffs on the opposite side of the river. Before the sound had died away they saw the men of the artillery batteries throw their weight against the locking levers. An instant later the arms of the ballistas snapped forward, releasing their deadly heavy bolts in a shallow arc towards the enemy defences. Behind the ballistas were ranged the catapults, throwing their rounded stones in a much higher trajectory. The artillery had been set up on a platform constructed by engineers during the night, high enough to prevent any stray missiles ploughing through the ranks of the legionaries formed up a short distance from the river.

General Ostorius had placed the Twentieth Legion, his strongest, in the front line. The second line comprised the Fourteenth and the detachment from the Ninth. For the first time since the garrison of Bruccium had joined the army, Cato was able to see the legions arrayed for battle. Many cohorts were clearly under-strength, some fielded less than half the men they should have. He estimated that there were no more than seven thousand in all. From what he had seen of the enemy forces, it was clear that the legionaries were outnumbered. Worse still, the enemy had the considerable advantage of defending the high ground. The legionaries had been ordered to leave their javelins in the camp as they were poor weapons to use against enemy on steep ground. The hill would be taken with the sword, the general had decided. One cavalry cohort, besides the Blood Crows, was all that was present of the auxiliary troops, the rest were spread around the far side of the hill, to block any retreat by Caratacus's army.

Or at least Cato hoped they were. He had heard no reports about their progress during the morning as the rest of the army marched out of the camp and took up their positions. Only the beggage train escort remained, lining the palisade as they watched their comrades prepare for battle. Overhead the clear sky that had greeted them at dawn was starting to cloud over ominously and the air stirred in flukey breaths of wind. A large number of camp followers had climbed on to a nearby knoll overlooking the section of the river where the legions would cross. Some had taken food and wine to consume as they watched the fighting.

'They're going to get a soaking,' Cato remarked.

Children chased each other up and down the gentle slope or sat and made daisy chains. It was little different to the crowds that went to see the gladiator games, Cato mused. Only on a vastly different scale. There was one other crucial difference. If the battle went against the Romans, the spectators would be put to the sword alongside the legionaries. He looked at the children again. Many of them would be the offspring of soldiers and he wondered how many would end the day as orphans.

The crack of the catapults drew Cato's attention back to the river and he watched as the shot flew up in an angled trajectory before seeming to hang motionless for an instant, then plunging down on to the enemy's defences. It was hard to gauge the impact on the native warriors as they had all gone to ground the moment the Roman artillery went into action. Before that they had lined their defences shouting insults at the legions, waving fists, brandishing weapons, and a handful even baring their buttocks in a crude display of defiance. As soon as the first bolts shot across the river they dived down and the steep slope which had been alive with cavorting warriors suddenly seemed quite lifeless and still. Those behind the second line of defences soon realised they were out of range and safe for the moment and slowly reappeared and gazed down on the scene below. The iron heads of the bolts clattered against the rocks in the barricades and buried themselves in the soil of the hillside. Most of the rocks thrown by the catapults seemed to do just as little damage as they thudded to the ground. A few landed close behind the barricades where the enemy were taking shelter and Cato could well imagine the carnage that would result: skulls and bodies crushed into a bloody pulp by the impact.

However, the main purpose of the barrage was not to batter the enemy defences; a siege train would be required for that. Rather, it was intended to force the warriors to keep their heads down while the legions crossed the river and climbed towards the barricade. Only as they approached the first line of defences would the barrage cease, then a deadly hand-to-hand engagement would follow. Cato raised his gaze and saw the standard of Caratacus flying above the second line of defences and there, standing on a boulder, hands on hips, was a tall warrior with fair hair and beard flowing from beneath his gleaming helmet. Cato pointed him out.

'Shame we haven't got the range. One lucky shot and it'd all be over.'

'You think?' Macro said doubtfully. 'Most of the barbarians on this island seem to hate our guts. One more or less isn't going to make a difference.'

'That particular Briton is the man who has been fighting us for the best part of a decade. He's inspired tens of thousands to follow him, even though we have defeated him time and again and driven him back into these mountains. Even here, he has talked the Silurians and Ordovicians into becoming allies under his leadership. If there had been no Caratacus then our problems here would have been over long ago.'

Macro glanced at Cato. 'There was a time you admired him.'

'I used to. That was before he came between me and my wife, and the child she is carrying. Now, all I want is for this to be over so I can return to Rome. To the first home of my own.'

'You'd miss the army. And you'd make a lousy civilian.'

'You once said I'd never make a decent soldier.'

'I did?'

Cato nodded.

'Hmmm.' Macro raised his eyebrows. 'Seems I can be wrong about some things.'

A shrill note sounded and the signal was taken up by the horns of the Twentieth Legion. Cato and Macro unconsciously leaned forward slightly as the gleaming helmets and armour of the leading ranks rippled forward, marching towards the fast-racing waters of the ford. The eagle standard and the staff bearing the image of the Emperor advanced side by side above the tips of the javelins. It was a stirring sight, as Cato always found, but he could not put aside his growing sense of anxiety over the wisdom of a frontal attack.

A light pinging noise distracted him, and the breeze suddenly strengthened. He glanced up and blinked as the first drops of rain struck his face and glanced off his helmet and armour. The clouds that had come up from the east now hung over the hill and edged towards the Roman camp, blotting out the sun. A vast shadow crept over the ground before the camp and then engulfed Cato and Macro on the gate tower as the rain started to fall in earnest.

'It's a wonder this bloody island manages to stay afloat,' said Macro as he pulled his cloak about his shoulders.

Cato made no comment as he watched the first wave of legionaries wade out into the river. The pace of the advance slowed to a crawl as the heavily armoured soldiers lifted their shields clear of the water and began to struggle to keep their footing. On the far bank Cato could see the faces of the enemy peering over the barricade as they watched the progress of the Romans. All the while the artillery continued hurling their missiles across the river, pinning the warriors down. The surface of the river was churned into white spray as the legionaries edged towards the far bank. At length, they reached the line of sharpened stakes and slowed down still further as they started to thread their way through the obstacles.

It was then that Caratacus sprang his first trap. The deep blast of a Celtic war horn echoed from the slopes of the hill and figures sprang up from the grass along the bank of the river. At first they seemed poorly armed, half naked with no helmets, shields or spears. Then Cato saw one of them raise his hand and twist it rapidly above his head.

'Slingers.'

The range was no more that thirty paces and the targets floundering amid the stakes would be impossible to miss. The first shots struck home with a sharp rattle that could be heard even from the gate tower of the camp and Cato and Macro saw the first men go down, crashing into the shallows. Those who had been knocked senseless disappeared beneath the surface of the water, dragged down by the weight of their armour, and creating a fresh obstacle for their comrades. The men of the Twentieth raised their shields to protect themselves and struggled on into the hail of stone and lead shot hurled in their faces.

'A nasty surprise, that,' Macro commented. 'But it won't hold the lads back for long.'

'No, but it will shake them. First round to Caratacus, I think.'

As the first legionaries struggled out of the water on to the bank, the slingers began to back off, keeping a safe distance as they continued to pelt their foes. One of the Romans, enraged, surged forward, clambering up the slope a short distance before his centurion bellowed at him and waved him back. But it was too late. His shield could only offer protection to the front and at once he was caught from the sides, the first shot smashing his knee so that he stumbled and fell. Unable to get up, he was struck again and fell, senseless, into the grass.

Macro hissed, 'Stupid, bloody fool.'

The centurions and optios steadily formed men into their units as they emerged from the stake-strewn shallows and as soon as the three leading cohorts were in line, they began to advance up the slope. The slingers retreated before them, keeping their distance. All at once Cato saw one of them fly backwards a short distance, pinned to the ground by a wooden shaft.

'They've been forced back into the artillery's killing zone.'

'Good!' Macro thumped his right hand into the palm of the other. 'Let's see how the bastards like a taste of their own medicine!'

More of the slingers were struck down, some by the catapult shot falling short of the first line of barricades. It was if they had been smashed into the ground by an invisible giant fist, Cato thought; like the wrath of Jupiter, best and greatest.

It couldn't go on, however, for risk of shot falling amongst the leading ranks of the Twentieth, and a horn sounded to cease the bombardment. The last of the catapults and ballistas cracked and the crews stood by their weapons to wait for further orders. On the far bank the slingers scurried over the barricades, passing between the ranks of the warriors who had risen from cover now the danger from the Roman artillery had passed. At first Caratacus's warriors hurled insults and challenges at the approaching wall of shields, then they followed up with rocks, a renewed hail of slingshot and arrows from archers who fired high over the heads of their comrades so that the arrows plunged down on the follow-up cohorts still crossing the river.

Cato felt a cold chill clench his heart as he saw the bodies littering the shallows and the far bank of the river. Some of the wounded who could walk were limping back across the current to seek treatment for their wounds. Well over a hundred had been lost so far, Cato estimated, and the fight for the first line of defences was only just beginning amid the dull gleam of the rain.

A blast of lightning dazzled the mountainous landscape, an image in stark white with dark shadows so that for an instant the scene looked like a monumental relief sculpture, scratched by the rain. Then the illusion passed and Cato beheld thousands of figures in combat as the men of the Twentieth closed with the enemy, swords and spears flickering in the gloom. A shattering crash and boom of thunder followed close on the heels of the lightning and then the hiss of the rain continued, pinging off Cato's helmet so loudly that he found it hard to hear above the din. Over on the knoll the camp followers were huddled in their cloaks. Already some had given up and were scurrying down the slope and back to the camp to find shelter from the downpour.

Macro was saying something, and Cato shook his head and leaned closer. Macro cupped a hand to his mouth and shouted, 'The general could have picked a better day for it. What do you think he'll do? Call it off until the rain has passed?'

'No. Not him. He intends to see this through whatever happens.'

'Then it's going to be tough on our lads.'

'Very tough.'

They turned their attention back to the fight along the nearest rock barricades, barely visible through the dense sheen of the rain. The enemy appeared to be holding their own and the legionaries could not break through. A steady stream of walking wounded were clambering out of the river, soaked through. They passed between the cohorts of the second line and slumped on to the ground to wait for the medical orderlies to treat them. Some of the green recruits glanced anxiously at the wounded until their optios bellowed at them to face front.

For a while the rain continued, then stopped as suddenly as it had started and sunlight broke through a jagged rent in the clouds, bathing the battlefield in a glow that revealed the terrible struggle in startling clarity. The legionaries had managed to force their way over in several places and were pressing their slender advantage to create space for their comrades to feed into the fight. Then, at one of the points where the enemy had seemed to build the barricade particularly high, it began to move. Cato strained his eyes and could see men on the far side heaving on beams of wood and instantly grasped the danger. But he could only watch helplessly as the rocks began to tumble down on to the legionaries below. The small avalanche swept through their ranks, knocking men over and carrying them away in a tangle of bodies, flailing limbs, shields, earth and mud. The enemy unleashed more rockslides, sweeping great gaps through the tightly packed Roman formations. Then the war horns sounded once more, and the defenders abruptly abandoned their first position and began to clamber up to the second line of defences.

'We've broken through,' Macro said with grim satisfaction. 'One last push.'

'If only it was that easy,' Cato replied. 'Look at the incline. Our boys are going to be exhausted by the climb. In full kit, heavier now thanks to that rain and the river crossing. And the ground is going to be churned into thick mud. Hard going.'

They could see their comrades struggling through the gaps in the barricades, slipping and slithering as they negotiated the saturated ground, each laboured step making conditions even worse for those that followed. The lightly armed enemy easily outpaced them and the more daring amongst them stopped to snatch up rocks and hurl them back down the slope, some finding their mark and shattering the jaws, knees or shins of the pursuing Romans. Very soon it was clear to Cato that the men of the Twentieth would soon be a spent force, too exhausted to close with the enemy and fight. They were not even halfway up the slope before their advance came to a halt, men and kit coated in the thick dark mud, some having sheathed their weapons as they went down on hands and knees to get greater purchase on the slope. The centurions, identifiable by their transverse crests, still led the way, urging their men on. Behind came the optios lashing out with their long wooden staffs to try and drive forward those who were floundering at the rear.

Their slow climb was made more hazardous yet by the defenders now that the men of the first line had joined their comrades defending the upper barricade. A steady rain of rocks and other missiles clattered down on the legionaries, inflicting more casualties, and halting those men who raised their shields to try and protect themselves.

'We're in danger of losing this,' Cato said quietly.

Macro grunted non-committally as he regarded the stalling attack. The first six cohorts had merged into one muddy mass, like maggots, and the remaining four cohorts were struggling to stay in formation as they began their climb from the riverbank. They reached the remains of the first barricade and picked their way over it before re-forming on the far side. At least their officers were keeping them in strict formation, Cato noted. Casualties stumbled past them and made for the river below, weakened by their wounds and the terrible exhaustion of the fight for the hill. Only once the four cohorts were ready did the officer commanding them give the order to advance. There was no steady progress as on a normal battlefield. Instead the front ranks seemed to inch forward as they started up the slope to reinforce the leading units. The glutinous mud made the going even harder for them.

The sprawling mass of the first six cohorts was at last approaching the upper barricade. The slope behind them was littered with men, few of whom had been wounded. Many simply sat, or lay, slumped in the mud, summoning up fresh reserves of strength before trying to continue. Before them a figure rose up on the barricade, brandishing a sword, and the blast of the enemy's war horns rang out along the breadth of the hill. Hundreds of warriors poured over the barricade in a wave and launched themselves down the slope, plunging in amongst the Romans only a short distance below them. Sword and axe blades flashed form side to side as the disorganised front ranks of the Twentieth Legion were engulfed by the frenzied attack. Still more of the enemy were flowing over the barricade, adding their weight to the charge. Incredibly, the legionaries seemed to be holding the line but then there was no mistaking it, they began to be driven back down the slope.

'Shit . . .' Macro gripped the wooden rail of the gate tower tightly. 'Now they're for it.'

Cato nodded. Caratacus had timed his attack to perfection, allowing his enemies to exhaust themselves as they tried to close with his men. Now his warriors had the advantage of the high ground, as well as being fresh from their rest behind the upper barricade. They threw themselves at the mud-plastered legionaries, hacking and slashing with their blades as they wrenched the heavy shields aside and fell on the heavily armoured Romans like wolves. The foremost legionaries were cut down or driven back on their comrades, slithering in the bloodied quagmire. Nothing could resist the pressure from above and their comrades on the far side of the river could only look on with a growing sense of horror at the disaster unfolding before them.

The worst of it was yet to come, Cato knew, as the last four cohorts became entangled with the retreating men from the first wave. More legionaries stumbled and slid back until the entire legion was swiftly turned into a leaden mass of armoured men flailing in the mud. The enemy pressed their advantage home, thrusting the Romans down the slope, falling on any legionary who had tumbled to the ground and hacking him to death without mercy.

Macro thrust his arm out towards General Ostorius and his command party watching the battle from the calm refuge of the near bank. 'For pity's sake, why doesn't he sound the call?'

'I don't know,' Cato muttered. 'I don't know.'

All semblance of cohesion had disappeared. There was no hope of forming up around the standards or centurions as the legion was pressed back relentlessly. Then, at last, the shrill call ordering the retreat sounded from the cornus to one side of the general and his officers. The men of the Twentieth responded to the signal at once, clambering down the hill to the river. As they fell back, a roar of triumph welled in the throats of the native warriors pursuing them. Small knots of legionaries kept their face to the enemy and tried to hold some semblance of a line as they covered their comrades.

As the first of the men reached the riverbank they picked their way through the remaining stakes in the shallows and began to wade to safety, no longer even able to hold their shields overhead to save them from the water. Some were lost as the current tore them from the exhausted grip of their owners and they sank from sight, tumbling over and over in the river, occasionally throwing an edge above the surface before being rapidly born away again. The first men began to stagger up on to the near bank and collapse on the wet grass, gasping for breath. Others helped wounded comrades to make the crossing before slumping down beside them as soon as they reached solid ground. Gradually the bank filled up, like a vast casualty clearing station, and still more men dragged themselves out of the river.

On the far bank the enemy had pushed the Romans back beyond the lower barricade and were pursuing them all the way to the river. Several groups of Romans still managed to fight on, shield to shield as they retreated off the slope and into the water.

The sudden crack of the ballistas made Cato flinch. He had been so absorbed by the scene that he had not noticed the crews making their weapons ready to resume the bombardment. Iron bolts shot across the river, over the heads of the scattered legionaries churning through the water. The missiles fell amongst the enemy, slamming men into the ground, pierced through. The catapults joined in, lobbing lethal rocks into high arcs that added to the enemy's casualties. A moment later the war horns sounded and the enemy began to break off, scrambling back up the slope to the cover of the first line of defences. Soon the last of them had gone to ground and the side of the hill lay almost still. Only the wounded still moved, writhing pitifully amid the glistening mud, tussocks of grass and grey rocks. Cato could see that there were still some Romans alive there who had somehow escaped the attentions of the enemy during their wild charge.

The fighting had stopped and the last men of the Twentieth made their way back to the near bank. The ballistas and catapults kept up their work for a little longer before being ordered to cease shooting. Then an awful stillness and quiet seemed to hang over the scene, as if both armies were giant fighters, bloodied and bowed, breaking away from each other a moment to draw breath. A handful of figures broke cover on the far side of the river and scurried out to retrieve their wounded, and cut the throats of any living Romans they encountered. They were too few and too far away for accurate shots from the ballistas and were permitted to go about their work unhindered.

Cato felt the nervous tension that had gripped his body during the attack begin to drain away and he found that he was sweating heavily and he felt a sudden tiredness. He lowered his head and closed his eyes for a moment, relieved that the disastrous attempt to take the hill with a frontal assault was over. At length he took a deep breath, opened his eyes and looked up. The last men from the Twentieth had returned across the river. But they had not been allowed to rest. A staff officer was riding along the edge of the water shouting orders and waving his arm frantically. The legion's officers began to stir the men to their feet and march them away from the crossing.

'What's going on there?' asked Macro. 'I hope it's not what I think it is.'

Cato did not reply. He had guessed the general's intention, but prayed that he was mistaken. As they watched, the men drew aside, leaving an open stretch of ground in front of the combined cohorts of the Fourteenth and Ninth Legions. When the way before them was finally cleared, General Ostorius raised his arm and held it aloft for a moment before dipping it towards the hill. The artillery crews sprang to their weapons and the quiet that had settled over the battlefield was broken by the crack of the ballistas and the crash of the catapults' throwing arms.

The cornus sounded the advance and the order was echoed along the lines of fresh legionaries facing the river crossing. Then, sunlight gleaming off their helmets, they tramped forward, as neatly as if they were performing a drill on the parade ground.

'What does the fool think he's doing?' Macro hissed. 'What the fuck is Ostorius up to?'

Cato shook his head. 'Madness . . .'

Cohort after cohort descended the gentle slope down towards the river and from the far side came the jeers and challenges of the enemy, sounding more defiant than ever to Cato's ears. Abruptly he turned from the rail and strode towards the ladder leading down to the ground.

'Sir!' Macro hurried after him and caught up with Cato as the prefect swung himself on to the topmost rungs of the ladder. Macro stared down at him. 'Where are you going?'

'Someone's got to try and put a stop to this,' Cato replied firmly. 'Before Ostorius turns defeat into a full-blown disaster.'

CHAPTER TEN

Before Macro could protest further, Cato rapidly descended the ladder and trotted over to where Thraxis was holding his horse. Cato snatched up the reins and swung himself up into the saddle. With a kick of his heels he turned Hannibal towards the gate and urged the animal into a gallop. The hoofs echoed off the wooden confines of the tower and then he was pounding over the bridge across the ditch and down the slope towards the general and his officers. Cato resolved to do whatever he could to prevent Ostorius repeating the first, futile attack and sending more men to their deaths needlessly.

The leading centuries of the Fourteenth were already wading into the river, with Quintatus at their head. The legate drew his horse up in the shallows and swung himself down from the saddle to splash in the current. Handing the reins to a servant he took a shield from one of his men and drew his sword and fell into step alongside the colour party carrying the legion's standards aloft, where all the men could see them. At the rear Cato caught sight of Tribune Otho astride a white horse, sword drawn as he waved it above his head in a circle, shouting encouragement to his men. They advanced in an earnest silence, fully aware of what lay in store for them. Thanks to the slope down to the river and the hill opposite, not a man amongst them had missed what had happened during the first attack. Now they were marching in the footsteps of their beaten comrades. Cato could not help marvelling at the discipline of soldiers who obeyed their orders without question, without the least sign of hesitation or dissent. The very qualities that made the men of the legions so effective in battle rendered them little better than lambs being led to the slaughter when under the command of foolhardy generals.

Perhaps Ostorius would relent, Cato hoped desperately. Perhaps he would issue the recall before it was too late, without Cato having to intervene. But there was no sign of movement from the officers gathered on the knoll a short distance away and Cato gritted his teeth, reined in his mount and slowed to a trot as he approached the general and his staff. A few faces turned at the sound of his approach but Ostorius's attention was fixed on the men crossing the river. The leading ranks, uneven now, reached the remaining stakes and began to rise up from the water towards the bank.

Once again the Roman artillery ceased shooting and as the last bolts and stones fell to earth, the defenders rose up from behind the barricade and unleashed their own barrage of missiles into the faces of the fresh legionaries. This time the Romans knew what to expect and the officers gave the order for the front rank to present a shield wall, with the following lines raising their shields above their heads so that the entire formation was sheltered from the hail of stones, arrows and slingshot rattling off the curved surfaces. While the men were better protected, the formation was unwieldy and tiring to maintain for any time and the inevitable gaps between the shields meant that there were still casualties.

Cato eased his horse forward to the side of the general and forced himself to draw a calming breath.

'Sir?'

Ostorius turned, a look of mild surprise on his face. 'Prefect Cato, what are you doing here? You should be with your men back in the camp.'

Cato ignored the question and sat erect in his saddle as he addressed his superior. 'Sir, you must call the men back.'

'What? What did you say?'

'General Ostorius, I respectfully suggest that you recall the Fourteenth and the Ninth.'

Cato was aware of the shocked glances that the officers around him were exchanging, as well as the darkening of the general's expression. Ostorius's nostrils flared as he breathed in deeply. 'You forget yourself, Prefect. You dare to question my orders?'

'Sir, I am urging you to reconsider. Before we lose any more men without result.'

'You young fool, can you not see that we are on the cusp of breaking through? One more push and they will flee. They will break and run and it will all be over. We had victory in our hands before those fools threw it away.' He gestured angrily at the men of the Twentieth slowly re-forming their units while the wounded, hundreds of them, were tended to by the legion's medical orderlies. 'It seems I was wrong to put so much faith in those men. But Quintatus and the second wave are made of sterner stuff. They won't stop until they have broken through the enemy lines and taken the hill.'

'They are still men, sir. The ground before them is a quagmire. They will tire long before they can defeat the enemy.'

'Enough, Prefect! Return to your post. I will deal with you later.'

'Sir—'

'Begone! Now!' Ostorius thrust his hand towards the camp.

Cato could see there was no further point to his protest. He had tried and failed. The men of the second wave were doomed to repeat the failure of their comrades. And if, by some miracle, the army survived the day, Cato would be subjected to the wrath of his commander. He had challenged his authority before witnesses. There would have to be a punishment.

He saluted stiffly and turned his horse around and cantered back to the camp. By the time he had returned to Macro's side, the Fourteenth had closed with the first barricade and the two sides were locked in combat. Macro looked at his friend with a concerned expression.

'I take it the general wouldn't listen to reason.'

Cato shook his head. 'I had to try.'

'Of course you did.' Macro smiled sadly. 'And I bet you pissed him off.'

'Oh yes.'

There was nothing more to say and they turned their attention back to the hill. The fighting was ferocious, with the more frenzied of the native warriors leaping on to the shields in a bid to smash gaps in the Roman line. But the legionaries held their discipline and steadily forced their way through the gaps in the line created during the first attack. Inch by inch they pushed Caratacus's men back. Then, as the horns sounded, the enemy broke off and clambered up towards the upper defences.

'That went better than last time,' Macro commented.

'There's still the slope to deal with, and more mud than ever this time. And more on the way.' Cato pointed towards the top of the hill. The sunny interlude was about to come to an end. More clouds were edging in from the west, dark and threatening further rain. The first drops were already falling by the time the native warriors had reached the second barricade. Cato saw that their ranks had been thinned out by the fighting and their leaders were pulling the men in from the flanks to oppose the Romans struggling up the slope towards them. Even as he watched he saw small parties of men abandon the rocky outcrops and crags that towered either side of the contested ground, which seemed to provide the only practicable route for an attack on the hill.

A fresh barrage of missiles struck the leading ranks of the Fourteenth as the shadow of the clouds cut off the sun so that the gleam of their armour dulled. A fine veil of drizzle swept down the hill and covered the enemy and a moment later the legionaries who had reached the point where easy footing gave way to the glutinous mud. Yet still they advanced, clawing their way up towards the waiting Britons. There was no further doubt in Cato's mind. This attack would fail just as certainly as the first. Caratacus had massed all of his men behind the barricade to make sure of it. Ostorius would be defeated, his men spent, and when the news spread across the province, every native who still nurtured a hatred of Rome would rejoice. Many would be encouraged to take up arms, and those tribes whose neutrality hung in the balance might finally join Caratacus's alliance. The consequences appalled Cato.

His mind worked feverishly as he surveyed the battlefield. Then he saw it, the faint trace of a path away to the left, beyond the crags that flanked the battlefield. He felt his pulse quicken as he framed his plan. It flew in the face of common sense and his duty to obey his orders. If he failed, then he would be killed. If he survived it was likely that he would be ruined and discharged from the army. But neither of those possibilities took into account the likely defeat of Ostorius's army. If that happened then Cato and his men would die anyway.

He made his decision and turned to Macro.

'Have the men form up outside the south gate at once. I want the Blood Crows with their mounts.'

Macro stared at him in astonishment. 'Cato, what are you doing?'

'At the moment, nothing. Nothing to prevent the disaster that's going to happen over there.' He jerked a thumb towards the hill. 'But there is something we can do that might make a difference. Get the men formed up. That's an order.'

'Your orders are to guard the camp, sir.'

'Macro, I'm doing this on my own authority. There's no time to waste. Trust me and do as I say.'

Macro rubbed his bristly jaw and then nodded. 'All right, you fool. The gods protect us!'

He turned and hurried to the ladder and a moment later Cato heard him bellowing orders for the officers to summon their men. Cato took a last look at the hill. The Fourteenth were no more than a hundred and fifty paces from the upper barricade and the rain was falling hard. There was still time to make a difference to the outcome, but only just. He thrust himself away from the wooden rail and descended from the tower and raced to his horse.

The two cohorts of the escort detachment stood formed up outside the camp in the hissing rain. Cato noticed the curious and anxious expressions on many of their faces. Just over two hundred soldiers in all. Barely enough for the task he had in mind, but these men were battle-hardened, veterans all, and if anyone could turn defeat into victory, they could.

Cato drew a breath and shouted to be heard above the rain. 'There's no time to explain. We must move and move fast. You'll know exactly what is expected of you when we are in position. All I ask is that you fight like demons when the time comes. Second Thracian! Fourth Cohort of the Fourteenth, advance!'

Cato turned his horse and urged it into a quick walk as he led the men away from the camp. Ahead and to the right stood the knoll on which a handful of civilians still stood watching the struggle on the other side of the river, in despairing silence. Cato led his men, cavalry first and the two understrength centuries of legionaries under Macro, at a brisk pace round the back of the knoll and behind a thin belt of trees that ran along the edge of the river. Through the trunks he could make out the slow flow, pockmarked with ripples from the rain. The river was much deeper here. Too deep to ford. Yet he recalled from Ostorius's briefing before the battle that there were a handful of crossing places unsuitable for a large-scale crossing further down. His plan depended on them not being guarded. If the enemy had not been recalled to the main body to help overwhelm the second attack, then Cato's plan would surely fail. Even if he could fight his way across the river he might lose too many men to see his desperate scheme through. On the far bank, a short distance ahead, loomed the crags, grey and foreboding.

The small column hurried on, passing by the crags until there, just beyond, the trees opened on to the riverbank and a narrow track led down to the river where the water raced over shallows, foaming around the scattered rocks on the river bed. Cato threw up his arm to halt his men, swung his leg over the saddle horns and dropped to the ground. Macro came trotting up, panting hard.

'What is it?'

'I need to see if the way is clear. Stay here. Soon as I give the command, get the men across as quickly as you can.'

Macro saluted and Cato turned towards the river. He followed the track down to the water's edge and paused, looking across the narrow ford to the far bank. There was no sign of movement. Glancing upriver he realised he could no longer see any sign of the battlefield, or the camp, and nodded with satisfaction. Then, steeling his nerve, he began to wade across, eyes constantly scouring the crags and the slope to the left where a steep track wound up towards the top of the mass of dark rocks. There was no sign of the enemy. Even though the water gushed around his calves he found that his footing was good and he was able to wade across with ease. At the midpoint the water reached no higher than his thighs and Cato breathed a deep sigh of relief as he splashed on, reached the shallows and emerged dripping on to the far bank. At once he turned and cupped a hand.

'Macro! Bring 'em over!' He beckoned with his arm in case his voice was lost in the sound of the rushing water. A moment later the first of the Blood Crows appeared, slipped off their saddles and led their mounts into the river, not risking any injury to themselves or their horses from slipping on the stones carpeting the river bed.

Behind the cavalry came the legionaries, instinctively holding their shields high, even though it was raining. Cato gestured to his senior decurion, Miro, and pointed to the track.

'Up there. Stop before you get to the top of the crags.'

'Yes, sir.' Miro saluted and ordered his men to follow him as he tugged on the reins and led his mount up from the river. Macro had Cato's horse and handed the reins over as the first legionaries reached the bank.

'Reminds me of the first real battle against Caratacus. Back in the early days of the invasion. Remember?'

Cato nodded. 'Hope our luck holds just as well this time.'

He turned towards the path and followed the rear of the Thracian cohort. The rest were picking their way up towards the crest and Cato set off, pushing himself and his mount to work his way back to the head of the column. By the time he caught up with Miro the decurion was a short distance from the top of the crag where the rain was being blown at an angle by the rising wind. Cato was relieved to hear the sounds of battle more clearly, the clash of blades and faint cheers and cries. It was proof that the Fourteenth were in action and holding their own, for now.

'Form the men up here,' Cato ordered. 'Hold my horse. I'll be back directly.'

Leaving the decurion with the reins, Cato jogged forward up the final rise and along the top of the crags. He slowed down as he saw the ground begin to fall away and continued in a crouch as he fumbled with the ties under his helmet and took it off in case the red plume and gleaming metal drew the enemy's attention. There was a stunted bush ahead, growing at an angle determined by the prevailing wind that swept across the mountains. He used that for cover as he gazed down on the battle raging along the side of the hill. The top of the crags were nearly a hundred feet above Caratacus's second line of defence and Cato could see clearly along the length of the battle line.

The legionaries had reached the barricade made of rocks and stone with roughly cut and sharpened branches embedded, the points angled down the slope. As Cato watched he saw parties of men sheltering beneath their broad shields while their comrades used their hands and swords to pull down sections of the barricade. The more courageous

110

of the legionaries had clambered up to engage the enemy. It was an unequal struggle as the Romans were heavily encumbered and could never get enough numbers forward before the enemy responded in overwhelming numbers, hacking the attackers down and driving the survivors back into the massed ranks below. A hundred paces further down, the men of the Ninth crouched down behind their shields. Tribune Otho, with his ostentatious red plume, had dismounted and was striding up and down in front of the colour party where the square drop of the vexillation standard hung limply in the rain. More bodies littered the slope behind the Ninth. Turning his gaze back to the fight, Cato saw that the native warriors were densely packed behind the cover of the barricade. Above them the ground evened out and there was a lumpy plateau stretching across the top of the hill where hundreds of crude shelters had been constructed in a haphazard fashion. A cluster of simple tents occupied the centre of the camp. Caratacus's headquarters, Cato guessed. Hundreds of wounded warriors sat or lay out of the rain and wind. Their injuries were tended by native women in cloaks, binding up cuts and broken limbs.

Cato had seen enough to grasp the lay of the land and crept back down out of sight before running back to join his column. The Blood Crows were standing by their horses in each of the three squadrons. Beside them stood Macro's two centuries of legionaries, one under his personal command, the other in the charge of the towering figure of Centurion Crispus, a man who had been promoted from optio after the siege at Bruccium.

'Officers! On me!' Cato called out as loudly as he dared. They hurried over to him and the cold rain and biting wind caused Cato to tremble as he waited for them. He cursed his weak body and forced it to be still, in case the other officers mistook his feeling cold for fear. They needed to have every confidence in him if they were to survive their part in the battle.

Cato gestured towards the top of the crags. 'The battle line is just the other side of the high ground. The general's second attack has reached the barricade, and there it will stall. Unless we intervene.' He looked round the small group of junior officers to make sure they understood. 'This is the plan. Centurion Macro and the infantry will go round the crags, staying out of sight as far as possible, before they launch an attack on the enemy's flank. Make as much noise as you can and go in hard. Drive 'em back. You won't have the element of surprise for long, nor be able to maintain the impetus of the charge. But you must drive them back far enough so that the lads of the Fourteenth can break through the flank and back you up. If we move quickly enough we can roll up their line from this end. Are you clear about that? Centurion Macro? Are your men up for it?'

Macro grinned and clapped his hands together. 'Just let the bastards try and stop us, sir!'

'That's the spirit!' Cato nodded, then turned to the three decurions. 'Miro, take your squadron and cover Macro's flank. You must stop them trying to get round our infantry. Charge any groups that look like forming up. Keep 'em on the move. Don't give them a chance to recover.'

Miro nodded grimly.

'I'll lead the other two squadrons. We'll head up to the top of the hill and ride through their camp. We'll scatter any fighting men up there and then wheel and charge over the crest and down the slope, straight into the rear of the enemy line. If all goes well, the attack from two directions will be enough to distract them just long enough for our lads in the Fourteenth to get round and over the barricade. Then it's all over . . . Everyone clear on what part they must play?'

Centurion Crispus shook his head in wonder. 'You don't fucking ask for much, sir.'

Macro punched his subordinate on the shoulder. 'You'll get used to his funny ways, if you live long enough.'

'That's it then, gentlemen. Let's do it.'

Macro and his men moved forward first, striding along the track and then branching off towards the battlefield. Cato and the horsemen followed. Where the track divided, Cato turned to Miro and nodded. 'Fortuna ride with you.'

'And you, sir.'

'I'll see you afterwards.'

They exchanged a salute and Cato waved the remaining two squadrons forward as he made for the crest of the hill and the enemy camp that lay beyond.

CHAPTER ELEVEN

The ache in Macro's limbs began to ease as he felt the blood pump through his veins. His muscles felt tense and tight and there was the familiar lightness in his heart as he anticipated the fight to come. Unlike Cato, he had no doubts that this was the reason why the gods had put him on the earth. This was what he had been born to do. He was a soldier, trained for this end, and by Mithras, he would do honour to his profession. Glancing over his shoulder he saw the line of men following him, breathing heavily and grim-faced. Although he had commanded them for less than half a year he knew them well. They fought hard and would not let him down.

They double-timed round the top of the crags as the rain lashed down from the dark clouds scudding overhead. Then the track levelled off for a short distance before dipping down towards the right flank of the enemy line. A flash of sheet lightning lit up the hillside, freezing men locked in combat. Then the light went and an instant later the air reverberated with the roar of thunder. The enemy's attention was fixed on the men of the Fourteenth, still struggling in vain to find a way over or through the defences. The nearest of them stood where the barricade ran up against a sheer cliff, fifty paces away. Macro stopped his men and waited until the two centuries were formed into a tight column behind him. Then he wiped his hand on the side of his tunic and drew his sword. He hefted his shield, raised his sword into the rain and swept it forward.

The soft thud of nailed boots and the chink of equipment blended with the patter of the rain on helmets and shoulders and the rising din of the battle. Macro increased the pace to a trot as they descended the gentle slope. To his left he saw movement and his gaze flickered to the horsemen fanning out to cover his flank. They were no more than twenty paces from the enemy when a robed man shouting encouragement a short distance behind his comrades paused as he heard the sound of men approaching. He turned and Macro saw his eyes widen in alarm before his jaw gaped and he let out a desperate cry.

'Fourth Cohort!' Macro bellowed. 'Charge!'

He increased his pace to a jog, the fastest any man could run in such heavy armour and equipment and roared the legion's name, 'Gemina!'

'GEMINA!' The cry echoed from his men's lips and Macro made for the man who had first seen them. Others had turned towards them now, the triumphant war cries of a moment earlier dying on their lips. Too late the robed man began to turn, and slipped, and then Macro smashed him to the ground with his shield and ran on. Hundreds of enemy warriors stretched out behind the barricade in front of him, but the sight only heartened Macro as he charged in amongst the hapless defenders at the end of the line. A spearman, stripped to the waist, braced himself and thrust the point at Macro. He flicked his sword and deflected the point down into the ground and then thrust his blade into the man's leading arm, tearing through flesh and muscle before ripping it free. He punched his shield out, feeling the heavy impact as it knocked the spearman back. Macro rushed by, feeling a limb squirm beneath his boot before he launched himself into a group of lightly armed men clustered at the end of the barricade.

A sword cracked against his shield and scraped down to the boss with a sharp clang. Macro punched the shield to one side and then recovered before stabbing his sword to the right. He felt a slight pressure as it inflicted a flesh wound, and then his men piled in on either side, punching their shields and thrusting their swords, just as they had been trained to do. Macro saw the barricade in front of him, a jumble of soil and rocks, with the body of a young warrior sprawled on top. Around him the legionaries had cleared the area at the base of the cliff and several of the enemy lay in the mud bleeding out.

'Go left!' Macros shouted. 'Roll up the bastards' flank!'

The frantic charge continued without mercy. The tribesmen were still reeling from the shock of the flank attack and Macro was determined to keep up the impetus for as long as he could before the enemy realised how few men he had. The moment the ruse was discovered Caratacus was sure to send his reserves to deal with the threat. The enemy were falling back ahead of the legionaries, running diagonally up the slope to escape their attackers, straight into the path of Miro and his squadron of Blood Crows. They slashed to the left and right, cutting down the fugitives and adding to the panic spreading through the right flank of Caratacus's army.

Macro drew up and looked round for Crispus. The centurion was a short distance behind, looming above his men as he ordered them to follow up Macro's century.

'Crispus! On me! Crispus!'

The centurion glanced round, saw Macro and nodded. A moment later the two officers stood together, gasping for breath. Macro pointed his sword at the barricade.

'Get your men to start pulling that apart. We have to let the lads on the other side through as quickly as possible.'

'Yes, sir.' Crispus bowed his head curtly and called the nearest two sections of his men to him and they lowered their shields, sheathed their blades and desperately began to pull the rocks aside.

'The rest of you follow me!' Macro beckoned to the remaining sections of Crispus's century and rejoined the charge. He passed more fallen warriors, and then the first of his men, lying on his back, his face smashed into a bloody pulp by an axe blow. Angling slightly up the slope for a better view, Macro could see that the enemy had been driven back over a hundred feet and were starting to bunch up. There was no escape for them, yet the dense mass of men would mean that the charge would stall as the legionaries could not press on. But for the moment there was still ground to be made and Macro roared to his men, 'On! On! Carve 'em up!'

Beyond, some distance away, he could see a large warrior on horseback riding down the line to investigate the disturbance on the flank. The rain had soaked the man's long hair and yet there was something about him that struck Macro as familiar and then he guessed he was looking at the commander. Caratacus himself. At once the rider gestured towards the flank and men began to pull away from the battle line and form a new line, thirty paces up the slope. As soon as he had gathered two or three hundred of his warriors, Caratacus led them along the slope at a trot. There was not much time before they reached the fighting and tipped the balance, Macro realised.

He looked back and saw Crispus and his men toiling away. They had removed the largest of the rocks and were working away at the earth, using their swords to shovel the muddy soil aside. Some of the legionaries from the other side, streaked in dirt, had clambered up on to the barricade to help them. But it would take a little while yet to open a gap large enough for a steady flow of men to reinforce Macro's weak cohort.

There was nothing more he could do, other than fight, and Macro strode forward to join his men in battle. Pushing his way to the front, he saw a heavyset warrior with a bedraggled white beard and a torso covered in swirling blue tattoos. The rain gleamed on his skin as he swung an axe above his head and then slammed it down on to the edge of a legionary's shield. The heavy blade shattered the metal trim and splintered the wood as it carved through the shield, and crushed the shoulder of the Roman behind. He let out a gasp as the air was driven from his lungs and then stumbled back, his ruined shield splashing into the mud. His foe let out a hiss of triumph and stepped forward, halting the advance of the Romans to his front and allowing his comrades to stop and gather their wits. '*Sa!*'

Macro met the mad gaze of the warrior as he began to swing his axe again. Before the man could strike, Macro feinted with his sword and his opponent instinctively flinched, lowering his axe as he retreated. Macro took another pace and followed up with a thrust of his shield, a light blow but it drove the man back against his comrades. Now Macro had the man trapped and he moved in for the kill, stabbing low, into the thigh, twisting the blade and withdrawing it before striking again, higher up, throwing his weight behind the blow which pierced the warrior's stomach. He let out an explosive groan and dropped his axe as he staggered back.

'Forwards!' Macro paused to shout. 'Come on, lads!'

Macro knew that the pace of the attack was slowing. His men were tiring, and the enemy was recovering from the shock of the sudden appearance of the small force on their flank. More men were angling up the slope to meet the Romans, and behind them Caratacus and his hastily gathered reserve were sweeping towards Macro. A quick glance back revealed Crispus and his men still toiling away and no sign yet of their comrades below coming to the support of the Fourth Cohort.

The impetus of the attack faded and Macro found himself merely standing his ground as he fought alongside his men and held the enemy at bay. A party of native spearman had got in amongst Miro and his squadron and were savagely piking the horses and riders, and driving the Thracians back, so that they threatened to uncover the flank of their legionary comrades. Macro looked further up the slope, towards the crest, for any sign of Cato and his two squadrons, but saw no movement there.

'Come on, lad,' he muttered. 'While there's still time.'

Caratacus and his men closed in, less than a hundred paces away, and their commander slowed their pace to allow the slowest to catch up so that the reinforcements would throw their full weight in when they charged down the slope and trapped Macro and his cohort against the barricade. There would be no escape if that happened.

A dull cheer caught Macro's ear and he saw that Crispus and his men had succeeded in opening a small breach, just wide enough for a single man to pass through. The first of the men from below scrambled through and ran to join Macro's small force holding the enemy at bay, then another, as Crispus urged his men to widen the gap. But it was too late. No more than twenty men had passed through the barricade by the time Caratacus and his party began their charge, surging at an angle down the slope towards Macro with a savage roar. The last of Miro's squadron was swept aside and the survivors turned and spurred their mounts back towards the top of the crag.

Macro felt his heart burn with frustration. If only there had been a little more time. A hundred more men would have made all the difference to holding the position while the breach was widened for the cohorts trapped on the other side to pour through and swing the balance of the battle in the Romans' favour. But he might as well wish for the moon, Macro realised, as he turned to face the oncoming enemy squarely, boots braced in the mud, his shield raised and his sword lowered, ready to strike. Above the trim of his shield he could see Caratacus looming high in his saddle, one hand clutching the reins,

117

the other waving his sword. His mouth gaped and the tendons on his neck stood out as he screamed his war cry.

'For fuck's sake, Cato,' Macro raged. 'Where are you?'

As the two squadrons reached the crest of the hill Cato gave the order to form line and the sixty horsemen fanned out across the uneven ground. Glancing right and left to make sure the line kept up, Cato walked them to the edge of the plateau. He lifted his oval shield up and held it close to his side as he reached for the long-bladed sword hanging in the saddle scabbard.

'Blood Crows! At the trot! Advance!'

The line edged into motion, towards the nearest shelters and the wounded men, and the women who tended them. The horsemen were quickly spotted and cries of alarm spread across the enemy camp as the dreaded Blood Crow banner was recognised. Those who could walk scrambled to their feet and turned to flee. The rest pressed themselves into whatever cover they could find, snatching up weapons to try and defend themselves.

Blinking away the raindrops that stung his face, Cato drew a breath and called out, 'At the canter!'

The men held formation as they burst upon the enemy camp, long blades hacking left and right, the riders leaning from their saddles to strike those on the ground. They killed scores of the helpless enemy and those who could ran for their lives, spreading the terror through the camp. Cato indulged his men a while longer, carefully gauging the distance they had advanced, anxious not to go too far before they changed direction. A third of the way across the plateau he reined in and raised his sword to draw the attention of his men.

'Blood Crows! Halt! Halt! Form up on me!'

Wheeling his mount to face the side of the hill where the battle was raging, Cato waited anxiously for his men to break off their butchering of the enemy wounded and take up position on either side of their commander. A quick glance round revealed only one riderless horse standing on the plateau. Cato nodded. It had gone well so far. If Macro and his men had played their part then the enemy's attention would be drawn to the attack on their flank, and they would not be prepared for a second blow from a different direction. But if Macro had failed then

Cato fully realised that he was about to lead what was left of the Blood Crows to complete annihilation. He felt a curious calm at the prospect. His only palpable regret was the thought of Julia grieving his death. He thrust all such thoughts aside and cleared his throat that he might give his order clearly and calmly.

'At the trot!'

The troopers dug their heels in and several of the horses whinnied, ears twitching, before they moved off. As the Blood Crows adjusted their pace to maintain an even line, Cato gauged that they had fifty paces to go before reaching the edge of the plateau. An effective cavalry charge was all about good timing, he knew. They must hold the line and then surge forward while there was still time to build up speed to a full charge and deliver as shattering an impact as possible on the enemy. Whatever the ideal might be, Cato's situation was complicated by the wet ground and the final approach down the slope. Some of the horses were bound to slip or fall, but that was a price that had to be paid.

'At the canter!'

Cato tapped his heels in and increased the pressure of his knees against the sides of his horse, leaning forward to tighten the grip of the tall saddle horns about his hips. The air filled with the slap and splash of hoofs on the sodden earth and drips flicked from the beast's mane into his face as Cato and his small force rapidly closed on the edge of the plateau and the ground began to dip. The sounds of battle were suddenly closer, sharper, and the ears of his horse twitched nervously. Cato did not want to give his men any chance to hesitate as they came in view of the battle and snatched a breath to give one last order.

'Blood Crows! Charge!'

CHAPTER TWELVE

The men let out a cheer and spurred their mounts on, surging over the trampled grass, up to the crest, from where the bloody struggle below was revealed in all its detail. In an instant, Cato took in the broad sweep of the spectacle. The enemy was holding their ground for full three-quarters of their defences, but the critical section of the battlefield was directly ahead and to the right where Macro's force was fighting for survival while the flank of the Fourteenth Legion was only just starting to feed into the battle. The hillside between Cato's men and their comrades was thick with enemy warriors charging down on the legionaries, yelling their war cries.

Cato's vision narrowed to the way directly ahead of him. The time to command was over. He was a fighting man now, just like the rest of the Blood Crows, who became no more than fleeting shapes on either side. Cato raised his cavalry sword up and out, ready to strike, and slashed down at the first warrior he came down upon, laying open his shoulder and back. Then the man was gone and the horse knocked another to the ground and there was a dull crack as a bone gave way beneath the hoofs pounding over the body. The horse shied at a third man who turned and roared at the mounted figure looming over him and Cato snatched at the reins to keep the beast from swerving too far and unseating him.

Cato's shield smashed into the warrior. Half turning in his saddle, Cato swung his sword across in an arc and the edge of the blade split his opponent's skull down to the jaw. The warrior's back arched as his arms snapped out and the movement threatened to wrench the sword from Cato's grasp. He held on and pulled with all his strength. He felt the blade give, and pulled again and it came free, causing him to lurch in his saddle. His horse had stopped, and Cato looked round.

The Blood Crows had broken the men who had been bearing down on Macro's cohort and the slope around Cato was a heaving mass of native warriors and horsemen. The enemy's cries of triumph had turned to panic and scores were fleeing towards the left of the line while their leaders tried to stop them and thrust them back towards the bloody melee on the flank. There were Druids there as well, Cato saw. Robed figures with wild hair, screaming curses at the Romans and those amongst their people who refused to turn and fight.

A movement to his side caught Cato's attention and he turned his head to see two men armed with spears rushing towards him. He pulled the reins and turned his horse towards them, digging his heels into the animal's flanks. The men were forced to either side and a spear thrust towards the right of Cato's chest. He cut down savagely with his sword and there was a ringing clash as the edge struck the iron spearhead and knocked it aside. The wet ground meant that it was hard for the man to change direction and his shoulder slammed into Cato's leg. The warrior looked up with a snarl, his eyes gleaming through the dark hair plastering his scalp. Cato instinctively smashed the pommel of his sword on the top of the man's skull and he fell away.

His shield hand suddenly jerked and the reins snapped tightly, causing the horse to turn. The second man staggered back, one hand still trying to rip the Roman's shield aside to open a gap through which his spear could strike. Cato pulled his shield back, throwing his weight to the other side and the spear point glanced off the flat surface and tore a shallow gash in the horse's side. The beast leaped beneath Cato and he clamped his legs to its sides as it kicked out, a hoof catching the warrior and knocking him on to his back.

It took a moment to regain control and Cato saw that Macro had re-formed his men into a line, two deep, extending from the barricade a short distance up the slope. The first men from the other cohorts were taking position to his left. All the time, more men were passing through the gap in the barricade as Crispus and his legionaries worked to widen the breach. The battle was beginning to turn in their favour, Cato realised. But he and his men had to keep the enemy distracted for as long as possible. The Blood Crows were scattered amongst the horde of warriors, fighting on in little knots, or singly, and Cato could

121

see he had already lost a quarter of his men. He must hold them together if they were to stand any chance of survival. The standard-bearer was a short distance away, together with four other men clustered around him as they struggled to prevent the enemy from capturing the standard. Cato spurred his horse over to them, keeping his shield close and his sword out, ready to strike or parry. One of the riders saw him approach and moved aside to let him pass. Cato reined in by the standard-bearer, sheathed his sword and cupped his hand to his mouth to call out over the battlefield, 'Blood Crows! Blood Crows on me! On me!'

Then Cato turned to the men about him. 'Keep close, lads. We'll make for the Fourth Cohort.'

One by one, his men worked themselves over to the standard and joined the growing party of riders as they cut a path through the native warriors towards the steadily strenghtening line of legionaries forming up the slope. Cato noticed that the enemy's spirit was wavering. Fewer men were willing to attack the small party of mounted Romans. Others were drifting away from the fight, seeking safety in the direction of the centre of their line. Only a handful grasped the importance of the desperate fight on the flank, Caratacus amongst them. He raged through their ranks, shouting and thrusting men towards the enemy, struggling to drive them forwards through the rain and the glistening mud.

By the time the last survivors of the two squadrons had rejoined the standard, they had forced their way through to the waiting legionaries, presenting their shields in an unbroken line.

'Make a gap!' Cato ordered as he urged his horse forward. 'Open ranks!'

The men directly ahead of him shuffled aside and Cato led the riders through and a short distance beyond before the shields closed behind him. Macro hurried to his side and looked up with a relieved expression.

'Fine work, sir! Bloody marvellous. You arrived just in time. Else Caratacus and his bastards would have been all over us and we'd have lost the breach.'

Cato grinned back, struggling to control the tremor in his limbs. He looked up and saw that at least two hundred men had already formed on the flank of Macro's cohort and more were taking position all the time. Ahead of them a gap had opened between the two sides and no amount of shouting and cajoling by their leaders could persuade the native warriors to return to the furious struggle that had erupted on their flank. The churned mud between the two sides was littered with bodies, splintered shields, abandoned weapons and puddles of bloodstained rainwater.

The tops of Roman standards appeared behind the breach and a moment later Legate Quintatus led his officers and the colour party through the gap and up to Cato.

'I heard what had happened at this end. Excellent work, Prefect!' He grinned. 'How the hell did you get up here? You're supposed to be guarding the camp.'

'We were the last reserve available to the general, sir. Once your attack stalled,' Cato explained briefly, not wanting to reveal that he had acted on his own initiative. There would be time for repercussions later, and Cato had little doubt that there would be. Whatever he may have achieved, he had also abandoned his post in the middle of a battle. He had left the army's camp defenceless.

'Desperate measures, eh?' Quintatus said. 'Still, no time to waste. We must press our advantage.'

The legate turned to the nearest of his junior tribunes. 'I want the flank cohorts up here on the double. Send word to Tribune Otho to reinforce us. The rest are to hold their position and cross the barricade when practicable. Go!'

The young officer saluted and turned to race back towards the breach.

'Prefect Cato, take your cavalry up to the crest. You'll cover our flank. You've had your fun, now leave the rest to the legions.'

'Yes, sir.' Cato saluted but the legate had already moved on, striding up the slope to take his place behind the centre of the line. Macro watched him briefly and shook his head.

'Fun, he says. I wonder what it's like when things get serious.'

Cato shrugged wearily. 'Perhaps one day we'll really find out. Meanwhile, well done, Macro.'

They exchanged a smile and then Cato gathered the remains of his cohort and led them back up the slope, behind the legionaries, to take their place on the crest. Miro, and a handful of the men he had rallied from his own squadron, joined them. The plateau had turned into a mass of fugitives. Fear and panic was spreading through Caratacus's army and hundreds of his men had joined the flight of the wounded, women and children streaming towards the far side of the hill as they sought to escape the legions. Cato regarded them with pity. All they would find was the screen of auxiliary troops sent to cut off their retreat. Even if the gathering storm provided some of them with cover to get away, most would be taken prisoner and condemned to slavery as spoils of war.

As soon as the first two cohorts had passed through the breach and formed up, the legate gave the order to advance and the legionaries tramped forward as their optios called the time. The large rectangular shields, spattered with mud, faced the enemy, while the points of short swords glimmered in the gaps between shields. Behind, the men peered over their shield trims, only exposing a fraction of their faces as they paced across the slope towards their foes. Cato and his men covered the open flank as the formation moved along the line of the barricade.

Only a handful of battle-crazed warriors dared to stand their ground, wielding their swords, spears and axes more with rage than skill, before they were cut down and trampled into the mud as the legionaries passed over them. Caratacus remained out in front of his men, imploring them to stand, before he too had to move to avoid death or capture. With a last look of anguish, he turned his horse and trotted through his men towards the centre of the line.

The dark rain clouds had grown thicker, blotting out the sky, and a shadowy gloom closed over the mountainous landscape as the rain fell even harder and the wind strengthened with moaning gusts that swept over the hill, chilling Cato to the bone. His fear for the fate of the army had left him. Caratacus had gambled on fighting a setpiece battle and lost. Ahead, Cato could see the enemy melting away and then there was a sudden surge in the distance and the glimmer of helmets revealed that the Romans had forced their way through, or round, the enemy's other flank and now they were caught, as if in an iron vice.

From his vantage point on the crest, Cato could see the centre of what remained of the enemy line. A body of armoured men with helmets and patterned cloaks still stood in formation a short distance back from the barricade. Above them flew the standard of Caratacus, rippling furiously in the wind. There were perhaps three hundred warriors in his bodyguard. Not nearly enough to retrieve the situation, Cato calculated. Sure enough, the formation did not move to engage the Romans, but instead began to climb the slope towards the camp, fending off those tribesmen hindering their progress. In the middle rode Caratacus and a small party of horseman, one of whom carried the standard, holding it steadily and keeping it aloft.

As they saw their commander falling back, the last of the men still holding their position along the barricade turned away and joined the rout. Soon nothing stood between the two Roman forces advancing towards each other and Quintatus ordered his men to make for the enemy general's bodyguard, moving in for the kill that would finally place the seal on the conquest of the new province.

Then, as the bodyguards reached the crest, Cato saw three riders leave the formation and gallop towards the tents in the centre of the camp. The standard still flew above the men who had halted and turned to face the Romans closing on them from either side. But the ruse was clear to Cato at once. The three horsemen must be Caratacus and his closest lieutenants, determined to escape the defeat and keep their struggle alive. Once again he faced a dilemma. If he pursued them he would be overriding his orders and leaving Quintatus's flank uncovered. Once again he knew what he must do.

'Blood Crows! Follow me!'

He spurred his horse forward towards the heart of the enemy camp. His men followed at once, spilling out on either side as they raced after their prefect. Cato saw that Caratacus and his companions had made good use of their head start and would reach the tents first. That could not be helped, but there was a chance that whatever they sought there would delay them long enough for Cato and his men to catch up. Around them the plateau was filled with drenched figures running for their lives. At the sound of the approach of the horsemen under the dreaded banner of the Blood Crows they turned aside and fled from the path of the riders. Some, too badly injured, or too tired, to move aside were run down and trampled into the sodden earth.

Ahead, Cato could just make out through the pouring rain that the

125

three riders had reached the tents. One slipped from his saddle and entered a tent, no more than two hundred paces away. Cato leaned forward in his saddle and slapped the flat of his blade against the flank of his mount, determined to wring the last measure of effort out of the blown horse. Saliva from its muzzle flicked back into his face as it pounded towards the tents. Then he saw the man emerge again, leading a small party of women and children. The other riders leaned down to help them up.

'Miro!' Cato called out. 'Go left. Cut them off!'

'Yes, sir!' came the instant reply and several of the riders sheared off to prevent Caratacus escaping. Cato charged on towards the tents. The riders looked up anxiously as the Roman horsemen reined in and surrounded them, swords out, ready to rush their enemy the moment their prefect gave the word.

Cato's chest heaved as he struggled for breath. Before him, not twenty feet away, he recognised Caratacus. At his side, clutching his arm, was a sturdy woman with dark hair. In her other hand she clutched the hand of a boy, no more than ten, Cato guessed. Behind her stood two teenage girls, with terrified expressions on their faces as they gazed at the Roman cavalrymen surrounding them. Caratacus snatched out his sword as he stepped forward to protect them. The other men dropped from their saddles, weapons in hand, to stand by their leader. From their features it was clear that they were related. Brothers, thought Cato, as he walked his horse forward and pointed his sword.

'Lay your arms down and surrender, Caratacus!'

'Fuck you, Roman!' one of his brothers snarled in Latin. 'Come and get them!'

Cato stared back in silence before he lowered his blade and spoke again. 'You cannot escape. You either surrender or die.'

'We can still fight, Roman!' Caratacus lifted his chin defiantly. 'You will not kill us before we have taken several of your men with us into the afterlife.'

'And what of them?' Cato pointed to the women and the boy.

Caratacus raised his spare hand and pulled a dagger from his belt and passed it to the woman with a brief exchange of words before he faced Cato again. 'I have told my wife to kill my children and then herself once I have fallen. Your men shall not rape my daughters. You will not raise my son as your slave!'

Cato quickly sheathed his sword and held out his hand. 'I swear, by all the gods that I worship, that your family will not be harmed. Nor will you, if you surrender.'

'And who are you to guarantee this?'

'I am your captor. Prefect Cato, commander of the Second Thracian Cavalry.'

'Prefect Cato?' Caratacus frowned. 'I know you . . .'

'Yes, sir. We have met before. I am a man of my word and you are my prisoner. I swear no harm will come to you before you are handed into the custody of the imperial palace. On my honour.'

Caratacus stared at him in an agony of indecision and Cato slipped his shield strap over a saddle horn and eased himself to the ground. He walked forward slowly and stopped a sword's length from the enemy commander. He spoke gently.

'Sir, there has been enough bloodshed today. Your army is defeated. Your war against Rome is over. All that remains is for you to choose life for you and your family, or death.'

Caratacus half lowered his sword and glanced over his shoulder at his wife and children, then he turned back to Cato and closed his eyes as he gave an order to his brothers. They stared at him with bitter reproach, but held on to their swords, until Caratacus straightened up again, and repeated his order firmly, eyes open and fixed on Cato. He threw his sword at the prefect's feet. His brothers hesitated a moment longer before they followed suit and then one slumped on to the ground and hugged his knees while the other folded his muscular arms and regarded Cato defiantly. Caratacus turned away and folded his arms about his wife and lowered his head on to her shoulder.

Cato let out a long, deep sigh of relief before he turned to the nearest of his men and gestured at the swords. 'Take those. The rest of you, form a cordon around the tents. Keep the enemy away!'

He turned his attention back to his prisoners again and regarded them with mixed emotions. The war was over, as he had said. There would be no more lives lost and for the first time the new province might live in peace. But there was something terribly affecting about the air of utter despair and exhaustion that hung about Caratacus, and the fear with which his children regarded their captors. Cato lowered his head, aware for the first time just how tired the battle had left him. He tied the reins of his horse to a tent pole and then stood a short distance from his prisoners while around them the shattered remains of the native army fled through the rain.

'Sir!'

Cato's head snapped up, immediately alert. 'What is it?' He strode towards the man who had called out.

'Officers approaching, sir. Looks like the general.'

Cato braced himself and took a calming breath as he ordered his men to clear a path for the general. A moment later the sound of horses' hoofs reached his ears and then he saw a large party of riders approaching through the rain. The gilded helmets, drenched plumes and scarlet military cloaks confirmed what Cato's man had said. He felt a cold dread clench his guts at the prospect of facing the general and justifying his actions. Around the tents the last of the enemy had left the plateau and small parties of legionaries were scouring the ground, looking for survivors hiding amongst the dead, and looting the bodies.

General Ostorius reined in and walked his horse towards Cato with a confused expression.

'Prefect Cato? What on earth are you doing here? I had heard that you had deserted your post. A capital offence in the face of the enemy, as you know. What is the meaning of this?'

It would take too long to make a full report, Cato decided. That could wait. Instead he stepped aside and gestured towards the desultory group of prisoners sitting in the rain. 'General Ostorius. It is my honour to present to you King Caratacus, his family and two brothers.'

Ostorius's jaw sagged as he looked on the enemy who had caused him so much trouble over the long years of his generalship. He swallowed and looked back at Cato.

'Caratacus?' His lips stretched into thin smile of relief. 'By the gods, then it's over . . . At last it's over.'

CHAPTER THIRTEEN

If the spectacle of a defeated army was one of the most miserable sights in the professional soldier's world, Cato reflected as they returned to camp, then sometimes the victors ran it a close second. Throughout the afternoon and into dusk the exhausted soldiers of the Roman army trudged back into the camp through the heavy rain. Many had been detailed to help recover their injured comrades and carry them back from the battlefield, groaning and crying out from the agony of their wounds. Others had been assigned to guard the prisoners. Hundreds had been taken and herded down from the hill under the watchful eye of their Roman captors. Outside the camp they were chained together and when the chains ran out, the remainder had their hands bound behind their backs and their feet were hobbled by ropes so that they could only take short steps. Then they were left exposed to the elements, shivering in the rain, and surrounded by guards. There would be many more taken by the auxiliary units that had been sent to block the enemy's escape. Some would slip through the cordon and return to their villages, chastened by the great defeat that they had suffered, and they would be wary of ever taking up arms against Rome again.

The men of the baggage train escort had been amongst the first units ordered back across the river. The Blood Crows and the survivors of Macro's two centuries formed a column around their prisoners and escorted them off the hill and back to the camp. The legionaries they passed along the way stood and stared, and then, as word of the capture of the enemy commander spread, they cheered Cato and his men, their acclaim drowning out the sound of the rain. Cato felt the warm glow of pride in his heart and glancing round at this men he saw his feeling mirrored in their expressions. He turned and could not help smiling at Macro, trudging along at his side. Macro laughed.

'Does you a power of good to hear that, eh, lad.'

'We've earned it.'

'You've earned it. You took quite a risk acting on your own initiative. If things had turned out differently . . .'

Cato pursed his lips. 'A risk, yes. But it was the best course of action in the circumstances.'

Macro raised his eyebrows. The prospect of abandoning his post in the middle of a battle would never have occurred to him. 'If you say so.'

'Think it over. If we had not acted, then it's likely the legions would have battered themselves to pieces on the enemy's defences. Caratacus only had to wait long enough for that to happen before unleashing his men and driving our lads back down the hill and routing them. In which case the camp would have fallen and we'd have been massacred along with the rest of the army. In such circumstances there is only one logical course of action, no matter what the risks involved.'

Macro puffed his cheeks and sighed. 'I'd hate to ever gamble against you, lad.'

'Gambling is only worthwhile if you have thoroughly appraised the odds.'

'Exactly. You'd take all the fun out of it.'

Cato turned to him with a frown and then saw the gently mocking expression on his friend's face and could not help a quick laugh. 'Whatever the reasoning, good fortune played its part, as ever. The nearest viable ford could have been much further along the river, delaying us until it was too late to make a difference. The enemy could have posted a flank guard – they should have. Even a small force would have stopped us in our tracks and given time to warn Caratacus.' He shrugged. 'The truth is that the battle could have gone either way for any number of reasons. We're lucky that it didn't, but that will never be the version given in the official record. Ostorius got his victory and by the time he celebrates it back in Rome, everyone will consider the outcome as inevitable. That's what the historians will say. A good general leading professional soldiers triumphing over the valiant but amateur barbarians. In time I dare say even we will look back on it as a foregone conclusion.'

'Instead of the fucked-up chaos and carnage that it was, eh?' Macro gave a dry laugh. 'Maybe. But right now, I don't give a shit about historians. I want a drink, something to eat, get this wound sorted out and then some sleep. A drink mostly.'

'That'll have to wait.' Cato's tone became serious. 'There's work to be done first.'

'I know.' Macro was quiet for a moment and then jerked his thumb towards the bedraggled prisoners. Caratacus was leading the forlorn-looking party, unbowed, head held high as he strode with a measured pace. 'What do you want done with our merry little band?'

Cato forced his weary mind to concentrate. 'They'll need stockades. A separate one for Caratacus, well away from the others. I want to keep him isolated from his kin in case he tries anything on.'

Macro nodded.

'And I want them all in chains.'

'They'll be bound to kick up a fuss.' Macro clicked his tongue. 'Prisoners they may be, but the quality are the same the world over. They think they can demand better treatment.'

'Then we'll have to disabuse them,' Cato replied firmly. 'They'll be treated well enough, but the days of being king are over for Caratacus.'

'What do you think the Emperor will decide to do with him? Be a damn shame if they did for him the same way they did for Vercingetorix.'

'It would be a shame,' Cato agreed, recalling the grim fate of the leader of the Gauls who had been defeated by Julius Caesar. Left to rot in a dark cell for several years, he had finally been dragged out and strangled when Caesar eventually came to celebrate his triumph over the Gauls. It had been a poor end for so noble and gifted an enemy and Cato shrank from the idea that Caratacus would meet such a death. Even though Caratacus had prolonged a struggle that had cost so many lives, he had done so out of a desire to resist the Roman invaders, if only to secure the primacy of his own tribe. Few men, Celt or Roman, could have done as much with the forces available. If it was up to Cato, he would spare the life of his enemy, and find a comfortable place of exile for Caratacus and his family. But the decision was not his. Emperor Claudius would pronounce the fate of this long-standing enemy of Rome, and the Emperor would be swayed by what he thought would please the mob most. Cato pushed thought of his prisoners' fate from his mind.

'Nothing we can do about it though. What we have to worry about is making sure they don't escape, and they don't do themselves in.'

'Do you think they would?'

'I don't know. But I don't want to take the risk. They're to be watched at all times, understand?'

'Yes, sir. I'll make sure of it.'

By the time the small column returned to the camp the storm had enveloped the mountainous landscape in earnest. Rain roared down from dark clouds in a constant torrent, turning the ground inside the ramparts into a muddy morass and forming growing puddles, shimmering with silvered spray. The wind had whipped up into a gale and moaned over the palisade like a frenzied giant beast, battering the tent lines and straining the guy ropes that held them up. Several of the tents had already collapsed and lay in sodden heaps.

Cato dismissed most of the men. The Blood Crows led their drenched horses away to feed them and check for wounds. The legionaries fell out and hurried off to secure their tents. Cato held Macro and his men back to construct the two stockades.

'I'll be back once I've written my report,' Cato said and turned towards his tent, leaving Macro to get on with it.

The larger stockade, for Caratacus's brothers and the rest of his family, was erected between the tents of the Blood Crows and those of the legionaries. The second, much smaller, was for Caratacus alone and that was placed a short distance from Cato's command tent. Night was falling as they were completed and the prisoners taken inside. There, despite their protests, they were placed in chains fastened to a stout post driven deep into the ground in the centre of each stockade. Macro ensured that the chains were secure.

When all was done he sent word to Cato and the prefect emerged from his tent to conduct a brief inspection of the work and pronounce himself satisfied. As he turned to leave the larger stockade, his gaze fell on the children huddled in the embrace of their mother. Even they had been placed in chains and now they squatted down, eyes wide in terror and limbs trembling with fear and cold. It was a pathetic sight

132

and despite his earlier resolve not to give his special prisoners any preferential treatment he was moved by their plight.

'Have a simple shelter erected for them, Macro. Nothing elaborate. just enough to keep them out of the rain.'

Macro looked at him in surprise but knew better than to question his friend. 'Yes, sir. There's some spare tent leather in the wagons. It's not much but it'll do.'

'Good.' Cato tore his eyes away from the children and left the stockade through the narrow gate at the side. He turned to the two legionaries taking the first watch. 'You watch 'em closely. No harm is to come to them for any reason. Even if they try to escape. Clear?'

'Yes, sir.'

Cato led the way back towards his tent and the other stockade. He paused at the roughtly hewn timbers of the gate. Two heavyset legionaries stood guard. Cato nodded at them as he and Macro approached. 'What about them? Good men?'

'The best. Picked 'em myself. As tough and reliable as they come. They'll be relieved at midnight by two more of my veterans. More than a match for Caratacus if he tries anything on.'

Cato nodded with satisfaction and then turned the conversation to a necessary but unpleasant topic 'Macro, I want the strength returns for both units as soon as possible.'

'Yes, sir,' the centurion replied. 'And the butcher's bill. I'll see to it. And anything else that needs doing. You should get some rest, sir. You look done in.'

'I'm fine.' Cato smiled wearily. 'Besides, in this storm, I doubt sleep will come easily.'

They exchanged a salute before Macro turned and strode off to his tent to begin work on the sober task of discovering the fate of the men who had gone into battle that day. Cato had done a rough count after the fighting and noted that two-thirds of his men had survived. There would be more rejoining his small command during the night – those who were having their wounds dressed. Some would be more seriously injured, carried off the battlefield to the tents of the legions' surgeons. Many would recover and return to their units, proudly displaying their fresh scars. For others their soldiering days would be over. They would eventually be discharged, with only their savings, share of booty and a small bonus from the imperial coffers to support them. There were few jobs that men crippled by war could find and unless they had family to return to, a dismal life awaited them. They would be only marginally more fortunate than those who perished from their wounds, Cato reflected.

There had been times when he had been tortured by visions of himself sharing such a plight. A broken man, eking out a precarious existence on the streets of Rome or some provincial town. With marriage to Julia the stakes had been raised even higher. Would she accept a husband mutilated by war? Even if she did not abandon him, Cato feared a worse fate – living with her pity as a constant companion. A pity shared by their child one day. That he could not endure. He would rather take his own life. But the chances of such a dismal fate had diminished considerably, he reminded himself. Today's victory would surely put an end to the gravest danger facing the new province. Without Caratacus to unite the tribes, resistance to Rome would crumble.

Taking a deep breath, he nodded to one of the legionaries standing guard by the door to the stockade. 'Open it.'

The man did as he was ordered and stepped to one side to let his superior pass. Cato ducked inside. The stockade was no more than eight feet on each side, with the sharpened posts rising up above the height of a man. Cato nodded his approval. There was little chance of escape, especially as the prisoner was securely chained about the wrists and ankles. Caratacus was sitting in the middle of his prison, leaning against the post to which his chains were fastened. He raised his head as he became aware of his visitor and stared defiantly at Cato through the rain.

'I've given orders for shelters to be erected for you and the others,' Cato told him.

His words were not met with any response. No hint of gratitude. Just the steady glare of an enemy.

'You will be fed soon. Aside from that, is there anything you need?' Cato gestured to his drenched and mud-stained tunic. 'Fresh clothes, for example? I have some spare tunics, cloaks.'

Caratacus hesitated and then shook his head. 'No. Not unless you have enough for all my men you hold prisoner.'

Cato smiled thinly. 'Sadly not.'

'What will become of them? Are they to be slaves? Or executed?'

'They are far too valuable to be executed. They will be sold into slavery.'

Caratacus sighed. 'Better that they were executed. Slavery is not life, Roman. And certainly no life for a Celt warrior.'

Cato shrugged, uncertain how to respond. He had come close to death enough times to value life with the same ferocity with which a drowning man will clutch at anything that floats upon a stormy sea. Yet slavery was a kind of living death for many. Some were treated well by their masters, but many were simply regarded as living tools, mere possessions. He could well imagine how that would shame the proud warriors who had followed Caratacus.

'I can't answer for slavery. All I know is that your followers will live. Unlike the tens of thousands that have died during the course of the war that you have waged against Rome.'

Caratacus stirred and his eyes blazed angrily. 'The war that *I* have waged? I was defending my home. It was you who invaded my lands. The bloodshed is on your hands, Roman.'

'Your lands?' Cato responded sharply. 'The same lands that you took when you conquered the Trinovantes and waged war against the Atrebates and the Cantii? Spoils of war, King Caratacus. Just as these lands are now our spoils of war. The difference is that Rome will bring peace and prosperity to the province.'

'Peace?' Caratacus spat the word. 'You create a wasteland out of our villages and towns, and sow the ruins with the corpses of our people, and you call it peace? Is your empire not yet vast enough for you that you have to gorge yourselves on the blood and land of our island? Could you not have traded with us for our silver? Our furs? Our dogs? Could you not have entreated us to be your allies? Why must Rome treat the world like a master treats his dogs? Why must we all be your slaves? Or perish if we refuse that humiliation?'

Cato mentally flinched from the accusations thrown at him. He knew the real reason behind the invasion well enough: Claudius had needed a military triumph for political reasons, and the conquest of Britannia had promised to be a ready solution. Cato sucked in a breath.

'I do not make policy. I am a soldier. I carry out orders. I suggest that you put your questions to the Emperor when you get the opportunity. Now, if you change your mind about dry clothes, let the guards know.'

Cato turned away and ducked out of the door. He was about to order the guard to close it when he saw two figures approaching him through the haze of rain. One was in the armour of a Roman officer. The other was a woman, attempting to pick her way across the muddy ground to spare her robe from the filth as much as possible.

'Prefect Cato!'

He recognised the voice of Otho and cursed under his breath. There were matters he needed to attend to, just as there should be for the tribune. Yet Otho seemed to have the time to take his wife for a stroll around the camp. He cleared his throat and called back, 'Tribune. What can I do for you?'

The younger officer and his wife hurried over and Cato saw at once the excited expression on the man's face. His wife, Poppaea, was somewhat less cheerful as she peered out of the hood covering her head. The rain had startd to soak through the cloth and wet tendrils of hair clung to her forehead. Otho reached out and grasped Cato's hand.

'First, let me congratulate the hero of the day. The man who won the battle and captured Caratacus.'

'Hmmm,' Cato grumbled in his throat, acutely irritated by the excessive praise. Excessive and dangerous. The last thing he wanted was to be seen to compete with General Ostorius for taking credit for the victory. Ostorius had powerful connections in Rome, while Cato had his father-in-law, a backwoods senator, and Narcissus, an imperial adviser who was struggling to retain his influence over the Emperor. It would be inadvisable to make unnecessary enemies.

Otho ignored his discomfort and continued, 'You deserve a triumph of your own, my dear Prefect! What an outstanding piece of work. Pompey the Great couldn't have done better himself. What do you think, my love?'

He turned, beaming, to his wife. Poppaea forced a smile and glanced down at the muddied hem of her robe.

'Oh yes ... Outstanding.'

'I, uh, was just doing my duty,' Cato muttered, wincing inwardly at the triteness of his words.

'You were doing hero's work, Cato,' Otho gushed, slapping his hand against his thigh. Then he peered past Cato and lowered his voice. 'Is the beast caged within?'

'If you are referring to King Caratacus, then yes.'

'Oh marvellous! We must see him.'

Cato frowned. 'See him? Why?'

Otho looked surprised. 'Why? Because he's the barbarian who has defied an empire. He's the barbarian it has taken the best part of ten years to bring to heel. When my wife returns to Rome she will be able to say she saw him on the very day he was humbled by our legions. She will be quite the envy of high society. Isn't that right, Poppaea?'

'Yes,' she responded curtly and fixed Cato with a hard stare. 'So let's hurry things along a bit so that I can return to my husband's quarters and change into dry clothes before I catch my death.'

Cato shook his head. 'My prisoner is resting. I suggest you come back in the morning, when the storm has passed and you can inspect him at your leisure.'

Otho's brow creased. 'I say, that's a bit off, Prefect. We've had to wade all the way across the camp to get here and now you're telling us we can't see the damned fellow?'

Too weary to get into an argument, and keen to see these aristocrats leave, Cato gritted his teeth. 'Very well. Quickly then. Open the door.'

The legionary slipped the locking bar out and swung the door back for the two visitors. The tribune stepped warily into the stockade and edged along the wall to make room for his wife. Cato watched from the threshold, pained to see Caratacus displayed like some exotic beast. Poppaea glanced round the close confines before fixing her attention on the man chained to the post.

'He doesn't look much like a king,' she said with disdain. 'More like a roadside beggar.'

Her young husband simply stared at the prisoner with an awed expression while his wife continued.

'I can't believe this . . . animal has been the cause of so much trouble,' Poppaea leaned a little closer as her nose wrinkled. 'I mean, really.'

Caratacus was staring straight ahead, apparently unmoved by her remarks. Then he lurched forward against his chains and let out a roar, his face contorting into a feral expression of savagery. Poppaea let out a high-pitched scream and stumbled back against the posts of the stockade. Her husband flinched then reached for his sword as his wife dived back through the door. Otho hurried out after her. Caratacus continued to rage, his chains clanking as he attempted to shake his fists.

'Bloody fellow is wild!' Otho exclaimed as he released his sword and put an arm round his wife to comfort her. 'Quite wild. Well, erm, I thank you, Prefect. And once again, well done. Now, my dear, it's time we got you into some warm, dry clothes. Come.'

They turned and hurried away towards the heart of the camp, pursued by a few more deep-throated cries and curses from Caratacus. Then he stopped, caught Cato's eye, and burst into laughter.

'Seems I'm not the only one who needs to change out of soiled clothing.'

Cato smiled, as did the legionaries on either side of the entrance, until their superior glanced severely at them and they faced forward and adopted the stern expression of sentries on duty. Caratacus's laughter subsided but there was still a slight smile on his face as he looked up at Cato.

'I think I'll take you up on that offer of a change of clothing, Prefect Cato.'

'I'll have my servant bring it to you.'

Their eyes met for a brief moment longer before Cato spoke again. 'It's a pity we had to be enemies. I should have counted it an honour to fight at your side.'

A flicker of surprise crossed the Celt's face. 'You may think that, Prefect Cato. But we could never have been anything but enemies. I know that now. And if you believe that were our positions reversed I would be offering you the comfort of dry clothes, then you are mistaken. I would have taken your head and mounted it on top of my standard.'

The warmth of a moment earlier had gone and Caratacus's eyes were filled with bitterness once again. Cato turned to the guards and nodded. The door was closed and secured.

'Once Thraxis has given him a fresh tunic and cloak, no one else is to disturb him. If anyone comes then tell them that they have to ask for permission from the general first. Understood?'

The two men nodded and Cato squelched over the mud to his tent. He was bone weary and looking forward to removing his armour and having Thraxis warm him some wine. He flipped the leather flaps open and ducked inside, then froze as he caught sight of the figure seated at his desk, warming his hands at the brazier.

CHAPTER FOURTEEN

'Good evening, Prefect Cato.' Septimus smiled without getting up. He had to speak loudly to be heard above the drumming of the rain on the leather above.

'What are you doing here?' Cato demanded. 'Where is Thraxis?'

'About now I should say he's in his cups. I sent for him saying that he could choose a wine jar as a gift from me to you in honour of your heroic feat today. I left him in the tender care of one of the camp whores who has been instructed to see that he is diverted, one way or another, long enough for me to have a little conversation with you.'

'I've had more than enough talk of bloody heroics,' Cato said sourly as he stretched up to his full height and undid the clasp of his cloak. He tossed the sodden folds on to a chest and unhooked the mail cape covering his shoulders.

'Take the credit.' Septimus smiled. 'No harm in building your reputation.'

'I did it to save the army. The capture of Caratacus was just luck.'

'Never knock luck, Prefect. In my experience it is the most important quality in a successful soldier. The gods favour some of us with good fortune. Skill and brains come a distant second.'

Cato arched an eyebrow. 'That's your view. I'd like to think that I make most of my own luck, whatever the will and whims of the gods.'

'How impious of you.'

Cato took a deep breath, gripped the hem of his mail vest and began to wriggle out of it. At length the heavy mass of rings passed over his head and he laid it on the chest beside his cape before turning back to the imperial agent. 'So, why are you here? And I'll thank you to get out of my chair.'

Septimus shrugged and eased himself to his feet and moved round to take one of the folding stools. Cato took his place and glanced into the jug on his desk. He was rewarded with the glimmer of dark wine at the bottom and he poured himself a small cup before turning to his uninvited guest. 'Well?'

'Thank you, but I've already had a drink.' Septimus smiled. 'As for my presence, I do truly wish to congratulate you on your fine work today.'

Cato raised his cup slightly in a mock toast, and then took a sip.

'Now that's out of the way,' Septimus continued, 'it's time to reassess the situation, in the light of today's developments.'

'Now who is underselling the victory? Doesn't that change everything? We have beaten Caratacus and destroyed his army. The campaign is over. Surely no tribe would dare to take up arms against us now, not even the Brigantes.'

'I wish I shared your confidence. With Caratacus out of the picture we still have to deal with Pallas and his schemes. His agent is still at large, and until Pallas gets the news of our victory, the orders he issued to the agent stand. Even then he may still decide that factional interests override completing the conquest of Britannia. As for me, I still have my orders too. I must find and eliminate Pallas's agent before he can do any mischief.' Septimus paused and leaned forward, resting his elbows on his knees. 'And let's not forget, you're in danger as well. You and Macro both.'

'I haven't forgotten.'

'Glad to hear it. You're the kind of officer that the empire can ill afford to lose. As you proved so singularly today.'

Cato set his cup down. 'Have you said your piece?'

'For now. I just wanted to make sure that you realised that my mission is not complete.'

'I understand,' Cato responded tersely. 'Now, if that's all, I'd be obliged if you left me alone. I have work to do.'

Septimus was still for an instant, then stood up. 'Very well, Prefect. I shall keep my distance for a bit. If I hear anything, I'll let you know. You know where to find me.' He bowed his head and slipped out of the tent.

Cato ran his hand over his head and closed his aching eyes.

Septimus's words echoed in his head and Cato despaired at the prospect of losing Britannia as a consequence of the political conflict playing out in the imperial palace back in Rome. So many lives, so much treasure and ten years had been invested in attempting to establish the new province. The thought of it all being thrown away burdened his heart like a lead weight.

At length he opened his eyes again, straightened his back and cracked his shoulders as he rolled his neck. Then, reaching for some bound waxed tablets stacked by his table so that he could write his report, something caught his eye. A small leather purse was lying on the ground next to the tablets. Cato reached down and picked it up. It felt heavy with coin and he noticed that one of the cord loops that fastened the purse to a belt had frayed and broken.

'Septimus,' he muttered to himself. He considered going after the agent but at that moment a sharper gust of wind blew overhead, battering the roof of the tent. 'Well, if he wants it back he can come and get it.'

Cato put the purse into his document chest to keep it safe and then picked up a stylus and began his report. Even though he had not yet been asked for it, Cato wanted to be sure to set down his decisions and their consequences while they were still fresh in his mind. If he was ever called to account for leaving the camp without orders from Ostorius, he would need to explain the necessity of his action. Perhaps it would be better to write two accounts, he reflected. One for Ostorius's immediate consumption which would downplay the chaos and near catastrophe of the general's frontal attack. The second account would tell the truth, or at least the truth from Cato's perspective, and hopefully other officers would vouch for it if the need ever arose.

He felt vexed by the need to think in terms of protecting himself from ambitious rivals. But there was no avoiding it. Promotion to senior rank came with a price and for a moment Cato felt a longing for earlier times when being a soldier had been a matter of day-to-day routine. Now he had to perpetually consider the future and guard against the consequences of the past, and he felt that he was becoming as much a politician as he was a soldier.

Cursing under his breath, he set to work and had drafted both accounts when he heard the leather tent flaps rasp lightly and looked up to see Macro enter, dripping.

'Got the final strength returns for the baggage train escort, sir.'

'Sit yourself down.' Cato gestured to the stool Septimus had used and indicated the jug. 'There's a drop left. If you want it.'

Macro grinned. 'Don't mind if I do.'

He took the cup Cato poured for him and sat with a sigh. 'I expect you'll want the butcher's bill first.'

Cato nodded.

Macro took out a slate from his sidebag and held it at an angle to the light of the flames in the brazier. 'The First Century took the brunt of the fighting. Sixteen dead, twenty-three wounded. Of which six will die, according to the surgeon. Two more may have mortal wounds. Five will have to be discharged when they recover. Three have light injuries and are expected make a full recovery. The rest are walking wounded. Crispus's century lost seven dead and nine wounded, only one of those seriously. The rest are flesh wounds. Which gives current strength returns of twenty-one and forty-two men, respectively.' Macro shook his head. 'Not even enough to fill out a single century. So much for the Fourth Cohort of the Fourteenth Legion.'

Cato sucked in a deep breath. Heavy losses indeed. 'What about my Blood Crows?'

Macro consulted his slate again. 'Not so bad. Twelve dead. Fourteen wounded. Sixty-four still in the saddle.'

'We've lost so many . . .'

Macro took a sip of wine. 'What did you expect? The attack on the enemy's flank was a desperate gamble. Look at it this way, if you hadn't given the order, it's likely there'd be none of us left alive now.'

'Perhaps, but we're too few to protect the baggage train.'

'From what? The enemy have been driven from the field. All we have to worry about now is keeping the peace amongst the camp followers. Doesn't take more than a few men to knock heads together when there's trouble. We'll be all right until we get replacements.'

'How long will that be, I wonder.'

'As soon as possible after the general marches the army back to its base at Cornoviorum, I should think. Of course they're likely to be pretty raw, but I'll soon get 'em into shape. Same goes for the Second Thracian Cavalry, though they'll be Thracian in name only. I expect they'll fill the ranks with Batavians or the like. Good horsemen, but not so wild-looking. Still, beggars can't be choosers. We'll have to take whatever they offer us, the same as the other units. The general's going to have a job of work explaining the losses he suffered today.' Macro paused and looked at his friend with a concerned expression. 'You look fit to drop, lad. We've done all we can for now. Best rest and let the storm pass and then we can pick things up in the morning.'

Cato shook his head. 'Nice thought . . . How are the prisoners?'

'They're fine. My lads can be relied on.'

The tent flaps rustled again and a headquarters orderly entered and saluted Cato.

'Yes?'

'General Ostorius sends his compliments, sir, and requests that you and Centurion Macro join him in the mess tent.'

'Oh? Did he say why?'

'No, sir. That's all.'

'Very well. Dismissed.'

The orderly saluted and left. Cato chuckled drily. 'So much for having a rest.'

The noise of the celebrations reached the ears of the two officers as they approached the centre of the camp. Around them the tent lines of the legionaries extended into the gloom. It would be dark soon but there would be no campfires that night due to the rain and the wind which beat down on the goatskin tents, causing them to shimmer and boom, like the sails of ships, Cato thought. There were few men out and about, the majority were taking shelter from the storm. Only those on duty, or heading to or from the latrine trenches, were braving the foul weather.

'Sounds like the booze is running freely,' said Macro, quickening his pace. 'Better be some left for us.'

Cato did not reply. He wondered if he had ever felt so tired and craved nothing more than a decent night's sleep. Even though he had put on a fresh cloak for the walk to headquarters, the rain had already started to seep through the waterproofing of fat that was worked into the cloth. He could not help trembling as he kept pace with his friend. Cato was in no mood to drink and celebrate and he silently cursed Ostorius for sending for them.

The headquarters tents in the heart of the camp were far more substantial than those of the legionaries and were securely fastened to the ground with doubled ropes and heavy stakes driven into the earth. But still they shimmered and shook in the wind. They glowed slightly from the illumination within and, despite his misgivings, Cato looked forward to warming himself at a brazier.

The guards standing outside were hunched in their cloaks but still stood to attention and saluted as the two officers passed by and entered the large mess tent. At once a wave of clammy warmth engulfed Cato and Macro and they looked round to see that the interior was packed with officers. The air was heavy with the smell of damp clothing, sweat, woodsmoke and wine. They slipped off their cloaks and hung them over the steaming material already covering most of the racks by the entrance to the mess tent, then made their way over to the counter where the wine merchant and his servant were struggling to keep up with the demands for refills from the officers crowding about. As they were recognised, Cato and Macro were loudly congratulated on their part in the battle and Cato tried not to wince as he was slapped heavily on the back and shoulders. He forced himself to nod gratefully and move on. Macro, by contrast, was revelling in the praise of his fellow centurions.

They reached the counter and were waved to the front of the queue by bleary-eyed comrades. As they turned away with two brass beakers filled to the brim, they were at once accosted by General Ostorius. The old man's lined face was split by a wide smile that exposed his stained teeth.

'Ah! Prefect Cato. The reason why we are all here celebrating.' He placed his hand on Cato's shoulder and his bony fingers squeezed tightly, just enough to be painful. Then he released his grip and turned to one of the junior tribunes near at hand. 'You, boy! Fetch me something to stand on. And be quick about it!'

The young man scurried into the throng and returned a moment later with a simple wooden stool. Ostorius climbed stiffly on to it and straightened up so that he was visible above the crowd.

'Gentlemen! Your attention!'

Those immediately surrounding their commander fell dutifully silent but there were pockets of raucous singing and laughter towards the far fringes of the tent and Ostorius scowled as he drew a deep breath and bellowed, 'Quiet!

As the last of the officers fell silent and turned to face him, there was a stillness inside the tent, though the goatskin walls shook and flapped and the rain drummed overhead, and dripped through whatever small gaps it could find. Ostorius gestured to Cato to stand at his side before he began to speak.

'Gentlemen, comrades, this has been a great day for us, for our men, for Emperor Claudius and for Rome! A victory!' He raised his cup, spilling some of the contents down the front of Cato's tunic as the other officers cheered. 'A victory that finally sets the seal on the conquest of Britannia. The enemy is beaten, humbled, and squats in chains as our prisoner. His army is shattered and thousands of them will be sold as spoils of war. Every man here and in the legions stands to make a small fortune from the proceeds!'

There was more cheering at the prospect of the flow of silver coins to come and Macro nudged Cato and grinned. 'That'll piss off the lads in the auxiliary cohorts sent to block the enemy's retreat. They won't be taking a share of the prisoners from the battlefield. Just those running away that they can net. All the more for us.' He laughed cheerfully at the thought of his comrades going short, in the long-standing tradition of rivalry between the legions and the men of the auxiliary cohorts.

The general raised a hand to calm the officers and the cheering died away. His expression grew more serious as he continued his address.

'A victory, yes, but a hard-won victory. The men fought like lions today, braving every arrow, rock and slingshot that the cowardly enemy rained down on them from the safety of their fortifications. We took them on, slogging our way to the top of the hill and scattering them like chaff in the wind. Their defeat was inevitable. But it cost us dear, and would have cost us more but for the timely intervention of Prefect Cato, Centurion Macro and their small band of heroes on the enemy's flank. It tipped the balance between a narrow victory and a shattering blow. For that we must raise our cups and toast Cato and Macro!' He beamed down at Cato and raised his cup high before taking a deep draft of wine.

'Cato and Macro!' the others echoed and downed their wine.

Ostorius stepped down unsteadily from the stool. 'I'll make sure you are given full credit for the role you played in the fight for the flank.' The general smiled. 'Who knows? You might even be invited to Rome when my victory is celebrated.'

'Thank you, sir,' Cato responded, while Macro merely nodded. Then the general turned away and disappeared into the crowd, and the officers returned to their loud conversation and laughter.

'Well, that was uncommonly decent of him,' Macro sniffed. 'You'd think we played a small part in some skirmish from the way he put it. Invited to *his* triumph . . . Fucking quality grab all the glory for themselves.'

'Well, what did you expect? A ride down the Sacred Way on a chariot all by yourself? Come on, Macro. That's just the way it is. Always will be. Doesn't change what we know really happened.' He forced a smile and held up his cup. 'To Centurion Macro, the hardest fighting officer in the Fourteenth, or any other legion.'

Macro's face cracked in a drunken smile and he raised his cup in turn. 'And to Prefect Cato, the hardest bullshitting thinker in the whole fucking army.'

Cato hesitated and then shrugged. 'Why not? I'll drink to that.'

They butted the brass beakers together and drained them before heading back to the counter for a refill.

CHAPTER FIFTEEN

The celebrations continued into the night, with officers arriving late, or leaving, as their duties dictated. Cato did not try to keep up with his friend, but drank just enough to allow himself to enter into the cheerful mood of his companions. Macro took his fill and assumed his customary role of a roaring drunk, singing his heart out along with the other centurions as they ran through their repertoire of marching songs. A number of officers had drunk themselves insensible and had stumbled over to the benches and tables to the side of the tent and slumped over their folded arms. A junior tribune leaned forward, hands on knees, vomiting just inside the entrance of the tent.

Later in the evening Cato spied a small group of women in the far corner, sitting on benches around a table. Officers' wives. Most were draped in simple cloaks, except for Poppaea, who had changed the clothes she had worn when she came to inspect Cato's prisoner. Her hair had dried, been combed and pinned up in an elegant bun. As he stared at her, she turned and caught his eye directly. Cato felt embarrassed and nearly succumbed to the urge to look away, but there was a challenge in her expression and he would not give Poppaea the satisfaction. At length she smiled thinly and raised her cup and bowed her head in salute. Cato nodded in reply and then turned away and worked his way towards the counter.

The wine merchant was sweating profusely and Cato waited patiently as he cleared away his empty jars and rushed out through the side flap to fetch some more stock from his cart. As Cato leaned on the counter, drumming his fingers, he suddenly smelt a sweet scent and turned to see Poppaea standing beside him. At once he pushed himself up and nodded a greeting.

'Poppaea Sabina.'

'Prefect Cato.' She smiled again. A very attractive smile, Cato thought. It reminded him of Julia, and he promptly wished it had not.

'It seems the good general is a little underwhelmed by the contribution you made to what he is claiming as *his* success.'

Cato struggled to focus his thoughts. Drink and tiredness were a distracting combination but he was determined not to say anything indiscreet to the wife of Tribune Otho. 'He gave me, and Centurion Macro, the credit we deserved.'

'Oh, come on. He hardly did that.' She poked him playfully in the chest. 'My husband told me exactly what happened on that miserable hill. You saved the day.'

'We played our part.'

'You did rather more than that. Why so modest? Surely it must irk you to see your actions pushed to the margins. You must know that by the time Ostorius reports to the Emperor, your part in the outcome will have been relegated to a minor detail.'

Cato stared at her. She was quite beautiful, and there was a playful intelligence in her expression that added to her allure. Yet her very directness discomforted him, and he did not trust her. Nor did he trust himself to speak as carefully as the situation required. Any comment that he made that could be remotely construed as disloyal to Ostorius would be bound to be repeated to Poppaea's husband and Otho did not seem the tight-lipped kind. Repetition engendered exaggeration and if word of his boasting reached the ears of Ostrorius then Cato would be viewed with disdain. All the good will he had won on the battlefield would vanish and Ostorius would be looking for any excuse to punish Cato with an appointment even less appetising than commanding the baggage train escort.

'I am a simple soldier, my lady,' he responded stiffly. 'I do my duty. What the general says and does are no concern of mine.'

She laughed. A light, pleasant sound. 'Oh dear. I seem to have upset you, Prefect. Allow me to get you another cup of wine.'

The wine merchant had returned, struggling with a large jar of wine under each arm. He set them down quickly as Poppaea waved him over.

'Yes, my lady?'

'I'll have a small jar of the Oscan wine you keep back for your best customers.'

'Oscan?'

Her eyes narrowed. 'Don't play the fool with me. I know all about it. My husband is Tribune Otho. Put it on his account.'

As soon as the name was mentioned the wine merchant bowed his head and turned his attention to the stack of jars behind the counter.

'That's not necessary,' Cato objected.

'Rubbish.' Poppaea smiled sweetly. 'You deserve to be rewarded, nay? Wine will have to do for now.' She lowered her voice. 'But there are other rewards that a man of your evident ability deserves.'

Cato froze. 'I, er, I'm not sure I understand.'

'Don't be a fool, Prefect. You know exactly what I am saying.'

'But your husband—'

'Has drunk himself insensible and is asleep in our tent. He's not quite the man I thought he was. Charming in public, but quiet and moody in private. He doesn't always fulfil all that a wife might require of a husband . . .'

Cato's jaw sagged for a moment, but he could not think of a safe reply. He was saved by the return of the wine merchant carrying a finely glazed jar. He took out the cork and carefully poured a measure into a cup he took from beneath the counter. Poppaea moved between Cato and the merchant to take the cup. Just then a strong gust of wind howled over the camp and the tent flaps slapped open and flapped wildly like the broken wings of a large bird. Cato looked round at the sound for a moment and turned back to see Poppaea close up, holding the cup out for him to take.

'Your reward. And there's more to come, if you wish it.' She leaned forward slightly to reveal the shadowy cleavage between her breasts.

The wind strengthened, roaring across the camp and abruptly the rear of the tent, where the women were seated, whipped up as the guy ropes on that side wrenched the wooden pegs out of the earth. The wind and rain blasted inside, sweeping away the thick atmosphere inside the tent. There were shouts of alarm from the women and anger from the men as they fled from the unwelcome intrusion of the elements. More guy ropes gave way and the far end of the tent began to collapse.

Cato's thoughts instantly turned to his men huddled in their shelters. His place was with them if the storm threatened the safety of the camp. He turned to Poppaea.

'Excuse me, I must go.'

Before she could protest he pressed the cup back into her hands and looked round for Macro. His friend was pushing through the throng towards him.

'Bloody fun and games, this.' Macro smiled ruefully. 'We'd better get back to the men.'

Cato nodded, noting that his friend seemed sober enough to make the walk to the tent lines, despite the amount he had drunk earlier. Several of the other officers were of a like mind and jostled for the cloaks at the entrance. Outside, Cato led the way, clutching the hood of his cloak tightly over his head. They had only gone a short distance before Macro stopped.

'A moment, lad.'

He moved to the side of the muddy thoroughfare and leaned forward. A torrent of vomit gushed from his gaping mouth as he made a deep heaving grunt. Most hit the ground but the wind whipped a small quantity back against his tunic and Macro swore before he lurched again, this time turning downwind as he let fly with another jet of vomit. He paused briefly then straightened up.

'You done?' Cato asked, hands on hips.

Macro nodded with a meek expression. 'Better out than in. And a word to the wise, always go downwind.' He gestured to the mess on his tunic.

Cato frowned with disgust. 'Let's go.'

The storm was raging across the mountains, the howling wind lashing the rain against the tents and every living thing inside the camp. There was a cry from behind and Cato looked back to see the end of the mess tent fly up in the air, tearing out the guy ropes and swirling violently, before collapsing. The general's guards had abandoned their weapons to hammer down the pegs holding the other tents in place. On all sides the storm was wreaking havoc and the men hurried from the shelter of their section tents to hold them down. Even with the chaos unfolding around him, Cato was gratified by the sight of the dim shapes of the sentries remaining at their posts on the ramparts.

'Jupiter's fucking balls!' Macro shook his head. 'Have you ever seen the like? Someone's got right up the noses of the gods and no mistake.'

'It's as well that it happens now rather than last night,' Cato responded, trying to look on the bright side. 'Can you imagine what that hill is going to be like after this lot?'

They struggled on, leaning into the gale, the hems of their cloaks whipping at their legs. At length they reached the partial shelter of the rampart and turned towards the corner of the camp where the baggage train was parked.

'What did the tribune's wife want with you?' asked Macro.

'Ah, you saw that.'

'Indeed. Looked rather cosy. Is she the kind of army wife who puts it about then?'

'I wouldn't know. She wanted to give me a pat on the back and buy me a drink. That's all.'

Macro chuckled. 'Sure. Pat on the back. Right.'

Cato sighed wearily. 'Macro, I'm a married man. And I love my wife.'

'So?'

'So, I'd rather we left it there, Centurion. That's an order.'

'Yes, sir.'

When they reached the tent lines of the escort, or what was left of them, Cato's heart sank. At least half the tents were down and the dark figures of men were struggling to save the rest. The Blood Crows had abandoned their tents to go and calm the horses and their shrill whinnies cut through the wild night.

'I'll see to the men,' said Cato. 'You check on the prisoners.'

'Prisoners? Fuck 'em. A little bit of rain won't hurt them.'

'Maybe, but I want them in good shape when they're handed over to the Emperor, whenever that is. Make sure they're safe and their chains are secure.'

'All right.' Macro dipped his head in salute and hurried off towards the larger of the stockades. Cato turned to his own tent first and was relieved to see that it was still standing. Thraxis was hammering down extra pegs as his commander approached.

'Any damage inside?' Cato asked.

His servant lowered his hammer and looked up. 'No, sir. I got most of your clothes into the chest earlier. Same with the paperwork and slates.'

'Good man!' Cato gestured to the tent. 'I'll leave you to secure this. I need to check on the others.'

Thraxis nodded quickly and turned back to his work as Cato strode towards the nearest line of tents belonging to the legionaries of Macro's cohort. He saw the giant outline of Centurion Crispus bellowing orders to his men and strode through the wind towards him.

'Centurion, report!'

Crispus wiped the streaks of rain from his face. 'Not good, sir. Lost most of the tents and we'll be lucky if we save any that are still left. I've told the lads to collapse them and sit on the bastards until the storm has passed.'

Cato yawned, weariness settling heavily on his tired limbs. 'Best thing, I suppose. As soon as the wind dies down get the tents back up and the men inside. They'll have to double up as best they can until daylight. We'll sort things out then.'

'It's going to get cosy in them tents, sir.'

'Then it'll help keep 'em warm.'

'Cato! Cato!'

The both turned towards the desperate shout and Cato could just make out Macro's stocky figure waving frantically in front of the smaller stockade. He ran to meet them.

'What is it?' Cato demanded.

'He's gone!' Macro shouted, eyes wide in alarm. 'Caratacus. The bastard's gone.'

CHAPTER SIXTEEN

'Gone?' Cato froze. His guts clenched with dread.

He didn't wait for any further clarification but sprinted across the mud and puddles towards the stockade. The door was open and it was too dark to see inside, but as he drew closer he saw two bundles lying on the ground just inside. The two sentries, he realised at once. He charged past them and into the stockade. The gloomy interior was empty, except for the post and the chains lying in the mud.

'No!' Cato bunched his hand into a fist and punched the wooden frame at his side. He crouched down and picked up the chains for closer examination. They were covered in mud but his probing fingers found no breaks in the links and the pins on the shackles had been cleanly knocked out. Rising quickly he turned and joined Macro and Crispus as they examined the bodies.

'Dead?'

'Both of them,' Macro answered. 'Throats slashed. Whoever did this got up close to them . . . Some bastard's going to pay for this.'

Cato tried to calm his racing mind. 'We'll deal with that later. Right now we must find Caratacus. Get the men. I want them to start searching at once. Send a runner to each of the gates. No one is to leave the camp. Go!'

The startled centurion ran off to the tent lines and Cato turned to Macro. 'What about the other prisoners?'

'I checked. They're all there.' Macro glanced round into the shadows. 'Caratacus could still be close if he thinks he can set them free as well.'

Cato shook his head. 'It's too late for him now. The alarm has been raised. If that was ever his plan he's not going to try it now. He'll want to get out of the camp and as far away as possible before daylight. I just hope we're not too late. You take charge here. Double the guard on the others. Find the cornicen and have him sound stand to.'

'What are you going to do, sir?'

'Report to headquarters. We have to rouse the camp at once.'

'Shouldn't we try and find Caratacus first? Before we tell the general?'

'It's too late for that. Move!'

They parted and Cato turned and began to run back towards the heart of the camp. He was in sight of the headquarters tents when he heard the thin notes of the horn sounding from behind him. He saw soldiers in the darkness pause from their efforts to salvage their tents and look round.

'What's going on?' a voice called out. 'Thought we'd seen to the enemy. What's that joker playing at?'

Cato stopped and cupped a hand to his mouth and shouted, 'Stand to! You heard the signal! Move your bloody arses!'

The spell was broken and men began to scramble for their kit. Optios and centurions relayed the order, straining to be heard above the storm. Cato plunged on, half running, half slithering over the mud as he made for headquarters. Miraculously, only the mess tent had gone, the rest still struggled against the wind and he slithered to a halt outside the entrance to the general's private quarters, gasping for breath.

'Let . . . me in.' He waved the guards aside.

'Just a moment, sir.' One made to block his path.

'There's no . . . time for this.' Cato thrust the man aside and pushed through the flaps. The glow from the oil lamps and the braziers seemed brilliant after the darkness outside and Cato looked round frantically as the only servant still awake started in alarm from cleaning his master's boots.

'Is the general here?' Cato demanded.

One of the guards entered the tent and hurried round Cato, hand moving to his sword. 'Sir! You'll have to wait outside!'

'Where is the general?' Cato repeated.

The curtain at the far end parted and Ostorius appeared in his tunic, barefoot. 'What in Jupiter's name is going on? Prefect Cato. What are

155

you doing here?' He paused and cocked his head. 'Who gave the order to stand to?'

Cato thrust his way past the guard and stood stiffly in front of his commander, heart pounding inside his heaving chest.

'Caratacus has escaped, sir.'

Ostorius stared at him, stunned into momentary silence. 'Escaped? How is that possible? You had the man in chains.'

'Yes, sir.'

'Then how could it happen?'

Cato swiftly collected his thoughts. 'He must have been helped, sir. The two men guarding him were killed and the pins of his chains were knocked out.'

'Helped? Who by?'

'I cannot say, sir. Not yet. But as soon as I discovered he was gone I sounded the alarm. My men are searching for him, and I've given orders that no one is to leave the camp. If he's still here, then we'll find the enemy commander, sir.'

Ostorius took the information in and his expression became severe. 'He had better be found, Prefect Cato. By the gods, he had better be found and put back in chains. If he has made good his escape then I swear those responsible will pay for this.'

'Yes, sir,' Cato responded helplessly.

The general turned to the guard. 'Send for my staff officers at once!'

The guard saluted and hurried from the tent. Ostorius's servant was still sitting on his stool, a boot in his hands. The general's glare turned on him. 'What are you waiting for? Get on with it!'

The servant began to scrub furiously, head down and hunched over his work. At that moment Cato would have willingly swapped places with the man. As it was, he stood still while Ostorius turned back, glowering.

'You'd better get on with your search for Caratacus, Prefect. Get out!'

Cato saluted and turned to hurry from the tent, grateful to quit the general's presence.

Once the general had briefed his officers, two cohorts were detailed to assist the escort detachment in the hunt for the escaped prisoner. The rest of the men were stood down and returned to whatever shelter they could find to see out the rest of the night. Cato returned to his headquarters to wait impatiently for reports to come in.

At last the storm began to abate and then pass on to the east, the wind easing as the storm drew the clouds in its wake. At last the rain stopped and the serene stars looked down from velvet heavens. As he stood at the entrance of his tent and stared up at the night sky, its very calmness seemed to mock Cato. His moment of triumph had lasted less than a day. The escape would no doubt transform him from the toast of the legion to scapegoat for this misfortune. Far from being the officer renowned for his capture of an enemy general, he would be doomed to be remembered for failing to prevent his flight. The real culprit was the man who had murdered the guards and set the enemy commander free. Cato swore that if he ever discovered the identity of that individual, he would be made to suffer. His only hope at this stage was that the culprit who had helped Caratacus was hiding him somewhere in the camp. The possibility that the enemy commander had found a way out was too painful for Cato to contemplate.

As the reports came in from the search parties, Cato felt his heart grow heavier at the lack of any sign of Caratacus.

As the first hint of dawn bled across the horizon, Macro brought him disturbing news.

'I've been questioning the guards on the gates. They've done as you ordered and let no one out. But then I had a thought. I asked them who had passed through the gates in the hours before the alarm was raised.'

'And?'

'You're not going to like this, there was nothing that stood out – the usual comings and goings of patrols. Except for a wine merchant's cart.'

Cato pressed his hand to his forehead. 'A cart. Did the sentries search it?'

'They gave it a quick look and it was empty. The driver's face was hidden by a cloak. Since it was raining, the duty optio didn't think it was unusual. The driver said he was returning to Viroconium to buy more stock since there was no more danger from the enemy. The optio passed him through.'

'What time was this?'

'Just before they closed the gate for the night. That was when we were in the mess tent. I've got the optio outside if you want a word with him.'

'Get him in here.'

Macro ducked his head through the flaps. 'Inside, you.'

He stood aside to let the optio enter. He was a seasoned-looking soldier but his uneasiness and dull expression did not create a good impression. To Cato he looked like the kind of soldier who was good enough to make optio but lacked those qualities that were essential for promotion to centurion. He stood to attention.

'Optio Domatus reporting, sir.'

'Centurion Macro informs me that you passed a cart out of the camp before you closed the gate last night.'

'Yes, sir.'

'A wine merchant, making for Viroconium.'

'That's right, sir.'

'And you didn't think it unusual for a wine merchant to be leaving the camp at that hour?'

The optio shifted uneasily. 'He sounded convincing enough to me, sir. Anyway, we're supposed to be keeping watch on threats coming from outside the camp, sir. He was leaving. Didn't see any harm in letting him pass.'

'Optio, the sentries on watch duty are looking out for the enemy. Your job is to carefully monitor who comes in or goes out.'

'As I said, sir. I didn't see no reason to be suspicious of the man. He gave me no cause to suspect he was an enemy. Let alone Caratacus himself, sir. Besides, he spoke Latin.'

Cato sighed. 'Did it not occur to you that at least one of the enemy might know our tongue?'

The optio opened his mouth to protest but had the sense to say nothing and clamped his lips together.

'Do you think it's him?' Macro intervened.

'It's possible. I'll send a patrol after him once we're done here. Just in case.' Cato turned his attention back to the optio. 'Domatus, is there anything else you can tell us about this wine merchant? Any description of the man?'

'As I told the centurion, sir, he had his hood over his head. Couldn't see much in the dark, and what with the rain and wind and all.'

'I see.' Cato sighed wearily. He was about to dismiss the man when the optio's expression lit up.

'I did get his name, sir. It was branded on to the side of the cart. I could just make it out as he passed through the gate.'

'Oh?'

'Hipparchus, he was called, sir.'

Cato stared at him.

'Oh, shit …' Macro growled.

Cato was on his feet at once, pushing past the optio. 'Macro, on me!'

He tried to run towards the baggage train and the battered sprawl of tents and shelters that belonged to the camp followers, but the mud made the going slow and slippery. Macro followed him as best he could. They hurried past the vehicle park where the army's carts and wagons were packed together, and on into the section allocated to the camp followers. There was little of the ordered layout of the soldiers' tents and the ramshackle shelters and colourful tents that were still standing sprawled around two intersecting thoroughfares. The sun had not yet stirred but there were plenty of civilians milling around. The storm had wreaked as much damage here as elsewhere in the camp; collapsed tents and overturned stalls surrounded the crossroads.

Cato stopped by the stall of a tinsmith which had survived intact. The proprietor was already setting out his stock, seemingly unperturbed and uncaring about the misfortune of his neighbours.

'Where do I find Hipparchus, the wine merchant?'

The man looked up and shrugged. 'Don't know the man. But if he deals in wine, you'll find him round the corner there, with the others.'

Cato ran on, turning into another muddy stretch lined with stalls. Close by he saw a stall with wine jars behind the counter. A fat man with greasy locks of grey hair was arguing with a customer as Cato approached him.

'I'm looking for Hipparchus.'

The merchant instantly turned his attention to the young officer and smiled. 'Sir, if you are looking for wine, then I guarantee you better quality at a lower price than Hipparchus.'

'I don't want your bloody wine. I want Hipparchus.'

The merchant shrugged and pointed to the stall on the opposite side of the way. Cato turned and saw a tall-sided wagon with an awning stretching out from one side to cover a sturdy wooden frame that formed the stall. He hurried over and clambered over the counter. His boots landed on something soft and yielding. He stumbled, recovered his balance and saw a body lying face down under the counter, hidden by the leather apron that fronted the stall. He knelt down and turned the body over. In the pale light he could see that it was not Septimus. From the soiled and tatty tunic and the clip in his ear he guessed that this must be a slave. The man groaned and raised an arm feebly. Cato grasped his shoulders and shook him.

'Where's Hipparchus?'

The slave's eyes flickered open and he tried to focus on the man looming over him. He stank of wine. Cato repeated his question with another shake for emphasis, but the man was still too dazed to think. With a hiss of frustration Cato released him and turned to Macro who was standing on the other side of the counter.

'Search the wagon.'

Macro nodded and hurried round to the rear of the wagon where he began to undo the ties securing the opening in the leather covering.

'What's going on then, sir?'

Cato looked up and saw the merchant he had spoken to earlier crossing over to him.

'Did you see anything over here last night?'

'See anything?'

'Anything out of the ordinary?'

'Well, I was a bit busy trying to keep my stall from blowing away, sir. Like most of us in the camp. But there was something a bit odd, like.'

'Tell me.'

'That Hipparchus, he ups and harnesses a mule to his cart just before the light faded. Him and that useless slave of his. Then he heads off. What with the storm and all, I'd have thought he'd stay close and look after his business. Ain't seen him since.'

'You sure it was him? Hipparchus?'

The merchant nodded. 'Recognised his cloak.'

'Cato!' Macro called out from the back of the wagon. 'He's in here!'

Cato turned away from the merchant and joined Macro at the rear of the wagon. In the gloom of the interior Cato could make out the imperial agent slumped against a rolled sleeping mat. He lay still, and for a moment Cato feared that he might be dead. Cato clambered up on to the bed of the wagon and made his way forward to the side of the body. He heard the man breathing and let out a sigh of relief.

'He's alive. Give me a hand here. Let's get him out of the wagon.'

They dragged the unconsious agent to the back and then eased him on to the ground. In the better light Cato saw that the hair on one side of his head was matted with dried blood. More blood caked his neck and the shoulder of his tunic.

Macro sucked in a breath. 'Some bastard's given him a sharp knock on the head. Caratacus, you think?'

Cato hesitated. 'Looks that way.'

Standing up, he called out to the wine merchant opposite to bring some water.

Macro gestured down at Septimus. 'What do we do with him?'

Cato scratched his jaw. 'We'll clean his wound and dress it. Then try and bring him round. If we can't get any sense out of him, we'll take him up to the infirmary for the surgeon to look after him. Either way, we need a word with him as soon as possible.'

Macro was about to say something when the wine merchant approached with a jug and small strip of linen. Cato took them off him.

'I want you to go to headquarters and report to the general.'

'I ain't a soldier,' the merchant protested. 'Go yourself.'

'Shut your mouth!' Cato snapped back. 'And do as I bloody well tell you. Tell the general that Caratacus has escaped from the camp in Hipparchus's cart. Tell him I'm sending my men out to try and find him. Now go!'

The merchant reluctantly hurried off, leaving the two officers with Septimus.

'Lift his head gently,' Cato instructed.

Macro did as he was told and Cato poured some water on the linen and started to clean off the dried blood as best he could. The scalp was torn but there seemed to be no damage to the bone beneath. As he worked on the rest of the wound, Septimus stirred and mumbled a protest before he slid back into unconsciousness.

'Something's not right about this,' said Macro.

Cato looked up. 'You mean aside from the fact that Caratacus has escaped and attacked an imperial agent in the process?'

Macro caught the strain in his friend's voice and bit his tongue rather than respond to the comment. There was a brief silence as Cato rinsed off the last of the blood from Septimus's neck, wrung the cloth out and then carefully tied it round the head, covering the wound. Macro eased the head back down.

Macro tried again. 'Someone helped Caratacus to escape and they just happened to pick on Septimus when they needed a cart and a disguise to get Caratacus out of the camp. Call me suspicious but that ain't bloody likely by a long way.'

'No,' Cato responded quietly. 'It does seem too much of a coincidence.' He tapped the imperial agent on the chest. 'You get him to the infirmary. I'll order the Blood Crows after Caratacus. I'll find you afterwards. I want to be there when Septimus regains consciousness. He's got some questions to answer.' Cato paused and winced. 'And, like as not, the general will have a few of his own to shoot at us.'

CHAPTER SEVENTEEN

'This is an unacceptable state of affairs,' General Ostorius said coldly as Cato and Macro stood in front of him. The patrols from the Blood Crows had reported to Cato an hour earlier, having discovered the abandoned cart but no trace of Caratacus.

The general glared at the two officers. 'You were entrusted with the care of the prisoner, the man who has been a constant threat to Roman interests on this island ever since we landed. The man we finally defeated in battle just yesterday and captured. And now, less than a day later, he has escaped. How exactly am I supposed to explain that to the Emperor?'

Even though the question was rhetorical, Macro was minded to point out to the general that it was his problem. Came with the rank. But promotion to the rank of centurion was not open to those who lacked the wit to keep their mouths shut and Macro remained at attention and said nothing.

Ostorius drew a breath and continued, 'More to the point, how do you explain yourselves to me? Well, Prefect?'

Macro cleared his throat and cut in before Cato could reply. 'It was my fault, sir. I was in charge of securing the prisoners and setting watch over them.'

'You?' Ostorius raised his eyebrows. 'Is this true?'

Cato saw the danger his friend was making for himself and felt a stab of anxiety. It was not Macro's fault any more than it was his own. It was almost certain to be the work of Pallas's agent. As was the attack on Septimus. It seemed that the imperial agent had underestimated his quarry, who must have penetrated his disguise. Cato could not risk divulging too many details of this to Ostorius, but he could at least intercede to save Macro from the ire of their commanding officer.

'Sir, Centurion Macro was acting on my orders. The responsibility is entirely mine, as is any punishment arising from the incident.'

'That is for *me* to decide, once I have the full facts. You'd better tell me what you know, Prefect.'

Cato fought off his exhaustion as he went over the details.

'I know that the escape occurred while Centurion Macro and I were in the officers' mess tent. I also know that he must have had assistance in his escape.'

'How so?'

'Because the two guards were stabbed in the throat, sir. Since Caratacus was unarmed and manacled, it follows that my men were victims of an armed assailant. Or more than one. Also, the pins on his shackles were knocked out. It takes a hammer and a special punch to do that.'

'So who helped him? One of the other natives? Have any more prisoners escaped?'

'No, sir. I checked with the centurion in command of the prisoners held outside the camp. They're all accounted for. Besides, even if one of them had escaped, he'd have to get across the ditch, over the rampart and past the sentries. Then he'd have to locate Caratacus, find a hammer and a weapon. It's a bit unlikely.'

'But not impossible.'

'As good as, sir,' Cato said firmly.

'What about the other members of his family and his brothers?'

'They're all still chained in their stockade. The guards there said that they noticed nothing suspicious all night.'

Ostorius nodded thoughtfully. 'Then why didn't Caratacus attempt to free his kin as well? Why would he leave them behind?'

Cato tilted his head slightly. 'My guess is that it was too difficult. There were four guards on the larger stockade and it was close to the tent lines of Centurion Macro's cohort. If the alarm was raised they'd be surrounded by armed men in short order. And even if they had managed to kill the guards and remove their chains, there would be several of them in the party and it would make getting out of the camp much harder to achieve. Caratacus alone might stand a chance. If he had tried to take the others with him then he was almost certain to fail.'

Ostorius arched an eyebrow. 'Are you saying that he sacrificed his family to save his own skin?'

'I'm saying that it was the most reasonable thing to do, sir.'

'Reasonable? Ruthless more like.'

Macro shrugged. 'Perhaps it's because he's ruthless that he's caused us as much trouble as he has, sir.'

The general glared at him. 'Thank you for those words of wisdom, Centurion.'

Macro flushed as his commander turned his attention back to Cato. 'So, assuming you are correct, what happened next?'

Cato thought swiftly. This was the part of the tale where he needed to exercise care if he was not to risk exposing Septimus. Regardless of the general's loyalty to his Emperor, he would not take kindly to the revelation that there was a spy in his army. Nor would he appreciate the fact that one of his officers had known of this and kept it from him. Cato cleared his throat and continued in a neutral tone. 'We know that Caratacus left the camp by the east gate disguised as a wine merchant called Hipparchus. I recognised the name as soon as the optio reported it to me.'

'So how did you come to know of him so conveniently?'

'The wine trader had sold me some wine two days ago. We tracked the merchant's business down and found Hipparchus unconscious in the rear of his wagon. His cart was missing.'

'I see. I wonder why Caratacus chose to attack that particular wine merchant?'

'Coincidence, sir.' Cato wondered the same thing. Hopefully he would discover the truth when he spoke to Septimus later on. He coughed and continued. 'Hipparchus had the kind of vehicle needed to get Caratacus out of the camp. Given the amount of wine the army consumes, his story of needing to return to Viroconium to buy more stock would sound credible.'

Cato felt his heart beat more quickly as the general mulled over the explanation. Ostorius folded his hands together and tapped his index fingers against his chin. 'Where is the wine merchant now?'

'Recovering in the infirmary of the Fourteenth, sir. He was struck on the head and knocked out. Surgeon reckons he'll recover his wits soon enough.'

'Good. I want you to question him the moment he comes round.'

'Yes, sir.' Cato did his best to conceal his relief that he had been handed the task and quickly moved on. 'Whoever helped free Caratacus was with him when he took the cart. Another wine merchant saw the two of them. In the dark he thought it was Hipparchus, with his slave helping to harness the mule to the cart. But we found the slave dead drunk. It's possible that Hipparchus will be able to identify the man who aided Caratacus in his escape.'

'How is that going to help us exactly?'

'Because the man in question is still here in the camp, sir.'

Ostorius lowered his hands and stared at Cato. 'How can you be sure of that?'

'Caratacus was the only one in the cart that left the camp. The optio on the gate said he looked it over quickly before letting it pass on. He's certain there was no one hidden inside.'

'Then we have a traitor in the camp.'

Cato nodded.

'Someone amongst the camp followers,' Ostorius decided, his expression darkening. 'When I find the bastard I'll have him crucified. It has to be a native trader. A spy, planted by Caratacus. I'll have them rounded up and questioned. Once the interrogators get to work on them someone will talk.'

'Yes, sir.'

'Let's hope we find that traitor. I've already given orders to send more cavalry patrols to scour the hills for Caratacus, but I don't hold out much hope. He knows the ground better than we do and can count on the help of the local native settlements to hide him and feed him. Jupiter only knows what he's planning to do next.'

'He'll go north, sir.'

Ostorius looked at the prefect in surprise. 'North? You seem very sure of yourself.'

'Where else can he go, sir? The Silurians suffered heavily yesterday and they won't be keen to follow Caratacus any more. Nor will the Ordovices when word of his defeat spreads. That leaves two possibilities. Either he'll make for the Druid stronghold on Mona. That's close and he can be sure of a warm welcome there. But it'll mean he's bottled up and I would imagine that you have plans to take Mona at some point in the near future.'

'I might,' Ostorius conceded. 'But go on. If not Mona then where will Caratacus make for, in your expert opinion?'

'Brigantia,' Cato answered without hesitation.

'But we have a treaty with the Brigantes. He'd be mad to hand himself over to our allies.'

'We have a treaty with Queen Cartimandua, sir. It's not quite the same thing. From what I understand, the queen does not enjoy the backing of all of her people. If there's a faction that stands against Rome, Caratacus will be sure to try and stir them up. If he can win the rest of the tribe over he'll have a powerful army at his back to continue his war against us.'

General Ostorius considered the notion for a moment and pursed his lips. 'Putting himself at the mercy of the Brigantes is a huge risk. I don't know. I'm not convinced. After the defeat we've inflicted on him, I think he's going to play safe. Retreat and lick his wounds while he considers what to do next.'

'I beg to disagree, sir. Caratacus is not the kind to lie low. He'll want to avenge his defeat at the first opportunity. He can only do that if he can raise fresh forces. And the only place he can do that now is in Brigantia.'

'Thank you for your opinion, Prefect Cato,' Ostorius said dismissively. 'I will take it under consideration. But for now we must concentrate on trying to track down and capture Caratacus while there is still a chance. We'll be breaking camp once the auxiliary units have returned and marching back to Viroconium. I shall want to know what the wine merchant has to say before then. Understood?'

'Yes, sir.'

'Then you're dismissed.'

Cato and Macro saluted and turned smartly to stride out of the tent.

When they were beyond earshot of the general's bodyguards they stopped and Macro let out a deep breath.

'It ain't right that he's trying to pin this one on us. It's not our fault some bastard sprang Caratacus. He's the general, it's his lookout.'

Cato smiled wearily. 'That's how the blame game plays out, Macro. This isn't about the army, this is about politics. Ostorius is thinking about what happens after he gives up command of the army. If there's any way of pinning the blame on a subordinate then he will. It's just our bad luck that we happen to be Junius-on-the-spot.'

Macro ground his teeth in frustration. 'Fucking politics.'

'Quite.'

They looked out over the camp, which was a scene of devastation. Most of the tents appeared to have been swept away by the previous night's storm and soldiers were picking their way through the churned mud and debris to retrieve their kit. Some were building fires, but Macro knew that it would take a while for the wood to dry out enough to be combustible. A mood of sullen misery stretched across the camp, despite the clear blue sky, the warm sunshine and the swifts darting through the air.

Macro sniffed. 'Anyone would think it was our side that lost the battle.'

'We won the battle but not the war. Not quite yet, at least. As long as Caratacus is at large we won't know any peace.'

'So what do we do now?'

Cato placed his palms against the small of his back and stretched. 'We have a word with Septimus, if he's up for it. Right now he's the only one who might be able to help us find the traitor in the camp.'

'Thought we were supposed to be looking for Caratacus.'

Cato shook his head. 'If I'm any judge of things, he's long gone. It'll be a miracle if the cavalry patrols pick him up. That's why we need to find the man who helped him escape. With the right inducement he may tell us where Caratacus is headed and what his plans are.'

'I suppose.'

Cato turned to his friend. 'If you've got a better idea, let's hear it.'

Macro concentrated a moment and then shrugged. 'Septimus it is.'

The surgeon looked strained as he sat at his camp desk at the entrance to the infirmary tent, one of the first to be erected again after the storm. The dim interior was filled with men lying on their sleeping mats. Some lay on the bare ground. Others sat up. The less seriously injured talked in mute tones or passed the time playing dice. The air was filled with the groans and cries of the wounded. Several orderlies moved through the tent tending to their patients. The surgeon was wearing a bloodstained apron over his black tunic and his face and arms were smeared with streaks of mud and blood.

'Who is it you want?'

'Hipparchus.'

'What unit?'

'He's a civilian. We brought him in first thing this morning with a head injury.'

'Oh, him. I remember. Fine, just a light tap. He's awake now.' The surgeon stood up and pointed to the far end of the tent. 'Last man on the right.'

Cato nodded his thanks and he and Macro made their way down the aisle running the length of the tent. As they passed through the densely packed rows of human suffering, Cato felt his anger towards the general rising up again. Most of these men would not be here but for Ostorius's decision to make a frontal attack on a strongly defended position. He could not help feeling that Legate Vespasian would not have made the same mistake had he been in charge. He recalled his first commander with admiration and a loyalty bordering on affection. If there was any justice in this world Vespasian would eventually achieve rank and position worthy of his talents, Cato thought. There was a man he would willingly follow into battle.

As they neared the end of the tent he saw Septimus sitting up, a fresh dressing wrapped neatly about his head. A small red stain showed where the blood had soaked through over the wound on his scalp. The agent glanced up as he became aware of their approach and smiled weakly.

'Prefect Cato and Centurion Macro!' He forced a smile. 'The two favourite customers of Hipparchus, purveyor of the finest wines in the camp!'

The wounded men immediately around him stirred and one shouted at him to shut his mouth and not disturb their rest. Septimus ignored them and propped himself up on his elbows.

'How's the head?' asked Cato as he and Macro hunkered down either side of the imperial agent.

'Not bad. Still feel a bit dizzy, but I'll be out of here before the end of the day. Don't think I could stand the company of these louts any longer than that.'

'Hey,' Macro growled. 'These louts are my comrades in arms.'

Septimus cocked an eyebrow. 'That explains a lot.'

He glanced round to make sure that none of his neigbours seemed to be listening and then lowered his voice as he continued. 'Have they caught Caratacus yet? There's been little talk of anything else in here.'

Cato shook his head. 'He escaped from the camp in your cart. Drove it out of the east gate and now he's disappeared into the mountains.'

Septimus grimaced. 'Oh shit . . .'

'What do you remember of last night?'

Septimus's brow creased as he tried to recall the details. 'I had caught my slave with one of my wine jars. I was going to give him a hiding but he was too drunk to notice, so I was going to save it until the morning. Then I went to find you, while there was still some light in the sky. I couldn't find my purse and I thought it might have slipped from my belt when we spoke earlier. I saw Thraxis leave your tent to go and help your men secure the rest, so I slipped inside. You weren't there so I thought I'd wait until you got back and ask about the purse. That was when I heard some commotion close by. I went out to have a look and saw that the door to the stockade was open.' He looked directly at Cato. 'That's when someone came up behind me and knocked me to the ground. Before I could react he was on my back, pressing my head down and holding a knife to my throat. He asked me who I was. I told him my cover story. I heard a brief exchange and then I was hauled up on my feet. I glimpsed the man who had knocked me down. Big, hairy brute.'

'Caratacus?'

'It had to be.'

'And the other one?'

'Couldn't see. He hung back and kept out of my line of sight.'

Cato thought a moment. 'When they spoke, was it in Latin?'

'Yes.'

Cato nodded. 'So what happened next?'

'Caratacus steered me ahead of him, and kept the point of his knife in my ribs. He told me to lead them to my wagon and not to try and run, raise the alarm or look back if I wanted to live.'

'And no one saw the three of you?' asked Macro. 'No one seemed suspicious?'

Septimus shook his head. 'Everyone had other things on their minds. Who was going to bother with three men making their way through the camp followers' canton when they were trying to save their livelihoods from the storm? So I led them back to my pitch and I was standing by the back of the wagon . . . That's the last thing I remember before I came round in here.'

'You don't remember us finding you? Macro and me?'

Septimus closed his eyes for an instant and then shook his head.

'All right then . . .' Cato sighed and reflected briefly on what he had been told. 'It was just unlucky for you that you came to my tent when you did.'

Septimus looked at him closely. 'What are you implying?'

'I'm not implying anything. Like I said, it was unlucky for you.'

Macro gave a thin smile. 'And bloody lucky for Caratacus and his friend.'

'That is in the nature of coincidences of this kind,' Septimus responded evenly. 'The gods will play their little games. Does the general know that someone else was involved?'

'Yes.'

Septimus hissed with disappointment. 'Then our man is going to know he's being hunted and he'll go to ground.'

'Maybe not. Ostorius is convinced that Caratacus was aided by one of the natives amongst the camp followers. He thinks that Caratacus planted a spy, and he's going to tear the native canton apart until he finds the man.'

'Ouch. But then again, it's where I'd look if I was the general.'

'If Ostorius is set on blaming a native spy then it's possible the culprit is going to think he's got away with it and not feel the need to lie low. That's to our advantage.'

'It is,' Septimus agreed. 'Very useful.'

Macro snorted. 'You're all heart, you two.'

Cato looked at his friend with a puzzled expression. 'What do you mean?'

'The general's going to tear the merchants' camp apart and hand any likely suspects over to the army's torturers for questioning, and all you can say is that you think it's useful.'

'Well, it is,' Septimus insisted. 'Why should I care what happens to a bunch of hairy-arsed tinkers? There are more important things to worry about, Centurion. We're talking about the fate of the province. And maybe the Emperor as well. I couldn't give a shit about a handful of Britons who fall foul of General Ostorius.'

Macro clicked his tongue. 'Like I said, you're all heart. It's moments like this that remind me why I'm a soldier and not some scheming snake in the pay of an imperial freedman.'

'Really?' Septimus fixed him with a cold stare. 'Frankly, the reason why you are not an imperial agent might have more to do with you lacking the necessary acumen.'

Macro gritted his teeth. 'Acumen? What the fuck's that supposed to mean? You calling me thick or something?'

Cato edged between them. 'That's enough! Jupiter's balls, we've got enough to worry about without you two kicking off. Keep your bloody feelings to yourselves, understand? I don't care if you hate each other's guts, we've got to find this traitor and put an end to Pallas's schemes. Macro?'

The centurion made a faint growling noise in his throat, then nodded. 'All right. But I'm telling you. Once this is over, I'm through with you and your kind.' He jabbed his finger at Septimus. 'You come near me and I'll break your neck.'

The imperial agent smiled coldly. 'Assuming you see me coming.'

Cato was utterly exhausted and his patience finally snapped. 'For fuck's sake! Enough!'

Around them heads turned towards the outburst and Cato abruptly stood up. He looked down at the imperial agent and spoke in a low voice. 'I'll report back to the general what you said, but not that they spoke in Latin. If he wants to question you himself, stick to that story.'

Septimus nodded.

'We'll talk more, when you're out of the infirmary. Come on, Macro.' Cato waved his friend towards the entrance of the long tent. 'Let's go.'

Once they were outside, back in the warm comfort of the sunshine,

Cato rounded on his friend. 'I know what you think of Narcissus and his kind but how do you think it helps us to bring it up all the time?'

Macro clenched his fists. 'They've fucked us about for years, Cato. One stinking job after another. Narcissus said he was done with us. When he left Rome he said he was sending us to Britannia and back to the army and our spying days were over. That's what he said. Fucking liar.'

'You think I don't feel the same?' Cato shot back bitterly. 'You think I enjoy playing the spy? We're in this, Macro, whether we like it or not. We can't avoid it. We can't decide to opt out. Septimus was right about there being a spy. And that means he was telling the truth about someone coming after us. Someone wants us dead. You really want to ignore that danger?'

Macro struggled to regain control of his temper and at length he shook his head. 'Of course not.'

'Then help me, Macro. Help me get through this so we find the traitor and make him disappear. So we can get back to being soldiers. Help me so that one day I can return to Julia. Well?' He held out his hand.

They clasped arms and Macro let out an exasperated sigh. 'I'm sorry, lad. I'm just thoroughly pissed off with Septimus and his kind.'

'Me too.' Cato flashed a tired smile.

Macro withdrew his arm. 'So what now?'

Cato puffed his cheeks and looked out over the camp. 'Caratacus is on the run. We're not likely to catch him. The general's about to turn the only friendly natives for miles around against him. There's a traitor in the camp who is prepared to go to any length to unseat the Emperor, and kill us the moment he gets the chance. What am I going to do now? I'll tell you. I'm going back to my tent and I am going to sleep the sleep of the dead. And when I wake up, I'm not going to rest until I find the bastard that set Caratacus free and murdered two of our men.'

CHAPTER EIGHTEEN

By the time the army returned to its base at Viroconium the men's spirits had fully recovered and there was a jaunty swagger to their step as they marched through the gates of the fortress behind their standards. General Ostorius and his staff rode at the head of the column, in gleaming breastplates and armour, in clean scarlet tunics. The garrison of the fortress had been forewarned of the general's return and lined the walls to cheer their victorious comrades. The men on the march returned the cheer with interest and looked forward to the comforts of their barracks, regular meals and a long anticipated visit to the bathhouse in the sprawling vicus a short distance from the wall and ditch of the great fortress.

The legionary units who had been involved in the battle had pride of place at the front of the column. Behind them came the auxiliary units who had been responsible for mopping up the remnants of the enemy army. The faint cheers from far ahead reached their ears and they smiled grudgingly at the celebrations of their legionary comrades, and shared their longing for the comforts of Viroconium.

Behind the auxiliaries came the long column of prisoners, chained and bound together, a shuffling tide of despairing misery, mostly men, but women and children too, the latter condemned to a life of slavery before they had any chance to savour the freedom that was the birthright of the offspring of the warriors of their tribe. A cohort of Batavian cavalry rode either side of the prisoners, watching over them and ensuring that they kept up the pace and did not cause the column to spread out too far. A thrust of a spear butt or prick of its point was sufficient to spur on any who began to lag.

Behind the prisoners came the baggage train, some miles back from the head of the column, and beyond earshot of the triumphant entry of the general and his legions. The army's wagons and carts came first, the latter carrying the dismantled artillery, a mix of ballistas and the larger catapults. The heavy wagons carried the grain and spare kit needed to feed and supply the army while on the march. Then came the wagons allocated to the legions' surgeons, filled with the men still recovering from the wounds they had suffered on the battlefield.

Those who had died from their wounds had been added to the huge funeral pyres that had burned outside the camp, while a handful who died later were buried outside the marching camps. Their graves were marked with simple stones hurriedly engraved with their names and units, and a brief request to the gods to look after their spirits. Even though they were wounded, the men in the wagons were in good humour, thanks to a generous issue of wine on the order of General Ostorius. Many were soon drunk and the warm country air resounded to tuneless marching songs, toasts and laughter.

At the rear of the column came the camp followers, several hundred merchants, traders, pimps, whores, entertainers, slave dealers and the long-suffering unofficial families of the soldiers. By law any man of the rank of centurion or below was not allowed to enter into a marriage. Nevertheless soldiers are creatures of flesh and blood and some had formed attachments with the women who lived outside the fortresses of the empire, and had children by them. These poor creatures, Cato reflected, were destined to trudge along in the wake of the army, wholly reliant on the meagre pay of the soldier to whom they were attached. If he fell in battle they might be left a small sum in the soldier's will, provided that he had written one. Otherwise they would be without support, until the mother could find another man. Around these small family groups trundled the carts of the commercial camp followers, piled high with the trinkets, drink and little luxuries that soldiers craved when they were off duty.

In the distance, behind the tail end of the camp followers, marched the auxiliary cohort of the rearguard. At the start of the march the ground had still been wet and the men of the Segovian Cohort had had to negotiate the churned ground left by the passage of thousands of boots, hoofs and wheels ahead of them. But the sun had now dried the ground and had yet to reach the almost as annoying point where the ground was so dry that the passage of a large army disturbed a cloud of dust that clung to every surface and filled mouths and eyes with a fine grit.

Macro and Cato were marching a short distance to one side of the baggage train, their men strung out in an extended screen on either side of the line of march. Having decided he could do with a break from the saddle, Cato had handed his mount to Thraxis and was walking the remainder of the way to Viroconium. So reduced were the escort's numbers that even a small raiding party could have caused mayhem and fled with their spoils long before Cato could have gathered a sufficient number of men to repel them. But there was no sign of any enemy on the march back to Viroconium.

From time to time they had passed a small village or settlement whose remaining inhabitants had run to hide as the army passed by. A few times Cato had seen distant figures on the tops of hills watching them. Never more than a handful. Hunting parties more than likely; rather than war bands. They had never ventured any closer and fled the moment any Roman horseman turned in their direction. The defeat of Caratatacus's army seemed to have broken the will to fight of the Silurian and Ordovician nations. But Cato knew that if Caratacus raised his standard again there would still be many who would rally to him, as they had in the past after previous defeats.

'I shan't be sorry to trade a tent and sleeping roll for a nice dry barracks and a proper bed,' said Macro, straining his eyes to scan the landscape ahead for the first sign of Viroconium.

'I wouldn't say no to that,' Cato agreed absently. He was preoccupied with the disappearance of Caratacus and the need to discover the identity of the agent Pallas had sent to kill them. The only advantage they had at the moment was that the agent was unaware that he was being hunted by Septimus. That was the only reason that he had been permitted to live when they took his cart, Cato reasoned. If Pallas's man had known Septimus for what he was, he would have been discovered with a knife in his back instead of a knock on the head. With luck, they would find and eliminate the enemy agent before he had a chance to do any more mischief.

'And there's the prospect of reinforcements,' Macro tried to get the conversation going again. 'Be good to flesh out our ranks. There's hardly any of us left. Let's hope the general's sent for some fresh draughts from the Second.'

At the mention of their old legion Cato recalled that the elite unit that Vespasian had once commanded was now stationed down at Isca Dumnoniorum. Apart from keeping a watchful eye on the local tribes, the legion was mainly a training establishment these days. It took in the convoys of recruits shipped over from Gaul and completed their basic training on British soil before sending them on to the other units of the army in Britannia. Cato decided that he would leave their induction into the Blood Crows to a veteran cavalryman like Miro. Yes, let Decurion Miro handle it, he decided. He had more important matters to deal with.

Conscious that he had not immediately replied to his friend, Cato quickly replayed their last exchange in his mind and cleared his throat. 'I wouldn't get your hopes up, Macro. The baggage train escort, and its commanding officers, are still very much in the general's black book. If there are any reinforcements available I rather fear that you and I are going to be at the back of a very long queue.'

'My, you are full of the joys of life, aren't you?'

'Can you blame me? Ostorius has pinned the blame for Caratacus's escape on us and you can be sure he'll make that known back in Rome. If his version of events is accepted, I'd be surprised if we were entrusted with any command larger than a latrine block in future.'

'Back in the shit again, eh?' Macro quipped.

Cato could not help a chuckle and Macro slapped him lightly on the back. 'There you go, lad! The boy can be taught to smile.'

'Seriously though, Macro, I don't see much to smile about at the moment. Our return to soldiering has hardly been a glorious success.'

'Oh, we haven't done so badly. We held Bruccium against Caratacus's army and we did for him back on the hill. No one can take that away from us. The lads here on the ground know what we did.'

Cato sighed. 'I suppose so. But that won't count for much back in Rome. We're in the lap of the gods now, Macro. And the gods tend to have an odd sense of humour at the best of times.'

'Then you'd get on well with them. Time for a sacrifice to Fortuna,

I'd say. Look here, Cato. There's nothing we can do about the situation at the moment, right?'

'True.'

'Then what's the point in spending all your time fretting about it? Tell you what. Tonight, once we're back in barracks, let's go into the vicus and get totally rat-arsed. The drinks are on me.'

Cato thought a moment and nodded. 'All right then. Rat-arsed it is.'

Two days later Cato and Macro were standing in front of the review platform outside Viroconium. The fortress had been extended to accommodate a second legion and a series of smaller forts had been constructed for the auxiliary units attached to the army for the campaigns against the mountain tribes. In front of the two officers lay the training ground, a vast rectangle cleared by the army's engineers when the fortress was first built two years earlier. The men of the escort detachment, their ranks bolstered by replacements, stood formed up facing their commanders.

With Caratacus still at large, the general had not yet issued orders for his forces to disperse and the vexillation from the Ninth Legion had added to the crowded barracks in the fortress. Despite the casualties from the recent battle, the arrival of a column of replacements had meant that some of the legionary cohorts had been assigned to the smaller forts. For that reason, and the faint possibility that the army might have to march to war again, the baggage train escort was retained and the legionaries and Thracians shared a fort on the far side of the training ground from the main fortress.

That suited Cato, who was keen to distance himself from General Ostorius. The arrangement also suited the men, who had plenty of space within the fort due to their losses. However, the luxury of space was short-lived when the two units received new recruits to bolster their depleted ranks. Just over two hundred men for Macro and a hundred and fifty Batavians for Cato, together with two hundred remounts. Not enough to bring them up to full strength but welcome nonetheless. As was the custom, the senior centurions of the First Cohorts of each legion had first pick of the replacements, then by order of declining seniority the commanders of the remaining cohorts

178

took their pick. Macro was none too pleased by the men that had been left when his time came.

'Not quite so impressive as they looked at Bruccium,' he commented.

Cato scanned the ranks before he responded. The new legionaries were well turned out in their new kit. Their helmets gleamed and were not yet marked by the scores of small dents, scratches and other imperfections that characterised the helmets of the veterans just returned from a campaign. The same was true of their shields. Nor had they customised their sword belts and scabbards like their more experienced comrades, and the plain leather and brass trims were all fresh from the armouries back in Gaul. Most of the men had already received their basic training after they landed at Isca Dumnoniorum, but they would need much more before they would be fit to stand alongside the veterans of the two cohorts.

'Let's have a closer look,' Cato decided.

They paced to the end of the front rank of the legionaries and began to walk slowly down the line. Macro had intended to allow the veterans to remain in their existing sections of eight and add to them from the new men. From his days as a ranker he knew the value of a close-knit team of men accustomed to living together and fighting alongside each other. But Cato had disagreed and instructed that the existing men were to form the kernels of the reconstituted centuries of the Fourth Cohort. They would be able to pass on their knowledge to the new men. There were six centuries in the cohort once again, albeit understrength, and it had been necessary to promote a number of men to the rank of optio, as well as promoting four existing optios to the centurionate. The dilution of experience through the cohort meant that Macro would have to train them hard to bring the unit to battle readiness, a task he was looking forward to. Today's parade was the first formal introduction of the recruits to their new commanders and Macro's experienced eye scrutinised each man they passed. Every so often the two officers would stop and examine one of the fresh-faced recruits in detail.

'You!' Macro barked, thrusting the tip of his vine cane at one man. 'Name?'

The tall, slender legionary presented his javelin and snapped to attention. It was neatly done, Cato noted approvingly.

'Legionary Gnaeus Lorenus, sir!'

'Where are you from?' Macro demanded.

'Massilia, sir.'

'Age?'

'Nineteen, sir.'

'Bollocks! You don't look old enough to shave.'

The recruit made the mistake of turning his face towards Macro in surprise.

'Don't fucking look at me! Look straight ahead!'

'Yes, sir! Sorry, sir.'

'And don't fucking apologise neither! You're on parade, not at some poncey actor's garden party!'

'Yes, sir.' The recruit committed his second offence by failing to stifle a smile at Macro's remark.

Quick as a flash Macro stepped closer to the man so that their faces were inches apart. The difference in height meant that the centurion had to tilt his head back to stare up at the recruit.

'Do I make you laugh, Legionary Lorenus?' he bawled.

'No, sir.'

'Then are you saying I haven't got a fucking sense of humour? Are you?

'No, sir.'

'Then you must be laughing at me, Lorenus! Is that it? Are you bloody making fun of me, you great big streak of piss?'

Again, the man's gaze wavered towards his superior and Macro jammed the head of his vine cane hard into the mail vest of the recruit. 'EYES FRONT! I asked if you are making fun of me?'

'N–no, sir,' the recruit gasped.

'I don't believe you. Optio!' Macro turned to the recruit's superior. 'Legionary Lorenus. Fatigues. Five days!'

'Yes, sir!' The optio inscribed a hurried note on his waxed tablet.

Cato had stood by impassively during the exchange. He readily recalled his own harsh treatment when he had first joined the Second Legion. The aptly named Centurion Bestia had made his life a misery and Cato mentally cringed at the fear the instructor had instilled in him. At the time he had believed that Bestia had been a cruel monster, but he had long since come to recognise the true purpose of the harsh treatment meted out during training. Soldiers had to keep a cool head in any conditions. They had to be disciplined from within as well as without. That process began on the training ground where they learned to keep their eyes ahead, answer directly and not let themselves become unsettled. It ended when they coolly faced an enemy in battle and put instinct behind them and placed their trust in their training.

Macro continued along the line with Cato in step beside him. Several more men received similar treatment before Macro handed over to their officers to begin the morning drill. As the First Century tramped off, Macro turned to his friend and rubbed his hands together in glee.

'Ah! I haven't lost my touch. I can still put the wind up 'em.'

'True. But I thought the point was to train them, not terrify them.'

'They'll pick it up soon enough, once they've stopped shitting themselves. Just like old times, eh? Proper soldiering. There's nothing like it! Every drill a bloodless battle and every battle a bloody drill.'

Cato smiled indulgently. This was Macro's ideal. The opportunity to mould men into tough, disciplined professional soldiers filled him with pride and a sense of achievement. What seemed to come to Macro so naturally was an onerous duty for Cato. He still felt self-conscious about shouting insults into the faces of fresh-faced soldiers and thanked the gods that he had been promoted to a rank that set him above such tasks.

The replacements allocated to the Second Thracian presented a different kind of problem. They were almost all from Batavia and already seasoned riders and fighters. Tall, big-boned and mostly fair-haired, their appearance was in stark contrast to the dark-featured Thracians who made up the original unit. The Batavians would need to accept the ethos of their comrades. The Blood Crows had a hard-won reputation for ferocity and had cultivated a look that made them appear more like a group of irregular cavalry than an established unit of the Roman army. That had served Cato well so far and he aimed to keep it that way.

As he began his inspection of the troopers standing with their mounts, the contrast between the Batavians and the Thracians concerned him. He stopped in front of the first of the decurions, a new man with a scarred, lined face. Clearly a veteran of some fights, not all of which he appeared to have won.

'What is your name?'

'Decurion Avergus.'

'Avergus? Is that all?'

'Yes, sir. That's the name I was given at birth. Don't see no reason to change it.' The man's Latin was good though accented and, like most of his people, he was inclined to talk more loudly than necessary. A good attribute for a soldier but a bit wearing socially, Cato felt.

He glanced at Macro. It was usual for auxiliaries from non-Roman backgrounds to adopt a Roman name on enlistment, especially as Roman citizenship was granted when the soldier had served out his time in the army. The choice to retain his tribal name meant that the decurion was either proud of his heritage or possibly disdainful of Roman ways. Cato decided he would need to keep an eye on Avergus.

'Avergus, were most of these men recruited along with you?'

'Yes, sir. Same tribe. Village on the banks of the Rhenus near Moguntum. The entire draught came from the settlement.'

'How many speak Latin?'

Avergus thought a moment before replying. 'Most of the lads from the village have a ready grasp, sir. Those from the outlying farms, none.'

'I see. What about you? You speak it fluently enough.'

'My dad's a fur trader, sir. Supplies the local Rhine garrisons. I spent more time in Roman forts than I did at home when I was growing up.'

'Then I'm making you the language instructor for the new men. Decurion Miro will supply you with the essential commands and terms. They'll need to grasp those at once. The rest you can teach them when they're ready.'

Avergus's thick brow knitted.

'Problem?'

'No, sir . . . Yes, sir. I ain't much of a teacher.'

'Just as well then,' said Macro. 'Because this is the army, not a fucking school. The prefect has given you an order and you hop to it. Clear?'

'Yes, Centurion.'

Cato nodded. 'Good.'

He moved on without stopping to beast any more of the new men, since there was little point in shouting at a man who did not understand a word being said to him. When he reached Decurion Miro, he halted.

'The new draught look like they have the makings of good men.'

'Yes, sir. They'll do well enough, once they've been drilled thoroughly. In time, they will be worthy of the Blood Crows.'

Cato smiled. 'Make sure they understand that's a name to be proud of. Carry on, Decurion Miro.'

They exchanged a salute and Miro took a pace back and turned to the men. 'Officers! On me!'

Cato nodded with satisfaction. Miro knew his business and could be trusted to get on with the training. He turned to Macro.

'Walk with me.'

They paced away from the two formations as the officers bellowed the orders for the men to begin their training rota: formation drilling, weapons practice and strength and stamina exercises. Cato strode up the ramp to the review stand and glanced over the men and horses of the escort detachment before turning his attention to Macro.

'The word from headquarters is the general has given the order to stop questioning the native camp followers and release them.'

'About time too. Did the interrogators find anything out that we don't already know?'

'Nothing. Whoever helped Caratacus to escape is one of ours.'

Macro cracked his knuckles. 'You're pretty certain this is the work of Pallas's agent, aren't you?'

Cato nodded. 'It seems to make sense. Given what Septimus told us.'

'And you trust him?'

'Not without reservation. He is his father's son, after all. But the escape of Caratacus proves what he said about Pallas's intention to scupper the province and destroy support for Claudius back in Rome.'

Macro nodded. 'But there's worse things that could happen. To us.'

'Exactly.' Cato sighed. 'Seems we'd better watch our backs, thanks to our dealings with Narcissus. We've been lucky so far . . .'

'So far.'

★ ★ ★

The following evening General Ostorius summoned his officers to a briefing at headquarters, the first such meeting for several days. The praetorium was a huge timber-framed structure that dominated the other large buildings clustered at the heart of the fortress: the granaries, tribunes' quarters, armoury, hospital and the stables for the mounts of the officers and the Twentieth Legion's scouts. It was just before dusk and a honeyed light slanted across the fortress, throwing long shadows up the street ahead of Macro and Cato as they approached the arched entrance.

They were surrounded by the subdued noises of the camp as the men ceased their duties and turned their attention towards preparing their evening meal. Those who had been issued with a pass would be looking forward to the delights of the vicus sprawling across the rolling countryside a short distance beyond the walls of Viroconium. After the hardships of the campaign, the army was content to slip into the peaceful routine of garrison life and a sense of well-being permeated the fortress.

Macro breathed in the tang of woodsmoke from the cooking fires and smiled with satisfaction. 'Life doesn't get much better than this.'

Cato's brow furrowed for a moment. 'Really? I could easily hope for better. I could do without the opprobrium of the general over the escape of Caratacus – which was hardly my fault. We have a wily enemy on the loose and I would prefer not to have to worry about an assassin sent from Rome to do us in. Right now, I really would prefer to be far from here, safely in the arms of my wife.'

Macro chuckled. 'I bet.'

They walked on in silence for a moment before Macro spoke again. 'I was only talking about this moment, Cato. Right now. Put everything else aside and tell me this isn't good.'

A short distance ahead of them one of the general's slaves was walking two of his master's hunting dogs. One of them abruptly stopped, directly in Cato's path, and hunched its back to defecate. Cato could not help smiling as he nodded towards the dog. 'That about sums up the situation from my point of view.'

'For fuck's sake,' Macro growled, then drew a breath and shouted at the slave, 'Oi! You clear that up, you hear?'

The slave turned anxiously and bowed his head. 'Yes, sir. Of course, sir.'

They turned into the gateway and strode across the courtyard, passing through the open doors into the cool shaded interior of the main hall. Most of the officers had already arrived and taken their places on the benches arranged before the dais at the far end. Cato saw a few spaces near the front and made towards them, until he saw Prefect Horatius sitting along the bench. He paused, but before he could change direction, Horatius glanced round, and beckoned.

'Here, Cato. There's enough space. You too, Centurion Macro.'

There was no choice and Cato and Macro did as they were bid. Horatius shifted towards them. 'How are the new Batavians working out?'

Cato shrugged. 'Good riders, but a little slow to adapt to our tactics. They'll come round soon enough if Decurion Miro has anything to do with it.'

'Bloody Batavians,' Horatius said with feeling. 'I had to make do with some as well. No love lost between them and the Hispanians. I've had three fights in the last two days, left one of my new men with a cracked skull. Surgeon reckons he'll be lucky not to come out of it witless. Not that you can tell with most Batavians, eh? How about you, Macro?'

'The replacements are a bit green, sir. But I'm knocking 'em into shape quick enough.'

'Just as well. With Caratacus still at large we may be on the march again before the summer is over.' Horatius lowered his voice and leaned closer. 'That's assuming the general is up for it.'

Cato said nothing but cocked an eyebrow.

'Word is that he's fallen ill. Been in his bed for days. That's why there's been no briefings.'

'Ill?' Macro shot a look towards the dais as if expecting the general to appear any moment. 'How ill?'

Horatius frowned. 'What am I? A bloody surgeon? Just repeating what I've heard. But you know what he's like. Tough as old boots. It'd have to be serious to keep Ostorius in bed. By the way, Cato, for what it's worth, I don't hold you to blame for Caratacus's escape. Could have happened on anyone's watch.'

'Thanks.'

'Still, if it had been up to me, I'd have doubled the number of guards you had. No point in taking a risk, eh?'

Cato forced himself to control his irritation at the remark and replied in a flat voice, 'I suppose not.'

He looked round in order to break eye contact with Horatius, and saw that the last of the officers was arriving and joining the others who were obliged to stand now that the benches had been filled. A moment later the camp prefect stepped up in front of the dais and barked the announcement, 'Commanding officer present!'

There was an instant din of scraping boots as the seated men rose and stood stiffly, then there was quiet and the sound of faltering footsteps echoed down the hall. Out of the corner of his eye Cato saw the general making his way along the side, accompanied by a tall young native in a finely woven cloak. Ostorius signalled to the tribesman to stand to the side of the dais and then climbed the three steps on to the platform. The general looked even more gaunt than usual and his skin had taken on an ashen pallor. He seemed to have shrunk inside his elaborately embroidered tunic and polished leather cuirass, like a decrepit tortoise in its shell, thought Cato.

The general paused a moment and then drew himself up in front of his officers, running the tip of his tongue across his lips to moisten them. He cleared his throat and began to speak.

'Gentlemen, I am the bearer of ill news. This afternoon I received a messenger from Queen Cartimandua of the Brigantes.' He gestured towards the native standing beside the stage. 'Our ally tells us that Caratacus has made his appearance at her tribal capital at Isurium. He is under the protection of her consort, Venutius, who has demanded that Caratacus be given a chance to plead his case before the assembled tribes of the Brigantian confederation.'

Ostorius paused as his officers stirred uneasily.

'Jupiter's cock,' Macro muttered. 'That's thrown the cat amongst the pigeons.'

Once he had his men's attention again the general continued. 'I need hardly warn you that if Caratacus gets his way he could stir the whole of the north against us. We know he is a powerful orator and if he can sway enough of the hotheads amongst the Brigantian leadership

186

then Cartimandua's authority will crumble, Venutius will become the new leader of his people and Caratacus will have a powerful army at his back to renew the struggle against us. It's bad timing. Our men are still recovering from the campaign in the mountains. We suffered heavy casualties and even though we have some replacements, they are unseasoned. The Brigantians outnumber us at least two to one. If I turn to counter the new threat then I must leave the west thinly defended. All that we have just won could be lost if the Silurians and the Ordovicians decide to take advantage of the situation. We'll face a war on two fronts. I will be forced to deal with the Brigantian threat first, then we may have to win back any ground we lose to the mountain tribes afterwards.'

'Assuming we beat the Brigantians,' Cato whispered.

Macro was only half listening to his friend. He was staring at the general, whose last words had sounded slurred. 'I don't believe it. The old man's drunk . . .'

Cato turned to look and saw that Ostorius was swaying slightly, his words crumbling into incoherence in his throat as one side of his mouth seemed to droop. The general staggered back, stumbled and collapsed on to the dais with a thud. At once the camp prefect rushed up the steps and hurried to the side of his superior. Several of the officers were already on their feet, including Cato. He knew at once that this had nothing to do with drink and turned to point to one of the centurions nearest the entrance to the hall.

'Get the surgeon! Go!' he called across the alarmed hubbub.

CHAPTER NINETEEN

'I thought we were supposed to be having a quiet word with Septimus,' said Macro as he took the chair opposite Cato's desk. Darkness had fallen outside the modest headquarters of the escort detachment's fort and the prefect's office was lit by two stands of oil lamps. Already a small cloud of insects swirled about the glow of the flames. 'Where is he?'

Cat shrugged. 'The first hour's only just sounded. Give the man a chance, Macro.'

Macro grumbled under his breath as he leaned back against the wall and folded his arms. 'What's the news on Ostorius?'

A day had passed since the general collapsed at the briefing. No official announcement had been made but rumours had rippled through the army, according to which the general had suffered every-thing from an over-indulgence of drinking to a sudden death brought on by poison administered by an agent of Caratacus. Cato had discovered the truth for himself by the simple expedient of visiting the general's headquarters and asking for information.

'He's alive. According to the camp prefect the surgeon says he's had some kind of a fit. He's lost control of the left side of his body and is rambling.'

'Is he going to recover?'

'The surgeon doesn't know. He's made Ostorius comfortable with some concoction from the east, and he's sacrificed a cockerel to Asclepius. Whatever good that will do.'

Macro frowned, never quite happy when his friend cast any doubt on the workings of the gods. It was a dangerous game to play, Macro thought. Even though he had never seen a god for himself, he considered it safer to pay the gods their dues, just in case. He cleared his throat softly.

'Do you think the old boy is going to get over it?'

'Like you say, Macro, he's old. That's the one ailment you can guarantee never recovering from.' Cato folded his hands together and stared at the door. 'This campaign has worn him out. He's been waging war against Caratacus and his allies from the moment he became governor five years ago. This was supposed to be his last post before retiring from public service. I think the prospect of Caratacus re-opening the war on a new front broke him. Even if he recovers, I doubt he will be in a fit state to command the army for another campaign season.'

'What then? Who will take over?'

'The senior legate is Quintatus. He'll be in command until the general recovers.'

'Quintatus. You told me you thought he's the one behind our posting to Bruccium, and that you think he did that to try and get rid of us.'

Cato nodded. Even though Quintatus had said he would not harm them Cato did not trust him.

'Shit. Now he's going to have a free hand to try that on again.'

'Quite. We'll have to try and keep out of his way. Give him no excuse to find fault with us. Speaking of which, how are the new men coming on?'

'I might have been a bit hasty in my judgement of them. They're learning fast. Good bunch of lads for the most part. But there's always a few who can't tell the business end of a javelin from the butt. I'll see what I can do about getting 'em transferred to the quartermaster's staff, where the rest of the lads will be safe from them.'

'That might be a mixed blessing. Who knows what harm they might cause with access to the army's rations and kit. What about the Batavians?'

Macro scratched his bristly jaw. 'Miro says they're good men. It'll be a while before they're good soldiers, though. And there's still tension between them and the Thracians, which threatens to kick off at any moment. I've told Miro to knock a few heads together and sort it out. Perhaps we should be threatening the Batavians that we'll send them to work in the quartermaster's stores. You know what they're like. They'd rather walk through fire then learn how to read, write and add up.'

They heard footsteps approaching in the corridor outside and there was a rap on the door before it opened and Thraxis ducked his head into the office. 'That wine merchant's here again, sir. Says you wanted to see him about ordering some more stock.'

'That's right. Show him in.'

Thraxis hesitated at the door. 'Sir, I can deal with him, if you wish.'

Cato fixed him with a steady look. In the normal course of events an officer of his rank would indeed entrust the purchase of his personal stores to his orderly. But Cato needed a cover story for his meetings with Septimus. If the Thracian took that as a sign of his superior's distrust then that was too bad. 'Do not question me again, Thraxis. Send the merchant in and then prepare a meal for me and the centurion.'

'Yes, sir.'

The door closed behind the servant and Macro clicked his tongue. 'Sooner or later someone's going to be wondering about Septimus's visits. And he's not helping matters, what with being a witness to the escape, and still new to the camp. It looks suspicious.'

'Can't be helped. Either he comes here to sell me wine or I have to trek into the vicus and buy it from him in person, and that would look even more odd.'

Macro shrugged.

Footsteps approached again and Thraxis opened the door to admit Septimus and closed it behind him without a word, just a scowl.

Septimus was carrying a jar under each arm and bowed his head before cheerfully greeting his customer. 'Honoured Prefect, a pleasure to be doing business with you again. I bring two samples from the latest stocks to reach Viroconium.'

As soon as Thraxis's footsteps had faded he dropped the act and set the jars down beside a spare stool and sat down. At once Macro gestured towards the wine. 'In the interests of maintaining your cover story I think we should test the quality of the wares.'

Septimus nodded. 'Very wise, and in the interests of maintaining my cover, I think you should pay me for the wine. A denarius for each jug.'

'What?' Macro feigned outrage. 'You would turn a profit on a comrade?'

'Why not? Anything an imperial agent can do to mitigate the costs of his services is simply an act of patriotism.'

'Is that what we call profiteering now?'

Septimus shrugged and held out his hand. With a curse Macro reached into his purse, plucked out a silver coin and tossed it to Septimus before helping himself to a jug and looking at Cato. 'Cups?'

'The shelf. Over there.'

Macro fetched the Samian ware cups and poured himself and Cato a generous helping before grudgingly pouring Septimus half a cup. The latter took a quick sip and then spoke.

'A sorry business,' he said wearily. 'The governor's illness does not help our cause.'

Macro shot him a cynical look. 'Our cause?'

Septimus stared back. 'My cause. My master's cause. The Emperor's cause. Rome's cause. And therefore your cause. Happy now?'

A smile flickered across Macro's face. 'It helps to be reminded from time to time.'

The imperial agent turned to Cato. 'You know this means that Quintatus will be assuming temporary command.'

'I'd worked that out for myself.'

Septimus ignored the jibe. 'I'd be wary of the legate. He's proved that he's sympathetic to the other side, even if he isn't actually an agent of Pallas. The situation is already dangerous enough with Caratacus on the loose amongst the Brigantes. With Quintatus in command of the army there's no telling what he might do to sabotage our position.'

Macro snorted. 'Are you suggesting that a Roman legate would deliberately sacrifice his men to satisfy the whims of an imperial freedman?'

Septimus gave him a withering look. 'This is all about what happens in Rome, Centurion. It is all about who sits on the throne and who stands at their side. Everything else that happens in the empire follows from that essential truth.'

'I think you have been playing your games for too long,' Macro replied coolly. 'Strikes me that you and your kind rather overplay your significance in this world. Your struggles are of little concern to the rest of us. We face more immediate dangers, like keeping the barbarians in their place.'

Septimus stared back and then laughed. 'You're priceless, Macro! Do you really think that's how the world works? Do you really think you soldiers have any say in what determines the paths taken by great powers?'

'As it happens, I do.' Macro patted the hilt of his sword. 'Want me to give you a demonstration?'

Cato waved his hand impatiently. 'Save it, Macro. This isn't the time to let our private grievances get in the way.' He turned back to the imperial agent. 'I don't think Quintatus will attempt anything too overt.'

'Oh?'

'Think about it. Even if he is working towards ensuring that Nero succeeds Claudius, he's hardly going to want to go down in history as the man who lost the province of Britannia. He'll be more subtle than that. If Quintatus is trying to fatally undermine our chances to bring peace to this island then he'll do it in such a way that it happens after he's left the scene. That way the blame will attach to someone else – the next governor, whoever that may be. Assuming Ostorius does not recover.' Cato paused to organise his thoughts. 'Now that Caratacus is in Brigantia there's every chance that the war will drag on. Long enough for Quintatus to serve out his tenure of the Fourteenth Legion and return to Rome. So it's in his interest to make sure that Caratacus talks the Brigantians round, while at the same time being seen to be doing all that he can to prevent it. The question is, how does he intend to achieve that? I think we'll find out soon enough.'

'What do you mean?' asked Septimus.

'Quintatus has summoned all senior officers to a briefing at first light. I imagine he is going to announce that he's assuming temporary command of the army, and the functions of governor of the province, until Ostorius recovers. And if the general dies, Quintatus will retain control until a new governor reaches Britannia. That's a lot of power to concentrate in the hands of a legate. Especially one who can't be trusted.'

'I'll have to report all this back to Narcissus at once. I'd better draft and code the message tonight.' Septimus stood up, taking care to pick up the spare jug before Macro could lay claim to it. At the door he looked back at the two officers. 'Given what's going to happen tomorrow, I'd take extra care to watch my back if I were you. I fear that the agent sent by Pallas is going to have a free hand.'

'We'll be careful,' Cato responded.

The officers gathering at headquarters the next morning could not hide their anxiety as they talked in muted tones while waiting for the camp prefect to bring them to order. They were not kept long before his voice echoed through the hall.

'Commanding officer present!'

Legate Quintatus strode briskly to the dais and climbed the steps to face the assembled officers. He was accompanied by the chief haruspex attached to the army. The priest was wearing his formal white robe. Behind him came a clerk carrying his bag of slates, scrolls, inkpot and pens. He clutched a large waxed tablet under his arm on which to make his notes of the meeting. Quintatus's gaze swept over them in silence for a moment before he coughed and began his address.

'It is the opinion of the surgeon of the Twentieth Legion that Publius Ostorius Scapula is medically unfit to continue command of the army for the present. It is his further opinion that the general may remain incapacitated for the foreseeable future. Therefore it falls to me, as senior officer present, to assume command of the army and control of the province until such time as Ostorius recovers. Is there any man who challenges my right to do so?'

It was the required custom to ask the question. There were no legitimate grounds for protesting and the officers remained still and silent.

'Very well then.' Quintatus nodded to the clerk standing at the side of the hall. 'Enter into the record that there was no objection. Furthermore, I have consulted the haruspex to ensure that my decision is in accordance with the will of the gods. The omens are favourable?'

It was more of a statement than a question and the priest nodded quickly as he replied in a sonorous tone, 'Indeed. The most propitious auspices I have ever witnessed, sir.' The haruspex drew breath to continue but Quintatus raised a hand to still the man's tongue.

'The gods have spoken and give me their blessing to proceed. Time is short, gentlemen. Our enemy is even now attempting to subvert the loyalty of our ally, Queen Cartimandua. If he succeeds, we shall be obliged to march against the northern tribes. It will be as big and bloody a campaign as any ever waged since the legions first landed on Britannia. The army must make ready. I will be sending for the Second Legion and two more cohorts of the Ninth to strengthen our ranks. In the meantime I require you to prepare your men for war. We must be ready to strike within days if the need arises. Questions?'

Cato steeled himself and raised his hand. 'Sir!'

Quintatus turned to him. 'What is it, Prefect Cato?'

'If we attack the Brigantes before they have decided what to do with Caratacus, we will precipitate a war between us. Surely it would be better to warn them of the consequences of siding with him first? While there is still a chance to resolve this peacefully.'

The legate smiled. 'Thank you for pointing out the obvious, Prefect.'

Cato felt himself flush with embarrassment and anger as some of the officers around him struggled to stifle their amusement. Quintatus allowed them a moment longer to enjoy his humbling of the commander of the baggage train escort before he continued.

'I will be sending an envoy at the head of a small column to persuade the Brigantes to hand Caratacus over to us. However, we must be prepared to act if the tribesmen reject my demand.' He turned his gaze away from Cato. 'Any other questions? Yes, Tribune Petillius?'

'Sir, how is the general?'

'Ostorius is recovering in his tent. If there is any change in his condition you will be notified. Anything else? No? Then, with the exception of Tribune Otho and Prefects Horatius and Cato, you are dismissed.'

The officers stood up smartly as Quintatus left the dais and made towards his clerk. As soon as he had climbed down the steps, the first of the officers turned to leave.

'What's that about?' asked Macro. 'Why would he want to see you?'

'Not sure, but I have a nasty feeling I can guess. You'd better get back to the men. Assemble our officers, the quartermaster, farrier, armourer and the horse master of the Blood Crows.'

'Yes, sir.' Macro saluted and turned to leave with the others.

The hall quickly emptied, leaving the three men picked out by Quintatus. Horatius was a short distance away from Cato and cocked an enquiring eyebrow, but Cato could only shake his head. Tribune Otho simply sat looking surprised. At length the doors thudded behind the last of the officers to leave the hall and the two soldiers of the headquarters guard resumed their positions on either side, spears and shields grounded. Quintatus dismissed the augur and had a quiet conversation with the clerk before the latter saluted and also left the hall, returning a moment later with the messenger sent by Cartimandua. The young warrior strode to the front of the hall and stood a short distance from the dais, arms folded in front of him. Cato scrutinised him. He was fair-haired, tall and well-built. His jaw was square and he had the muscular good looks that would have made him very popular with the kind of women who worship gladiators in Rome, Cato mused.

Turning back to his subordinates, Quintatus announced, 'This is Vellocatus, the personal representative of Queen Cartimandua. He speaks our tongue.' It was as much a gentle warning as an introduction. The Brigantian nodded a brief greeting to the other officers before Quintatus continued.

'Prefect Cato, you asked about making an attempt to negotiate with the Brigantes and so avoid war. In which case you will be pleased to know that I have chosen you to accompany the envoy to speak to Queen Cartimandua and her people on my behalf. The envoy in question will be Tribune Otho.' He turned to the young aristocrat. 'It is a vital task. Do you consider yourself the right man to carry it out?'

Otho could not help beaming as he replied effusively, 'Yes, sir!'

'Good. Then you will take command of the column leaving here at dawn tomorrow. Vellocatus will accompany you to act as a guide and translator. You will take two of your cohorts from the Ninth as well as the auxiliary cohort of Prefect Horatius and the baggage train escort of Prefect Cato. These are the only forces I am prepared to risk. If we send any more men it will look like an invasion. Any less, and they won't be able to fight their way out in case of trouble. Although you will speak for me, and are the ranking officer, I require that Prefect Horatius be in command of the column for military purposes. If it comes to a fight I want an experienced officer in charge. Is that clear?'

'Yes, sir.' Otho nodded, then a slight frown formed on his smooth forehead. 'Might I ask why you honour me with this mission?'

'Honour has nothing to do with it. I need a good man on the spot. Someone with breeding who can speak with the authority of the Senate behind him and, through them, the Emperor. You are best placed for such a role.'

'Yes, sir.'

Quintatus smiled warmly. 'Play this well, Tribune Otho, and you will win a name for yourself as the man who brought peace to Britannia.'

'Yes, sir.'

Quintatus addressed the two prefects. 'Horatius, you will support the tribune as best you can. Your duty will be to guard him and, if need be, Queen Cartimandua. If the negotiations fail, you may have to conduct a fighting retreat. Are you the man for the job?'

'Sir!' Horatius nodded.

The legate faced Cato. 'I imagine you're wondering why the baggage train escort will be joining the column.'

'The question had crossed my mind, sir.'

'You are no fool, Prefect. You have also proved yourself an adept at adjusting to circumstances and acting with initiative. Just the kind of officer I need to support Tribune Otho and Prefect Horatius. Serve them well.'

'I know my duty, sir.'

'I'm sure you do. Look on this as a chance to redeem yourself.'

Cato's eyes narrowed. 'Redeem myself. For what, sir?'

'The general took the view that you shoulder much of the blame for the escape of Caratacus. I am sure you feel it's unfair. That's as maybe, but what matters is how the news is received back in Rome. If we can come out of this with Caratacus in the bag and having broken the will of the natives to resist, we will all be rewarded and any unfortunate details will be quietly forgotten. In that lies your chance for redemption, Prefect Cato. Do I make myself clear?'

'Painfully, sir.'

'Good. Then you all know what parts you have to play. I'll have the clerks draft your orders and you'll have them before the day is out. You'll leave at dawn.'

The legate fixed each of them with a quick stare. 'Good luck, gentlemen. You'll need it.'

CHAPTER TWENTY

'What's this?' Cato asked as he unbuckled his helmet and mopped the sweat from his brow. He indicated the folded papyrus lying on his desk. His name was neatly written on the outside.

Thraxis paused from unhooking Cato's mail shoulder cape to glance at the desk. 'It's from the wife of Tribune Otho, sir. Her slave brought it this afternoon, while you were exercising the cohort.'

Cato grunted. He had been out with his men since the morning's briefing ended. The baggage train escort had barely had the chance to settle back into the routine of garrison life before being thrown into the preparations for the march up into Brigantian territory. There were some grumblers – there always were. Cato recalled his first experiences as optio to Macro when he had been constantly frustrated by the need to be ready at a moment's notice for any duty, or frequently none at all while waiting for new orders. Now that he commanded a unit, that world had gone. The myriad duties of a prefect meant that boredom had become a rare luxury.

The morning had been spent requisitioning transport for the horses' feed, carts for the ballistas of Macro's cohort, rations for the march and, most pressing of all, leather to repair or replace the tents damaged in the storm. The stock of leather at Viroconium was scarce and he had been obliged to bribe the quartermaster to let him have a barely sufficient quantity for his men. The afternoon had been taken up with observing the men drilling on the parade ground. There was still much work to be done with the Batavian recruits who had mastered the basic formations and squadron manoeuvres but still tended to respond slowly and clumsily when required to perform the more refined deployments into wedges and wheeling about the axis of each flank.

Still, they were fine riders and spirited. If it came to a fight, Cato was sure that they would acquit themselves as well as the rest of the Blood Crows.

Macro had drilled his new legionaries hard in the few days since they had joined the cohort and they could be trusted to march and deploy as required. Their skill at arms was still rudimentary. In battle the more experienced men in their sections would have to set the example in holding formation and giving no ground. It was late in the afternoon before Cato dismissed the two cohorts and sent the men to their barracks to prepare their marching yokes and saddle packs. He was hot, tired and thirsty and had been looking forward to a session in the bathhouse to ease his muscles before leaving Viroconium on the morrow.

'What does Poppaea Sabina want?'

Thraxis did not look at him but answered after the most fleeting hesitation. 'I'm sure I don't know, sir.'

'You didn't read it then?'

'I barely know more than a few words, sir.'

'But enough to know her purpose, eh?'

'Actually, sir, I got the details from her slave girl.'

'And not just the details,' Cato added shrewdly, before he relented. His servant's private life was his own. He raised his arms as Thraxis helped him out of his mail vest. 'What does the tribune's wife want?'

'Her husband has invited you to dine after the first change of watch, sir. Together with Prefect Horatius, and the three senior centurions commanding the legionary cohorts.'

Cato ground his teeth in frustration. He had intended to complete his preparations for the march and get a good night's rest in a proper bed. Now he would have to satisfy the social whims of some broad-stripe tribune and his wife. He felt embarrassed by the memory of her unwanted attention the night after the battle and had no desire to spend the evening in her company. Besides, if he was any judge of such events, it would drag on and be late in the night before he could finally sleep. He toyed briefly with the idea of turning the invitation down, but knew that would put him in Otho's black books. If he was going to have to serve under the tribune for the next month or so it would be better not to offend him at the outset.

The last of the heavy links slid up over his head and Thraxis took the vest away to carefully lay it over the frame with the rest of the prefect's armour. Cato rolled his neck, relishing the feeling of being released from the burden.

'Once you've finished here, you can take my acceptance to the tribune's quarters.'

'You mean his house, sir?'

'House?'

'Yes, sir. The tribune's wife was not satisfied with the accommodation in the fort so she persuaded her husband to rent the villa of a wool merchant on the edge of the vicus. It's not far. No more than a mile away, sir.'

Cato pursed his lips. It seemed that Tribune Otho was in the habit of indulging his wife's every whim. But then no doubt he could afford to. Cato could well imagine the tribune's wealthy background. Like most aristocratic families there would be a fine home in Rome, a villa in the Tuscan hills to retire to during the hot summer months, and another down by the sea in the wide curve of the bay stretching from Puteoli to Pompeii. Otho would have known the best tutors and enjoyed the best seats at the theatre, the games and the great circus. After his brief stint in the army he would go on to enter the Senate and if he kept his nose clean he could look forward to a lucrative posting as governor of a province, or commander of a legion, in due course. Cato felt a stab of envy at the easy path life granted to some, while others toiled hard for their meagre rewards.

Cato bitterly tried to thrust his envy aside. Very well, he would go to the tribune's damn dinner. But he would be formal and curt and be such a dour guest that they would be delighted to be relieved of his presence and never seek to repeat the experience. He smiled with satisfaction at the thought as he thrust a strigil and small pot of oil into a haversack and left his quarters to join Macro at the bathhouse complex that served the officers and men of the garrison at Viroconium.

'So, what's this all about?' Macro asked as they made their way through the vicus. Beneath a crescent moon the evening air was thick with the cries of traders and small parties of boisterous off-duty soldiers in search of a drink, dice games and whorehouses. Many of the small towns that grew up close to army fortresses were ramshackle affairs of filthy winding streets, but the settlement at Viroconium had been laid out in a far more ordered fashion from the outset on the orders of General Ostorius. The streets were straight, wide and drained, and many of the temporary structures had been replaced by timber-framed buildings built on stone foundations. There was even a small basilica at the heart of the settlement where a council met to order the affairs of the inhabitants. Cato had been musing over the speed with which Rome stamped its mark on newly conquered territories and so missed his friend's question.

'Sorry? What was that?'

'This bloody invitation from the tribune? What does he really want with us?'

'A chance to get better acquainted, I expect. It's his first independent command. Otho wants to make a decent job of it.'

Macro had been to the barber's stall at the baths and was clean-shaven. His dark curly hair had been neatly cropped and his tunic was freshly laundered. Every so often Macro reached up to the neckline of his tunic and scratched his skin, as if its freshly cleaned state was the source of an itch. He still smelled of the aromatic oils the barber had massaged into his jowls after the shave.

'So we have to get all tarted up to make a good impression?'

Cato had undergone similar treatment but was more comfortable with his appearance. He shrugged. 'It can't do any harm.'

Macro cast a longing look into the dark entrance of a brothel as they passed. A small queue of soldiers leaned against the wall sharing a wineskin. A thickset woman with red-tinged cheeks and long lank hair emerged from the doorway, lifted the hem of her short tunic and curled a finger suggestively at the nearest soldier. He instantly hurried inside with her. Macro sniffed at the scent on his skin.

'I'll put it to good use on the way back. Last chance before we head up into barbarian territory.'

'I think you will find they are called the Brigantes.'

'Don't care what they're called, as long as they behave and hand that bastard Caratacus back to us.'

Cato turned to him and shook his head. 'And there was I thinking that this was essentially a diplomatic mission.'

'Waste of time. Better to just put the stick about and let 'em know who is in charge. That's my kind of diplomacy.'

'Clearly.'

They reached the edge of the settlement and could just pick out the walled villa a short distance down the road against the dark greys of the surrounding landscape. The wool merchant must have made a small fortune from his trade with the army, Cato thought, as he took in the proportions of the building. As they approached he could make out the gatehouse leading into a courtyard while the main building rose up beyond with what looked like a tiled roof, though it must be wooden shingles, Cato realised. It would be a while yet before tiles reached Viroconium.

A section of legionaries from the Ninth were guarding the entrance and stood to as the two officers emerged from the darkness. The optio looked them over and saluted.

'Prefect Cato and Centurion Macro,' Cato announced. 'Here to see the tribune.'

'You're expected, sir. The other guests have already arrived. If you'll follow me?'

The optio turned and led the way through the arch. By the dim light of the moon Cato saw that the courtyard followed the familiar style of covered sides given over to stables and stores. Ahead lay the main building. The door was open and the interior was illuminated by lamps whose glow bled out across the cobbles of the courtyard. They followed the optio into the house and saw that it gave out on to an enclosed garden. Lamps hung from brackets fixed to the wooden frame of the house. A shallow colonnade ran around the garden, providing shelter for the walkway in front of the living rooms, kitchen, latrine and bedrooms. The garden itself was no more than ten paces across and the space was mostly taken up by the dining couches arranged around a low table. The wool merchant's house was modest by Roman standards but palatial compared to the simple round huts of the island's tribes. It also enjoyed a more peaceful setting than the cramped, noisy quarters available in the satellite forts clustered about the main fortress. Cato could see why Tribune Otho and his wife might prefer it.

'Prefect Cato and Centurion Macro!' the optio announced.

Looking past him, Cato could see Horatius and the other officers on the side couches while the tribune and his wife occupied those at the head of the table. Otho looked up and smiled as he beckoned his guests over.

'Ah! I was wondering if something had happened to you two!'

Mindful of his earlier decision to play the taciturn professional, Cato did not return the smile and simply bowed his head slightly before he responded. 'The centurion and I had to finish our preparations for the march, sir.'

'Good. That's good.' Otho indicated the bench to his left where two spaces were left. Horatius lay opposite, the more privileged position, according to his superior rank. When they had taken their places, Otho indicated the two centurions lying beside Horatius. 'In case you haven't met, that's Gaius Statillus and Marcus Polemus Acer, senior centurions of the Seventh and Eighth Cohorts of the Ninth Legion.'

Cato cast his eye over the centurions and instinctively assessed them. Statillus was perhaps fifty, and coming to the end of his enlistment. His hair was thin and watery blue eyes stared back from his weathered features. Acer was younger. Recently promoted, Cato guessed. His gaze flickered constantly round the table as if he was not convinced he belonged with such exotic company. He was the bigger of the two, built like a champion secutor with light hair and broad features that betrayed his Celtic origins.

Otho settled back on his couch and reached for a silver goblet. 'That should complete the introductions.'

His wife reached over and touched his arm. 'Not quite, my dear. I don't believe I know the delightful creature next to Prefect Cato.'

Macro gritted his teeth at her comment.

'No?' Otho smiled and raised her hand to kiss it. 'That, my dear, is Centurion Macro, senior centurion of the Fourth Cohort of the Fourteenth Legion.'

'So many numbers to remember!' she protested. 'How do you all cope? I'm sure I would not know where to begin were I a soldier. All these ranks, names, numbers and detachments.'

Horatius and the other centurions smiled politely but Cato kept his expression neutral as Poppaea shifted her position to address him directly.

'Ah yes, I have it now. Centurion Macro's men, and those rough-looking horsemen you command, are in charge of the army's luggage. Is that not so, Prefect?'

'Baggage, my lady,' Cato corrected her flatly. 'I command the baggage train escort.'

She tilted her head to one side and smiled briefly, revealing neat white teeth that looked sharp. Like her tongue, Cato mused as she continued. 'It does not sound like a particularly onerous or significant duty, and yet you were the toast of the army for your actions on the day of the battle.'

'And rightly so!' Centurion Acer interrupted, raising his cup to Cato. 'A bloody fine piece of work, sir. Pulled our arses out of the fire that day and no mistake.'

'Such a kind endorsement of your comrade,' Poppaea said sweetly. 'May I continue? You are quite right, the prefect seems to have covered himself in glory that day. Though the moment passed exceedingly quickly with the escape of Caratacus. You see, yet another detail of the military world that a simple civilian finds bewildering. One moment you are a hero, the next, some sort of miscreant. What is one to make of that?'

Cato was silent a moment, brimming with bitter self-justification, and then he forced the feelings aside and concentrated his efforts on maintaining his indifferent appearance. 'It's the way of the army, my lady. All a soldier can do is serve to the best of his ability and take the bad along with the good.'

She gave him a level look. 'So stoical, and so typical of the professional soldiers I have encountered while in Britannia. And yet you are too young a prefect to come from such a background. I assume you have breeding.'

'If by that you infer a wealthy background, then no.'

'I inferred nothing as crass as wealth. I spoke of breeding.'

'I have none of that either. I rose through the ranks.'

'Then you must have proved yourself a consummate soldier to have risen so swiftly, nay?'

Cato shrugged diffidently but did not reply.

Poppaea shifted her gaze back to Macro. 'And what of you, Centurion? What is your background?'

Macro sniffed and cuffed his nose. 'Joined up as a lad. Took eight years to reach the rank of optio, then two more years before I got the promotion to the centurionate. That's when I met the prefect. He served as my optio back then.'

Her neatly plucked eyebrows lifted a little in surprise. 'Prefect Cato was *your* subordinate? And how do you feel about that now?'

'How do I feel?' Macro shifted and puffed his cheeks. 'Prefect Cato is my commanding officer, Lady Poppaea. I obey his orders. That's how I feel about it.'

She stared at him for a moment and let out a brief laugh before reaching for her goblet and taking a delicate sip. 'I can see we are in for an evening of the most animating conversation.'

Otho shot her a concerned look and then raised his goblet. 'A toast, gentlemen. To the successful pursuit and apprehension of the fugitive, Caratacus. And the peace and prosperity that will ensue.'

The other officers dutifully raised their cups and did their best to repeat the lengthy toast, mumbling through the final phrase. Poppaea looked on with wry amusement as her husband gestured to the slave standing silently to one side. 'You may bring the first course now.'

'Yes, master.' The slave bowed and disappeared through a door beneath the colonnade.

Macro looked around the garden and nodded. 'Nice place you've got here, sir.'

'Nice? I suppose so. In a clean, basic sort of way. Of course, it's a seller's market out here on the frontier of the empire. The rent I pay for this hovel would cover a modest palace back in Rome. But it's a small price to pay for the comfort and privacy that it affords.'

'Hovel?' Macro muttered under his breath.

Poppaea wafted a hand around the garden. 'It'll be a shame for us to swap this for the hardship of sleeping in a tent for the next month or some, but duty calls.'

Cato coughed. 'Do you intend your wife to accompany us to Brigantia, sir?'

'Of course. My dear Poppaea and I cannot bear to be parted from one another. Besides, it's a diplomatic mission. The presence of my wife will demonstrate our peaceful intent. I'm sure that Queen

Cartimandua would appreciate some female company during the course of our negotiations.'

Macro was not so sure. He recalled his brief dalliance with a young Iceni woman during his first tour in Britannia. Boudica had been a spirited individual who enjoyed a drink and other earthy pursuits. He did not think there were many interests she would share with this brittle-looking aristocrat. Perhaps Cartimandua was different, but he doubted it.

'Is that wise, sir?' asked Cato. 'It may be a diplomatic mission but there is a good chance it might turn into a military action. In which case Lady Poppaea would be in grave danger.'

'Oh, I very much doubt it will come to that,' Otho responded confidently. 'It will be Queen Cartimandua who is in grave danger if she fails to comply with our demands. If she is rash enough to side with Caratacus she will be swept away with the other malcontents when Legate Quintatus brings the rest of the army up. Frankly, I think she will know the game is up the moment my column arrives. But I trust we can keep things on a civil basis, and in that I am sure my wife can assist with smoothing things over between Rome and those benighted barbarians. Isn't that so, my love?'

'I shall play my part. That is my duty.'

'There!' Otho smiled at Cato. 'You see?'

Cato shrugged.

They were interrupted by the arrival of the first course, a large shallow dish carried by the slave. He set it down on the table and a rich aroma wafted over the guests.

'Strips of mutton, quick fried with a garum and vinegar glaze,' Poppaea explained. 'To a recipe passed on to our cook from that of Agrippina.'

The slave served neatly presented portions on small silver platters, handing the first to the hosts before the other officers. As soon as Otho began eating, the others joined in with gusto, using their knife points to pick up the strips of meat and popping them into their mouths. Macro quickly finished and gestured to the slave for another helping, while Cato proceeded at a more sedate pace, refusing to show that he found the flavour quite delicious.

'Damn fine dish!' Horatius enthused, reaching out for more. The other centurions nodded heartily. Cato noted that Statillus was making hard work of it and then, as his lips parted, he understood the reason why. The man had no teeth. Cato realised the veteran must be older than he had first thought.

'It's simple enough,' said Poppaea. 'Sadly our cook was only able to bring one chest of spices and other ingredients with him. And there's precious little variety of meat and fruit available in this wretched island. So we make do. It is a little more sophisticated than the fare of the common legionary, I imagine.'

'It's bloody delicious,' Macro commented, mouth still half full.

Poppaea flashed him a smile before turning to Cato. 'And what do you think, Prefect Cato?'

He chewed and swallowed and licked his lips before replying, 'Salty.'

'Salty?' She frowned, but before she could respond, Otho clapped his hands to attract the attention of the slave and indicated that the first course should be removed.

In the interval another slave brought more wine and filled the cups.

'Now, gentlemen, if you don't mind, I would like to turn our attention to the business at hand. You already have your orders from headquarters and know the nature of our task. The question is, how best to go about it. And what contingencies we may have to prepare depending upon a variety of possible outcomes.'

Cato noticed that the tribune had adopted a more businesslike demeanour and there was now a shrewd glint to his eyes that Cato had not noticed before. Otho propped himself up on his elbows and folded his hands together as he continued to address his officers.

'Caratacus has a head start on us. He will have had plenty of time to address the leaders of the tribe. We know that he is very persuasive and will already have talked some round to his side. We will have some ground to make up when we reach Isurium. From what I have gleaned from Vellocatus, we may be given a hostile reception. If that happens, we'll fall back here at once. If they receive us in peace, we'll state our demand that the Brigantes honour the alliance they have agreed with Rome. I don't expect Cartimandua will come to a decision instantly. She will need to be confident that she can carry the majority of her people with her.'

207

As he listened to the tribune, Cato could not help being aware of the clarity of the young man's thinking. It seemed somewhat at odds with the naive hail-fellow-well-met persona he had adopted on most occasions so far. There was clearly another side to his character that was far more shrewd and calculating.

'Of course,' Otho continued, 'it may go the other way, in which case we'll be facing a new leader of the tribe. At the moment, the most likely candidate is Venutius, a staunch supporter of Caratacus. If that's the case, we'll have a fight on our hands. It's my intention to play safe. We'll make camp outside Isurium, even if they offer us the hospitality of their capital. It won't be your standard marching camp. The ditches will be deeper and wider and the rampart higher. We'll mount ballistas on the corner towers. The natives have little knowledge of siege-craft so we will be able to hold them at bay until relieved by Legate Quintatus.'

He paused and smiled. 'But let's assume things go our way and Cartimandua agrees to hand the enemy over to us. In that event I want him taken out of Brigantia as quickly as possible. That will be your job, Prefect Cato.'

'Yes, sir. I assume you mean just the Blood Crows.'

'I mean the escort detachment, Prefect.'

'Begging your pardon, sir, but it would make most sense if my cohort alone brought Caratacus back to the fortress. Otherwise we'll have to march at the same pace as Macro's infantry. That would give Venutius and his followers plenty of opportunity to set an ambush for us. Far better that we ride hard for Viroconium and that Macro's cohort add its strength to the men remaining in the camp.'

'Who says we will remain in the camp?' Otho countered. 'Once we've concluded our business with Cartimandua I plan to quit Brigantian territory at once and return to join the army.'

Cato hesitated before putting his objection to his superior. He wanted to ensure that his reasons were explained clearly, and accepted. 'Sir, even if the queen agrees to hand him over, that is no guarantee that the campaign to subdue Britannia is over. Whatever Cartimandua decides is bound to divide her people. It's more than likely that surrendering Caratacus to us will provoke Venutius into action. There may be violence between the supporters of Caratacus and the pro-Roman faction. In which case, if your men are at hand you might be able to tip the scales in the queen's favour. In my opinion it would be best for Rome to maintain a military presence outside Isurium until it is clear that Cartimandua has her people firmly under her control.'

'Easy for you to say when you'll be in the clear.'

A tense silence fell over the dinner table and Cato felt a surge of anger at the accusation. Before he could respond, Otho laughed good-naturedly and grinned at him. 'Just joking, Prefect. Just joking . . . You are right, of course. Very well, if we get our hands on Caratacus, you will return here and report to the legate that I intend to remain in Brigantia until relieved, or I deem it safe to leave, or I receive orders from Quintatus to break camp.'

'Yes, sir.'

'Then I think we have every eventuality covered.' He looked round at the other officers questioningly. 'Horatius, anything to add?'

The prefect in command of the military side of the mission thought a moment and shook his head. 'No, sir. You can rest assured that I will do my duty.'

'Good! Then we can enjoy the rest of the meal without talking shop, to the eternal gratitude of Poppaea, whose boredom over such matters is positively deafening.' He turned to her with a grin as she scowled back, and then darted his head forward to kiss her on the lips. She made to resist and swat his attentions away but then kissed him back. The officers looked away from the open display of affection awkwardly and Horatius turned to talk to the two centurions next to him. Cato watched a moment longer, painfully reminded of the wife he had left in Rome, yet knowing that he would find it difficult to split himself between his duties as an officer and a husband. Although Tribune Otho seemed to carry it off with aplomb, Cato could not help having reservations about his superior's decision to bring his wife with him on the march to Brigantia. Aside from the danger to the woman, there was the question of the distraction she would present, just when her husband would need to fully concentrate on negotiating an end to the conflict in Britannia.

A small column of slaves emerged from the kitchen. The first two carried a long tray holding a small glazed piglet, surrounded by delicately patterned pastries. Another followed with a basket of bread loaves, then came another with a tray of mushrooms, roasted onions and other vegetables. The confusion of mouth-watering smells drew the compliments of the officers. Otho and his wife drew apart and smiled at the delight of their guests. Beside Cato, Macro rubbed his hands as he eyed up the pig.

'Ah, will you look at that crackling! Mmmm!'

Only Cato remained stern and silent, unable to shake off the shroud of misgivings he had over the dangers presented by the mission that lay ahead.

CHAPTER TWENTY-ONE

'What's he doing here?' asked Centurion Acer as he gestured towards the wine merchant easing his wagon into position at the end of the small column of carts and wagons that carried the supplies and artillery.

Horatius looked round. 'The tribune gave him permission to join our happy throng. His name's Hipparchus. Just another Greek latching on to the cloak tails of the Roman army and trying to make his fortune.'

The other officers laughed and Cato and Macro joined in half-heartedly.

'Seriously, though,' Acer continued, 'I thought we were supposed to leave anything that might slow us down behind. No unnecessary clutter was what the tribune's orders said.'

'That was just for us, lad,' said Macro. 'The tribune clearly thinks that his wife and a ready supply of wine are necessary to ensure the success of his mission.'

The others laughed again.

'There's a little more to it than that,' said Horatius. 'The merchant's here to trade with the Brigantes. There's nothing the natives like more than our wine. By the gods, they'd sell their own mothers for a jar of decent Falernian. And they once did, according to my father who served at Gesoriacum, many years before the invasion. A steady flow of wine shipped out to Britannia, with the ships coming back with furs and slaves. The tribune hopes that a supply of wine to the natives might help to grease the wheels and make the natives a little more open to persuasion. Besides, you know how these Greek merchants are. If there's any useful gossip to pick up on, it reaches their ears first.'

The sun had just risen over the sprawl of the forts and civilian settlement at Viroconium. The first trails of rekindled fires trickled into the rosy hue of a clear sky. The men of Otho's column were standing in loose formation on the parade ground waiting for the order to march. The horses of the two auxiliary cohorts were saddled and laden with the kit of their riders and nets stuffed with feed. They sensed the expectant mood of the men around them, and pointed ears and delicate muzzles twitched this way and that, accompanied by the light chinking of their metal bits. The mules harnessed to the carts and wagons seemed, by contrast, utterly uncurious and stood still in their harnesses as their drivers walked the lines of their beasts, making slight adjustments to straps and yokes as necessary. The wagon of Poppaea Sabina was the largest vehicle in the column and had been positioned at the front where she would not be troubled by the dust stirred from the wheels and hoofs of the others.

'Here they come,' Macro announced quietly and the officers saw the tribune, arm in arm with his wife, stroll up from the direction of their rented villa. 'No rush then.'

When they reached the wagon, Otho handed his wife up the steps at the rear and then rose on his toes to take one last kiss before he stretched his shoulders and strode past the legionaries and the contingent of auxiliary infantry from Horatius's mixed cohort. He rubbed his hands together as he approached his officers.

'Brisk morning, nay?'

Macro whispered to Cato out of the corner of his mouth, 'What's with this naying?'

Cato shrugged. 'Some fad from Rome, I expect.'

'Well, it's annoying the shit out of me. Every time, I feel like I should throw 'em a handful of oats.'

'What's that, Centurion?' Otho asked cheerfully.

'Just saying, sir. It's good to see a man who dotes. On his wife, I mean.'

'Poor effort,' Cato muttered, barely moving his lips.

The tribune nodded happily. 'I give thanks to the gods every day that Poppaea is my wife. Now, to business, gentlemen. All is ready, I take it?'

Horatius nodded. 'Just waiting for the order, sir.'

'Then let's be off. We have the small matter of a conquest to complete.'

Horatius hesitated, unhappy at the casual manner of his superior. Then he sighed and nodded. 'Yes, sir. Officers! To your units.'

The centurions turned and quickly paced to their positions while the prefect strode towards the head of the column. Cato and Macro exchanged a brief nod before the latter made for the cohort formed up behind the wagons. Cato strode towards the trooper holding his horse and swung himself up into the saddle and adjusted his seat before he gave the nod to Decurion Miro. The latter drew a deep breath and cupped a hand to his mouth.

'Second Thracian! Mount!'

With some scuffling of hoofs and grunts from the men and whinnies from the horses the troopers quickly mounted their beasts and steadied them.

Across the parade ground Cato saw a slave lead the tribune's horse to him, a finely groomed white stallion whose coat gleamed where it was not covered by the red and gold saddle blanket and tassels hanging from the leather tackle. The slave bent down and cupped his hands to provide a leg up. Once Otho had finished fastening the straps of his helmet he climbed into his saddle and sat stiffly as he surveyed his small force. In his flowing red cape, trimmed with gold lace, shining breastplate and helmet topped with an elaborate red plume he looked impressive, thought Cato. The kind of appearance that he could imagine Pompey the Great affecting in his younger days. Certainly the young officer's accoutrements outshone those of General Ostorius himself, let alone the legionary legates whose rank far exceeded that of Otho. Cato smiled as he thought of the Brigantian queen being dazzled by this display when the Romans reached her capital at Isurium.

The tribune lightly spurred his horse into motion and trotted to the head of the column where Horatius was waiting, along with the native translator, Vellocatus. A short distance beyond stood Horatius's mounted contingent which formed the vanguard of the column and would scout ahead the moment they moved beyond the official frontier of the new province. Otho nodded to his second-in-command and Horatius's voice carried clearly down the line of men, vehicles and beasts behind him.

'Column! Advance!'

Behind the two officers the standards of the units attached to the column moved forward, then the leading ranks of the first legionary cohort, commanded by Centurion Statillius, then Acer's men, followed by the baggage train and Macro's cohort. The Blood Crows were assigned to the rearguard from where they could easily advance to protect the flanks of the column if the need arose.

The column marched out of the parade ground and joined the road leading north from Viroconium. A handful of women from the vicus had gathered to watch them leave, a few of them unable to contain the tears at being parted from their men. Due to the need to reach Isurium swiftly, Otho had given strict orders that no camp followers would be permitted to join the column, where they might become stragglers. His wife would be the only woman permitted to accompany the soldiers, and the wine merchant the only other civilian.

A small party of officers from the fortress stood outside the main gate to bid farewell to the tribune and his men. Quintatus stepped forward as the head of the column passed by.

'Good fortune go with you, Tribune Otho, and good hunting.'

The young man smiled back. 'I'll bring back Caratacus, dead or alive, sir. You have my word.'

'And I will see you again within a month. One way or another.'

They exchanged a brief salute and then the tribune edged his horse forward again and led his column towards the land of the Brigantes. Whether they were still an ally of Rome or had become a bitter enemy would soon be discovered.

The first two days they marched through the lands of the Cornovii, a tribe that had sued for peace with the invaders shortly after the legions had landed. But it was only after Ostorius had driven the enemy back into the mountains that the people of the tribe had lived free of raids from their neighbours for the first time in generations. As a consequence the rolling hills were dotted with farms and the column passed herdsmen and traders travelling freely from settlement to settlement, unburdened by the dread of bands of marauders lurking in the forests that spread across the hills.

It was a vision of how the entire province might appear one day,

Cato reflected as he rode at the head of his men through the lush green countryside sprinkled with the bright colours of wild flowers. There was a soft beauty to these lands that touched his soul. Quite different to the dramatic scenery of Italia, frequently disfigured by the huge agricultural estates where chain gangs of slaves toiled miserably from first light to last. He offered a prayer to Jupiter that Britannia be spared such excesses. If a lasting peace could be won, then he would bring Julia to see the island for herself and perhaps she too would feel its attraction. A moment later he sniffed with contempt for such easy idealism. He was surrendering to the serenity of the island's summer. For much of the rest of the year it was wet and cold, and in the depths of winter the short days bathed the bare landscape with a thin light. Julia would hate it, just as Macro did, or claimed to.

They passed through the band of small turf forts and turrets manned by auxiliary detachments on the third day and advanced beyond the frontier of the Roman province. That night the tribune ordered that the men construct a marching camp 'in the face of the enemy', as the army termed the construction of a deeper ditch and higher ramparts topped with a palisade. The horses and mules were no longer hobbled and left to graze in roped-off enclosures outside the camp, but were brought in at dusk and herded into far smaller enclosures within the defences where they were safe from raids. The night watch was doubled in strength and the sentries were tense and alert as they surveyed the dark loom of the surrounding landscape cloaked by darkness.

Cato was aware that the mood of the men had shifted. The light humour of the first two days had faded and they had a more watchful, professional edge to them now. They all knew the broad purpose of the mission they had been sent to accomplish and the danger they might face. Caratacus had become something of a legend to his Roman opponents, as Cato could well understand. Rome had fought few men for so long and the Catuvellaunian king refused to capitulate, even after his kingdom had fallen years before. No defeat had swayed him from his fanatical devotion to the cause of defying Emperor Claudius. And now it seemed to the common soldiers that he possessed magical powers that had enabled him to walk free from his chains in the very heart of the Roman camp on the same day that he had been captured.

215

No such man could be permitted to defy Rome for any longer. He must join the ranks of those who had tested her might and been found wanting, like Hannibal, Mithridates and Spartacus before him.

The following day Cato's flank guard sighted a small party of horsemen tracking them just below the crest of the hills to their right. Decurion Miro pointed them out to his superior and it took Cato a moment before he spotted the distant movement amid the heather and gorse growing on the steep slope. There were five riders, wearing tunics, leggings and carrying spears. There was no glint of armour, nor any sign of shields.

'Looks like a hunting party.'

'Want me to send out a squadron after them, sir?'

Cato considered briefly and then shook his head. 'No point. They'd outrun us easily enough. Besides, we're not here to make war. If they are Cornovii, then they're our allies. If they're Brigantians the same applies, until we discover otherwise. Leave them be.'

Miro bowed his head but made no effort to conceal his misgivings. He turned his horse aside and trotted back to his men. Cato continued to watch the riders from time to time and noted that they kept pace with the convoy. They made no effort to come any closer or ride further off. If they were hunters, they had clearly abandoned their original intent in order to keep watch on the Romans. More than likely the instant they had caught sight of the column they had sent off some of their number to report its presence. Despite the existing treaty with the Cornovii and the Brigantian queen, Cato could not help feeling anxious about the route that lay ahead. Tribune Otho would be leading them far beyond the established frontier of the province. In the distance Cato could see a line of hills stretching from north to south. That, according to Vellocatus, marked the boundary of Cartimandua's nation. It was possible that Caratacus had won them over to his cause already and they were even now mobilising a fresh army for him to lead against the Romans. If the column was ambushed in the hills, or the lands that lay beyond, there would be no hope of rescue.

Nor was the only danger from without, Cato reflected sourly. There was a good chance that someone in the column was planning to sabotage Tribune Otho's mission to arrest Caratacus. But who? Cato

216

turned his attention to the column trudging through the peaceful countryside: the infantry, labouring under the burden of their marching yokes, many with soiled strips of cloth tied around their heads to soak up the sweat; the cavalry leading their mounts, their kit hanging from the sturdy saddlehorns; and the wagons and carts rumbling over the dry track leading towards the line of hills rendered indistinct by the haze. Cato picked out the covered wagon of Septimus and saw the imperial agent sitting beside his slave on the driver's bench, arms crossed, his body trembling from the vibrations of the vehicle as it passed over the uneven ground.

Septimus had mentioned his suspects but Cato had seen no clear evidence of treachery from any of them. Horatius seemed too much a soldier to be capable of conspiracy, and while there were hidden depths to Tribune Otho and his wife, there was no evidence to indicate they were involved in any treachery. Yet someone had aided the escape of Caratacus, and had been ruthless enough to murder two soldiers in the process. Such a person was a dangerous threat. Particularly if Septimus was right about their intention to eliminate Macro and himself as well. For a while Cato had been content to be back with the army with the clear-cut purpose of defeating the enemy. Since the arrival of the imperial agent with his news of Pallas's plot, Cato had been forced to live in a state of heightened awareness. His restless mind was looking for any sign of treachery and it was difficult to sleep well. Even then, he had ensured that his sword was within easy reach and his dagger rested beside his bolster. Not that he was under any illusion that a resourceful enemy would not find a way to kill him if the chance presented itself. It was unlikely to happen in the routine course of events since such a murder would entail too much risk for minimal rewards. It was far more likely that Pallas's man would wait until he could make their deaths look like an accident or, better still, he would use their deaths to further his wider cause, Cato calculated. Supposing he and Macro were killed during the negotiations with Cartimandua? If their deaths were blamed on the tribesmen, it would cause a rift between Rome and the Britgantes. There was one glimmer of hope in all this, Cato mused. Caratacus knew who the traitor was. If it was not already too late to negotiate a peaceful resolution, Cato would keep a close watch on the enemy fugitive and try to discover if he was in contact with someone in the Roman column. Once that happened, Cato would strike, without pity.

Late in the afternoon, just after Otho had given the order to halt and make camp, a larger party of horsemen appeared on the crest of a hill little more than a mile from the column. Cato was standing with Macro as the legionaries broke up the ground with their picks ready to commence constructing their allotted section of the defences. The alarm had been raised amongst the men of Centurion Acer's cohort and now the rest turned to look, craning their necks to stare towards the hill. Cato calculated that there must be at least fifty in the party. This time it was immediately apparent that these were no hunters. The angled light from the sun gleamed on polished helmets and shield bosses. Cato turned towards the centre of the camp where the tribune was standing with Vellocatus and some of the other officers. Otho gazed towards the horsemen but made no effort to order the cornicen to call the men to arms. Instead he turned briefly to one of his orderlies and pointed in Cato's direction. The man nodded and began to run over.

Macro had seen the brief exchange. 'What's he want with us?'

'We'll find out soon enough,' Cato replied and then glanced round to see that Macro's men had all stopped to scrutinise the distant natives.

'Macro . . .' Cato nodded towards the work detail.

The flesh around his friend's eyes puckered into an angry glare and he drew a breath. 'What is this? A fucking public holiday?' he roared at his men, brandishing his vine cane. 'Lift those picks and put your bloody backs into it!'

At once the legionaries returned to their work and the air filled with the sound of iron points thudding into the earth, accompanied by the grunts of the men wielding them. Macro paced down the line to make sure none of them was slacking, just as the orderly drew up in front of Cato, short of breath after his quick dash.

'Tribune Otho sends his respects, sir, and requires that you lead one of your squadrons out to confront those horsemen.'

'Confront? Does he wish me to chase them off?'

'No, sir. Just discourage them from coming any closer.'

Cato stared hard at the orderly for an instant, wondering just what discouraging the native warriors might entail if they did decide to approach. 'Very well. Tell the tribune I'll not be the first to strike a blow if I can avoid it.'

'Yes, sir.' The orderly saluted and turned to trot back to his commander.

Cato sought out Decurion Miro who had just unfastened the girth of his saddle and was lowering his heavy leather burden to the ground.

'Miro! On me!'

A short while later Cato led the first squadron of the Blood Crows out towards the horsemen watching over the camp. He kept the pace to a steady walk in order not to alarm the natives. The dull clink of the picks was drowned out by the easy rumble of horses' hoofs. The sun was sinking towards the horizon and bathing the countryside in a warm golden hue. The shadows of the Roman riders stretched out across the grass to their side as a faint haze of dust rose gently in their wake. Decurion Miro was clenching his free hand over and over again as he rode beside Cato.

'We should have brought the whole cohort with us, sir.'

'The tribune just wants us to keep an eye on them,' Cato responded calmly.

'We could have done that from the camp.'

'But that might have encouraged them to venture a little closer. It's better we keep them at a distance for now. We have our orders, Decurion,' he concluded firmly, disapproving of the way his subordinate allowed his anxiety to interfere with his duty.

They advanced in silence until they reached the foot of the hill where the native horsemen waited, unmoving. Cato raised his arm and ordered his men to halt and form line, and the Blood Crows fanned out on either side and turned to face the slope. The Thracians were tense and held their spears and shields at the ready. Cato could understand their nervousness. The unit had been campaigning for two years against the hill tribes and every native they had seen in that time had been an enemy. Why should the men at the top of the hill be any different? Nevertheless, Cato was determined that his men should not inadvertently cause any hostilities.

As the shadows lengthened and the grass and heather were tinged with the flare of the fading sun, the work of constructing the marching camp continued. Every so often Cato would turn and look back and see that the rampart had risen a little higher, while below, the men toiling in the ditch seemed to sink lower into the ground. Eventually only their heads showed above ground, and later all that was visible was the flicker of picks and clods of earth thrown up to add to the rampart. Beyond, other men had started to erect the tents, long, neat lines of brown leather held taut by pegged ropes. The duty cohort formed a cordon round the camp and watched for the approach of any enemy. Once the defences were complete, they were called in and the first watch manned the rampart while their comrades removed their armour and began to prepare the evening meal.

'How much longer are we going to be kept out here?' Miro fretted to himself but just loud enough to provoke a response from his superior.

'Until we hear the recall, that's how long.'

Miro made ready to reply, thought better of it and clamped his jaw shut.

'Sir!' A trooper raised his spear and gestured up the slope.

Cato followed the direction indicated and saw that one of the horsemen had left the rest of the group and had started down the slope at a nonchalant pace, his horse flicking its tail lazily from side to side. At once the Blood Crows began to stir, tightening their grips on reins and spears.

'Easy there!' Cato called out. 'No one is to do anything without my express order! Hold your ground and wait for my order. I'll have the skin off the back of the first man who acts out of turn!'

The line steadied and waited in tense silence as the rider slowly descended from the crest of the hill. As he approached, Cato could see that he sat tall in the saddle of his finely groomed chestnut stallion whose coat gleamed in the fiery light. He wore a patterned tunic and blue leggings bound with leather straps. An oval shield hung from his saddle and he held a long lance in his right hand. His arms were thickly muscled and his dark hair hung in plaits on his broad shoulders. There was no trace of fear in his expression as he walked his horse towards Cato's squadron and halted a mere ten paces from its commander. He stared at Cato a moment and then wheeled his horse to the right and rode towards the flank, glaring at the Blood Crows. At the end of the line he turned round and walked back until he stopped in front of

Cato again and jabbed the tip of his spear at the Roman officer. Miro instinctively made to draw his sword.

'Don't!' Cato growled. 'Do nothing until I say so.'

Miro hesitated a moment and then forced himself to release his grip and eased his hand up on to his saddle horn.

The rider began to speak in a deep voice, tinged with pride and anger as he addressed Cato in his native tongue, pointing his spear at the Romans to emphasise his words. It took a moment before Cato realised that he was indicating the camp as much as the line of horsemen he was confronting.

'What's he on about, sir?' Miro asked in an undertone.

'I imagine he's demanding to know what we're doing here. And it's a fair enough question. We may be allies but we might look like an invading column.'

'What we need is that translator the tribune's brought along. Shall I fetch him, sir?'

'No. Stand firm, and keep your mouth shut.'

The rider continued his tirade and his eyes glittered from time to time as they caught the glare of the setting sun so that he seemed the very embodiment of outrage, on the cusp of spurring his horse forward to try and impale Cato on the tip of his spear. Then Cato became aware of the thrumming of hoofs and risked a look over his shoulder to see a horseman racing towards them from the fort. He swiftly recognised him as Vellocatus and smiled thinly as he addressed the decurion.

'Seems like the tribune has second-guessed you.'

The shouting stopped as the rider craned his neck to look past Cato. A moment later Vellocatus reined in and eased himself into a space beside Cato. The other man's expression creased into a contemptuous sneer and he spat into the grass in front of the new arrival.

Cato scratched his earlobe casually. 'Friend of yours?'

'A cousin. Belmatus. Younger brother of Venutius.'

'Ah, now I understand something of his pleasure in seeing you here.' Cato nodded in the direction of the fiery native. 'Better find out exactly what he wants.'

Vellocatus cleared his throat and addressed his relative. Cato had learned some of the tongue of the tribes further to the south but he could not follow the more guttural dialect of the two northerners. There was a sharp exchange before the translator turned back to Cato.

'Besides some colourful insults directed at me, Belmatus demands to know why the Romans have ventured beyond the frontier of the lands they lay claim to.'

'I see.' Cato tilted his head slightly as a worrying thought struck him. 'Do I take it that your queen has not yet informed her people that she has requested our assistance?'

Vellocatus shifted uncomfortably in his saddle before he replied. 'I do not know, sir. I merely carried the message.'

'I don't believe you. Try again.'

The young nobleman lowered his gaze as he replied, 'She said it would be better not to give too much warning of your approach.'

'It seems that events have rather overtaken her intention.' Cato nodded to the waiting native. 'Word of our advance is going to reach Isurium a while before we arrive.'

Vellocatus shrugged. Before Cato could continue, they were interrupted by Belmatus who spoke quickly and harshly.

'He demands an answer.'

'Then we'd better tell him the truth.'

The translator shot Cato an anxious look. 'I don't think that's wise.'

'What choice have we got? If we don't tell the truth then it looks like we're invading Brigantian territory. Tell him we're here at the request of his queen. She has asked to speak to a representative of the Roman governor.' Cato lowered his voice. 'Don't mention anything about who we have come to arrest. They'll guess our true purpose quickly enough, but let's not give it to them on a plate. Tell him what I said.'

There was another exchange, more lengthy this time and more heated, before Belmatus gritted his teeth and thrust his arm out, pointing south, back the way the column had marched.

'Let me guess,' Cato said drily. 'He demands that we turn back and return to the province.'

Vellocatus nodded. 'He says that he has heard nothing about Cartimandua's request. In any case, he takes his orders from his brother. If your column continues then the Brigantes will take it as a declaration of war.'

222

Cato stiffened. That changed the situation rather unpleasantly. This had gone beyond the scope of his authority. He must report back to Tribune Otho and allow him to consider matters before deciding how to proceed.

'Hrrrmm.' Cato cleared his throat. 'Tell Belmatus that I will convey his message to my commander, and tell him that we mean no harm to his people. Remind him that we come here at the request of Queen Cartimandua, our ally. I advise him to confirm that with her before he carries out any action that his people might have cause to regret.'

Vellocatus spoke and there was a sharp retort from the other native that seemed to strike the translator like a blow. He turned to Cato and winced. 'My cousin says that if your column takes another step in the direction of Isurium then he, and the warriors of his tribe, will cut you down and take your heads as trophies.'

The warrior had been watching Cato closely as his words were conveyed and now he smiled coldly and drew his finger slowly across his throat. Then he turned his horse round and spurred it back towards his men waiting on the crest of the hill. The sun was setting on the horizon and even though the evening was warm and close, Cato felt a cold shiver trace its way down his spine.

CHAPTER TWENTY-TWO

'How could your queen possibly think it a good idea to conceal from your people the fact that she had asked for our assistance?' Tribune Otho demanded.

Vellocatus took a moment to unpick the convoluted question before he replied. 'As I explained to Legate Quintatus, her position is delicate. Our people are divided over our relations with Rome. Most want peace, but there are many who hate or fear you. They feel that they must join those that continue to fight against the invader. Or else Brigantia will be swallowed up like all the tribes to the south of our lands. My queen decided that it would be best not to let her court know that she had asked for your help. At least not until you were on the march.'

Otho rubbed his weary eyes as he digested the explanation. Around the table the other senior officers of his column sat in silence. Cato tucked a finger under the hem of his tunic and pulled the cloth away from his clammy skin. It was stifling in the tribune's tent thanks to the fact that Otho had ordered the tent flaps to be closed to keep the insects out. Even so, a small swirling cloud of gnats and mosquitoes clustered around the flames of the oil lamps and with a muttered curse Macro raised a hand to swat away those that came too close to his face.

The tribune, however, was ignoring the nuisance. His attention was fixed on the young Brigantian nobleman. 'Will your cousin really attack us if we attempt to continue our march tomorrow?'

'If?' Horatius interrupted. 'Sir, we have orders to—'

'I know my damn orders, thank you!' Otho snapped. 'And I am in command here. I make the decisions. I'll thank you to remember that, Prefect Horatius.'

The sudden outburst was the first time Cato had seen the young tribune's temper and he and the other officers sat still and waited for the moment to pass. Otho sucked in a calming breath and gestured to his translator. 'So, will your cousin fight us?'

Vellocatus closed his eyes for a moment and frowned before he looked up and replied. 'I don't know. Belmatus is a hothead. Always has been. But he takes his lead from Venutius. He's the one you should be concerned about. If he has given his brother the order to fight, then fight he will.'

'But that would be foolish,' Prefect Horatius interrupted. 'He has no more than fifty men. If he attempts to stop us we'll wipe him out.'

'And that's bound to be well received at the court of Queen Cartimandua,' said Cato with heavy irony, so that Horatius could not miss the point. 'Before her Roman allies have even reached Isurium they'll have the blood of her people on their swords. I can imagine how that will play out. Venutius will lay the responsibility for their deaths at our door and say that this is proof of Rome's intention to wage war on the Brigantes, and that his people have no choice but to join Caratacus's struggle against us.' He turned to the tribune. 'Sir, we have to make sure that there is no bloodshed tomorrow, at least as far as we can help it.'

Otho rubbed his brow slowly. 'Are you suggesting that if we are opposed then we should turn back?'

'Not at all, sir. If we turn back Venutius will claim the credit for it and it will weaken the queen's position.'

'Either way, the situation at Isurium gets worse for us. We are damned if we do push on, and damned if we don't.'

Cato repressed his irritation. He disliked this kind of categoric thinking. It forced all real possibilities of outcome into two channels and limited the scope for action as a result.

'No, sir. I'm just pointing out that the decision isn't between going on and turning back. Either of those will damage any support that we have amongst the Brigantes. Therefore neither is the best course of action.'

'Then what is?' Otho demanded in frustration.

'We must continue our advance tomorrow,' Cato said patiently. 'Besides, as Horatius has pointed out, those are our orders – unless the

225

legate has included a contingency against proceeding if we are opposed.'

Otho shook his head.

'Then we go on,' Cato said firmly. 'But we must not provoke any violence. We must avoid it at all costs.'

Horatius leaned forward. 'At all costs short of defending ourselves.'

'That's right,' Cato conceded. 'But if any blows are struck, then we have to ensure that theirs is the first.'

There was a brief pause before Macro spoke. 'The lads ain't going to like that. They're not trained to stand there and take it from the enemy.'

'But they aren't the enemy,' Cato responded. 'Not yet, at least, and that's how we want to keep things. If it comes to a fight then we may lose a few men to start with. Better that than be the cause of a war that costs many more lives, all because our men lack the discipline to see this through.' He turned his attention back to the tribune. 'Sir, you need to change the marching order tomorrow. If we are confronted, then we're going to need the right men in the vanguard. Men we can trust to do exactly as they are told.'

Tribune Otho gave a thin smile. 'Your men, I suppose?'

'Yes, sir.'

'But haven't they something of an unfortunate reputation amongst the natives? I'd heard that your men are a bloodthirsty lot, Cato. Hardly the sort we can entrust with keeping the peace.'

'That's the point, sir. Their reputation will march ahead of them. When Belmatus and his men see the Blood Crows' standard at the head of the column, it may cause them to think twice before they engage us.'

'It's not their side that concerns me. What if you can't control your men? What if they strike first?'

'They won't,' Cato said firmly. 'I'll pick the men myself, and make sure they understand what I require of them. I trust them, sir. So can you.'

Otho stared at Cato and weighed up the choices available to him. At length he folded his hands together and glanced round at the other officers. 'Any comment?'

No one responded and there was a short silence before Otho sighed. 'Then it seems I am obliged to continue the advance towards Isurium.

Given the situation, we will march as if in enemy territory. Besides the nightly fortifications, we'll double the guard on the camp. We'll also advance in close formation. On the morrow, Prefect Cato and half of his cohort will lead the vanguard. Prefect Horatius, your men will guard the flanks of the column. Gentlemen, make sure that your officers tell their men that it is vital they not let themselves be provoked by the tribesmen. Nor, if we pass any settlements, are they to take anything from the natives. If there is any theft, any violence, then I will shit on the man responsible, and his commanding officer, from a very great height. Do I make myself clear?'

The officers nodded and muttered their assent.

Otho turned his eyes back to Cato. 'You'll be leading the way. If anything happens, I'll hold you directly responsible, Prefect. If a conflict breaks out between Rome and Brigantia, I will make sure that everyone from Legate Quintatus up to the Emperor himself knows that you were the cause of it.'

Cato stared back, struggling to retain his composed expression. Inside he felt contempt for the tribune's readiness to shift responsibility from his shoulders to that of his subordinate. The column was Otho's command. He had his orders. He knew his duty. And yet he shirked from exposing himself to the full consequences of assuming the rank he had been entrusted with. Cato felt disappointed in the man. Much as Otho seemed typical of his class, he had been spirited enough in the battle against Caratacus and his army. Perhaps he had exceeded the measure of confidence that was innate to his nature. That was what ultimately separated the lesser officers from the best, Cato had come to learn. Confidence was the source of competence. Arrogance might also help a man, but it was a brittle quality and founded on delusion rather than good judgement and therefore dangerous. Was that Otho's weak spot? His Achilles' heel?

Then a dark suspicion seeped into Cato's mind. What if he was misjudging the tribune? What if he was deliberately, albeit very cautiously, seeking to undermine his mission? It might be that he was the enemy agent sent to Britannia by Pallas to do all that he could to deny peace to the province. His eagerness to place Cato in charge of the vanguard might be motivated by the chance that Cato would be amongst the first to perish if there was a confrontation with the tribesmen. It would be a most economical solution, Cato thought with a touch of admiration. Pallas would have provoked the war with Brigantia that he wanted and the elimination of his prey at one stroke. Otho's column would be forced to withdraw and Macro could be disposed of later.

Cato took a long deep breath before he responded to his commanding officer. 'I will do my duty, sir. I will not provide the excuse for a new war.'

'I'm delighted to hear it,' Otho replied flatly. 'Now, unless there's any other matter that anyone wants to raise? No? Then you're dismissed.'

The officers rose from their stools and left the tent. Macro let out a relieved puff as they emerged into the cool night. Above them the sky was completely clear and the stars glimmered like tiny gems. A half-moon hung low in the sky, not far above the line of the hills, and by its light they could just make out a single horseman watching over the Roman camp from the nearest crest. The other officers turned and strode back towards their units. Macro and Cato lingered a moment a short distance from the tribune's headquarters tent.

'What are you thinking?' asked Macro. 'Is there going to be trouble tomorrow?'

'Who knows? All I can do is play my part in seeing that our side doesn't cause it.'

'Yes. Nice of the tribune to finger you for the job.'

Cato gave a dry chuckle. 'It was my idea. I'll take responsibility for it.'

Macro glanced at his friend. The pale glow of the moon made the prefect's skin look cold, like marble. 'You take care, lad. I don't care what you said back in the tent. If one of them barbarians comes at you tomorrow then take no risks. Skewer the bastard before he gets the chance to do the same.'

Cato's lips parted in a quick smile. 'I'll have to see about that.' His expression hardened. 'Actually, it's not just the danger from the barbarians that concerns me.'

'What do you mean?'

They were interrupted by the soft laughter of the tribune's wife, carrying easily to their ears. Four of the tribune's bodyguards stood silently by the entrance to the tent, within listening distance. Cato steered his friend away from the tent. 'Not here. I think it's time we had a little drink.'

Macro's eyes twinkled in the moonlight. 'Ah! Now, you're talking.'

Then he grasped the true import behind Cato's words and his shoulders sagged a little as they turned to make their way across to the small wagon parked in the corner of the camp.

A brazier lit the open area in front of the wine merchant's wagons and a modest crowd stood, or sat, in small clusters as they sipped from simple clay beakers and talked in the quiet manner of soldiers who were weary from the day's march but broadly content with their lot. The men parted to let the two officers through to the counter set up a short distance from the side of the wagon. Septimus's slave was busy serving customers while his master stood to one side mixing cheap wine with water.

'We'll have two cups,' Cato announced as he reached into his purse and took out a few brass coins. 'Decent wine, mind you.'

Septimus had looked up the moment he recognised the prefect's voice. He lowered the jug he was holding and smiled obsequiously. 'Alas, no wine, my dear sirs. Only posca, carefully blended with fresh spring water by my own hand. Most refreshing.'

'We want wine,' Macro insisted.

Septimus raised his hands and shrugged his regret. 'I cannot, on the orders of his excellency, Tribune Otho. He does not wish any man under his command to become drunk. So watered wine it is. Or no wine.' Septimus lowered his voice, just enough so that he could still be heard by the nearest soldiers. 'But, for my special customers, dear sirs, there is always wine. I have a few choice jars in my wagon, if you are interested?'

Cato nodded and Septimus casually waved them in the direction of the end of the wagon. Some of the nearest men shot glances at their superiors and exchanged brief grumbles about the privileges of rank before returning to their original muted conversations. Septimus led the two officers to the tailgate and reached through the leather flaps of the cover to extract a small jar. He gestured at it occasionally as he spoke.

'It's best if we keep this brief. What's the matter?'

'You saw the men watching us earlier in the day?'

Septimus nodded.

'They're threatening to block our way tomorrow.'

'I heard as much from your Decurion Miro. He was here a short time ago, trying to drown his sorrows.'

'He's not going to get far down that road on posca,' said Macro.

'Just as well. Don't think the man would like a hangover on top of his other woes.' Septimus turned his attention back to Cato. 'So?'

Cato hesitated a moment. 'Otho's looking for an excuse to turn the column round.' He briefly recounted the briefing that he and Macro had attended at headquarters.

'I see . . . And you think there may be more to it than a case of rattled nerves?'

'The tribune didn't lack for courage in his first battle,' Macro pointed out. 'He'd hardly turn tail because a sorry-arsed bunch of tribesmen told him not to trespass on their turf.'

'Exactly,' said Cato. 'I think there's more to it than that.'

Septimus scratched his nose. 'You think he's our man? Pallas's agent?'

'He could be. He's in a perfect position to make sure this mission fails, long before we even get close enough to Caratacus to take him into our custody.'

'That's true,' Septimus conceded. 'And the fact that he's keen to put you in harm's way would seem to support your interpretation. But it's hardly conclusive proof.'

'He has to play this carefully,' Cato continued. 'Whoever turns out to be the agent has to cover his tracks. Not only to protect himself, but to protect Pallas. If there's a crisis here in Britannia, and someone can trace the origins back to the Emperor's freedman then Pallas is going to get nailed to a cross, and all those associated with him.'

'I hardly think that extends to all associated with him. Not the Emperor's wife, nor Nero.'

'You think not? He had Messalina put to death for plotting against him. And Claudius loved her. He married Agrippina for political reasons as much as anything else. If it was proven that she had acted with Pallas in attempting to undermine the Emperor then I'm not so sure Pallas would be the only one for the chop.' Cato paused. 'Anyway, as I said, Pallas's agent cannot afford to act in the open. He has to be cautious. Right now, that makes Otho a likely suspect. Unless you know anything you haven't shared with us.'

'I'm no closer to the truth than you are,' Septimus admitted. 'It's possible that the agent is not even in the column. It could be someone back at Viroconium. The legate, for example.'

'I don't think so,' Cato decided. 'Quintatus came clean about being told to make life difficult for Macro and me.'

Macro snorted. 'And that makes you less suspicious of him?'

'Precisely,' said Septimus. 'Look here, Prefect Cato. We're dealing with Pallas and his circuit of agents. They've every bit as cunning and deadly as anyone used by Narcissus. And I know what they're capable of. It could be Otho. It could be his wife . . .'

'What?' Macro snorted. 'You think she cut down two of my men and set Caratacus free?'

'Why not? Can you think of anyone less likely to put two men on their guard if they were approached by her? You really think that there aren't any female imperial agents? By Jupiter's cock, you've got a lot to learn, Centurion Macro! And you'd better learn it fast if you don't want anyone to cut your throat.' He paused, and moderated his tone. 'Of course I suspect her. And anyone else who has the means to do what Pallas wants. That could be Otho, his wife, Horatius, almost anyone.'

'Even you?' Macro growled.

Septimus scowled. 'I serve Narcissus. He serves the Emperor. That makes me above suspicion. About the only people I don't suspect are you two. If only because your lives are in danger from the man we're looking for. Or woman,' he added.

'The way I'm feeling about your boss Narcissus right now, I might as well be Pallas's agent. I'd happily do you and Narcissus in just to get you off our backs, no matter what happened to the empire as a result.'

The two men glared at each other in the baleful gloom of the moonlight and Cato eased himself away from the wagon. 'This isn't getting us anywhere. I've said what I've come to say. You should keep a close eye on Otho. That's what I think.'

'Duly noted. Now, I'd better get back to my customers, before someone starts wondering why we've got so much to talk about.'

231

Septimus shoved the jar back into the wagon and moved towards his counter, raising his voice a little. 'I am sorry, dear sirs, if my price is too high. I had assumed Roman officers had sufficient coin to live like gentlemen.' He added with a critical note to his voice, 'Things are not always what they seem.'

The two officers nodded curtly to him and threaded their way back through the crowd and away from the makeshift inn.

'A fat lot of use that was, talking to him,' Macro complained.

'Yes,' Cato said softly. 'Not helpful . . . Not helpful at all.'

CHAPTER TWENTY-THREE

Cato sat silently in his saddle as he cast his eyes over the men he had selected for the mounted vanguard. There were fifty of them, standing by their horses as they waited for him to address them. He had given orders for their kit to be carried on the baggage carts so that they would be unburdened and ready to respond to any threat. Most were Thracians, men who had followed him into battle before. Their discipline had been vouched for by their squadron commanders. A handful were drawn from the recent intake of Batavians who had proven themselves reliable.

'They look like good men,' Cato said quietly to Decurion Miro, standing by his side.

'Yes, sir. Our best. More than a match for that mob on the hill.'

Both men's gaze shifted upwards to where a thin line of horsemen stood on a ridge less than a mile away. They had changed position during the night and now stretched across the track that the column would have to climb when they broke camp. That task was already well under way. The wooden palisade had been taken down and the pointed stakes packed on to the wagons. The last section of the rampart was being swiftly shovelled back into the ditch so that only the raised spoil marked the outline of the previous night's camp. The tents had been struck and the last of them were being tied over the saddle packs of the column's mules. The draught animals were hitched to the wagons and carts and the drivers steered them into line. Ahead and behind, the infantry were forming up, marching yokes resting against their shoulders. The cavalry of Horatius's cohort and the balance of the Blood Crows had formed up on the flanks and rear of the column, no more than twenty paces from the infantry. Poppaea Sabina's carriage was positioned in the middle of the short baggage train, with a section of legionaries assigned to protect her.

'Let's hope we don't have to put it to the test,' Cato responded. Then he cleared his throat and spoke formally. 'Thank you, Decurion. You may join the main column now.'

'Sir?' Miro turned to him.

'I'll take command here. You'll be in command of the rest of the cohort, until further notice.' Cato had been anticipating this moment. He had already made his mind up to exclude the decurion from the vanguard. Miro's nerves the previous day had betrayed his unsuitability for the job. Cato needed men who could be relied on to be steady in testing circumstances. But he had no desire to say as much to the decurion. Even though Miro lacked the correct temperament for command, or even the task at hand, he was a competent enough officer and did not deserve to be offended. He had risen in rank as high as he was going to go and would serve out his enlistment as a decurion. His value to Cato lay in him serving contentedly in that capacity.

Miro hesitated and Cato smiled patiently. 'I need someone I can rely on to take over if anything happens to me. Do you understand?'

The decurion nodded and then saluted. 'Yes, sir. You can count on me.'

'Very well.' Cato returned the salute.

Miro turned and briskly made his way to where the rest of the cohort was waiting for the column to set off. Cato turned his attention back to the men of the vanguard.

'You all know why you were picked for this duty! You are the best men in the cohort. And that marks you out from every other cavalry unit in the army. There is no finer cohort than the Second Thracian – the Blood Crows. But that honour comes with a price. Our reputation has been hard won over the years that the cohort has been campaigning in Britannia. And like all reputations, what takes years to build can be torn down in a single moment of disgrace . . .' Cato paused to look sternly at his men. 'That I will not allow. Today we may face a stern test of our self-discipline and courage. I want every man here to understand what I require of him. And that is, absolute obedience. Whatever happens, however you are goaded or provoked, you will ignore it. You will not react. You will do nothing unless I explicitly

234

order it. I do not care if some stinking, hairy Brigantian goatherd leaps up into your saddle and fucks you in the arse. If it happens, it happens, and if you so much as wince, then I'll have you shovelling the shit from the latrine of Centurion Macro's cohort for the rest of your days!'

There was a smattering of laughter at the comment, and Cato blessed the rivalry between the two units that had served together for the best part of a year. Although he had made a joke of it, he knew his men would heed his stricture all the more avidly for fear of being shamed in front of their comrades.

'Blood Crows!' His smile faded. 'Mount!'

The horsemen turned towards their saddles, paused for the standard silent count of one-two-three and then swung themselves up into their saddles and took up their reins to steady their mounts and dress their ranks. When they were ready, Cato turned his horse towards the front of the column and swept his arm forward.

'In column of fours, advance!'

They walked past the infantry of Horatius's cohort and then began to pass the men of Macro's cohort who would back them up in the event of a fight. Macro was waiting at the head of the First Century and saluted as his friend approached.

'Good luck, sir.'

'And you, Centurion.'

A formal exchange, and yet both men were conscious of the deep bond they shared. How many times over the years had they faced such moments? Cato wondered. And yet this was different. A new kind of courage was required to hold back all the training that had taught them to strike first at an enemy. Training and an instinct for self-preservation, thought Cato.

'If anything goes wrong, I want you to be the one who tells Julia.'

'Perish the thought, sir.'

'Interesting choice of words.' Cato smiled and continued forward on to the track until the rearmost rank of the vanguard was ten paces ahead of Macro's cohort.

'Blood Crows! Halt!'

The horsemen drew up and their mounts stood ready, ears twitching, and the occasional thud or scrape of a hoof on the packed earth of the track. There was nothing to do now until the command was given for the column to advance. The sun had already risen and was washing the landscape with warm glow. The tribesmen waiting ahead of them were bathed in the same light, which somehow made them seem larger than life to Cato's eyes. He wondered if it was simply the tension gnawing at his stomach. Even though he could not quite believe that Belmatus and his handful of men would really sacrifice themselves so willingly to start a war, he could not still his nerves. Something was not quite right about the situation, and he could not pin the doubt down.

There was only a brief delay before the last element of the column was in position and then a horn sounded through the morning air, a clear, carrying note that echoed back off the slopes of the closest hills.

Cato filled his lungs and called over his shoulder, 'Blood Crows! Advance!'

With a click of his tongue and a gentle nudge of his heels he urged his mount to walk forward, eyes fixed on the tribesmen blocking his path no more than half a mile ahead. The air filled with the clop of hoofs, the dull pounding of nailed boots and the rumble of the baggage train. Above, flights of swifts whipped through the air in search of their first meal of the day, some soaring above while others flashed between the shrubs and longer clumps of grass, speckled with yellow and white flowers. All of which imposed themselves on Cato's heightened senses as he steadily climbed the gentle rise to the crest of the hill where Belmatus and his men were waiting.

He could already pick their leader out. The warrior sat on his stallion in the middle of the track, hand on hip in a haughty pose that Cato had come to recognise as typical of the men who led the tribes of the island. For a moment he wished he had Vellocatus at hand to translate if there was any exchange of words. But Vellocatus had been ordered to travel in Poppaea's carriage where he would be out of sight. The tribune had been right to do that, Cato reflected. The sight of one of their own, riding with the Romans, could well stir the passions of the natives into an act of violence that all would regret. And, Cato reasoned, there was no need for a translator. He knew exactly what he must do and words would be superfluous, and possibly dangerous in such a situation. At the root of it all Cato recognised that he was only wishing for the man's presence because he felt exposed riding at the front of the column alone. His heart was beating quickly and he felt the blood racing through his veins as he maintained a composed air and stared straight ahead.

Then, when he was no more than a hundred paces from the crest, a great roar filled the air, startling birds into flight. Beyond the small party of waiting horsemen, the ground was suddenly alive with more men, hundreds of them, surging forward to swell the ranks of the riders. A cold stab of fear thrust up inside Cato's chest but he clenched his jaw and continued advancing, true to his orders. He looked back quickly and noted with pride that none of his men had faltered, even though they had readied their spears and raised their shields to cover their bodies. Cato did the same with his own shield and shifted his reins to the right hand to remove the temptation to rest it on the pommel of his sword.

The tribesmen made no attempt to move forward but stood and jeered, brandishing fists and weapons. As Cato closed on them, a thin young warrior darted forward and turned his back to the oncoming Romans. Grasping the hem of his tunic, he hauled it up to reveal his buttocks and then bent forward to thrust the pale cheeks towards Cato. He stifled a smirk at the youngster's hubris and pretended to ignore the gesture. The youth darted aside at the last moment and left Cato face to face with Belmatus.

The Brigantian nobleman stood his ground and Cato subtly tweaked his reins so as to pass just to the side of the man. No words were spoken, only their eyes clashed, a steely, unbending exchange of glares, and then Cato passed by him. Beyond lay a mass of shouting, gesticulating tribesmen, and Cato looked over their heads as he walked his horse on. Like all cavalry mounts it had long since been battle-trained and was inured to the sounds of shouting, the blasts of horns and the clash of weapons. Even so, the beast snorted and jerked its neck as it raised its head away from the men in its path.

Cato felt a man brush past his leg and tried not to flinch. No attempt was made to stop his horse, nor to lay a hand on it, or him. Then there was a flicker of movement to his right and some muck landed on his chest, splattering his chin. The smell of shit assaulted his nostrils, but he forced himself not to react. Not even to brush it off. Then he was through the line of tribesmen and emerged, unscathed, on to the crest of the hill. Before him the track continued into the hills of Brigantia. He rode on a short distance before looking back and saw that his men were holding their discipline, ignoring the abuse and filth thrown at them. Then he caught sight of Belmatus, who had shifted to the side of the track. The nobleman turned and saw Cato at the same time and Cato could see the frustration in his expression.

At once, all the tension seemed to drain from Cato's body and he felt an urgent desire to laugh out loud as he realised that Belmatus and his men had been given precisely the same orders as he had. They, too, had been instructed not to land the first blow, but were free to do anything short of that to provoke the Romans to violence. Now that the bluff had been exposed, that was not going to happen, Cato thought with relief.

The column trudged forward through the heart of the baying mob but not one blow was exchanged, not one Roman turned to hurl abuse back at the Brigantians, and a short time later the vanguard left Belmatus and his men in its wake. From the top of the next hill Cato turned aside to look back and saw the nobleman wave his arm angrily at his men until they fell silent and stood still, watching the backs of the Roman soldiers as they marched off across the serene sprawl of the countryside. Cato took out his canteen and rinsed off as much of the shit as he could. The next time, he might not be so lucky, he mused. It would be an arrow, spear or slingshot that was hurled at him.

The column continued into the hills that stretched into the distance on both sides and the natives kept pace with them on either flank. There were no more attempts to stand in their way and that night the two forces set up camp less than a mile apart. The sprawl of the Brigantian fires illuminated the natives in a ruddy glow as they gathered about the flames and talked in the animated way of the Celts. Their voices carried to the orderly lines of the ramparts where Roman soldiers patrolled in silence, stopping from time to time to cast a wary eye on their neighbours, before resuming their steady pace as their eyes scanned the darkness for any sign of danger. As the night drew on, the natives fell to singing. At first the tunes were raucous and good-spirited, but by and by they fell to more gentle, soulful songs that sounded sorrowful to Cato's ear as he walked the section of the perimeter entrusted to his men.

In the normal course of events it was the duty of the optio in charge of the watch to ensure that the men remained alert, but Cato had not been able to sleep. Taking up his cloak he had made his way on to the sentry walk and passed from post to post, giving the password each time he was challenged. Cato approached one of the corner platforms where the dark mass of a ballista loomed against the lighter shades of the landscape, barely lit by the distant curved gleam of a crescent moon, no wider than the lethal curve of the daggers Cato had once seen in Judaea. He heard a muttered exchange between two men and his lips pressed together in an angry line as he prepared to berate the sentries. Then he made out Macro's voice.

'Tuneful lot, ain't they? What are they singing about now?'

There was a pause before the other man replied. 'It's a lament . . . About the wife of a warrior waiting for her man to return from battle. She doesn't know it, but her man has fallen. A hero's death. She stands at the gate of her village with the other women and searches for the face of her beloved amongst those returning, until the last of them has passed. And then she knows . . .'

Cato recognised the voice of Vellocatus as he spoke. The Brigantian was interrupted by a gruff snort.

'Not very cheerful,' said Macro. 'Still, the tune isn't too bad. Not too bad at all. You'll have to teach it to me some day . . .'

He turned as he sensed Cato's presence and nodded a greeting as he recognised his friend. 'Evening, sir.'

'Centurion.' Cato nodded and his eyes shifted to the native translator. The man's features were just discernible in the faint glow of the moon. Enough to see the pained expression as he glanced towards the distant campfires. 'Anything to report?'

'No. Belmatus and his boys are being as good as gold. And they're providing a bit of entertainment.'

'Let's hope they continue to behave.' Cato stepped up to the palisade beside them and looked out over the intervening ground. 'I wonder if they're going to keep this up all the way to Isurium.'

'The singing I can live with. But, if they want a fight, then they'll come off worst.'

'Unless they're reinforced. Besides, the further we go into their territory, the longer the retreat, if it comes to that.'

'Do you know,' Macro responded, 'I had worked that out for myself.'

Cato was irritated with himself for the unnecessary comment. It betrayed his nerves. He flashed his friend a quick smile. 'Sorry.'

The three men fell silent as they listened to the soft sound of the singing drifting through the night. Then Cato was aware that Vellocatus was quietly humming along with the melody and it occurred to him that the translator would rather be with his compatriots than here on the rampart. He cleared his throat.

'Why are you here, Vellocatus?'

The Brigantian turned to him sharply. 'What do you mean?'

'I mean, why are you with us rather than with them?' Cato gestured towards the distant figures gathered round the campfires.

Vellocatus looked at the Roman officer shrewdly. 'You mean, why am I helping you rather than my compatriots?'

'Yes.'

'I am here on the orders of my queen.'

'Why did she choose you?'

'Because I speak your tongue. Because she trusts me. Those are reasons enough. Besides, she ordered me to. I have no choice in the matter.'

'We all have choices. You could have chosen to side with those who would rather not hand Caratacus over to us. You could have joined the faction of Venutius. But you didn't. I'm curious to know why.'

The other man casually rubbed the back of his neck. 'In truth, I am a shield-bearer of Venutius. Something of an honour in our tribe. I will not deny I was proud that he chose me. Venutius is a great warrior. As courageous as he is strong. Our people admire him. That is why he came to the attention of Cartimandua in the first place. That is why she took him as her consort. With Venutius at her side she purposed to strengthen her hold over our people and unite them.' Vellocatus gave a wry smile. 'Unity is a quality that most of the tribes on this island pay scant heed to, as you Romans may have noticed. If we had placed greater value in uniting against you then your legions would have been driven back into the sea long ago.'

'You think so?' Macro intervened. 'I think our determination to see a job through is more than a match for your unity.'

'Good as your legions are, even they would never be able to overcome the combined might of our tribes. If the Brigantes go to war against Rome, there is a very real prospect that you will be defeated.'

'I think you overestimate your chances, young man.'

'Vellocatus,' Cato turned to face him. 'If what you say is true, then why doesn't every man in your tribe choose to follow Venutius?'

The translator hesitated. 'There are two main factions amongst the Brigantes, the western tribes and those in the east. Venutius comes from the western tribes and there are many there who have ties to the Ordovices. Their sympathies are with Caratacus and his allies. There are some who would willingly fight Rome. That's why the queen chose Venutius for a consort, to hold our people together. She, and I, come from the eastern lands. We have less cause to hate Rome. Besides, there is always the risk of defeat, and the queen is cautious of exposing her people to the consequences. I agree with her.'

'Spoken like a true warrior,' Macro jibed.

Vellocatus stiffened. 'Even a shield-bearer to a hero like Venutius can understand that war is not the answer to everything, Centurion. I saw that my queen was right to tread carefully. The certainty of peace with Rome is better than the risk of defeat and the crushing of our people under your heel. I have no desire to share the fate of the Catuvellauni or the Durotriges. Nor do many in our tribe. The queen knows this, and shares their concerns.'

'You seem to know the queen's mind rather well,' Cato said evenly. 'For someone who serves as the shield-bearer of Venutius.'

The young nobleman opened his mouth to reply, but hesitated, then looked away.

Cato sensed he had stepped on troubled ground and needed to proceed more tactfully. He changed the line of enquiry. 'And what does the queen's consort make of her caution?'

'Venutius is a warrior, born and bred. He has led our tribe in battle many times. But being a leader is not the same thing as being a ruler. That requires wisdom along with courage, as I have come to learn through my service to the queen. He is no longer content to be her consort but has ambition to rule in her place so that he can lead his people in a war with Rome, with Caratacus at his side.'

'Caratacus is the not the kind of man to stand at anyone's side,' said

241

Cato. 'He won't be content to let Venutius command your people. That is the role he wants for himself. And another army to oppose us with. He'll fight us to the last drop of blood of any man in Britannia that he can talk into following him. Only Queen Cartimandua stands in his way.'

'Not just her. There are still many of us who are loyal to her,' Vellocatus replied fiercely. 'We'll not stand by and let Ventius take the throne.'

Macro cocked his head. 'Loyal to the queen, but not loyal to your warlord, eh?'

'My duty is to my people, my queen and then Venutius.'

'Very laudable.' Macro nodded to Cato. 'Wouldn't you say?'

'Oh, yes.' Cato replied, and then kept quiet as he waited for the young man to continue. Instead, Vellocatus took one last look at the glow of the fires before he turned back to the two Roman officers.

'I'm exhausted. I shall retire if you don't mind.'

Cato stared fixedly at him and then nodded. 'Of course. Sleep well.'

The Brigantian nobleman nodded curtly and hurried down the interior slope of the rampart before striding in the direction of the headquarters tent.

'Well, well . . .' Macro said softly. 'It seems the lad was caught between two stools. Glad he's come down on the right side, at least as far as we're concerned.'

Cato nodded slowly. 'I think there's more to it than that.'

'What do you mean?'

'There was something in his tone when he spoke about Cartimandua. Did you hear it?'

'I heard what he said.'

'Not quite the same thing.

Macro sucked in a breath. 'For fuck's sake, give it to me straight.'

'I mean that there's more to this than his loyalty to the queen over the loyalty he owes to the man who honoured him with the role of shield-bearer . . .'

Macro considered this for a moment before he swore softly. 'You mean he's taken a shine to the woman?'

'Somewhat more than that. And I think the affection is returned.'

'How can you know that?'

'She sent us someone she could trust, who happens to be the servant of the man who is an ally of Caratacus. Venutius isn't in on the secret of their relationship. Why would he be? I'm sure the queen and Vellocatus are being careful how they play it. You know how easily passions are stirred up amongst the Celts.'

'That I do,' Macro replied with feeling.

'She's been clever.' Cato scratched his chin. 'And Vellocatus hasn't been very honest with us. At least we know that his first loyalty is to Cartimandua.'

'What if you're wrong?' asked Macro. 'What if he's really working for Venutius?'

Cato considered this and then shook his head. 'As I said, there was something in his voice when he spoke about Cartimandua . . . I'm sure of it.'

Macro stretched his shoulders wearily. 'Sweet Jupiter, that must make for an uneasy relationship at Isurium. The queen's playing the boy against her husband. If the truth gets out, that'll put an end to their domestic bliss. And how!'

'Quite.' Cato nodded. 'As if we didn't have enough to deal with as things stand. The last thing we need is a civil war in Brigantia. If the difference of opinion over handing Caratacus into our custody doesn't spark things off, then Cartimandua's infidelity might well be the excuse Venutius needs. And we've got an agent in our own ranks to worry about.'

'Danger on every side then,' Macro mused sourly. 'Sounds about right. Tell me, Cato, what have we ever done that the gods have decided they're going to drop us in the shit right up to our necks at every available opportunity? Eh? Tell me that.'

The singing had come to an end and the natives began to stretch out on the ground, warmed by the dying flames. Cato shrugged.

'The gods play their games, and we play ours, Macro. And it seems there's nothing we can do about it except try to stay alive. That's all.'

CHAPTER TWENTY-FOUR

They reached the Brigantian capital at dusk three days later. Isurium had once been a hill fort whose ditches circled the crest of a steep-sided hill overlooking a river valley. Now the crest was covered with the thatched roofs of scores of huts of varying sizes. A large timber hall had been constructed on the highest point and dominated the fort. A narrow track curved through the lines of ditches and palisades and led down to a large settlement at the foot of the hill. Small farmsteads dotted the surrounding valley.

The shadows were lengthening by the time the Roman column halted half a mile from the track leading up into Isurium. The native force that had shadowed them continued into the settlement while the horsemen climbed the hill and disappeared from view amongst the complex of earthworks guarding the entrance to the fort. As soon as the column halted, the soldiers began their usual routine. A screen of pickets was sent out to guard their site while their comrades downed packs and took up their picks to start work on the ditch and rampart.

As the shadows lengthened, scores of natives, more daring than most of their tribe, ventured closer for the first view any of them had ever had of the Romans who had swept all before them in the lands to the south. They kept to a safe distance and simply watched as the camp rose from the ground before their eyes. Before the light had completely faded, the palisade was in place and the ballistas were being assembled on strongpoints at each corner.

'I want gate towers constructed tomorrow,' Tribune Otho ordered as he inspected the camp with his senior officers. 'We may be here for several days. Or longer if the situation turns against us.' He turned to Centurion Statillus. 'I want the camp's defences improved as far as possible. We've no caltrops, so we'll have to make do with stakes and whatever other obstacles we can deploy. See to it.'

'Yes, sir.'

They were standing on the rampart nearest Isurium and the dark mass of the hill loomed high above them in the night. The hall was lit by braziers positioned a safe distance from the thatched roofs and in the red hue the structure seemed even larger than it had in natural light. All the officers were looking in the same direction and there was a brief silence before Prefect Horatius cleared his throat and spoke for all of them.

'When are they going to acknowledge us?'

There had been no contact with the queen or any of her officials since the column had arrived and that struck Cato as ominous. He turned to Vellocatus.

'These are your people. Why do you think the queen hasn't sent someone to greet us?'

'I don't know,' Vellocatus admitted. 'But if I was allowed to ride up there, I can find out and report back.'

Otho shook his head. 'No. I need you here in case anyone approaches the camp with a message. If there's nothing by tomorrow morning, then I'll send a small party with you to present greetings from General Ostorius. We'll gauge the queen's mood then. And that of the rest of her court.'

'But I could do it tonight, sir. Right now, if you give the word.'

Otho thought a moment and shook his head. 'Too dark. It might be dangerous to leave the camp. We'll wait until we have light. I wouldn't want to put you at any risk.'

'Risk?' The Brigantian was not fooled. 'You would prefer to keep me hostage, you mean.'

For an instant Cato was sure that the tribune was going to protest but then Otho nodded. 'Of course. You could be leading us into a trap, for all I know. You might not realise it, but that's irrelevant. If your queen, or whoever is in charge, values your life then it might give us something to bargain with. If not, and the Brigantes have betrayed our trust, you will be the first of your people to die. You had better pray to your gods that Cartimandua's guarantee of free passage for my column holds true. In the meantime, you will not leave my side. If you attempt to escape the camp I will assume your motives are treacherous and I will have you executed. Understand?'

Otho issued his threat firmly and the native nobleman simply nodded. Cato arched an eyebrow at the ruthless streak revealed by the young tribune.

'Very well.' Otho turned to address the others. 'We'll set one cohort on watch at a time. Half the men on the ramparts and half resting in the dead ground behind, ready to man the palisade at once if the alarm is raised.'

He sensed the uneasiness of his officers and explained his thinking. 'I know the men are exhausted, but I'd rather be cautious than caught by surprise. We're far beyond the frontier, gentlemen, in the heart of Brigantian territory. Even though they are supposed to be our allies, we've already seen that there is little love for Rome amongst their warriors, some of them at least. So a full cohort will stand each watch. That is my decision. We'll discover the true situation in the morning. One way or another. You are dismissed, gentlemen.'

The party exchanged salutes before Otho strode away with his staff officers, Vellocatus and his personal bodyguards. The remainder waited until their commander was out of earshot before they began to speak quietly.

'I don't like it,' Centurion Acer muttered. 'If we're still at peace with the Brigantians then why haven't they come out to greet us?'

'Any number of reasons,' Cato responded.

Acer rounded on him. 'Such as?'

'Such as, *sir*,' Cato reminded him of the requirement to defer to his rank. He paused to let the point sink in and then continued. 'The queen might want to keep it formal. We arrived too late for her to put on any ceremony. If she's going to make a show of it, then it would better to do it in broad daylight. In front of her people. There's nothing sinister in that.'

'Assuming you're right, sir.'

'If he's not, we'll find out soon enough,' said Macro.

The summons arrived at dawn. A rider approached the camp with a message from the ruler of the Brigantes. Cartimandua requested the attendance of the commander of the Roman column, together with a small party of officers and bodyguards should he feel the need for such protection. The queen gave her word that no harm would come to the Romans while they enjoyed the hospitality of her people. Her guests were to attend on her at noon, in the royal hall atop the hill fort. Once her envoy had received Otho's acknowledgement, he mounted his horse and rode out of the camp.

'Do we trust her, gentlemen?' Otho looked round at the officers in his tent. 'Or do we insist that she comes to us?'

'I don't like the look of it, sir,' Horatius spoke up. 'If you go up there and it's a trap, they're going to have hostages.'

'But we already have one of our own,' Otho pointed out. 'Vellocatus.'

'Which gives us a slight advantage, sir. If they take some of ours then we lose the advantage.'

Cato cleared his throat. 'Which is why I don't consider it a good idea to keep Vellocatus here, sir. If the Brigantes think that we're holding one of their noblemen against his will it might encourage them to do the same if the opportunity arises. We should let him leave the camp, or at least you should take him with you when you meet Cartimandua.'

Otho arched an eyebrow. 'If I go.'

'With respect, sir, you have to.'

'Why is that, Prefect?'

'For two reasons,' Cato explained. 'Firstly, the Brigantes are watching us closely. This is the first military column to march into the heartland. Like it or not, we are being judged by them. If you fail to respond to the queen's summons, it will cause offence. Worse, it will damage her authority, in front of her own people. That will only strengthen the hand of those who support Venutius, and his friend, Caratacus.' Cato paused. 'Then there's the other matter. If we are seen to be too nervous to venture out of the camp and enter the tribal capital, Venutius will accuse us of being cowards. He is sure to use that line when he tries to whip up support for war with Rome.'

Otho nodded thoughtfully as he considered Cato's remarks. 'Then it seems I have no real choice in the matter.'

'You do have a choice, sir,' Horatius protested. 'We're Romans. We don't take orders from barbarians. That's what you tell her. You order her to come to us. That will show 'em who is in charge. And it means we won't have to take any risks.'

Otho smiled thinly. 'For a diplomat you make a damn fine soldier, Horatius. Therein lies your problem. We're here to take possession of Caratacus, at the request of Queen Cartimandua, our ally. It ill becomes us to treat an ally so shamefully, even if they happen to be, as you say, a barbarian. For that reason I shall be leaving you here, in command of the camp, when I meet Cartimandua. You will be under strict orders to remain behind these walls until I return.'

Horatius pressed his lips together as he controlled his anger at the rebuff, before he replied stiffly, 'Assuming you do return, sir.'

'If I do not return by nightfall, or I do not send word that I am safe, then you are to assume that I, and those with me, have been taken prisoner. In which case you will not enter into negotiations for our release. You will demand it. If that fails then send a message back to report to Legate Quintatus. The column must remain here until instructed otherwise. Clear?'

'Yes, sir,' Horatius replied with a show of reluctance.

'Good.' Otho looked round at the others in the tent. 'I will take Prefect Cato with me, as I need a man with quick wits. And you, Centurion Macro, just in case there is any trouble and I need a man with a ready sword. Vellocatus will come too, and a pair of my bodyguards, and also my wife.'

'Your wife?' Macro raised his eyebrows. 'I'm sorry, sir. Your wife?'

'Why not? As Prefect Cato has pointed out, we cannot be seen to be nervous of these people. It will create a favourable impression amongst the locals. I doubt even a barbarian would have the effrontery to attack an unarmed woman.'

'Sir, there's a reason why they are called barbarians,' Macro protested.

'Stuff and nonsense!' Otho dismissed the objection with a curt flick of his hand. 'I've made my decision. I want you, the prefect, and my guards to be smartly turned out. I want the natives' first impression to be as favourable as possible. Horatius?'

'Sir?'

'You'll have your orders in writing before I leave. And you'll obey them to the letter.'

'Yes, sir.'

'That's all, gentlemen. Dismissed.'

'What the fuck is he playing out?' Macro growled as they strode back through their camp to their tents. 'It's madness to bring his wife along. What does he think this is? Some bloody picnic in the Tuscan countryside?'

Cato shook his head. 'He's right. It demonstrates that the tribune trusts Cartimandua. If he's wrong, and there's trouble, then I doubt Poppaea Sabina is going to be much safer back here in the camp. The column won't be able to hold out for long once the Brigantes mobilise their warriors.'

Macro looked up and pointed. 'There's one who's getting out while he can.'

Cato followed the direction Macro indicated and saw the wine merchant's wagon a short distance from the gate facing Isurium. A small cart, harnessed to two mules, stood beside the wagon and Septimus was loading a heavy wine jar on to the back of the cart. He heaved it into position and stopped to mop his brow before he caught sight of the two officers approaching him. An anxious expression flitted across his face before he slipped back into his role as a wine trader.

'What's this?' Macro demanded. 'Leaving us already?'

'Hardly, my dear Centurion!' Septimus called back, affecting his tradesman's patter. 'I would never abandon such good customers. No, I seek to trade with the natives. Wine for furs or, better still, silver and gold.'

Cato glanced into the cart and saw several large jars and twenty or so small vessels, each marked with the name of the wine inside. 'You're selling them the cheap wine, then?'

'Of course. Gives me a chance to shift the stuff no Roman in his right mind would touch.' Septimus's eyes glanced round quickly to make sure that no one would overhear them. 'I saw that native enter the camp earlier. What's happening?'

Macro jerked his thumb in the direction of headquarters. 'Their queen's sent for the tribune. He's going up there at noon. Together with Cato and me, a few men, and his wife.'

'His wife?' Septimus's eyes widened in surprise.

Macro held up a hand. 'Don't ask. Apparently, it's a good idea.'

'So what are you really up to?' asked Cato.

'You know how it is with wine and the Celts. If anything is going to loosen their tongues, it's this stuff.' Septimus patted one of his jars. 'I'll try it out on those around the queen. With luck someone might let some useful information slip. The trail's gone cold on my traitor.'

'If you hear anything, make sure you share it with us,' said Cato.

'Same goes for you two.'

Macro affected a horrified expression. 'What, don't you trust us?'

'Just reminding you that we're on the same side, Centurion.'

'Are we? Which side would that be? You're working for Narcissus. The traitor is working for Pallas. On top of that we have Caratacus, and Venutius. And then there's Vellocatus and his queen.' Macro scratched his head theatrically. 'There are so many sides in this I'm losing track.'

The imperial agent stared back coldly. 'There are only two sides. Those who serve the true interests of Rome, and those who oppose them. That's the plain and simple reality, Macro.'

Macro leaned forward and whispered menacingly, 'Where your dad is concerned there's no such thing as plain and simple reality, my friend.'

Septimus glared back and then smiled. 'Watch your back, Macro. You too, Prefect.' Then he turned away and made for the rear of the wagon to fetch another jar. Macro clenched his fists and his jaw set into the familiar line that meant he was bracing himself for a fight. Cato recognised the symptoms well enough and steered Macro away from the back of the cart.

'Come on. There's no time for this. We've got to make sure our kit is spick and span for the royalty.'

Macro shifted reluctantly and cracked his jaw. 'All right. I'll leave it, for now. But next time that bastard makes a crack about watching our backs, I'll have him.'

'Of course you will,' Cato said soothingly and his friend shot him such an angry look that Cato could not help laughing at his expression. 'That's the spirit. Now save it for the enemy, eh?'

CHAPTER TWENTY-FIVE

As the sun blazed down from its zenith, the gates of the camp opened and Tribune Otho led his small party out of the camp. At his side rode his wife, her stola hitched up around her pale legs as she sat astride her saddle. In Rome she would have insisted on a litter, Cato thought wryly. But here on the frontier such niceties were unheard of and Poppaea sat erectly and tried to affect as much grace and dignity as she could. Behind them rode Cato, Macro, Vellocatus and two of the tribune's bodyguards. All three officers had polished breastplates and helmets with fresh red-stained crests that stood up stiffly in the warm summer air. Each man wore a clean cloak flicked back from the shoulders to avoid the stifling embrace of the scarlet wool. The Brigantian nobleman had chosen a plain green tunic and check-patterned breeches.

Cato and Macro wore their medal harnesses and the silver discs gleamed in the sunlight. A large gold torc encircled Macro's neck, a trophy he had taken from the brother of Caratacus whom he had killed in single combat shortly after he and Cato first landed on the island many years before. It was a valuable item and Macro usually kept it wrapped in a cloth at the bottom of his kitbag, away from the prying eyes of camp servants and any light-fingered soldiers. Their decorations were in stark contrast to the unadorned chest of their commanding officer, but Otho affected a proud air that he no doubt hoped would impress the natives as much as the gold and silver awards for valour that adorned his subordinates.

The small party was watched by Horatius and the other officers from the gatehouse that had been constructed that morning, but neither Otho nor the others deigned to turn back for one last glance towards the safety of the camp. Instead they fixed their gaze on the settlement before them, nestling beneath the steep grassy slopes of the hill upon which the fortified capital of the Brigantes stood. They were not the only party making for the court of the queen, Cato noticed. Another small band was climbing the track from the settlement ahead of them and two more groups approached from the direction of the hills to the north. He pointed them out to Macro.

'A gathering of the nobles?' the centurion wondered.

Cato nodded. 'Caratacus's fate is going to be witnessed by quite an audience, I imagine. Cartimandua wants to make certain that they all get the message that her authority is not to be questioned. And we're here so that her nobles know that she has powerful friends. Isn't that the case, Vellocatus?'

The Brigantian shrugged. 'It does no harm to impress the fact upon those fools who follow Venutius.'

By the time they reached the settlement a small crowd had gathered to watch them pass. They stood in silence, dressed in the worn tunics and leggings of peasants. The warrior caste would be accommodated up in the hill fort, Cato knew. The people who lived in the huts and hovels at the foot of the hill cared little for the distant wars affecting other tribes. Their lives were far more concerned with the daily struggle to feed their families. Some regarded the Romans and their native translator with curiosity, some with suspicion and some with fear but none made any attempt to address them. Macro met the gaze of a teenage girl leaning against the gateposts of the settlement and nodded a subtle greeting to her. She smiled back shyly, until her father cuffed her on the head and shoved her away into the crowd.

Poppaea glanced from side to side and muttered, 'If this is what passes for their capital city then we are surely amongst savages, far beyond the very fringes of the civilised world.'

The tribune shot her a warning look. 'My dear, I would be obliged if you kept such thoughts to yourself. Some of the, uh, savages speak our tongue.'

Cato overheard the exchange and felt a stab of embarrassment as he glanced sidelong at Vellocatus. The younger man pressed his lips tightly together and clenched his fist round the reins but made no attempt to respond, Cato noted approvingly. The kind of man who knew how to bite back on his pride and keep his mouth shut was likely to be an asset in the coming days.

The track continued through the settlement, winding between small clusters of huts and pens holding goats and swine. It was a hot summer day and the smell of animals, sweat and sewage was being cooked to a ripe odour that hung heavily in the still air. The track passed out of the settlement and began to zigzag up the hill towards the fort, four hundred feet above. A small cluster of wide-eyed children followed them a short distance before being called back by their parents, or losing interest now that a steep climb was involved.

As they approached the outer defences of the fort, Cato and Macro cast a professional eye over the earthworks.

'Smaller than that place Legate Vespasian knocked over down south. You remember? That bloody huge fort held by the Durotriges.'

'I remember,' Cato replied. Macro had been wounded at the time and had not taken part in the attack, only seeing it once it had fallen. For Cato it had been very different. He had infiltrated the fort to rescue hostages while the rest of the Second Legion had mounted the main assault. 'This one would be a tougher nut to crack.'

'You think?'

'Much steeper slopes, and any attacker would be exposed to missile fire all the way to the gate complex. It's a good thing the Brigantes are allies. I'd hate to have to try and take this place. It's a well-chosen position – a natural fortress.'

They continued up the slope until they reached the first turn alongside the fort's outer defences. An outlying bastion rose above them and a handful of sentries gazed down at them as they passed by. Fifty paces further on, the track doubled back into a narrow ravine between the earthworks, and ahead lay the gate, a sturdy pair of timber doors on the far side of a drawbridge. Above the gates was a fortified walkway that gave out on to two palisaded mounds each side of the gate. More sentries looked down on them. Now that they had climbed up from the valley floor a welcome breeze was blowing lightly and the yellow banner of the Brigantes billowed above the gate of Isurium. As the cloth rippled, they could clearly see the outline of the black boar at the centre of the banner, seemingly alive with the movement of the material.

253

A small party of warriors holding spears and shields were visible through the opening and Otho turned in his saddle to beckon to Vellocatus.

'I'll need you in a moment.'

The other man nodded and spurred his horse forward, edging past Poppaea and taking up position beside the tribune. The drawbridge clattered under their hoofs as the riders crossed the ditch and passed through the gate. A line of men barred their way and Otho halted just in front of them and boldly announced, 'We're here as guests of Queen Cartimandua. Step aside.'

Vellocatus interpreted and the natives' leader, a large warrior with grey-streaked hair tied back with a leather headband, stared at the Roman before he replied.

'This is Trabus, captain of the queen's bodyguard,' Vellocatus translated. 'He has been sent to escort us to the hall.'

'Then thank him.' Otho bowed his head. 'And ask him to lead on.'

The escort formed up on either side of the riders while Trabus strode ahead. In contrast to the settlement below, the inside of the fort was a much more ordered affair. The huts were arranged round the inside of the rampart, leaving a large open area in front of the royal hall. Twenty or so men were training to one side, engaged in mock duels under the eye of a wiry older warrior whose bare torso was covered in blue tattoos. Six more men, wearing ochre tunics and armed with spears, stood guard at the entrance to the hall and they formed up in front of the open doorway as they saw the party approaching across the training ground.

Casting his gaze around, Cato took in more details, keenly observing anything that might serve him well at a later time. To one side of the hall stood two lines of stables where a large party of men were standing with some horses, exchanging greetings in loud cheery voices. Just beyond them stood Septimus's cart and Cato caught a glimpse of him going through his patter with one of the noblemen.

'Must be those riders we saw earlier,' Macro commented.

'Yes.' Cato looked them over and then glanced to the other side of the hall where several smaller huts were arranged around a number of fire pits with spit trestles at each end. Women and children were busy butchering lambs and pigs and preparing the fire pits with bundles of kindling. Trabus led them to the hall and then turned and gestured at them to dismount. Two of his men stepped forward to hold the horses as they eased themselves on to the ground where they landed with a clink of armour accoutrements. Macro stretched his head back and looked up at the front of the hall. The lintel above the two doors was a massive length of oak, inlaid with carvings of horses and the swirling designs beloved of the Celts.

'Nice work.'

Cato looked up. 'Makes a change from the skulls some of the other tribes collect.'

'Give 'em time.'

Otho had taken the arm of his wife and turned to his men. 'Let's keep this nice and calm. We're here as guests.'

Macro made a quick adjustment to his helmet so that it sat squarely on his head. 'Just as long as they remember that, sir.'

The tribune took a deep breath then flashed a smile at his wife before turning towards the entrance to the hall and stepping forward with as much purposeful dignity as he could muster. The remaining men followed him, Macro, Cato and Vellocatus together and the two bodyguards bringing up the rear.

After the bright sunlight it took a moment to adjust to the dim light inside the hall, then Cato could see that it was lit by gaps along the ridge where shafts of sunlight penetrated the gloomy interior, catching dust motes and insects in their honeyed glow. The floor was paved with smooth slabs of slate and their boots sounded loudly as they entered. Scores of tribespeople, men and women, lined each side of the hall, standing in silence. A broad avenue stretched towards the far end which was dominated by a large wooden throne raised up on a stone platform. It had been positioned beneath a large opening in the thatched roof and the angled light caught the top half of the throne, bathing it in a golden hue. Seated there, still and silent, was a tall, slender woman with a mass of strawberry-blond hair which seemed to glow about her fine features. Cartimandua looked to be in her forties, as far as Cato could judge from his initial impression.

No one spoke, or even murmured, as the Romans and their translator paced down the length of the hall and approached the queen of the Brigantes, the most powerful tribe in Britannia. To her right

255

Cato could see a powerfully built warrior with plaited hair hanging over his tunic, beneath which his muscular shoulders bulged. He stood with folded arms and eyed the newcomers defiantly. Venutius, Cato guessed.

Tribune Otho slowed the pace as they approached and stopped a short distance from the step leading up to the throne. Now that Cartimandua was no more than ten feet from him, Cato could see that she was quite beautiful, even though she had left her youth behind many years before. Her eyes were brown, dark and penetrating and her cheekbones were high and made her jaw look slim and deep. She scrutinised each Roman in turn, starting and ending with Poppaea.

The tribune bowed his head. 'I am Marcus Salvius Otho, senior tribune of the Ninth Legion. This is my wife, Poppaea Sabina.'

Poppaea bowed her head stiffly.

'And these officers are Prefect Quintus Licinius Cato, commander of the Second Thracian Cavalry, and Centurion Lucius Cornelius Macro of the Fourteenth Legion.'

Cato and Macro saluted.

'We have come here on the orders of General Ostorius, who sends warm messages of friendship to Queen Cartimandua and her people, to apprehend an enemy of Rome. And therefore an enemy of us both.'

Cartimandua smiled faintly before she turned to Vellocatus and spoke for the first time in a commanding tone, more deep and resonating than was typical for a woman. Vellocatus quickly stepped forward and dropped to one knee in front of her as he intoned a formal greeting. Cartimandua's eyes fell on him and Cato saw the corners of her mouth lift momentarily in pleasure. She reached forward and cupped his cheek in a slender hand and then patted him lightly.

Cato's eyes flickered to the man he had taken to be Venutius; he glared coldly at Cartimandua and her young favourite.

'No love lost there,' Macro whispered. 'And she's not exactly hiding her affections.'

Cartimandua lowered her hand and sat back, fixing her eyes on the tribune. She was still for a moment, and the rest of the hall took their lead from her so that the new arrivals felt the gaze of hundreds of eyes upon them. She spoke to Vellocatus and he nodded before he rose to his feet and took his station beside the Romans. Then Cartimandua spoke again for all to hear, and her words were translated for the tribune and his companions.

'I bid our Roman guests and allies welcome to the great hall of the Brigantes. They will be shown every courtesy by our royal order. We have pledged our friendship to Rome, as they have pledged to support our interests and independence and gifted us gold and silver as guarantee of their intent to honour the treaty between us. All here know this and are bound by the sacred oath I swore as our pledge to Rome. Now comes the first great test of that treaty.'

Cato saw her left hand give the merest flicker of movement and a figure to the side of the platform eased himself towards a small doorway at the side of the hall as the queen continued.

'There comes amongst us a fugitive who was once a great king in the south of the island. A great warrior who has been an unflinching enemy of Rome since they first set foot on Britannia. In the course of his struggle, he has been defeated time and again by the legions of Rome. Losing his realm, he chose to lead other tribes against Rome and all have been defeated and destroyed and their lands are filled with cries of lamentation and despair. A fate the Brigantes have been spared. A fate we shall not countenance for our people.' Her gaze travelled across the assembled nobles, daring any of them to defy her will. 'This king, having been defeated and driven from the mountains of the Silures and the Ordovices, now comes to us to ask for shelter and sustenance, demanding our hospitality, which our custom obliges us to provide. But there are limits to such obligations when they endanger their hosts and a decision has to be made between our customs and our very survival. It is for this reason that we have summoned you to bear witness to the fate of this king . . . Caratacus.'

As her words echoed down the length of the hall, Cato saw the man emerge from the side door at the head of a small party. Four large warriors in ochre tunics and wearing swords in shoulder slings escorted an even larger man in their midst. Caratacus was finely dressed in a blue tunic and white leggings. His hair had been plaited and hung down his broad back. A gold torc gleamed about his neck. He strode towards the platform with his head tilted slightly so that he seemed to

257

tower over those around him. His appearance and demeanour was not so much that of a prisoner of the Brigantes as a king advancing into the hall with his personal bodyguard.

Despite the fact he was the sworn enemy of Rome, Cato could not help feeling admiration for his proud bearing. He sensed the same mood in the rest of the hall and felt a sickening sense of foreboding in his stomach. The enemy leader was a man who commanded instant respect by his very presence. It was small wonder that so many had been willing to follow him to defeat and death across the long years of conflict with Rome.

The one-time king of the Catuvellauni made to address the gathering but he was cut off by a sharp word from Cartimandua and she glared at him threateningly. Caratacus bowed his head with a small smile and the queen drew a fresh breath to address the hall.

'We are bound by our treaty with Rome to deliver this man into their custody,' Vellocatus translated, 'and we shall honour that obligation.'

What seemed like a sigh swept through the crowd and there were pockets of muttering. The queen rose to her feet and spoke again in a cold, determined voice.

'We have made our decision and it will not be undone!' She glared round defiantly before she continued in a more moderate tone, 'However, there is no need to abandon our good reputation for hospitality. Tonight, there will be a feast in honour of Caratacus, before he is taken into Roman custody.'

'Feast?' Macro sucked in a breath through his teeth. 'For that bastard?'

'Shh!' Cato hissed softly.

Tribune Otho could not help revealing his surprise and then a flash of anger at the announcement. He turned swiftly to Vellocatus. 'Tell your queen that is not acceptable. This man is an enemy of Rome, a fugitive from our justice. He should be in chains.'

'No!' She stabbed a finger at him to silence the Roman and spoke in Latin. 'You too are guests here and it ill behoves a guest to dictate terms to their host. So you will keep such thoughts to yourself, Tribune, if you have even the slightest conception of civilised manners. Is that understood?'

Otho was taken aback by her outburst, delivered in his tongue, and his jaw sagged briefly before he nodded. But his wife was not so easily discomforted and she took half a step forward and tilted her head towards the Brigantian queen. 'Now you listen here, no one speaks to a Roman like that. No one.'

'But I just did,' Cartimandua replied evenly. 'And if you wish for a place at the feast you would do well to speak only when spoken to, Lady Poppaea.'

Poppaea's carefully plucked eyebrows shot up in outrage and her husband took her arm. 'No more, my dear. This is not the time or place for it.'

Caratacus had been watching the brief altercation with wry amusement and now his gaze turned to Cato.

'Ah, Prefect Cato. My short-lived captor. I trust that my escape did not cause you too much personal inconvenience.'

Cato bowed his head to the enemy king. 'Sir, I will not deny that it displeased General Ostorius. However, it now seems that it is your escape that is short-lived.'

'You think so? Truly?'

'The queen has spoken. You will be back in our hands come the morrow. We already have your brothers, your wife, your children, and tomorrow we shall have you. The war you have waged against Rome is over. There will be peace. So I suggest you enjoy the feast tonight, sir. It will be the last one you enjoy as a free man.'

Caratacus's expression darkened for a moment before he smiled coldly and spoke in a menacing undertone. 'Perhaps it is you who should be enjoying the feast, Prefect Cato. Who knows? It might well be the last meal you ever eat.'

CHAPTER TWENTY-SIX

During the afternoon more groups of nobles and their entourages arrived at the hill fort and soon there was no further stabling available for their mounts and they were obliged to leave them down in the settlement below the fort. Trestle tables and benches were carried into the hall and arranged in three rows stretching down the length of the building. Outside, the queen's servants built up the cooking fires and then lit them in the afternoon to allow them time to burn down to embers to roast the meat over.

Following her announcement about the feast, Queen Cartimandua retired into a private hut to the rear of the hall, together with her Roman guests. The tribune ordered his bodyguards to wait with their horses. As the mounts were led away, Cato saw Caratacus escorted to a smaller dwelling that had been assigned to him, where he was kept under guard. Cartimandua's private quarters had been prepared for the meeting. A small circle of stools had been placed on the flagstoned floor and a larger, padded seat dominated the far side of the circle. Once Cartimandua was seated, the rest followed suit and there was a short period of shuffling before Cartimandua smiled at them.

'I apologise for speaking in my tongue in the hall, but there are those amongst my people who tend to regard my understanding of Latin as a sign of treachery rather than a useful skill. That is why I had Vellocatus translate most of my words.'

'And how do your people regard Vellocatus, your majesty?' asked Otho.

She smiled at her husband's shield-bearer. 'He is young and of little importance and so is easily forgotten. In time, he will take a prominent role in our nation, but for now his command of your tongue is a vice that most are prepared to overlook.' Cartimandua turned back to the tribune and the brief look of pleasure in her expression faded and was replaced by the implacable face of a queen.

'I have honoured my agreement with Rome. Caratacus will become your prisoner. I would be obliged if you removed him from my lands as swiftly as possible once the feast is over.'

'Then why give him the feast?' Macro asked bluntly and then registered the sharp intake of breaths before he swallowed and continued in a more respectful tone, 'I apologise, your majesty. I meant to say, why not just hand him over to us right now and send us on our way?'

'I wish it were so easy, Roman. To tell the truth, his unwelcome arrival at Isurium has been a source of considerable difficulty for me. I understand he managed to escape from inside your general's camp the night after the battle in which you defeated and captured him.'

'That is true,' Otho conceded. He indicated Cato. 'This officer was in charge of guarding the prisoners.'

'You're the fool responsible?'

Cato stiffened at the accusation and insult, and he sensed Macro bristling at his side. He took a calming breath before he responded. 'I captured him on the battlefield and the general charged me with looking after the prisoner as a reward for the deed.'

'And yet he escaped. How very careless of you. One would think that so dangerous an opponent might be looked after more diligently,' Cartimandua said with heavy irony. 'So you will understand my disappointment with your general when Caratacus arrived in my court demanding protection, as well as taking the opportunity to call on my people to join him in a new war against Rome.'

Otho shifted on his stool. 'He was helped to escape. Someone betrayed us.'

'That's your concern not mine. Except that it has become my concern. Especially when Caratacus has talked my consort into supporting his appeal for the Brigantes to go to war. Fortunately my people have a more mercenary nature than most. They won't fight unless they are promised gold and silver. Their loyalty to me can be bought for the same reason. As a result, I have all but exhausted the

261

treasure advanced to me by your Emperor to keep the peace with Rome. That is the only reason why I have not been deposed by Venutius and his faction. If Rome wants to keep things that way then I shall need more coin.'

Cato grasped the point at once. 'You want a reward for Caratacus, your majesty?'

Her gaze turned to Cato and her eyes narrowed fractionally as she reappraised him. 'Of course. An alliance places obligations on both parties, Prefect.'

'As far as I understand it, Rome pays you to stay neutral. Handing Caratacus over would seem to satisfy that condition.'

'You bought our neutrality. There was no mention of acting as jailers on your behalf. That will cost you a little extra. I shall want payment for Caratacus.'

'Now just hang on,' Poppaea butted in. 'A treaty is a treaty. Who do you think you are to change that? Some jumped-up barbarian woman, is what. How dare you?'

Cartimandua glanced at her before addressing her husband. 'Women are respected amongst our people. That is why I am queen. I realise that the very idea of a female ruler causes you Romans acute discomfort. Even your women share that view. But we are not in Rome. We are in Isurium. I would be grateful if you respected our customs.'

Poppaea opened her mouth to renew her protest, but Otho shushed her and instead she clenched her jaw and glared down at her feet. Her husband addressed the queen in an emollient tone.

'Your majesty, I shall take your request for payment back to General Ostorius. That is the best I can do.'

'It's not enough,' Cartimandua countered. 'I want a hundred thousand denarians for Caratacus and I want you to set your seal to a document stating those terms before you leave Isurium with your prisoner.'

'A hundred thousand denarians?' Tribune Otho shook his head in astonishment. 'By the gods, I can tell you now that the general will never agree to that.'

'Why not? It is the price of peace in your province, and cheaply bought when you consider the possibility of a renewed onslaught by Caratacus, with thousands of my warriors at his back.'

Cato saw that his superior was momentarily speechless and he cleared his throat and intervened. 'Your majesty, the presence of Caratacus at your court is as much a problem for you as it is for us. You said so yourself. In which case, it could be argued that our taking him into custody is doing *you* a favour. If we were to leave him here, how long do you think your reign might endure?'

Cartimandua fixed him with a steely glare and then gave a light laugh and turned to Otho. 'Oh, he's a shrewd one, your prefect. And he is right, to a point. I want Caratacus removed as soon as possible. He's undermined my position enough since he arrived here. And it has cost me dearly to buy the loyalty of my people thus far. At the very least, I should be reimbursed for what I have paid out for the sake of preserving peace with Rome.'

Macro chuckled. 'Not to mention for the sake of preserving your place on the throne, your majesty.'

She shot him a withering look. 'This one, I do not like, Tribune. He lacks the sense to phrase things palatably. Kindly order him not to address me again.'

Macro's cheeks flushed angrily and he leaned forward to protest, but Cato raised a hand and gave him an imploring look. With a hiss Macro subsided and clamped his lips together.

'That's better,' Cartimandua continued. 'Now then, we were discussing the price for Caratacus. I am not unreasonable. Shall we say ninety thousand?'

Otho thought for a moment and shook his head. 'Sixty.'

Cato winced and could not help wishing Macro's mother, Portia, was haggling on their behalf. The sharp-minded old woman had a knack for it, unlike the young aristocrat.

'Eighty?'

Otho chewed his lip. 'Seventy-five.'

'Seventy-five it is, then.' Cartimandua nodded. 'I shall want that within two months and you will put it in writing, along with your seal, before you leave Isurium. Agreed?'

Otho nodded helplessly.

'Then our business is complete, and we are free to enjoy the feast tonight.'

'Must it be in Caratacus's honour?' asked Cato.

'Indeed it must. For the sake of appearances. He is a king, at least until tomorrow. Many of my nobles and their warriors hold him in high regard. It would anger them if I simply handed him over to you in chains. Instead he has been treated as an honoured guest. The feast permits us to maintain that illusion. The truth is he was a prisoner the moment he showed his face at my court.'

'And you are certain there is no real danger from the those who support his cause, your majesty?'

'None. Whatever they think of Caratacus you can be sure they think rather more highly of the coin they have been paid from my treasury. The feast is a matter of form. I will play the part of a generous host and win the respect of my people. They will be able to toast him and glory in his deeds without the frightening prospect of having to shed their blood for him. Honour is satisfied all round.' She paused and folded her hands together in her lap. 'Of course, the question of the price to be paid for the prisoner will remain a secret between myself and Rome. That would be best for both of us.'

'I understand, your majesty.'

'Then we have an agreement?'

'We do,' Otho reaffirmed.

'I suggest that you enjoy the hospitality of Isurium before the feast begins.'

'Thank you. First I must send word to my second-in-command that we will be returning to the camp later than anticipated.'

'Very well.' Cartimandua inclined her head towards the entrance of the hut. 'You may leave.'

The others rose from their stools and made for the opening. The queen spoke softly in her tongue and Vellocatus stopped and turned towards her. There was a brief exchange before he turned back to the Romans.

'I must stay. My queen needs me.'

Macro forced his expression to remain neutral as Cato replied, 'Of course. We'll see you at the feast, I expect.'

'Yes. At the feast then.'

Cato was the last out of the hut and Vellocatus drew the leather curtain across the entrance behind them. As they followed the tribune and his wife back towards the hall, Macro chuckled and was about to speak when Cato got in first. 'Be careful what you say, Macro.'

'I was merely going to make a point about the burdens of duty. The lucky lad!'

'That's what you say now,' Cato replied then gestured discreetly towards the open ground in front of the hall. Venutius stood with a group of nobles, but he was not listening to their conversation. Instead he stood, arms folded, glaring bitterly in the direction of his wife's hut.

Cato continued in an undertone. 'I don't think the queen's amorous tryst is much of a secret and her consort doesn't look the type to turn a blind eye.'

'Enjoy the hospitality of this squalid dump indeed,' Poppaea muttered as she plucked at the folds of her stola to raise it above the ground. It was a hot day and the ground was dry and Cato saw it for the spiteful gesture of disdain that it was.

'Oh, I'm sure there must be something to see here,' her husband replied with forced cheerfulness. 'A native market perhaps. Somewhere you can pick up a few charming little native trinkets for your friends back in Rome, my love.'

She flashed him a dark look. 'The only thing I'm likely to pick up here is some vile native sickness. I'm sure my friends would love to receive that as a memento of my visit to this charming, rustic haven.'

They were interrupted by the flash of a red tunic as a Roman came running towards them from where the bodyguards and the tethered horses were waiting.

'What now?' Macro demanded under his breath.

Tribune Otho halted and the others stopped at his side as the soldier approached, a closed waxed tablet in his hand. He saluted the tribune and offered the tablet to him. 'With the compliments of Prefect Horatius, sir. I was ordered to find you and give you this at once, but those bastards wouldn't let me past.' He nodded to the men in ochre tunics.

'Mind your fucking tongue, soldier!' Macro snapped. 'Some of the bastards speak Latin. Keep it civil.'

Otho raised an eyebrow. 'Thank you, Centurion.'

The tribune took the tablet and moved off a short distance as he broke the seal and flipped the waxed tablet open. The others watched

265

in silence as he read the message, trying to gauge its contents from his reaction. Otho sucked in a deep breath as he closed the tablet. Turning to the soldier he spoke curtly. 'Wait by the horses. I'll have a message to send back.'

'Yes, sir!' The man saluted and turned and strode off.

When he was out of earshot, Otho returned to the others and glanced round briefly before he muttered, 'Ostorius is dead.'

All three stared at him in silence. Cato's mind raced. Foul play? Fallen in battle? An accident? 'Dead? How?'

Poppaea sighed. 'The poor man.'

'Horatius doesn't give any detail other than to say the general died in his tent.'

'Who's taken command?' asked Cato.

Otho shook his head. 'Horatius doesn't say.'

'Legate Quintatus,' Macro suggested. 'Has to be.'

Cato nodded. It made sense. Quintatus was the next in seniority in the army at Viroconium, and had already taken temporary command of the army. But there were also the legates of the three other legions in the province and one of them might take the chance to assert their right to the temporary command. There would be a brief opportunity to grab some glory from running the new province before Rome appointed a new governor. Especially if Ostorius's replacement was able to take credit for sending Caratacus to Rome in chains. If there was any dissent among the legates then Cato feared that their enemies would take full advantage of the situation while the power struggle was resolved. Another anxious thought struck him.

'If his death is common knowledge back at Viroconium, it's only a matter of time before the news reaches Isurium.'

Otho stared at him. 'So?'

'It might strengthen Venutius's position. If he can persuade others that the death leaves our forces leaderless for the moment he might talk enough Brigantian nobles around to his side to cause us a few problems. You heard the queen, sir. Her grip on power is slipping.'

Otho nodded thoughtfully. 'Then we'd better see to it that she gets that money as soon as possible.'

'Yes, sir. As long as there's an acting commander in place to authorise the payment.'

'Damn, you're right.' He frowned and then his eyes lit up. 'We have our own pay chest. We could use that.'

Macro spluttered. 'No! That's the men's money. That's their pay and savings. You touch that, sir, and you'll piss our lads right off.'

Cato knew his friend was right. The pay chest of each unit was almost as sacred as the standards the men marched under and would give their lives to protect. The sturdy iron-bound boxes contained all the men's wealth in the world, all their dreams and ambitions for what they would do after they had served out their enlistment. If the tribune emptied the pay chests and handed the contents over to the Brigantian queen then his men would be as outraged as Macro. Cato stood to lose out as well, but he at least could see that the money would help to buy peace in the province.

'What does that matter?' Poppaea said to her husband. 'They're your men. Your soldiers. They'll do as they're told, and like it.'

Macro drew a deep breath and tried to control his anger as he addressed his commander's wife. 'Begging your pardon, my lady, but you don't know what you're talking about. This is soldier's business. Believe me, if you take the men's money then I can't answer for the consequences.'

'You can, Centurion. You must. You're an officer. You swore an oath to obey the Emperor and those officers above you in rank. If my husband gives an order then you must obey it and see that it is obeyed by others.'

Macro glared at her, burning with the desire to tell her to shut her mouth and mind her own business. But before he could speak, Otho cleared his throat and spoke calmly. 'You are quite right, my dearest, but I will deal with the situation. Not you.'

'Pfft!' Poppaea sniffed and flicked her hand. 'Deal with it then.'

Otho flashed a condescending smile at her before turning back to the others. 'You think it's inadvisable to use the contents of the pay chests then?'

Macro ground his teeth. 'Inadvisable is putting it mildly, sir.'

Otho shifted his gaze to Cato. 'And you, Prefect? What do you think?'

'We're a long way from the rest of the army, sir. It's a delicate situation. The last thing we need is to have to worry about the

267

mood of our men. Besides, even if we did as you suggest, there might not be enough to serve Cartimandua's needs. In that case we'd be facing big trouble on both fronts. I advise you, most strongly, not to do it, sir.'

'Then what? If I give my word that we'll send her coin the moment we return to Viroconium only for there to be no one in a position to authorise the payment, Queen Cartimandua is going to feel a little angry.'

'Completely pissed off, more like,' Macro said darkly. 'And she'll lose face in front of the rest of her tribe.'

'We'll have to deal with that when the time comes,' said Cato. 'The vital thing is that we take custody of Caratacus and get him far away from here as quickly as possible. Sir, we have to keep news of Ostorius's death to ourselves. There's no way of knowing how it might affect the situation. Meanwhile we attend the feast, go along with the queen's honouring of Caratacus. We take charge of him at first light and break camp and march back to Viroconium as fast as we can. By the time the Brigantians find out about Ostorius it will be too late to change the situation. Of course, you'll have to make a good case to whoever assumes command of the province about paying the queen off.'

'Quite.' Otho nodded sourly. 'And if the payment isn't made after I have given my word then I am dishonoured.'

'If that's the price to pay for taking our most dangerous enemy out of the game then it's worth paying, sir.'

'Easy for you to say. I'm the one in command.'

'Goes with the rank, sir.' Macro pursed his lips. 'Sometimes you eat the wolf. Sometimes the wolf eats you.'

Otho frowned. 'What the bloody hell does that mean?'

'Just a saying, sir. It's your decision.'

'Thank you for pointing that out, Centurion Macro. You're very helpful.' Otho clenched his eyes shut for a moment, sucked in a deep breath and sighed bitterly before his eyes snapped open. 'Right. We take Caratacus at the first opportunity and get out of here. Meanwhile, no one is to breathe a word about Ostorius.'

'You'll have to notify Horatius to do the same in the camp, sir,' Cato pointed out.

'Yes . . . Of course. At once.' Otho flipped open the waxed tablet and hesitated. He glanced up. 'Stylus, anyone?'

Macro looked at him blankly and Cato instinctively began to reach for his sidebag before realising he had left it back in camp.

'Terrific,' Otho muttered, then drew his dagger and as carefully as he could with the clumsy instrument, he inscribed a brief response to Horatius. Snapping the wooden tablet shut he sheathed his dagger and beckoned to the messenger. The soldier had been watching and ran across to the tribune.

'Take this back to camp. It is to be handed directly to Prefect Horatius. Tell him to act upon my orders precisely. Understood?'

'Yes, sir.'

'Then go.'

The messenger turned hurriedly.

'Wait,' Otho growled. 'Don't rush. That will only draw the natives' attention to you. Show 'em that Romans keep cool heads, eh?'

'Yes, sir.' The soldier walked steadily towards the horses, swung himself up into the saddle and urged it into a gentle trot as he made for the gatehouse and disappeared out of sight down the track towards the settlement.

'That's that, then,' Otho concluded. 'The die is cast. Nothing to do now but wait for the feast to begin.'

Cato smiled encouragingly, relieved that the tribune had made the best possible decision under the circumstances. It hardly equated to crossing the Rubicon but if that thought allowed the young aristocrat to flatter himself that he was making a difficult but right decision then Cato was content to let it pass.

'Speaking of dice ...' Macro nodded towards the two bodyguards. 'Might as well pass the time usefully. Sir?'

Otho raised an eyebrow. 'What? Oh, yes. As you wish, Centurion.'

Macro saluted and glanced at Cato. 'How about you?'

Cato was tempted to turn the offer down. There was too much to think about. Then he realised that there was nothing he could do about the situation. He had done all that he could to influence the matter. Now it was up to the gods to look kindly on their plans, or throw a completely new twist of fate in their path. He nodded at Macro.

'Why not? Our luck has to change for the better some day.'

CHAPTER TWENTY-SEVEN

The open ground in front of the royal hall began to fill with those invited to the feast as the sun dipped towards the horizon. The day had been hot and those who had stood in the sunshine for much of it were feeling the prickle of skin that had been burned in the glare of the sun. The beasts that had been slaughtered earlier in the afternoon were roasting over the raked coals of the fire pits, a safe distance from the thatched roofs of the nearest buildings. The air was thick with the delicious smell of roasting meat and Macro lifted his nose and breathed in with a beatific smile.

'Mmmm. I'm bloody starving. Make a change from marching rations.'

Cato shifted beside him on one of the long benches that had been placed outside the entrance of the hall for the queen's guests to rest while they waited to be summoned inside.

'I suppose so,' he replied absently. He was preoccupied by observing the comings and goings of the Brigantian nobles. The dice game had finished late in the afternoon, once Macro had won all the ready coin from the tribune's bodyguards, and most of Cato's. Small wonder that his friend was in such a fine humour, Cato brooded.

Tribune Otho and his wife had returned from their exploration of the settlement below the fort shortly afterwards. Both were flushed and sweating from the exertion of struggling back up the hill, and a small party of children followed them, carrying baskets of fruit, bundles of furs and small rolls of the thick patterned cloth favoured by the natives. Otho directed them to leave their burdens in the charge of his bodyguard and paid them off with some bronze coins from his purse. The queen's guards then herded them back out of the fort as the tribune and his wife made their way across the fort to Cato and Macro.

In the warm glow and long shadows of dusk, Poppaea sat beside her husband, opposite the other Roman officers, attempting to cool herself with a straw fan while struggling to drive off the cloud of gnats that swirled round her head like tiny flakes of gold.

'When is this wretched feast going to start?'

Her husband was idly eating an apple he had taken from a small basket sitting on the bench between them. 'If you're hungry, try one. Quite delicious.'

Otho took another bite and offered the basket to her. Poppaea stared back coldly.

'You look like a suckling pig if you want to. I'll keep up the civilised standards on your behalf.'

Cato glanced at her and bit his tongue. Like the rest of them, Poppaea looked hot and dishevelled and her stola clung to her flesh where she had been perspiring. He doubted whether she would have cut a very fine figure amongst her society friends in Rome at the precise moment.

'Hello, at least someone looks happy.' Macro broke into his thoughts and pointed. Cato followed the direction indicated and saw Septimus approaching. The imperial agent had tied a strip of cloth round his head to keep the sweat from his eyes.

'Centurion! Prefect!' Septimus called out cheerfully then adopted a more respectful manner as he caught sight of the tribune and his wife. 'I bid you good afternoon, sir, and to your fine lady.'

'You look like a pig in clover,' Macro remarked. 'Had a good day's trading? You seemed busy enough earlier on. I saw that Venutius and some his mates buying up most of your stock.'

Cato smiled. He had also watched the queen's consort making his purchases before taking the small hoard of wine jars off to one of the larger huts.

'You know how it is with these Celts.' Septimus smiled knowingly and patted the heavy purse hanging at his side. 'They do love their wine. I sold the lot. Auctioned the last three jars, and they bid like it was their last day on earth.'

Cato looked past him towards the noblemen standing in small groups nearby. Many were talking loudly and most were clearly under the influence. He turned to smile at Septimus. 'Just as long as it has the desired effect.'

The imperial agent gave him a faint nod before he replied. 'As long as they're in their cups, and I'm deep into their purses, then all's well. I can see this is going to prove a fine market for the first trader who can bring his business regularly to Isurium.' He paused. 'Of course, that all depends on there being peace in this part of the world.'

'We'll see to that all right.' Macro nodded. 'Even if we have to give them a bloody thrashing to make sure of it. Rome doesn't care who she has to destroy in order to bring peace.'

Cato glanced at his friend and tried to reassure himself that Macro was dusting off his seldom-used sense of irony.

'Er, yes.' Septimus frowned. 'I'll have to be off. Need to fetch more stock from the camp.'

He knuckled his forehead and then bowed respectfully to Otho and his wife before heading back to fetch his empty cart.

'Dreadfully boring man,' Poppaea drawled. 'Like all tradesmen. All they ever talk about is money. That's all Rome means to them. It's our class who dedicates itself to the expansion of the empire and spills our blood to win new lands. And it's the likes of that wine merchant who profit from our labours. I went to buy some wine from him earlier this afternoon and he would only sell it to me at a ridiculous price, the scoundrel.'

Cato suppressed a smile at this proof of the imperial agent's skill in playing out his cover story.

Otho swallowed and inspected his half-eaten apple as he replied. 'Perhaps, but you are hardly labouring in the service of Rome, my dear.'

'No? You think it is easy for me to live like a common soldier and share all their hardships?'

Macro choked and hurriedly looked down at the ground between his boots as he fought to suppress his laughter.

'I am beginning to wish I hadn't been so insistent on accompanying you to this squalid island. It would had been better if I had remained in Rome.'

'That's true . . .' Otho said pleasantly and then, realising how his response might be taken, he gushed, 'I mean, it would be better for you to be in your natural element, my darling. You are like a rose amongst nettles here. I fear for you. My mind would be less troubled if I knew you were safely back in Rome.'

Macro leaned a little closer to Cato and muttered, 'Not half.'

Poppaea shot her husband a suspicious look, but before she could speak the shrill note of a horn blasted through the evening air. Conversation stopped as everyone turned towards the noise. A large warrior blew several more notes before lowering his shining bronze instrument. Beside him stood Vellocatus. The latter drew a deep breath before he made his announcement. He spoke in the native tongue before he turned to the Romans and repeated his words in Latin.

'Her majesty, Queen Cartimandua, entreats you to enter her hall and take your place at the feast.'

The noblemen, and their women, immediately began to edge towards the entrance to the hall as the doors were drawn inwards by two of the queen's servants. Cato watched as Otho made to rise but his wife tugged at his arm and made him sit down, hissing, 'Wait! I will not see us herded in there like swine. We will enter as Romans should, in a dignified manner that sets us apart from these barbarians.'

The tribune gave a resigned sigh while Cato could clearly hear the sound of Macro grinding his teeth. Vellocatus slipped round the edge of the crowd to join them a moment later.

'The queen has set aside a place for you at her left. I will sit with you.'

Poppaea arched a plucked eyebrow. 'To her left? Then who is sitting to her right?'

'Her consort, Venutius. As is his rightful place.'

Cato could not help picking up on the strained note of bitterness in the young nobleman's voice.

'And who is sitting with Venutius?' He asked.

'His closest comrades.'

'And that includes Caratacus, I expect.'

Vellocatus nodded.

Poppaea's eyes narrowed. 'Our enemy is be seated in a place of honour, second to the queen, and above us? No. It cannot be permitted.'

The Brigantian's brow twitched. 'It cannot be avoided, my lady. It is arranged.'

She turned to her husband. 'That woman intends to humiliate us. We are her allies and she gives the place of honour to our enemy instead. You cannot permit it, Otho. Tell him.'

'My love, I can't—'

'Tell him! Or tell that woman.'

'Silence!' the tribune snapped at her, his expression instantly turning into a savage glare. Poppaea recoiled and he continued in the same angry tone, 'You keep your tongue still. I don't want to hear another word of complaint from you. We're in enough difficulty as it is, without your whining making it worse.'

'Whining . . .' she pouted, her lower lip trembling.

'Yes, whining. You wanted to come to the frontier with me. An adventure, you said. And I've heard nothing but complaints since we arrived. Right now I need you to shut your mouth until spoken to. And if you have cause to speak then you will be polite and courteous. Is that understood?'

She stared at him, eyes wide in surprise and shock at his uncharacteristic outburst. 'But, Otho my love, I . . .'

'I asked if you understood. Yes or no? If it's no, you go straight back to the camp. And then back to Rome the moment we reach Viroconium.'

'You don't mean that.'

'I do.' He stood up and loomed over her. 'So what's it to be?'

She looked up at him with a pained expression and tears glistened in the corner of her eyes. 'Yes.'

'That's better.' Otho softened his tone and offered her his hand. She took it hesitantly and rose to her feet. The tribune turned to Vellocatus and his two subordinates. 'I apologise for that little scene.'

Cato said nothing but tilted his head in acknowledgement. Macro merely gave muted, meaningless mumble, while Vellocatus smiled tolerantly.

'Now, if you would be so good as to lead us to our places.' Otho gestured towards the entrance and Vellocatus led them into the hall.

'About bloody time,' Macro whispered to his friend. 'She's had it coming to her.'

274

'Indeed,' Cato replied softly and shot him a quick grin.

By the time the small group had entered the hall, most of the other guests had already taken their places on the benches either side of the long tables stretching the length of the hall. There was none of the polished silver platters and delicate snacks that one might have expected at a banquet in Rome, thought Cato. Instead, bread and cheeses had been set down along the middle of each table and each man and woman either had a Samian ware cup, or had brought their own drinking horn or decorated cup. There were jugs of mead and beer. Some had already downed their first helping and the air was filled with the cheery din of their laughter and noisy exchanges. Vellocatus led his guests down the centre of the hall and Cato tried to keep looking directly ahead and ignoring the curious and hostile glances on either side. Ahead of them he could see that Cartimandua's throne had been removed to the rear of the hall and three trestle tables had been placed on the royal dais with simple chairs set up behind. The queen's place was empty but Venutius and several other men were already seated and talking animatedly. Cato felt his blood grow cold as he picked out Caratacus. Their eyes met and the Catuvellaunian king froze. Those around him picked up on his sudden change of mood and turned to stare with undisguised hostility at the approaching Romans.

'So much for Brigantian hospitality,' said Macro.

'No surprises there,' Cato responded. 'But let's keep it peaceful.'

'I will if they will.'

'You will, come what may, my friend.'

Macro frowned at him. 'Killjoy.'

'And that's the only killing that'll be on the menu tonight,' Cato concluded firmly, resolving to make quite sure that Macro kept the peace. He would need watching, especially as far as the drink was concerned. When Macro was the worse for wear, things tended towards outbreaks of violence, Cato knew of old. Under the circumstances, a drunken brawl might not be the best conclusion to the feast.

They climbed on to the dais and Otho took the seat nearest the queen's table. Then came his wife, Vellocatus, Cato and Macro. Directly opposite, Venutius and his comrades stared at them with cold, unyielding expressions of hatred and contempt.

'Well, this is awkward,' said Macro. He picked up the cup sitting in

275

front of him and reached for the nearest jug. He sniffed the contents suspiciously before giving an approving nod. He made to pour his cup, then remembered his manners and turned to the others.

'Want some?'

Poppaea shook her head and looked down at the weathered tabletop.

'Perhaps later,' Otho answered.

Vellocatus and Cato held out their cups and Macro filled them close to the brim before turning to his own and then setting the jug down. Raising his cup, he held it up and out in the direction of Caratacus. 'To the guest of honour.'

Venutius looked furious and was on the verge of rising when the Catuvellaunian king placed his hand firmly on his companion's arm to keep him in his seat. With an amused smile, Caratacus filled his drinking horn, a finely decorated affair with a bull's head on the base, and returned Macro's toast, calling across the gap, 'To my redoubtable Roman enemies.'

'Redoubtable,' Macro repeated with pleasure. 'That's us all right.'

He lifted his cup and took a sip. The brew was sweet and tasted lighter than the Gaulish beers Macro had drunk before. Beside him, Cato also drank, while Vellocatus refused to touch his cup.

'Quite a nice drop,' Macro said, and then took a healthy swig. 'Better than that Kourmi crap back in Gaul.'

'Very pleasant,' Cato agreed and glanced at his friend. 'But go easy on it, eh?'

Macro leaned forward to peer round his friend at Vellocatus. 'What's up with you, lad? Why aren't you drinking?'

'I will not share a toast with the man who plots against my queen,' Vellocatus answered.

'What, him?' Macro gestured across towards Caratacus. 'His plotting days are over, my friend. This time tomorrow he'll be in our hands and on his way to Viroconium. He's not going to trouble us, or you, ever again. Trust me. Meanwhile, let the man enjoy his last night of liberty, eh?'

The consort's shield-bearer remained silent, and folded his arms to emphasise his protest.

'Suit yourself.' Macro topped up his cup and cracked his shoulders as he looked round. The smell of the roasting meat pervaded the stuffy interior of the hall, lit by the gleam of the evening sun pouring through the entrance. 'Where's the queen, then?'

As if in answer to his question, a figure stepped out of the gloom at the side of the hall and gracefully ascended the dais. At once there was a deafening scraping of chairs and benches and the conversation died away. Cartimandua eased herself down into her seat and sat, straight backed, as she surveyed her guests. Then she raised a hand and ushered them down into their seats. Again there was a scraping and the conversation began to resume, rising slowly in volume.

There was no preamble to the eating. No entertainment. Servants laden with platters of cut meat entered through side doors and served them to those at the furthest end of the hall first, so that the queen would have her meat hot when she was served last and ate first. Macro's stomach began to rumble at the sight of the glistening piles of roast meats and he licked his lips.

Then Venutius abruptly stood up and raised his arms wide to draw attention to himself as he called out above the din of the other voices filling the hall.

'What is he playing at?' asked Cato. He glanced to his right and saw the look of alarm on Cartimandua's face as she beheld her consort's intervention. 'What's he saying, Vellocatus?'

There was a brief pause before he translated. 'He demands to be heard. He says he has an announcement to make, he must inform us that our gods have revealed an omen to him. They have sent a sign that they have cursed Rome.'

'Curse?' Otho's brow knitted. 'What rubbish is this?'

But Cato could already guess. The queen stabbed her finger at her consort and spoke imperiously. Venutius turned to her with a sneer and shook his head. Before she could repeat her command, he turned to face the Roman tribune directly and called out to him in a loud voice that carried to the furthest corners of the hall. As he spoke, Cato nudged Vellocatus sharply.

'What is he saying?'

'He says that Governor Ostorius is dead.'

Cato and Otho exchanged an anxious glance, but it was enough for

Venutius to seize upon and he bounded across to their table and bellowed at them.

'He demands to know if that is true.'

'Fuck,' Macro growled. 'He knows.'

'How can that be?' Otho shook his head. 'How could he have found out so soon?'

Venutius rested his hands on the edge of the table and Poppaea flinched as he repeated his question in a voice laced with menace.

When he received no reply, Venutius moved away from the Romans, turned his back on the glowering features of Cartimandua, and addressed those in the hall.

'He says your silence proves that what he said is true. It is a sign from the gods. A sign that they have turned against Rome. A sign that the Brigantes should rise up and wage war on Rome. Our gods will strike down the legions just as surely as they struck down their general.'

Most of the queen's guests looked on aghast, but Cato could see some nodding, a defiant gleam in their eyes as they listened to Venutius.

'He says that the gods are angry with our queen's alliance with Rome. They are angry with her decision to hand Caratacus over to the enemy.'

'We have to shut him up,' said Macro, hand slipping down to the pommel of his sword. 'Quickly.'

'No,' Cato ordered. 'We draw a weapon in here and we're dead.'

'But we can't do nothing. We can't let the bastard stir them up.'

Cato nodded, thinking quickly. Glancing at Otho, he saw that the tribune's face was frozen in horror. Snatching a deep breath, Cato stood up and filled his lungs and bellowed at the top of his voice to drown out Venutius.

'Enough! Enough! Hear me! Brigantians, hear me!' He turned to Vellocatus. 'Tell them what I say. Exactly what I say.'

The nobleman nodded.

Venutius did not try to compete with Cato but stepped aside and folded his arms and smiled coldly.

'It is true that General Ostorius is dead. But it is not a sign from the gods. He was old and ill. Even as I speak another officer is taking his place. The legions will serve him just as effectively as they ever served Ostorius. They will crush any tribe that opposes them. Venutius speaks falsely when he says that your gods have cursed us.'

As soon as the words were translated, Venutius interposed himself between Cato and the rest of the hall. There was a fresh note of triumph in his voice as he addressed his people again. Cato looked round and gestured to Vellocatus to resume his translation.

'He says that he can prove the gods are against Rome . . .'

Venutius paused and thrust his hand towards the entrance to the hall where the dying sun painted the wooden frame in a fiery glow. A tall, robed figure stepped on to the threshold and spread his arms wide, black against the bloody red hue of the sky.

'A Druid,' said Cato. 'Shit . . .'

At once the new arrival began to speak in a rich, deep timbre, uttering his words in a spell-like rhythm.

'He says he is Druid of the order of the Dark Moon.'

'Oh no,' Cato whispered to himself as he felt an icy trickle of dread flow down his spine. He had encountered the order before, and had nearly paid for it with his life, as had Macro. At the same time he knew that the performance had been carefully planned, even down to his own attempt to deny the omens that Venutius had claimed. While the natives might not wholly believe the queen's consort, they would readily accept the word of a Druid. Cato looked across to the other table and saw Caratacus smiling at him as Vellocatus continued to translate.

'The Druid says Venutius speaks the truth. He has seen the omens. The death of the Roman general is a sign that the gods are calling on the Brigantes to rise up and follow the example of Caratacus. They call for war against Rome. They have shown him a vision of a golden eagle drowning in a sea of Roman blood.'

Before the Druid could speak on, Cartimandua was on her feet shouting her reply. She was forced to raise her voice and where it had been mellifluous earlier in the day it now sounded shrill. The Druid fell silent before her edgy onslaught and then she turned her wrath on her consort who gave as good as he got.

Vellocatus had stopped translating, shocked into silence by the bitter confrontation taking place before him.

'What are they saying?' Otho demanded, then grabbed his arm and shook him. 'Translate, damn you!'

Vellocatus blinked and nodded. 'She tells him to send his Druid away and to leave Isurium at once. Now Venutius says he refuses to leave. He demands a meeting of the tribal council to discuss the omens and the decision to hand Caratacus over to the Romans.'

A chorus of shouts greeted Venutius's words and his supporters were joined by others, while the remainder looked to their queen with fearful expressions. Some stood up and shouted angrily at those on the side of Venutius.

'The situation's turning to shit,' said Macro. 'We have to grab Caratacus now and get out of here, before it's too late.'

'It's already too late,' said Cato. 'If we touch him, then we're as good as dead.'

As the angry exchanges in the hall continued, Cartimandua approached her Roman guests and spoke earnestly in Latin. 'You must go. Get back to your camp. I'll deal with this.'

Otho shook his head. 'We can't leave without Caratacus.'

She gritted her teeth. 'Are you a fool, Roman? I tell you, go now. Leave by the side entrance and take to your horses.'

'What will you do?' Cato asked.

Cartimandua glanced at her consort. 'I'll give Venutius his hearing in front of the council. Then I'll banish him from my court, and from my realm. I'll have him cut down the moment he ever shows his face here again.'

'And Caratacus?'

'He'll be sent to you at first light. You have my word on it. Now go!'

Cato turned to Tribune Otho who nodded reluctantly and rose from his seat, helping Poppaea up before steering her towards the side entrance Cartimandua had indicated. Cato and Macro followed, keeping a wary eye on those nearest them. A handful of Venutius's men jeered and whistled. Outside the hall the Romans hurried along its length in the direction of the hill fort's gate. Otho wrapped his arm protectively round his wife's shoulder. Macro and Cato grasped their sword handles, ready to draw them the instant there was any danger. On the far side of the open ground, the bodyguards were waiting anxiously, roused to their feet by the uproar. Cato looked up and saw that the sky along the western horizon was stained a deep crimson. Far above the band of light a crescent moon shone against the backdrop of velvet night, like the blade of a scythe. He shuddered at the sight and could not prevent the thought that perhaps the Druid was right about the omens after all.

CHAPTER TWENTY-EIGHT

Tribune Otho gave the order for the men of his column to stand to the moment he returned to the camp. The optios and centurions bawled at their soldiers and the Romans stumbled out of their tents in the last glimmer of the failing light and hurriedly put on their armour and began to form up. Meanwhile, the senior officers met in the tribune's tent. His wife had retired to their sleeping quarters and drawn the curtain behind her, as if that would shut out the danger that she felt herself to be in. Cato could understand her fears. The mission that her husband had been sent out to accomplish had been overturned by events. Now there was a very real possibility that instead of being welcomed as allies of the Brigantian tribe, their hosts might be persuaded into becoming the enemies of Rome. The prospect of the most powerful tribe in Britannia throwing its support behind someone as wily and determined as Caratacus filled Cato with dread.

Nor was he the only officer who feared the outcome of the confrontation between Queen Cartimandua and her consort taking place in the hill fort that towered above the Roman camp. A sombre mood settled on the Roman officers as they sat around the tribune's desk. Otho had briefly described the evening's events and now paused to let his officers consider the situation. He cleared his throat so that he might sound calm when he continued.

'What are our options, gentlemen?'

'Options?' Cato folded his hands together. 'Sir, we have no idea what is happening up there. Until we know otherwise we have to hope that Cartimandua can calm her people down. We should stay in camp until we find out what has happened.'

Prefect Horatius shook his head. 'By then it could be too late. We can't afford to sit on our hands, sir. I say we send a cohort of legionaries in to support the queen. They can arrest those who oppose her and get their hands on Caratacus. Come the morning it will all be over. Order will be restored and no one will dare to question the queen's authority.'

Otho nodded slowly before he replied. 'Do you think one cohort will be sufficient? What if we sent two? There must have been at least several hundred men up there earlier.'

Cato felt his heart grow heavy as he listened to the exchange and forced himself to expand on the concerns that plagued his mind. 'Sir, if we send men up to the fort, there will be violence. It doesn't matter who starts it – blood will be shed. The moment the rest of the tribe hears that Roman soldiers have killed some of their people, no matter what the circumstances, it will turn them against us. We will be playing directly into the hands of Venutius and Caratacus. They will hold it up as an example of what Rome intends for the Brigantes.'

'Not if we clap those two in irons first,' Horatius responded. 'If we arrest the ringleaders of the anti-Roman faction we can put an end to their opposition to Rome right now.'

'Or we might just provoke the rest of the tribe into war,' Cato countered. 'We can be certain of one thing. Whatever the differences between the factions and tribes of the Brigantian nation, they will bury those differences and turn on us the moment we are seen to be using force against them. Besides, with this moonlight, the moment Roman soldiers advance on the fort they will be seen. Venutius and Caratacus will have plenty of time to make their escape.'

'True, but in that case, they'll be running with their tails between their legs. We'll demonstrate our support for the queen's authority and restore some order at Isurium.'

Cato bit back on his frustration and forced himself to keep his tone even. 'It will only serve to make her look powerless. To her people she will seem like a Roman puppet. Any authority over her people that she has right now will collapse.' He turned to the tribune. 'We have to give Cartimandua the chance to settle this by herself, sir. You've seen that she has a forceful personality. She may yet persuade her nobles to back her against Venutius. We must give her a chance.'

Otho's brow creased as he tried to think the matter through. 'You

283

may be right, Prefect Cato. It could be dangerous to intervene.'

Horatius snorted. 'And it might be even more dangerous to sit here and wait on events, sir. I say we go in.'

'And I say I am considering our options,' Otho replied curtly. 'We were sent here on a diplomatic mission, Horatius. Not to invade Brigantia.'

Horatius chewed his lip and was quiet for a moment before he spoke again. 'If you recall, sir, the legate said that I was to assume command if military action was required.'

'But it isn't required yet,' protested Cato. 'I say we should wait until we know what has happened.'

'And I say we don't take the risk of letting things get out of control. The time for action is now.' Horatius slapped his hand on the table. 'If Prefect Cato is nervous, then he can remain in the camp with his men, and protect our baggage. After all, that's what he's good at.'

This was too much for Macro and he leaned forward aggressively. 'It was Prefect Cato who turned the battle against Caratacus, in case you'd forgotten, sir. And there's many of our men still alive now thanks to his quick thinking, and courage, who might otherwise have been killed on that fucking hill.'

'I don't deny it,' Horatius replied. 'Then again, it's because of Cato that we're here at all. If he'd kept a better eye on Caratacus . . .'

'That's enough!' Otho called out. 'Be quiet, gentlemen!'

There was a tense silence before Macro eased himself back, his jaw clenched. Horatius stared back angrily but restrained himself from further comment, for the moment.

'Prefect Cato is right to point out that this is not yet a military matter. I pray to Jupiter that remains the case. We'll not precipitate any action until we find out what has happened. If it comes to a fight then I will relinquish control of the column to you, Horatius, but not before. Is that clear?'

'Yes, sir.'

'In the meantime, we'll keep a double watch on the camp walls. Stand down the other units. They can rest behind the ramparts between watches. Horatius, Cato, remain here. The rest of you are dismissed.'

Once the other officers had filed out of the tent, Otho waited a moment to be sure that they were still not within hearing before he turned his furious expression on his subordinates.

'I swear to the gods that if ever you two cause a scene like that again, I'll have you relieved of command. That is in my power to do, Horatius, despite the legate's instructions concerning military command of this column. I'll thank you to remember that.'

'Yes, sir,' Horatius acknowledged through clenched teeth.

Cato kept his mouth shut. He was angry over being accorded the joint responsibility for the confrontation. He had only been doing his duty in advising his commander of the risks attached to any military action. And the slur Horatius had made about his courage had cut him to the quick. Nevertheless, Otho fixed him with a stern look.

'And you, Cato.'

'Yes, sir,' he responded flatly, unhappy at being treated like a badly behaved child by a man some years younger than he was.

'Then there's no more to be said, gentlemen. Join your units. We'll know which of you is right when the morning comes. Or even before then. Dismissed.'

Cato could not sleep and spent the first hours of the night in the wooden tower above the main gate. Macro stood with him for a while as they gazed towards the hill fort. Torches flared along the palisade and the loom of fires illuminated the roofs of the huts and the hall. There was no sign of flames and Cato guessed that the distant light came from the fire pits used for cooking and others used to light the interior of the fort.

At one point, just after the midnight watch change was sounded in the Roman camp, there had been loud shouting that seemed to resolve into a chant that continued for a while before fading away. Afterwards there had been no more sounds from the hill fort and its inhabitants might well have been sleeping off the wine, beer and mead they had consumed, for all Cato knew. Or, his thoughts continued, they might be quietly, soberly, drawing up their plans to attack the Roman camp as a prelude to launching a full-scale war against the forces of Emperor Claudius. The tribespeople in the settlement at the foot of the hill seemed to share Cato's foreboding and there was no sign of light, or life, amid the huts dimly visible in the moonlight. Indeed, the only sign of life came from within the Roman camp as the sentries paced steadily up and down between the towers and turrets along the wall.

'What do you reckon's happening up there?' Macro asked softly.

Cato's shoulders heaved as he drew a deep breath and organised his thoughts. 'I've no more idea than you, Macro. All we can hope is that Cartimandua has persuaded enough of her people to remain loyal to her. If not, and Venutius has taken control, then we'll have a war on our hands.'

'In which event Isurium is not going to be a great place to be a Roman.'

'It'll take a while to summon the tribes. We'll have a few days' grace to try and rescue the situation here. That, or get a decent head start on any force that Venutius sends after us.'

Macro turned to his friend and cocked an eyebrow. 'Better to make a run for it, you think?'

'I don't know . . . We'd have to make some attempt to take the fort and capture Caratacus before we considered a retreat. But it's going to be a difficult and bloody job. You've seen the defences up there. Even with half our number, Venutius could hold us off until he's relieved. And those men up there are the cream of the tribes' warriors. They'll put up a stiff fight.'

'They've done that before, and it hasn't done 'em much good,' Macro replied with a grin, his teeth gleaming dully in the pale moonlight. 'One hill fort's just the same as any other.'

'Not this one.' Cato gestured towards the line of earthworks, visible only as shadowy bands stretching round the crest of the hill below the line of the palisade. 'Steeper slopes than most, and higher. There's only one practical line of attack and that's covered by the outer redoubt. And there are hard-fighting men behind the defences.'

Macro considered this for a moment before he responded. 'Do you think Horatius is up to the job?'

'I don't know. He's certainly no Vespasian.'

'True enough.' Macro chuckled. 'The legate went through those hill forts like grease through a goose, from what I heard. We could do with him now. Instead we've got that wet-behind-the-ears tribune and his nursemaid, Horatius. A sorry lookout all round.'

Cato pursed his lips briefly. 'They might surprise us both yet.'

'And then again they might not.'

Cato turned to him with a light smile. 'I thought I was the one who was inclined to see the downside of everything.'

'That's you all right.' Macro laughed and patted his friend on the shoulder. 'Seems like you've finally worn me down to your way of seeing things.'

Cato shrugged. 'What can I say?'

'Best you didn't, eh?' Macro yawned and stretched his shoulders. 'As long as it's quiet I'll get some rest. Could be busy tomorrow.'

The centurion crossed to the rear of the tower and took off his helmet and unclasped his cloak. Folding the cloth into a tight bundle, Macro lay down and rested his head on his makeshift bolster. He breathed easily for a while before settling into a deep slumber. A smile flickered across Cato's lips as he heard the familiar faint rumbling that acted as a prelude to his friend's usual snoring.

Then he caught a flicker of light out of the corner of his eye and turned to look towards the hill fort as sparks burst into the air a short distance below the palisade. There was a short-lived pool of light on the grass slope before it died away. Another torch arced into the air, followed by others, falling in a fiery arc against the darkness before they, too, hit the ground with distant bursts of flame. This time there was enough light for Cato to pick out a figure scrambling down the slope. Then the scene was plunged into darkness again. He strained his eyes and ears and caught the faint sound of shouting before the note of a horn pierced the quiet night and echoed briefly off the surrounding hills.

Cato turned and called over his shoulder. 'Macro!'

His friend seemed to stir before turning his back to Cato and grumbling something about a tent. Cato hurried across and bent down to shake his shoulder vigorously. 'Wake up, Centurion!'

This time Macro's eyes shuddered open and he blinked as he focused. As soon as he made out Cato's anxious expression, he snapped back into full consciousness and climbed to his feet, helmet in hand. 'What is it, sir?'

'Someone's making a bid to escape the fort. Looked like they're heading this way. I want a half-century of your men ready by the gate, now.'

Macro fastened his chinstrap and nodded before turning towards the ladder. 'Right, lads! First Century, Fourth Cohort! On your feet!'

As the figures lying at the base of the rampart stirred, Cato returned to the front of the tower to try and follow the action close to the hill fort. A few more torches were descending the slope, this time held above the men bearing them as they half ran, half slid down the slope in pursuit. There were more torches rippling along the palisade in the direction of the fort's gate complex. Cato felt his pulse quicken. Whoever had come out on top in the struggle between Queen Cartimandua and her consort, it did not look like it had ended peacefully.

It might have been a trick of the moonlight but Cato thought he detected movement on the dark grey landscape stretching out towards Isurium. A moment later he was certain of it. A figure was running towards the Roman camp. He felt tempted to raise the alarm and call the entire column to readiness. But there was only one man as yet, and it would be better for his soldiers to be left to rest and save their strength for the morrow.

He cupped a hand to his mouth. 'Macro?'

'Sir!' The reply sounded from below and behind the gate.

'Are your men ready?'

'Any moment, sir.'

'Good. Stand by the gate.'

The runner was no more than a quarter of a mile away, racing through the long grass in the stifling heat of the hot summer night. Then, above the clink of armour and shuffling of the boots of Macro's men, Cato heard another unmistakable sound. The pounding of horses' hoofs. They came from the settlement and he saw them at once, several riders, fanning out slightly as they galloped after their prey, determined to run him to ground before he could reach the Roman camp.

Cato hurried to the rear of the tower and leaned over as he spotted Macro's foreshortened figure.

'Open the gate! There's someone approaching from the fort. With horsemen not far behind. Get out there and bring the man in.'

Macro's dimly visible face stared up. 'Yes, sir!'

He glanced round to the front rank of the First Century of his cohort. 'You heard the prefect! Get that locking bar out!'

Dark shapes rushed forward and Cato heard the men gasp as they lifted the heavy timber beam from its brackets. A moment later the hinges groaned as the gates were hauled aside. Then Macro issued a curt command.

'First Century! At the double . . . Advance!'

CHAPTER TWENTY-NINE

Their boots pounded across the packed earth of the narrow causeway as they poured out of the gate, across the ditch and into the night. Macro instinctively held his shield tightly to his side to keep his balance as best he could. His right hand hung loose as there was no need for his sword just yet. He scanned the moonlit landscape ahead until he saw the figure hurrying towards him. Altering direction to meet the fugitive, he also saw the horsemen angling in towards him. It would be a close thing, Macro decided. He steadily increased his pace and ordered his men to keep up. The riders posed little threat to the legionaries. There were too few of them. Yet they came on in a frantic charge, heedless of the risk to their mounts as they plunged through the night. He could hear them now, uttering savage cries as they urged their horses on, like hunters closing in for the kill.

'This way!' Macro called out. 'Over here!'

The figure plunging through the grass ran straight at Macro. Behind him galloped the horsemen, and Macro could see that they carried spears. The leading rider lowered his weapon and took aim with the point.

'Shields to the front! Form wedge!' Macro bellowed as he swung his round and snatched out his sword, pressing the flat of the blade against the shield trim. He slowed to allow the men of the front rank to take position either side of him, and the men following fanned out as they continued forward.

The fugitive glanced back over his shoulder and saw the nearest of the riders a short distance behind. He put on a last desperate sprint for the safety of the Roman formation, but Macro could see that he would not make it before the riders caught up with him.

'Drop down! Down!' Macro shouted frantically as the first horseman thundered up to the man. Whether he heard the warning or acted on instinct, the fugitive threw himself to the side and rolled on the ground. The rider stabbed and missed and then snatched at his reins as his horse plunged towards the Romans. Macro felt the blow on his shield as the chest of the horse struck. Then the animal reared above him, the rider cursing as he stabbed with his spear. The iron point glanced off the curve of the shield and Macro punched his sword up, feeling the point drive home into flesh.

Then the horse was gone, wheeling away towards the other horsemen. Macro looked for the man they had been chasing and saw a tall figure rise up from the grass. He could make out the flowing hair and the left hand clasped to the opposite shoulder. Then the man plunged forward, pushing past Macro into the safety of the Roman formation. There were still others to deal with and Macro did not spare him a glance as he closed ranks and raised his shield towards the oncoming riders.

'First Century! Halt!'

Their boots ground to a stop and their panting breath filled the air as they faced the horsemen. At the last moment the riders veered down the sides of the wedge, stabbing their spears at the dark shapes of the legionaries. The clatter of iron on wood and the brass bosses of the shields stung the air but none of the spears struck home. Macro edged back into the formation and ordered the men on either side to close up. Then he turned and saw that the man they had rescued was on his knees gasping for breath.

'You all right, lad?'

The man looked up at Macro, his features clear to see in the moonlight. Macro started. 'By the gods, Vellocatus!'

The nobleman nodded and struggled to catch his breath. 'Your tribune . . . Have to speak to him . . . At once.'

'Right, then.' Macro sheathed his blade and helped the Brigantian to his feet. There was a dark stain on the cloth on his right shoulder where he still pressed his hand to control the bleeding. Macro steered him into the heart of the formation and covered his body with his shield. Around the compact formation of the legionaries the horsemen were wheeling round, trying in vain to find a way past the large rectangular shields. Macro looked back towards the fort and estimated that it was over two hundred paces away. The blast of a trumpet announced that the general alarm had been given.

'Fall back on my count! One . . . two . . .'

With the centurion calling the pace, the men tramped back in the direction of the camp, with Vellocatus safe in the middle of the formation. As they approached the camp, a squadron of cavalry disgorged from the gate and galloped towards them and Macro smiled as he recognised the shape of the Blood Crows' banner.

'It's our prefect, boys! Come to escort us into camp.'

The native horsemen broke away as they became aware of the threat. Macro saw one of them turn back and raise his spear in an overhand grip. The man gave an enraged shout and hurled his weapon at Vellocatus. Macro instinctively threw himself at the intended victim and both men crashed to the ground as the spear whipped over their heads and struck one of the legionaries in the thigh, bursting through his flesh and out the other side. The Roman staggered under the impact and then looked down in a disbelieving stupor at the shaft piercing his leg.

There was a shout of command and the riders wheeled away and galloped back towards Isurium. The wounded legionary sheathed his sword and calmly lowered his shield to the ground as he inspected his wound with a trembling hand.

'Get that out of him, and bind the wound up,' Macro ordered.

A heartbeat later the auxiliary cavalrymen reined in either side of the formation and Cato called out, 'All right there, Macro?'

'Fine, sir.'

'Did you get to our man in time?'

'He's here. It's Vellocatus.'

There was a pause as Cato took in the information and felt a sickening dread at its implications. 'Get him into camp. I'll send for the tribune. I don't think he's going to like what our friend has to say.'

The surgeon from the Ninth Legion concentrated on cleaning the wound on his shoulder as Vellocatus gave his account to the officers standing around him. They had gathered just inside the gate where Cato had ordered a brazier to be lit to provide sufficient light for the surgeon to tend to his patient.

'They've taken the queen prisoner,' Vellocatus said bitterly. 'Venutius had her arrested. Her guards have been disarmed and Venutius's men were rounding up anyone who was loyal to Cartimandua. There was a struggle in one part of the hall and that's when I managed to get out by the side door. They spotted me at once and one of them got his blade into my shoulder before I went over the wall and made for your camp. You must help. You've got to rescue the queen,' he insisted.

Otho and his officers exchanged anxious glances before Cato spoke up. 'What happened? Precisely. We have to know before we can act.'

'What's there to know that we don't already?' Horatius countered. 'She's failed to take control of her people. Now this renegade's in charge. Him, and Caratacus. So we'll have to go in there and sort 'em out.'

'Wait,' Cato protested. 'We need to know more.'

Horatius cooked his head. 'Why exactly?'

'Because it doesn't make sense.' Cato turned to Otho. 'Sir, yesterday when we had the private audience with Cartimandua, she said that she had paid her people off. She said their loyalty had been bought. Remember?'

The tribune nodded. 'That's right. Seems she was wrong.'

'She seemed confident of it at the time. And again in the hall last night. There was support for Venutius, but a minority of those present. I'm sure of it.'

Otho thought a moment. 'You're right. What of it?'

'There's only one way Venutius could have swung enough support round in his favour to depose the queen. He offered them more gold.'

'That's right,' Vellocatus interrupted. 'He did. Silver coin for every man who sided with him against the queen.'

'Did he show them the silver?' asked Cato. 'Did you see it?'

Vellocatus nodded. 'One of his men brought in a chest. Filled with coins.'

Horatius sighed impatiently. 'I fail to see what the point of this is. It doesn't change anything.'

Cato turned to him. 'But where did he get the silver? He must have ready access to a fortune. You don't just scrape that together by having a whip-round amongst your tribal supporters.'

'All right,' Horatius conceded. 'So how did he get hold of it?'

Cato glanced at Macro before he replied. 'He's been helped by someone on our side. A spy.'

Horatius stared at him and then suddenly laughed. 'Oh, fuck off! We've got a native spy on our side? He's blended in and passed himself off as Roman, has he?'

'I didn't say he was a native.'

'What then? You mean a Roman? One of us?'

'That's exactly what I mean. Someone sent to help Venutius depose the queen and get the Brigantes to support Caratacus.'

Horatius shook his head and smiled mockingly. 'Just listen to yourself, Cato. It's absurd.'

'Prefect Cato's right,' Macro interrupted. 'There's a spy in our camp, and he's out to undermine the security of the province.'

Horatius and the others turned to Macro in surprise. Horatius sucked in a breath before he responded. 'You too? What, is it something in the rations you boys in the baggage train escort have been eating? Some of those mushrooms the Druids are so fond of?'

'It's the truth.' Macro spoke as calmly as he could. 'The prefect and me were briefed that there's a faction in Rome that want to abandon Britannia. The spy is working for them.'

'And why would you be briefed?'

'Because we've done work for the side that's against the faction I'm talking about.'

Horatius frowned. 'What's this? You and the prefect are also spies?'

'No,' Cato cut in now that Macro had blurted out the truth. 'Not any longer. Not since we returned to the province. I give you my word on that. We were informed in case we could assist in frustrating their plans.'

Tribune Otho stared at him. 'Informed? Who informed you?'

Cato shook his head. 'We're not at liberty to say.'

'Bah!' Horatius growled. 'Utter bollocks, whichever way you look at it. And it doesn't change a thing. We've got to get up there. Sort Venutius and his lads out, and put Cartimandua back on her throne.'

'That's right.' Vellocatus nodded. He shifted round to face Otho, and the surgeon had to hurriedly withdraw the needle and thread he had been about to use to sew up the wound on the Brigantian's shoulder. 'That's what you must do. You have no choice.'

Otho avoided his gaze as he considered the prospect. 'I have just over two thousand men under my command, and we are now in the heart of what has become enemy territory. Aside from the hundreds of men Venutius now has at his command, there will be tens of thousands more that will rally to his standard in a matter of days.' He looked up. 'Gentlemen, as far as I see it there is no choice. We have to retreat. At once.'

There was a stunned silence before Vellocatus spoke in an anguished voice. 'You would betray your ally? You would abandon Cartimandua to her fate? Is this how Rome honours her treaties?'

'I'm sorry,' Otho responded. 'There's nothing we can do. It would be suicide to attempt to rescue her. I will not risk my men's lives in a futile gesture.'

Horatius regarded the tribune with contempt. 'Your men, or your wife?'

Otho glared at him. 'What are you suggesting?'

'I always said you should never have brought your wife along. Women have no place in such a campaign.'

Macro nodded in agreement.

'That's my decision, Prefect. And I am in command here.'

'No, sir. You are not. Not any longer. The legate's orders were clear. If it comes to a fight then you are to cede command to me.'

'But we can avoid a fight if we retreat at once.'

'We're not going to retreat. There will be a fight. And I will be in command. Until it's over.' Horatius smiled wryly. He turned to look round the faces of the other officers. 'In accordance with orders, I am taking command from Tribune Otho. Is there any objection?'

Centurion Statillus shook his head, and Acer followed his lead. Horatius's eyes shifted to Cato. 'Well?'

Despite his instinct that it was the right thing to attempt a rescue, Cato made himself quickly run through the options. Retreat was possible. It would avoid the bloody loss of life of any attack on the hill fort. Both native and Roman. But there was no guarantee that they would make it back across the frontier before Venutius and his warriors caught up with them and forced them to turn and fight. They could lay siege to the fort, but every day they spent waiting for Venutius to run out of food and surrender was a day the enemy could mobilise reinforcements amongst the tribes and then march on Isurium. No, there was only one logical course of action, Cato concluded. They must crush the rebellion before it could spread, and restore Cartimandua to power. And that meant agreeing to the change in command of the forces in the camp.

'I have no objection.'

'Macro?'

'I agree.'

Horatius nodded. 'Then it's settled. I have command. I'll make plans for an attack on the fort at first light.'

'Why wait, sir?' asked Macro. 'What if they try and get out under cover of darkness? If Venutius and Caratacus flee then we'll never track them down.'

'No, they'll stay where they are,' Horatius replied. 'They think they're safe up there. Though I dare say they will have already sent word to the tribes to concentrate at Isurium as soon as possible. That's why we have to settle this tomorrow.'

The surgeon had finished sewing up Vellocatus's wound and was tying a dressing over his handiwork. The Brigantian shield-bearer stood up and bowed his head gratefully to Prefect Horatius. 'I thank you, sir.'

'Don't thank me until the job is done, young man. The rest of you, brief your officers and prepare your men for the attack. I suggest you feed 'em at dawn, and let 'em rest as much as they can before then. You'll have your orders as soon they're ready.'

'What about me?' Otho asked quietly.

Horatius regarded him for an instant before he shrugged. 'Do as you will, sir. Join us, or stay here in the camp with the unit left on watch, and your wife. It's your decision.'

'I see.'

'That's all. I'll be at headquarters if I'm needed.' Horatius turned to the Brigantian. 'You come with me. I need to know the layout of the fort, and anything else that might cause us a nasty surprise.'

He strode off and Vellocatus hurried to catch up with the new

296

commander. The rest stood and watched in an uncomfortable silence, refusing to turn and meet the tribune's eyes. Otho cleared his throat and made to speak. Then thought better of it and turned away and slowly paced off into the night, in Horatius's footsteps, as he made for the tent he shared with his wife.

'Poor bastard,' said Macro. 'He'll never live this down.'

'Maybe.' Cato scratched his jaw. 'Or he may yet be proved right. It could all go wrong, and we'd be better off having retreated like he wants.'

Macro sucked his teeth and then shrugged. 'Look on the bright side.'

'The bright side?'

'Sure.' Macro nodded. 'If the tribune is proved right and it all goes tits up, he's not going to be around to say I told you so.'

CHAPTER THIRTY

By the time the Roman soldiers began to enter the settlement most of the inhabitants had already fled. Once word reached them that Venutius had seized power many had feared that the Romans in the nearby camp would intervene. Hurriedly packing their few valuables into bundles, they herded their families out of the settlement and made for the safety of the surrounding hills from where they could watch events unfold. Only a few still remained, silently hiding behind closed doors and praying to their gods that they were overlooked or ignored.

Prefect Horatius had left the mounted contingent of his cohort to protect the camp, under the command of Tribune Otho, while he led the rest of the soldiers out to attack the fort. He rode at the head of his troops, sitting stiff-backed in his saddle. Ahead of him a screen of legionaries warily entered the settlement, watching for signs of ambush as they pushed forward along the narrow lanes towards the track leading up to the fort. The sun had only just risen and shadows lurked between the huts and pens of the natives. Horatius halted the main column outside the settlement and summoned the unit commanders. It was still cool enough to warrant wearing a cloak, but Cato had to suppress a shudder as he craned his neck to look up the slope towards the palisade far above.

'There's only one way to do this,' Horatius began. 'And that's to attack the main gate.'

A party of men had been sent out during the night to fell a suitable tree for use as a ram and now two sections of legionaries were carrying the heavy burden towards the settlement.

'Centurion Statillus, your cohort will launch the first assault up the track. A covering century in the vanguard. Then the ram, and the rest of your men.'

Statillus nodded.

'You will, of course, ensure that the men carrying the ram are screened by their comrades. I don't want any unnecessary casualties. Climb the track as quick as you can and batter through the main gate. Your cohort should be sufficient to take the fort, but Centurion Acer's men will be on hand if you need reinforcing. Unfortunately we cannot deploy our ballistas to cover your attack because the angle of the slope is too great.'

'A pity, that,' Macro commented. 'The natives really don't like being on the receiving end of our artillery.'

'It can't be helped. We'll just have to take the fort head on. Roman courage and Roman steel will be enough to crush Venutius and his supporters.' Horatius turned to Cato. 'The only remaining task will be to ensure that no one escapes. If Vellocatus can get out over the wall, you can be sure others will give it a try. We don't want the ringleaders to escape, or Caratacus. That's your responsibility, Prefect Cato. The Blood Crows are to surround the hill and round up anyone who gets down the slope. Clear?'

'Yes, sir.'

'Good. Then everyone knows what they have to do. We'll commence the attack as soon as the Seventh Cohort is formed up at the foot of the hill.' He glanced round and concluded confidently, 'Good luck, gentlemen. Do your job and this will all be over by noon. Dismissed.'

The other officers saluted and turned away to rejoin their commands. Cato walked with Macro as they paced down the side of the column of legionaries. Macro's cohort was at the end, just before the contingent of auxiliary infantry from Horatius's unit. The Blood Crows stood by their horses at the very rear of the column.

'What do you think?' Cato asked.

'About?'

'The prefect's plan?'

Macro pursed his lips. 'It's simple enough.'

'That's the problem.'

Macro sighed. 'You know, sometimes simple is best.'

'True,' Cato conceded. 'But not in this case. A frontal assault is going to be costly. There's no avoiding heavy losses if we go directly for the main gate.' He paused and pointed up at the outlying bastion round which the track curved in its final approach to the ditch and gate of the fort. Already there were scores of warriors lining the palisade, watching the approach of the Roman forces. 'That's what we should go for first, before we bring the ram up.'

Macro stared up at the formidable earthwork. 'That would take too long. Horatius is right, we need to get this over with as soon as possible, even if it means we have to accept a few extra casualties.' He smiled grimly. 'Hills . . . Taking 'em seems to be our speciality these days.'

Cato was still for a moment as he envisaged the perils of the coming assault. 'Let's hope we don't have a repeat of that bloodbath we got ourselves into with the Silurians.'

'Amen to that, brother.'

They resumed their march down the column until they reached the standard at the head of Macro's cohort. Cato held out his hand and they clasped arms.

'Watch yourself, Macro. If you get sent up the hill then it'll be sticky.'

'If I get sent up the hill, Horatius will have fucked it up spectacularly. That ain't going to happen. Just make sure you let none of those bastards slip away.'

'There's no way Caratacus is going to do that again. I swear it, by all the gods.'

'I wouldn't tempt them if I were you. The gods like to have their fun with the pair of us. That much I've learned.'

Cato laughed. 'Very well. I'll see you later, in the fort.'

They released their grip and Cato continued down the column towards the waiting horsemen. By the time he had swung himself up into the saddle and given the command to mount he could see the glint of the early morning sun on the helmets of the Seventh Cohort as they emerged from the settlement and formed up in their centuries on the track leading up the slope. Above them, in the outer bastion, thin trails of smoke were rising into the clear sky as the defenders made their preparations to drive off the coming assault.

'Decurion Miro!'

'Sir!'

Cato pointed to the hill. 'I want our men positioned a short distance out from the bottom of the slope. Two men every fifty paces should cover it. I'll keep one squadron in reserve to the right of the settlement. We're not to let one man get past us. And we want prisoners. Only kill if we have to. We must take Caratacus alive.' Cato wheeled his horse round and raised his voice so that all of his men would hear. 'You all know what Caratacus looks like. He won't escape us this time. If you see him, I promise a hundred denariians for the man who captures him. And ten for every other prisoner.'

He could see the excited gleam in their faces and knew that he could count on them, Thracians and the replacements alike. They would do their duty and fight well for him, even more so now that there was money involved. Cato had no fear of being out of pocket. He would make it back from the sale of captives to the traders waiting back at Viroconium.

'Second Thracian! Advance!'

He spurred his horse into an easy walk and led the cohort out across the knee-deep grass towards the hill. He stopped the leading squadron a short distance from the nearest of the huts and indicated to Miro to begin dispersing the rest of the men around the slope. Ahead he could see the last of the legionaries of the Seventh Cohort moving into column on the track. Close to the front the ram lay on the ground, eight men on either side, shields strapped over their backs. They had the unenviable task of carrying the heavy ram all the way to the top of the hill before swinging it against the gates. All the time they would be targeted by the defenders and would have to rely on their comrades to protect them as far as possible.

The rumble of wheels drew Cato's attention and he turned to see Septimus on the driving bench of his cart as he approached from the camp. The imperial agent waved a hand in greeting and drew up beside Cato's squadron.

'A fine morning, Prefect!'

'What brings you here, Hipparchus?'

'Trade, sir. Trade. What else?' He pointed to the legionaries. 'It's going to be hot work today. Men will need refreshment, and what better than a cup of my fine wine? Besides, I can watch things closely,' he added in a deliberate tone. 'Who knows what a humble civilian might learn today.'

A horn announced the start of the attack and both men focused their attention on the Seventh Cohort as the leading century began to edge forward.

'I'd better be off then, sir.' Septimus knuckled his forehead and flicked his whip to urge his mules forward. The cart rattled on over the uneven surface and disappeared into the settlement. As he sat in the saddle, Cato felt stiff and tired. He had not slept the previous night and his mind was clouded by fatigue. It seemed that Septimus, and his master Narcissus, had been right all along and there were traitors conspiring to bring about the collapse of Roman ambitions in Britannia. No doubt if Caratacus was taken alive he would be taken back to Rome and questioned closely about the identities of those Romans who had secretly abetted his cause.

As strong and tough as Caratacus was, Cato had no illusions about the enemy king's ability to hold out against the skilled torturers of the imperial secretary. He would reveal all that he knew, and then there would be the consequent discreet bloodletting of those uncovered in plotting against Emperor Claudius. It would be better for them if Caratacus were to perish here today, fighting his Roman foes to the last breath. That was the fate he better deserved than being broken by Narcissus's thugs, Cato conceded. After all, he had fought for the liberty of his people. He had fought on when lesser kings had bowed to Rome, or accepted Roman coin to become the lapdogs of the Emperor. There was something of the hero about him, and Cato wished him a better end than painfully expiring in a dark, dank dungeon in the bowels of the imperial palace.

A dark smudge traced an arc through the air as a fire arrow reached the zenith of its flight and plunged down towards the leading ranks of the Seventh Cohort. The signal given, the archers in the bastion loosed a barrage of arrows down the slope and Cato saw shafts shatter against the red shields of the legionaries. Some lodged where they pierced the wood and looked like fine hairs sprouting on the back of a long, scaly insect as the cohort trudged round the first bend in the track that zigzagged up to the fort.

The first man fell out of line shortly after the legionaries set out along the next straight length of the track, an arrow protruding from his leg at a steep angle. The man hobbled out of the path of his comrades and, keeping his shield up, he picked his way down the grassy slope. The second casualty soon followed as one of the men carrying the ram was felled by an arrow tearing through his neck under his cheekguard. He fell on to the track and an optio ordered another man forward before he dragged the stricken legionary aside.

The cohort turned another corner and began to pass directly beneath the outer bastion. Cato saw the flicker of flames along the parapet and swirling smoke as men heaved blazing bundles of faggots up on the end of pitchforks and swung them over the rampart. The faggots flared brilliantly as they flew through the air. The angle of the slope was such that they did not burst apart on impact but continued rolling down the slope straight at the exposed right flank of the column of Roman soldiers. The column halted where the legionaries tried to get out of the way of the blazing bundles of wood splashed with pitch. Cato saw a complete file of men knocked to the ground and when one rose up he was alight from where the burning pitch had stuck to his tunic. He threw down his shield and started to beat at the flames as his comrades backed away. Then he was hit by an arrow, and another, and he stumbled off the track and rolled down the slope, desperately trying to extinguish the flames.

More men were knocked down by the flaming bundles and scorched before the optios and centurions ordered the men on the right of the column to switch their shields to their other hand. A section ran up to guard the flank of those carrying the ram, three of whom had been burned or struck down by arrows. The column edged forward again, under a steady bombardment of arrows, rocks, javelins and blazing faggots.

Cato watched with a growing feeling of despair as more legionaries were hit and the slope below the track was dotted with the gleam of armour and red tunics of the wounded struggling to reach the safety of the bottom of the hill. Above them the palisade of the bastion was thick with Brigantian warriors, and hundreds more lined the wall of the main fort, cheering their comrades on, their cries clearly audible to the Roman units watching in silence as the Seventh Cohort struggled on. At length, the survivors of the leading century turned the last corner, between the bastion and the main fort, and approached the gate, and passed out of Cato's field of vision. The ram followed, though Cato wondered how many of the original party still lived to carry their burden. The following centuries edged forward, more and more slowly until they ground to a halt.

A glint lower down the slope caught his eye and he saw an officer on a horse galloping up the track. Horatius, Cato realised. The prefect slowed as he passed the first of the casualties and then he was forced to walk his horse as he reached the end of the column. Drawing his sword, Horatius raised it high and stabbed the point up at the fort, urging his men on as he passed by them, making for the head of the cohort. He reached the last corner and then seemed to be snatched from view, gone. Cato strained his eyes but could make out no sign of him. No plumed helmet, nor even his horse. Then he saw the beast, empty-saddled and streaked with blood, as it bolted down the slope. Behind it the legionaries began to edge away.

Cato's heart filled with a leaden sense of frustration as he watched the retreat. There was no sign of the ram, abandoned in the killing zone between the fort and the bastion, as its bearers fell back with their comrades, free at last to unsling their shields and hold them overhead to protect them from the missiles raining down. More men fell, and the fortunate were helped up and supported by their comrades as the Seventh Cohort retreated down the track and out of the range of the rocks, and then the spears and last of all the arrows. The more hopeful of the defenders tried a few final shots before it was clear that their enemy was beyond the reach of their arrows. A triumphant cheering rose up from the throats of the Brigantians as they surveyed the bodies and discarded equipment scattered below the fort. The remains of several bundles of wood still burned at the end of the streaks of scorched ground that scarred the slope. Some of the wounded tried to crawl to safety before they attracted the attention of the enemy.

Cato shook his head in despair. The attack had failed, just as he had feared it would, and it seemed that Horatius had placed himself in danger and been knocked off his horse into the bargain. The Seventh Cohort had suffered heavy losses and would be very wary of making another such attack, as would the rest of the column who had witnessed their battering.

'Well, what now?' a voice sounded from the men at Cato's back. He glanced over his shoulder and saw Thraxis shaking his head. 'Bloody waste that was.'

Cato stared at him a moment, tempted to share his own doubts. Then he determined not to undermine the authority of another officer in front of his men. Instead he growled, 'Silence in the ranks!'

He turned back and wondered what would happen next. Once Horatius had reached the safety of the settlement he would have to rethink his plan as he had any injuries seen to. Cato hoped that he would try something different. The bastion had to be the priority. Until it was reduced, the Romans would never even reach the fort's gate, let alone breach it with the ram, without suffering appalling losses.

Cato was still considering the situation when he saw a rider gallop out of the settlement and turn his mount towards the squadron from the Blood Crows. A moment later the headquarters orderly reined in and saluted.

'Centurion Macro sends his compliments, sir,' he breathed deeply. 'Prefect Horatius is dead.'

'Dead?'

The orderly nodded. 'Killed outright by a slingshot, sir. Struck him in the face. His body was brought down a short time ago. Centurion Macro sent me to tell you.'

'I see.'

'There's more, sir . . . Centurion Macro begs to inform you that you are in command now.'

Cato froze. Of course. His friend was right. He was the next in the chain of command. To him passed the responsibility. He turned in his saddle to face Thraxis. 'Ride to Decurion Miro and tell him to take over. Tell him what's happened, and tell him I'll be in the settlement.'

'Yes, sir!' Thraxis flashed a salute and spurred his mount out of the formation and galloped off around the hill.

Cato turned back to the orderly. 'Let's go.'

CHAPTER THIRTY-ONE

'Stupid fool,' Macro grumbled as they looked down on the body of Prefect Horatius which had been placed on a bier in one of the huts. He and Cato were alone with the corpse and the surgeon who had attempted to treat Horatius's wound. The prefect was still in his armour but his helmet had been removed, but even without the helmet it would have been difficult for his closest friend to recognise him. The slingshot had struck slightly to the right of the bridge of his nose, pulverising the cartilage and shattering his brow before plunging through his eye into his brain. In its wake the shot had left a crater of bone, torn flesh and blood that utterly disfigured the face of Horatius. Beside him, on the ground, lay Centurion Statillus. Also dead. Killed when an arrow had severed an artery inside his thigh. He had bled out on the track before the men carrying him had reached the settlement.

'What was Horatius doing up on the hill anyway?'

Macro thought back. 'He could see that the cohort was stalling and lost his temper. I tried to talk him out of it. But he took his horse and galloped up there. Stood out like a sore thumb. Every native worth his salt took aim at him. It's a miracle he got as far as he did before someone hit him.' Macro cracked his knuckles. 'Still, it's an ill wind and all that . . .'

'Meaning?'

'Now we've got someone in charge who knows how to do his job.' Macro raised his chin. 'What are your orders, sir?'

Cato had had little time to think through the situation as he rode over from the Blood Crows. He hurriedly collected his thoughts. 'Firstly, the casualties. I want the walking wounded to make their own way to the camp. The rest can be collected in carts. Bring forward the ballistas at the same time.'

'What are we going to need them for? Horatius was right about one thing. The angle's too great to use them.'

'From down here it is,' Cato conceded. 'Have the ballistas broken down into their components and brought forward. They'll serve us well yet.'

Macro frowned, but Cato continued before he could speak. 'Then I want axes and picks, enough for ten men, and rope, from stores. And as many slings and shot as we have. I'll choose a new commander of the Eighth Cohort. Acer can look after the Seventh until this is over. They'll need a little time to get over their rough handling. Your cohort is the next one to go up the hill.'

'We're under strength. Even now we've got less men than the Seventh. Mind you, they're tough lads.' He fixed Cato with a steady gaze. 'We're up for it, sir. Just give the order.'

Cato smiled. 'All in good time, Macro. We've a few preparations to make first.' He turned to the surgeon. 'Have Statillus and Horatius taken back to the camp, then see to the wounded.'

'Yes, sir.' The surgeon saluted.

Cato and Macro left him in the hut and emerged into the sunlight. It was not yet mid-morning and the day was bright and warm. On either side the street was filled with wounded men, many lying on the ground, while others sat or stood with strained expressions as they waited to be seen to.

'Macro, I want you to return to camp and gather together what I've asked for. Get back here with the equipment as soon as you can.'

Macro saluted and turned away to carry out his orders. Cato picked his way through the injured and emerged on the edge of the village facing the fort. Macro's cohort, and the Eighth, were resting on the open ground, waiting for orders. They looked round expectantly as their new commander came into view but when he simply stood and concentrated his attention on the bastion, they returned to their quiet conversation.

Cato scrutinised the bastion from end to end and noted that the timber posts of the palisade were lower on the side furthest from the corner where the track approached the gate. Either the Brigantians who had built the fort had used uneven lengths of timber, or the ground had shifted beneath the end of the fort, Cato mused. If that was the case, then it would help his plan. At least the first step of it. There would still be a savage contest for the bastion, but if it could be taken then the rest of the fort would soon fall. Everything depended on taking the outwork, he knew. It would be dangerous, and the men would need to be led by officers who would set an example of the courage needed to see it through. He smiled grimly. A job for himself and Macro then.

It was noon before the equipment was ready and the men had been briefed. The auxiliary infantry had been paired up. One man carried a legionary shield to cover himself and his companion, while the other was armed with a sling and a bag of shot. They were already advancing directly up the slope to get into position to cover the small force led by Cato. Two sections of Macro's cohort were carrying the tools and rope while the rest of the First Century would form a testudo to provide protection.

Cato gave a last look over the men gathered around him. 'Remember, when we reach the bastion we have to work fast. They'll be throwing everything they have at us. I don't want to lose one man more than absolutely necessary to get this done.'

He turned to the senior centurion he had chosen to lead the Eighth Cohort. Lebauscus was a big man. He towered over the others and was just as broad. His Germanic roots were obvious to all. Fair-haired and square-jawed, with piercing blue eyes.

'When I give the signal, you get the men up the slope at the double. You don't stop for anything. You don't stop until we've cut down every one of those bastards in the bastion.'

Lebauscus grinned. 'You can rely on me, sir. And the lads. We'll not let you down.'

'Glad to hear it.' Cato glanced towards the last officer to play his part in the coming attack. 'Acer, your teams will follow the Eighth the moment they set off. I'll want those ballistas ready to set up the instant we've taken the bastion. Together with the ammunition. We'll clear the gatehouse of defenders before they even know what's happening.' He paused and addressed them all. 'I want this to be quick and bloody. By the end of the day these natives are going to see just how swiftly the Roman army can bring them to their knees. I want word of this to go out to the rest of the Brigantes. Let 'em know what's in store for them if they ever think of giving us any trouble again. One last thing. Caratacus. He's to be taken alive. Wound him if you have to, but the gods help the man who fancies getting a reputation for himself by claiming the life of Caratacus. That's one the Emperor wants all to himself. Any questions?'

The officers and the men chosen for the work party stared back silently.

'Good.' Cato clapped his hands. 'Then let's go to it, gentlemen!'

Acer and Lebauscus strode off to their units. Cato undid the clasp of his cloak and let it slip from his shoulders. He caught it before it reached the ground and folded it carefully and then paused to smile as he patted the loose folds. 'Julia gave me this, before I left Rome.'

'Then she'll be glad it's given you good service,' Macro said gently. 'And it'll please her to see you wearing it on your return.'

'Yes.'

There was a brief silence before Macro spoke again. 'Listen, there's no need for you to do this. I can handle it.'

Cato shook his head. 'I don't mind getting my hands dirty.'

'I know you don't.' Macro's expression became serious. 'I'm more concerned about what happens to the rest of us if you get yourself killed. We've already lost two senior officers. If you get the chop then it's down to me or Tribune Otho to see it through, or get the lads back across the frontier. I'm not sure either of us are up to the job.'

'You'll manage. Besides, I've given the orders. The men are expecting me to lead them. What will they think if I duck out of it now? I have to go up there.'

Macro puffed his cheeks and nodded. 'All right. But keep your head down.'

Cato felt sweat on his palms and bent down to pick up some of the loose, dry soil beside the track. He rubbed some between his hands to get rid of the moisture and improve his grip. Then, picking up an axe and a coil of rope, he took a deep breath and loosened his shoulders. 'Let's get started.'

They strode out towards the men of Macro's cohort who were waiting on the track, shields grounded. There was a gap in the centre of the formation and Cato and the work party filed into place before Macro took up his shield and moved to the front.

'First Century, Fourth Cohort! Prepare to advance.'

The men took up their shields and stood, booted feet ready. When they were all still, Macro faced forward. 'Advance!'

The century paced forward, one rank at a time until the whole unit was advancing up the track. Above them Cato could see faces appearing above the palisade of the bastion as the enemy were alerted to the fresh attack being made by the Romans. As soon as the legionaries started up the track, the auxiliaries also began to move forward, climbing warily up through the grass to get close enough to the defences to use their slings. They had only gone a short distance before the first of the arrows whirred down towards them. Keeping an eye out for the shafts, the auxiliaries kept climbing, occasionally darting aside or sheltering together beneath a shield. It did not take them long to get into range and soon a steady exchange of missiles zipped to and fro between the defenders and the auxiliaries.

Cato nodded with satisfaction. The slingers were intended to serve as a distraction as much as a danger to the warriors defending the bastion. It would take some of the pressure off Macro's men as they moved into position. Glancing back he saw Lebauscus leading his cohort forward to their start position, and behind him came the men laden down by the components of the ballistas and baskets filled with the deadly iron-headed shafts that had proved so effective against the tribes that Rome had fought since landing in Britannia.

Macro led the century on, up the first length of track before swinging round the corner and beginning the next climb. The first arrows began to land close by, slender feathered lengths seeming to spring up amid the grass like tall flowers.

'Halt!' Macro commanded. The grinding of boots ceased. 'Shields up!'

The heavy wooden rectangles clunked together as the legionaries raised them above their heads and took some of the weight on the crowns of their helmets.

'Close up!'

The legionaries edged together and Cato was cut off from the sunlight and cast into the shaded world of sweating men, breathing heavily. The work party was squeezed between their comrades and bent down to give them space to let their shields meet in the middle of the column.

'Advance!'

They moved forward again, the sounds of the men around him louder than ever in Cato's ears. Above, arrows and stones clattered off the shields, or occasionally pierced the surfaces with a splintering crack. The urge to escape the confines of the formation was overwhelming and it took all Cato's willpower to keep in pace with the others. At the next corner they slowed to a crawl as they turned on to the last stretch directly below the bastion.

'This is it,' Cato called out to Macro. 'Get ready.'

They went on a few more paces before Cato ordered them to halt. He felt his heart pumping furiously from the exertion of the climb and the fear of what was to come. He tensed his muscles, waiting to give the command.

'Break ranks! Go right!'

Instantly the shields were wrenched aside and bright light poured on to Cato, making him blink. Bodies swerved away, off the track, and started up the short climb to the nearest end of the bastion. Cato ran with them, axe haft clutched in his right hand as he used his left to help him climb. The legionaries around him grunted and gasped with the effort of the ascent, and arrows and stones flew down at them from the palisade. On either side the auxiliary slingers hurled their missiles back with renewed effort, doing their best to put the defenders off their aim and force them back into cover. Even so, Cato saw a man go down to his right, an arrow shaft piercing the base of the spine just below his cuirass. Another was struck on the helmet by a rock and he sprawled, senseless, into the grass before a comrade clambered over him. Cato came up to two men sheltering behind their shields, heads hunched down, waiting there for their torment to come to an end. He reached out and shook the nearest man roughly.

'Keep going! Keep going, or you'll die here!'

The man seemed to come out of a daze and nodded. He gave his companion a shove and they both started forward again. Cato gave him an encouraging grin and the next moment he heard rather than felt the thud of an arrow. He looked down and saw the feathers of the arrow, then the shaft and then the base of it disappearing through the back of his left hand. Instinctively he tried to pull his hand away but the point of the arrow was embedded in the soil. Dropping the axe, he grabbed the shaft just above his hand and pulled the arrow free of the ground and felt a peculiar relief that it was only a narrow bodkin, the kind designed to punch through armour rather than cause horrific flesh injuries. Gritting his teeth, Cato grasped the shaft tightly. There was no time to hesitate, to imagine the pain. He wrenched it back, feeling the bones of his hand lurch as the iron head grated back through them and came free with flare of agony and a bright spray of blood.

Cato dropped the arrow, snatched up the axe and bunched his injured hand into a fist to try and stop the bleeding and still give him support as he moved on, jaws tightly clenched. He looked up and saw that Macro and several of his men had already reached the foot of the palisade and were starting to form a roof with their shields to shelter the work party. Cato scrambled up the last stretch of slope and into cover, throwing his axe down and slipping the coiled rope over his head and dropping it. He winced as he quickly examined the wound, an ugly puckered hole bleeding freely. Macro saw him and grimaced.

'Bet that smarts, sir.'

'Hurts like fuck.' Cato unwound his neck cloth and gestured to the nearest of the work party. 'Bind my hand.'

The legionary did as he was ordered while Cato examined the ground at the foot of the palisade. He could see that the soil had dropped a foot or so around the corner of the bastion, evidence of a landslip in the past.

'There! Get digging.'

Several of the men took up their picks and went to work, breaking up the ground and frantically scraping the soil aside. Above them the arrows and rocks continued to fall, and then there was a brief roaring sound and a wave of heat as a faggot burst on the shields and burning debris flickered down into the grass on either side of the shield men. The soil came away easily and soon they had worked two feet down the length of the wooden posts.

'Keep going,' Cato urged, leaning forward to feel the surface of the wood, dark and soft with age and damp. He turned to one of the work party. 'Take an axe to it, here. Cut around it as best you can.'

The soldier nodded and Cato backed away to give him space to wield the tool. The man struck as hard as the confined space allowed and a sharp thud reverberated in the close air. He struck again and a small chip of wood flew to one side. Again and again he struck, sweat flying from his brow, as he cut a channel in the timber, nearly a foot in diameter. He knew his task and did not need further instruction from Cato. As soon as he had a created a gap around the edge of the post wide enough for his purpose he set the axe down, drew his dagger and dug at the soil behind, working the blade around the back of the wood until there was enough room to pass a rope round. Cato reached down and handed him a coil and the soldier fed it round with clumsy speed, and once again, before tying the end off and throwing the rest of the rope down the slope.

'That's the first,' Cato called over to Macro. 'Two more should do it.'

'Hurry it up!' Macro shouted as his shield lurched under the impact of a rock. 'They're getting really pissed off up there.'

The men with the picks attacked the ground in a renewed frenzy, striking clods away in flurries of blows, until the bases of several of the posts were exposed, like old blackened teeth. A fresh man stepped forward to replace the axeman and cut the next two channels, and another fastened the ropes. Cato tested the knots with his good hand. Satisfied that they would hold, he ordered, 'That's it! Get on the ropes!'

The work party downed their tools and joined the others sliding down the slope and taking up position along the lengths stretched over the grass. Cato remained by the posts, standing between two of the ropes with his back to the wood.

'Take up the slack!'

Even though they were exposed to the enemy's missiles, Macro's men took the rope in both hands and braced their boots and waited for the order.

'Pull!'

The ropes went taut and Cato touched the nearest lightly with his fingers, feeling the tension, and searching for the telltale lurch that would indicate the post was moving.

'Together!' Macro called out. 'On my command . . . heave!'

313

The men on the three lines groaned, grunted and swore as they threw all their weight and strength into their efforts and pulled on the ropes. But Cato could sense no movement, and touched another of the ropes, fearing that he had not allowed the work party to dig deep enough around the bases of the posts. 'Move, you bastards . . .'

A loud cry drew his eyes to one of the men on the ropes. He had let go and was clawing at the shaft of a throwing spear that had pierced the mail armour over his shoulder. The tension on the rope slackened.

'Keep pulling!' Macro bellowed and the line snapped tight again. This time, Cato felt certain he sensed movement beneath his fingertips. No more than a slight tremor.

'It's moving!' he called out. 'Macro, another heave!'

'Ready, lads! Together. One, two, three, heave!'

This time it was more noticeable, and Cato even felt the rope shift a fraction downhill, and the wood moved a little behind his back. 'It's going to work!' he shouted with glee. 'It's moving! Heave!'

The soil at the bottom of the post began to trickle away and Cato looked up and saw the top of the post move against the clear background of the sky. Another post also edged out of place and for a moment Cato was oblivious to the pain in his hand as he grinned like an excited child. He felt cold soil sprinkle on to his arms as gaps opened above him and he laughed as he met Macro's gaze. But there was only an acute look of alarm in his friend's expression.

'It's going! Get out of the way, you fool!' Macro shouted at him.

Cato felt the post shift behind him and heard the strained groan of timber grinding on timber. His exultation of an instant before changed to icy dread as he thrust himself away from the corner of the fort and leaped down the slope. Ahead of him the legionaries had abandoned one of the ropes and were sprinting to either side. The post swept close by him in a blur.

'Get clear!' he heard Macro bellow to his men.

Another post thudded down to the other side of Cato and suddenly the ground seemed to move under his feet like water and a great weight struck him in the back, pitching him head first a short distance before there was only blackness, silence and he could not move.

At first Cato wondered if this was what death was like. An endless cold darkness enveloping his disembodied mind. It made a kind of sense if there was some irreducible essence to a person's being. He was surprised to find himself thinking so calmly, and then he felt the pain in his hand again, and found that he was straining to breathe. So much for the afterlife, he chided himself as he tried to move. He felt the soil shift as he wriggled his fingers. He thrust out his arm as far as he could and tried to move his legs at the same time. A burning sensation tingled in his lungs and the air about his mouth and nostrils felt hot and stifling and the first stab of fear pricked his mind. Buried alive. Suffocated to death. He renewed his efforts to struggle free but could not work out which direction he was facing. Then panic fully seized him.

CHAPTER THIRTY-TWO

'Where the fuck is the prefect?' Macro shouted as he rose to his feet and covered his body with his shield. Around him the other men were picking themselves up and shaking off the dirt that had poured down the slope when the corner of the bastion had collapsed. One of the legionaries had been crushed by the end of the post and lay unmoving where he was pinned to the ground. The Romans were not alone on the slope. Several of the enemy had been caught up in the small avalanche and were struggling to free themselves from the mound of earth beneath the breach. The posts that the Romans had pulled free had caused a collapse of the earth behind them and had carried away more posts on either side, leaving some hanging out at angles either side of the breached palisade.

Snatching out his sword, Macro knew he must take advantage of the moment. He thrust the point up the mound of earth towards the gap in the bastion's defences.

'First Century! Get stuck in!'

His men let out a roar and surged back up the slope and on to the loose earth, scrambling towards the breach. Macro charged at a dazed Brigantian with a dark plaited beard and knocked him down with a blow from his shield and quickly stabbed him three or four times with his sword. As the man rolled away he caused a small slide of earth to go with him and exposed the tips of a red crest. Macro kicked the body aside and fell on to his knees. He dropped his sword and frantically scooped the soil away until he could see the gleam of a helmet.

He turned and beckoned to a legionary climbing past. 'You, give me a hand here!'

They hurriedly worked to dig round the helmet and as they exposed the face, Cato's eyes blinked open and he spat to clear his mouth.

'Macro . . .' he muttered.

'Fuck me, lad, you lead a charmed life,' Macro laughed as he and the legionary pulled more earth away to free the prefect. Cato sat up with a small cascade of dirt. He was facing down the slope and he could see that Centurion Lebauscus and his men were streaming up towards the breach, and behind them the men of the Seventh, laden with the wooden parts of the ballistas. He turned and looked up at the bastion and saw that the enemy had recovered from the shock of the collapse of the corner and were making ready to contest the breach as the legionaries swarmed up towards them.

Macro helped him up and gestured to the legionary to get forward. 'Anything broken?'

Cato tested his limbs and shook his head. 'I'm fine.'

His wiped his left hand on the hem of his tunic to clear the earth from his wound and saw that the hand was trembling wildly. He gritted his teeth and clenched his fist tightly and tucked it against his chest before he drew his sword. 'Let's go.'

Macro retrieved his sword and side by side they joined the men struggling up over the loose soil. Ahead, the last of the enemy caught in the collapse of the corner of the bastion was cut down as he tried to rejoin his comrades and the legionaries clambered over him to get at his comrades waiting above. There was space for several men to defend the breach and they hefted their swords and axes as they raised their oval shields and prepared to fight. The first of the Romans came up, shield held over his head, and a Brigantian warrior swung his axe down viciously, the impact driving the legionary on to his knees. He struck again and as the blow split the wood, the legionary thrust with his sword, stabbing the man in the shin. His opponent bellowed a curse and reached down to wrench the shield aside and smashed his axe into the side of the legionary's helmet. The Roman slumped on to the earth close to the top of the ramp and immediately two of the Brigantian's companions bent over him, hacking at the body with their swords.

The next legionaries to climb into the breach were more wary, pausing to brace their boots and present their shields before advancing

317

together. The defenders swung their swords and axes at them, trying to beat them back. More Brigantians pressed round the breach and those to the side hurled stones down on the Romans clambering up towards them.

Macro and Cato pressed forward with their men, gasping for breath with the effort of climbing the bank of soil that slid down under their boots and made their progress slow and laborious. The first group of legionaries into the breach were engaging the enemy and the clatter of blades and thuds of blows striking shields filled the air. As more men filled the breach, they added their weight to the struggle and pressed forward. The two officers stopped behind the closely packed ranks of their men and while Macro held his shield up, Cato stood and peered over the heads of the legionaries ahead of him.

'We have to get the lads moving.'

Macro nodded. 'I'll see to it.'

Cato saw two of the Brigantians pointing him out, picking out the red crest of an officer. Cato recognised one. Belmatus. The other raised a bow and took aim, the head of the arrow foreshortening to a point as he took a steadying breath. His fingers released the string and Cato ducked down at the same time and the arrow deflected off his helmet with a glancing blow. Macro had pressed through the ranks until he was close to the front and then called out, 'First Century! Push and pace! On my count . . . One!'

The Romans had braced themselves, ready for the order, and let out a deep grunt as they threw their weight behind their shields.

'Two!'

The men took a step forward and braced themselves for the next thrust.

'One!'

Cato pushed forward with them, using his good hand to keep his balance. He had escaped death once this day and was desperate not to slip and be trampled into the ground by his own men. The tight mass of armoured men slowly gained ground, driving the natives back as they beat at the shield wall with their weapons in a wild frenzy. Risking a quick glance, Cato saw that he had passed between the posts still standing on either side. He took another step and his boot pressed on something solid. Looking down he saw the first legionary who had entered the breach, and died for the honour. There would be no award of a rampart crown for the man now.

Four more paces and then there was flattened grass under his boots as he entered the bastion. The legionaries were spreading out on either side and had won a foothold inside the defences, and all the time more men were pressing forward. Cato could see over the heads of those in front now. The interior of the bastion was an oval, eighty or so paces long and no more than thirty at the widest point. There were perhaps two hundred defenders and a brazier burned brightly a short distance from the few remaining faggots. Only a handful of the Brigantian rebels were still manning the rest of the palisade, loosing arrows at the Romans on the slope below.

Clutching his wounded hand to his breast, Cato drew his sword, dropping the point to make sure he did not accidently wound any of his comrades. He was surrounded by laboured breathing; this was tiring work for his men, having climbed the hill and the breach with the dead weight of their armour. Cato spared a moment's gratitude for the lighter burden of the mail vest he had bought from the Syrian merchant, then he focused his mind again. They had to clear the bastion while they still had the strength to.

'Keep going!' he shouted above the din of the battle. 'Forward!'

Macro took up the cry. He had found a space in the leading rank and stood shoulder to shoulder with the men facing the enemy. Advancing in a balanced crouch, he peered over the bronze trim of his shield, short sword stabbing out at any of the Brigantians who came within reach. The enemy had lost the contest to keep the Romans out and had backed off far enough to wield their weapons again. They fought with the desperate courage of their race, fearlessly lurching forward to hack at the line of Roman shields. The more cool-headed of them struck low, attempting crippling blows at the booted feet and shins of the Romans, or going high, over the top of the shields, to strike down at heads and shoulders. Either way, they risked exposing themselves to a quick thrust of a legionary sword.

Directly before Macro, a warrior in a mailed vest and carrying a heavy axe emerged from the press. His shaven head was adorned with swirling tattoos and a red moustache trailed either side of his snarling teeth. He roared at Macro and lifted his axe in both hands to strike.

There was just time for Macro to punch the shield out and then the shield split as the axehead smashed through the trim and splintered down almost as far as the brass boss.

'Shit . . .' Macro hissed, momentarily awed by the force of the blow.

The axehead shifted as the warrior tried to pull it free. But it was jammed and Macro pulled back savagely, trying to rip it from the man's hands. But the Brigantian was strong and held on and axe and shield shifted to and fro briefly before the warrior let out a roar and hurled himself forward, knocking the shield back into Macro and causing him to loose balance, until he was saved by the shield of the legionary behind him. With a mighty effort the Brigantian ripped his axe free and swung it back to strike again. The backswing caught one of his comrades and the iron head crushed his nose. Then it swept forward in a powerful arc, smashing across the shield of the man to Macro's right before passing narrowly in front of his own. The momentum of the swing reached its maximum force just as it struck the helmet of the legionary on the other side, right on the hinge of the cheekguard. The metal flap leaped aside as the edge of the axe smashed on through the soldier's skull, bursting out through his eye sockets and bridge of his nose before reaching the end of its arc.

'Sa!' the Brigantian shouted in triumph. He retrieved his weapon and kicked at the shield of the stricken man as he collapsed, spraying blood across the armour of his neighbours.

Macro leaped forward, punching his ruined shield up into his opponent's face, and was rewarded with a solid impact and a pained grunt as the splintered surface gouged into the warrior's face. He punched forward again, driving the man back before he withdrew his shield and braced his sword to strike. He saw the man's face, streaked with blood where a long splinter had torn open his cheek. Then he thrust his sword, the point catching the warrior in the stomach. He folded over the blade but, to Macro's astonishment, the finely made mail vest kept the point of the sword out. The blow winded the Brigantian, however, and he staggered back into the press of warriors and out of sight.

Macro found himself in space and uttered a savage roar as he swept his sword out in a wide arc. It was sufficient to discourage his enemies just long enough for a quick glance around to assess the situation. Half the survivors of the First Century had climbed through the breach and were pushing further into the bastion. A short distance behind him he glimpsed the crest of Cato's helmet. Then he turned back, boots braced, his ruined shield raised, sword poised, and let the ragged line of legionaries edge up beside him. Several of the defenders had been struck and lay writhing on the ground and were finished off as the Romans passed over them.

There was a shout and the enemy hurriedly pulled back. Macro paused, and saw a tall warrior standing defiantly ten paces away, Belmatus, in front of a line of archers, arrows notched. The warrior stepped back amid them and raised his sword.

'Front rank down!' Macro yelled. 'Second rank, shields up!'

He went down on one knee, letting his shield drop to the ground. The man behind raised his shield and rested it at an angle on top of Macro's. Those on either side were following suit when the warrior barked a command and the first volley of arrows struck the Roman line with a shattering chorus of rattles and cracking as many of the iron heads pierced the shields, while others deflected overhead, some shafts shattering on impact. A more ragged volley followed, then a third before it became a steady series of impacts as the less skilled archers began to lag behind.

'Macro!'

He turned and saw that Cato had crept forward and was squatting to one side, just behind him. He had tucked his wounded hand inside the soiled strip of ribbon that passed round his waist. His other stabbed his sword into the ground to help him balance as he settled on his haunches.

'Hot work!' Macro grinned, blinking as a bead of sweat dripped from his brow and made his cheek itch as it rolled down to his stubbled jaw. 'In every way. How are we doing, sir?'

'We hold the breach. The Eighth Cohort have started up the ramp. It's about time to unleash the men. The rate the enemy's been going through their arrows they'll be out of them any moment.'

'Let 'em shoot. The lads could use the chance to catch their breath before we get stuck in.'

Cato nodded. 'All right. But be ready when I give the word. And go in hard. I want the bastion cleared as swiftly as we can. Did you see the man giving the order to the archers?'

'The tall bastard? Yes.'

'That's Venutius's brother, Belmatus. If you get the chance, take him down. I reckon he's the commander of the bastion. If he goes . . .'

'I'll see to it.'

Already the barrage of arrows was beginning to slacken and Cato edged back to the rear of the century and looked down the earth ramp. Centurion Lebauscus was powering up the loose surface, barely out of breath. He paused at the top to nod a greeting to Cato and then turned to bellow at his men.

'What the fuck's keeping you, you 'orrible lot? Up here on the double! Last man is on a charge!'

The fittest of his men struggled up, then the standard-bearer, leaning on his staff as his chest heaved.

'What happened to you, sir?' Lebauscus asked as he looked Cato, still covered in loose soil, over. 'You look like a bloody mole. When there's trouble, you're supposed to go to ground, not in it.'

'Very funny, Centurion. You'll back up Macro the moment he gets moving again. Like I said to him, go in hard. We'll worry about taking prisoners later.'

Lebauscus grinned cruelly. 'Yes, sir.'

The new arrivals rested behind their shields as occasional arrows whipped overhead. Cato waited until they had filled the space behind the First Century of Macro's cohort, then he took a deep breath and called out, 'Macro! Now!'

Macro half rose and squinted warily through the split in his shield. Most of the archers had exhausted their arrows and fallen back to join the men massing around Belmatus, tossing their bows aside and drawing their swords. Macro drew a breath.

'First Century! Prepare to charge, and make it loud!'

The men on either side made ready, limbs tense as they awaited the order.

Macro filled his lungs and roared, 'CHARGE!'

A great cry tore from the lips of his men as they powered forward behind their shields, swords levelled and ready to strike. The sudden eruption of battle rage momentarily stunned their opponents and the first of the legionaries plunged in amongst them before they could react. Macro slammed into one of the archers who had begun to back away and was knocked flying by the impact, crashing into two of his companions a short distance beyond. Macro followed through, striking with his shield again before delivering a vicious series of stabs at each of the men. One, armed with a short axe, leaped back after he took a wound to his side, and hurled the axe at Macro's head. He jerked aside and felt the rush of air on his ear as the weapon spun by end over end and cracked against the shield of a legionary behind him. Macro made sure that the other two were out of the fight before he moved on. He was aware of the surge of red tunics and shields on either side of him as his men shouted the name of their legion.

'Gemina!'

The legionaries surged forward, striking their opponents down efficiently and mercilessly. But the Brigantians quickly recovered their wits and rushed forward to meet the Romans, sword and axe against shield and armour. Only a handful had mail vests worn over padded tunics. The rest fought without armour, or even bare-chested, putting their faith in raw courage and disdain for the heavily protected enemy. It was an uneven contest and they fell one by one, inflicting only a few casualties as the men of Rome ploughed through them.

Macro paused to search for Belmatus. Then he saw him, standing beside a tattooed warrior waving a standard steadily from side to side so that all would see the golden bull on a green background in the breathless air of the baking summer's day. A different standard flew over the Brigantian capital today, Macro mused, but he resolved that it would fall before the day was out.

He advanced on Belmatus, only lifting his shield or sword to those directly in his path. Steering a path through the wild melee, exchanging blows when necessary, he confronted the enemy leader. Belmatus had seen the crest of the centurion weaving towards him and moved to intercept him, keen to have the honour of killing an officer. Another warrior rushed in at an angle until Belmatus turned to him and bellowed angrily and the man backed off and turned to find another enemy to fight.

'You want me all for yourself, do you?' Macro growled as he inscribed a small ellipse with the point of his sword. 'Then come and get me.'

For a heartbeat the two men sized each other up as Belmatus raised his longer sword and buckler and lowered himself into a crouch. The Brigantian muttered something. A curse perhaps, Macro thought, or a challenge like his own, as if they were meeting as paired fighters in the arena, and not amid the frenzy of the battle taking place for the possession of the bastion. He decided to make the first move, a feint to test the reactions of his opponent. Macro drew back his sword to make a thrust at the centre of the warrior's chest.

Before he could strike, there was a blur of motion and a legionary slammed into Belmatus's side, his sword taking the warrior under the armpit and disappearing deep into his chest. He let out an explosive grunt and was lifted bodily off his feet and carried another pace before he crumpled on to the ground, spluttering blood.

'What the fuck d'you think you're doing?' Macro howled in rage. 'The bastard was mine!'

The legionary braced his boot on the fallen man's chest and ripped his blade free. He shrugged at the centurion, mumbled an apology and hurried off into the fray, leaving Macro staring at Belmatus with a disappointed expression as the latter writhed feebly on the ground, blood coursing from the fatal wound.

A short distance away the native standard-bearer was also staring at the body in horror, then he looked up as Macro advanced on him, brandishing his sword.

'You'll have to do instead, my friend.'

'*Na!*' The man shook his head and backed off, then turned and ran with the standard towards the rear of the bastion. As the banner fluttered over the heads of the combatants, there were groans of despair from the natives and some turned away from the fight and followed the fleeing standard-bearer. Then Macro saw what the man was heading towards: a small gate on the palisade, opposite the main fort, clearly visible in the background as it was slightly more elevated than the bastion. Panic spread quickly and the Brigantians broke away, retreating a few steps before turning and running. The legionaries went after them, slowed by the weight of their equipment. But as the natives struggled to escape the bottleneck at the gate, the Romans caught up and laid into them. Pressed together, with no space to wield their weapons, the tribesmen were at the mercy of the legionaries. But there was no mercy. Only the urge to kill. And they went about it with violent abandon, thrusting again and again. Mortally wounded men slumped down, some prevented from reaching the ground by the crush around them.

Over the slaughter, Macro saw the standard pass through the gate and disappear from sight as the standard-bearer descended the steps on the far side of the earthwork. More men fought to get through, desperate to escape the crimson blades of the Romans pressing in around them. A small party of legionaries reached the palisade and began to work along it towards the gate and then closed off the only line of retreat for the Brigantians. They began to force the survivors back towards the centre of the bastion.

Macro saw that there was no escape for the fifty or so that remained, surrounded by low mounds of their fallen comrades. He suddenly felt an intolerable ache in his limbs and the full burden of his armour, as well as the stifling heat. He licked his dry lips and forced himself to stand erect as he shouted an order.

'Enough! Stand back!' His voice was hoarse. Too hoarse for his men to hear clearly. He quickly spat and coughed and called out again. 'Pull back!'

It took a moment for the order to penetrate the minds of men caught up in the fiery madness of butchery, but one by one they withdrew from the knot of defenders that still lived until a small gap opened between the two sides. Macro stepped forward, sheathing his blade. He set his split shield down on the ground and pointed a finger at the nearest Brigantian's weapon and then at the ground.

'Drop it!' he snarled to emphasise his demand.

The man nervously did as he was told and tossed his sword a short distance away, beyond the bodies. At once the rest followed suit. Macro glanced round and saw the century's optio. 'Get 'em over to the other side and sit them down. One section to guard them.'

'Yes, sir.' The optio bowed his head and turned to summon men to carry out the order.

Most of the interior of the bastion was devoid of any signs of the struggle. The fighting had been most fierce at the end that had been pulled down and scores of bodies lay on the ground. There were a few more scattered across the rest of the flattened ground, men who had tried to get away but had been hunted down and killed by the first legionaries of the Eighth Cohort to enter the breach. Macro was looking over the bodies when he caught sight of the shaven-headed warrior he had fought earlier. The man lay on his back, head propped up on the bloodied torso of another warrior. Macro squatted down at his side and took a fold of the mail, pursing his lips at the quality of the joints. No wonder it had kept his blade out. Macro removed the dead man's belt, took hold of the sleeves and pulled the armour from his body. He bundled it up and deposited the mail vest with one of the men guarding the prisoners.

'Here. Look after it. I'll want it when this is over.' He wagged a finger at the soldier. 'You'd better make sure it's still here. Understand?'

As the man saluted, Macro caught sight of Cato conferring with Centurion Lebauscus, who nodded and disappeared back down the collapsed bank of earth. Turning towards his friend, Cato came striding across.

'I saw Belmatus back there. You got him then?'

'I would have if some bugger hadn't got in the way. Still, he's dead.'

Cato looked at the heaps of bodies close to the rear gate and let out a low whistle. 'Sweet Jupiter. What a bloodbath . . .' He crossed to the palisade and looked down in time to see the last of those who had escaped running across the narrow strip of open ground and in through the gate of the main fort. A moment later the doors shut with a dull thud and then there was the scrape of the locking bar being eased back into its brackets.

'Let's hope they give a good account of what happened here. Enough to persuade Venutius and his friends that they don't want to share the same fate.'

There were warriors above them on the fort's gatehouse and along the palisade, and some were carrying bows. Cato turned and looked at the prisoners the optio and his men were herding away from the dead. 'Better keep them on this side of the bastion. Might discourage their friends from trying any potshots.'

Macro nodded. 'Good idea.'

Cato looked down the track that Horatius had chosen as his route for the first attack. The ram lay abandoned inside the final bend, surrounded by bodies of the men of the Seventh Cohort. Macro saw them and shook his head in dismay.

'They didn't even come close. What a waste.'

'Indeed.' Cato sighed. 'And we're only halfway there.'

He gestured towards the massive defensive earthworks and the gatehouse opposite them. 'We have the bastion. Now comes the hard part.'

CHAPTER THIRTY-THREE

By the time the Seventh Cohort had dragged the dismantled light ballistas up into the bastion, Lebauscus's men had begun constructing protective screens along the rear wall. The legionaries used the enemy's shields and smaller timbers taken from the front of the fortification. Hurriedly lashed together, they provided cover from missiles directed from the main fort. Then the auxiliaries, armed with slings, moved into position along the length of the palisade facing the gate.

Cato's strategy of using the prisoners to discourage Venutius from shooting across into the bastion had worked for a while, but as soon as the first screens were set up, the enemy reluctantly accepted the risk to their captured comrades and unleashed their arrows. After an initial flurry, which claimed more native lives than Roman, the Brigantians contented themselves with occasional harassing shots to conserve their ammunition.

'Over here!' Cato called across to Centurion Acer, and indicated the makeshift embrasures opposite the fort's gatehouse. 'Set 'em up along the palisade.'

The sweating legionaries carried their burdens over the blood-stained grass and set them down behind the cover of the wooden wall. As more men came up with the baskets of three-foot-long bolts and rounded stones, their comrades set to work reassembling the weapons. The largest component was the heavy wooden frame containing the thick cords of twisted sinew that gave the ballistas their extraordinary power. These were heaved up on to the sturdy wooden stands and secured with wooden pegs and wedges, hammered home with mallets. Finally the missile beds and the throwing arms were slotted home and the loading handles fitted to the torsion ratchets.

'They're ready now, sir,' Centurion Acer reported to Cato as he conferred with Lebauscus, Macro and Vellocatus. The latter, his arm in a sling, had climbed up to the bastion along with the Eighth Cohort.

'Shall I give the order to start shooting?' Acer asked.

'Not yet,' Cato decided. 'When we strike, I want to hit 'em with our full strength. If we can shake them badly from the off then the battle is more than half won. One thing I have learned from fighting these Britons is that if you go at them with speed and ferocity, they have a tendency to lose their nerve. Shock them, gentlemen. That's the trick of it.'

'Nice words,' said Lebauscus. 'But they don't win battles, sir. That's down to men and cold steel.'

Cato nodded. 'And the mind that directs them, Centurion.'

He paused and quickly considered the men at his disposal and the ground before them. It was vital that the officers were clear about their roles in the coming action and the need to co-ordinate their efforts if the attack was to succeed with minimal casualties. They could ill afford to lose any more men. Cato had already considered the consequences if they failed. The column would be obliged to retreat across the frontier as quickly as possible. As soon as Venutius and Caratacus had gathered sufficient men they would pursue the Romans and harry them all the way. The depleted column would need every man to hold the enemy off. He put aside thoughts of retreat and focused on the immediate task.

'Centurion Horatius was right on one count, the only way we're going to get into the fort is by battering down the gate. His method, however, was too direct.'

'That's putting it mildly,' said Macro.

'We still need that ram,' Cato resumed. 'The enemy will be determined to make us pay a high price to recover it. The ram is in full view of the earthworks either side of the gate and the party we send out to fetch it is going to be exposed to a barrage of arrows, spears, rocks and whatever else they have prepared for us. That said, they in turn are going to have to expose themselves when they target our men retrieving the ram. That's where you come in, Acer. I want those ballistas worked hard. Keep the defenders' heads down. You'll command the auxiliary slingmen as well. When the command is given, hit the enemy as hard as you can. Anything to put them off their aim and give our lads the chance to fetch the ram without suffering too many losses.'

'Yes, sir.'

'Which brings us to the small job of retrieving the ram.' Cato turned to Macro with a weary smile. 'How many men are left in your First Century?'

Macro had accounted for his losses during the brief pause in action while the ballistas were set up. 'Forty-eight still on their feet, sir. More than enough.'

'Good. You'll take them out of the breach and go round the front of the bastion. When you hear the signal, you make a dash for the ram, pick it up and carry it to the gate. Then smash the bastard in.'

Macro grinned. 'With pleasure.'

'Excuse me, sir,' Lebauscus cut in. 'But why send in Macro's men? They've done their bit. Better to let my lads do it. They're fresh and at full strength.'

Cato shook his head. 'That's why I'm saving them to deliver the main blow. The Eighth Cohort will be up here, ready to assault the fort through the bastion's gate the moment the ram has done its work. Besides, you're going to have a hard time talking Macro out of the job. Isn't that right?'

Macro laughed and wagged a finger at the other centurion. 'Try and stop me, my friend.'

Lebauscus smiled. 'It's your funeral, Macro. Just trying to help.'

'You'll have the chance to play your part after Macro has succeeded,' said Cato. 'When the gate is down, you'll go in fast and hard. Kill any that resist, but spare any that abandon their weapons. You need to make that point clear to your men. I don't want to kill any Brigantians we don't have to. As far as we're concerned, those who have sided with Venutius and Caratacus have been misled and made a mistake. So we let them live and be grateful for it.'

Lebauscus looked doubtful. 'That'll be hard on the men, sir. You know what they're like when their blood's up.'

'I do. And that's why you need to rein them in, Centurion. When

330

this is over, the Brigantes are going to be our allies again. I'd rather we didn't give them any more pain than we have to. We do not want to leave behind a legacy of bitterness or resentment. Is that understood?'

'Yes, sir. But what about captives?'

'There won't be any. Anyone we capture will be handed over to Queen Cartimandua to decide their fate.'

'No captives?' Lebauscus could not hide his disappointment. 'The men aren't going to like that. I've already overheard some of them talking about their share of the loot.'

'I don't care what they do and don't like,' Cato replied tersely. 'Those are my orders. There will be no captives taken to sell as slaves, and no looting. Any man caught looting or raping will be subjected to the harshest discipline. You will explain that to them as well, and you will be responsible for their actions, Centurion Lebauscus. Clear?'

'Yes, sir.'

Cato looked round. 'Is everyone clear about what they have to do?'

The others nodded and Lebauscus asked, 'What about you, sir?'

'I'll be going in with your cohort. Me and Vellocatus.'

Lebauscus raised an eyebrow. 'With respect, sir. Both of you are wounded. You'd be more of a hindrance than a help.'

'I thank you for your concern,' Cato replied acidly. 'We'll need Vellocatus to call on them to surrender. I'll be there because I am in command.'

'As you wish, sir.'

Cato paused but there were no further questions. 'Very well, then. The signal for Macro to go for the ram and for Acer to start shooting will be one blast of the horn, repeated at intervals until we're under way. Then two blasts for the main attack to begin, and Acer to cease shooting. To your units, gentlemen. Macro, get your men round the back of the bastion. Keep out of sight and be ready to act the moment you hear the signal.'

The officers saluted and strode off to join their men and Cato turned to Vellocatus. 'Time for one last appeal to reason. Ready?'

Vellocatus nodded. 'Do you really think Venutius will surrender?'

Cato stared at him. 'You're Venutius's shield-bearer. You know him far better than I do. What do *you* think?'

'He'll fight,' the Brigantian replied at once. 'He's been a warrior all his life. All he knows is fighting.'

'That's what I feared you would say. But we have to give him a chance. In any case, he'll probably be taking his cue from Caratacus.' Cato smiled ruefully. 'You can imagine what that means.'

'Then why even make them the offer?'

Cato exhaled wearily. 'If there's a chance to end this before another man has to die, then I have to take it.'

He led the way to the auxiliaries crouching behind the palisade and peered cautiously between the hastily erected screens. The fort's gatehouse was no more than forty paces away. The track below the bastion's gate was a short distance below, and then open ground to the ditch and the raised drawbridge. Many of the enemy were in clear view, some of them archers. There was no reason for them to take cover. Not yet, Cato reflected grimly. He turned to Vellocatus.

'You're up. Tell them the Roman commander wants to speak to Venutius.'

'Just Venutius?'

Cato nodded. 'If it helps to undermine Caratacus's standing over there then it's worth a try.'

Vellocatus smiled. 'You understand my people too well.'

The Brigantian cupped a hand to his mouth and drew a deep breath before he shouted across to his compatriots. There was no immediate response, so he repeated his call and this time there was a brief pause and then angry shouts and jeering whistles. Vellocatus turned to Cato who shook his head.

'No need to translate. I got the gist of it.'

The voices from the fort swiftly fell silent, save one, and Vellocatus risked a quick glance over the palisade. 'It's Caratacus.'

'Damn . . .' Cato frowned. It seemed that the Catuvellaunian king had already assumed command of the rebels. 'Say that I want to speak to Venutius.'

Vellocatus called out and there was a beat before Cato heard his enemy's voice reply, in Latin, 'I'm speaking to the Roman commander! Not his treacherous lapdog. You have my word that no one will try to stick an arrow in you. I expect the same in return. Stand up, where I can see you and talk.'

Cato thought quickly. It was too late to try and undermine Caratacus. If he refused to speak to him, Caratacus would tell his supporters that the Roman commander was afraid. And if they spoke in Latin, there would be only a handful of natives who understood enough to follow the exchange. 'I want you to keep translating. Keep it loud, so that as many of them can hear as possible.'

Vellocatus nodded.

Cato took a deep breath and eased himself up on to his feet and warily moved into the open, exposing the top of his body above the palisade. He indicated to Vellocatus to stand but keep behind the screen. The young nobleman shook his head, and moved close to Cato's side as he whispered fiercely, 'I'll not show any fear to those traitors.'

'Good for you,' Cato replied quietly. 'But you get down at the first sign of trouble. You'll be needed later on.'

'Is that my old adversary, Prefect Cato, under that helmet?' Caratacus called out.

'Say that I want to speak to Venutius.'

Caratacus listened to the reply and shook his head. 'I speak for the patriots of the Brigantes. Venutius has honoured me with the command of his men. And I will speak with Prefect Cato and not his lackey.'

Cato raised his voice. 'I demand that the rebels in the fort release Queen Cartimandua and all other hostages, and surrender. I give you my word that all who surrender will not be enslaved or otherwise mistreated. I further guarantee that I will insist that there will be no reprisals by our ally, the queen. My only demand will be the delivery of the fugitive, Caratacus, into our hands.' He turned and nodded to Vellocatus who began to translate his words, until he was interrupted by Caratacus shouting over the top of him.

'And these are my terms, Roman. Abandon your attack and leave Isurium and I will guarantee that you will be given free passage as far as the frontier. I, and my new host of warriors, will spare your lives if you leave Isurium before the day is out. If you are still here at dawn then I swear by our war god, Camulos, that you will all die and your heads will decorate the huts of the warriors of Brigantia. What say you?'

Cato glanced at Vellocatus. 'Tell them what I said again.'

Vellocatus began, but was swiftly drowned out once more. This time Caratacus ended by turning to his men and shouting an order.

'Get down!' Vellocatus grabbed Cato's good arm and pulled him into cover and the first arrow hammered into the screen a moment later. Several more followed, one bursting through the surface of a native shield and showering them with splinters. Cato reached up with his good hand and carefully brushed them from his shoulders. 'That would seem to conclude our attempt to negotiate a peaceful resolution. Time for something more emphatic, I think. Come!'

Staying in a crouch, Cato led the way along the palisade to the end nearest the ram. Then, taking a native shield to protect himself, he dashed over the open ground and peered over the palisade. Macro and his men were in position on the grass slope below, waiting for the signal to begin the attack. Cato turned back and looked across the bastion. Lebauscus had ordered his cohort to kneel and shelter behind their shields. Acer's men were crouched beside their light ballistas and the auxiliaries had the first shots carefully placed into the leather pouches of their slings. All was ready, Cato decided. It was time to put his plan to the test.

The colour party of the Eighth Cohort clustered around the standard. Amongst them Cato could see the shining bronze curve of the horn carried by the soldier responsible for transmitting the commands to the six centuries led by Lebauscus. Cato gestured to Vellocatus to stay close to him and trotted over. One of his men alerted Lebauscus to the approach of his superior and he turned and saluted as Cato reached him.

'It's time.'

Lebauscus nodded.

Cato could see Acer watching, fist clenching over and over as he waited for the order to unleash the Roman barrage. Cato turned to the legionary holding the horn.

'Give the signal.'

The legionary raised the mouthpiece and spat to clear his mouth. Pursing his lips, he drew a deep breath and blew. The horn blared loudly, one long sustained note. He stopped, paused to take another breath and count to five before repeating the note. Before the second blast carried across the bastion, the whirring of slings and the crack of the light ballistas shattered the comparative quiet of the lull in the fighting that had followed the capture of the bastion. From over the palisade came a chorus of shouts as Macro and the remaining men of the First Century bolted from cover and raced towards the ram lying a short distance up the last stretch of track leading up to the fort's gate.

CHAPTER THIRTY-FOUR

'On me, lads!' Macro shouted as he ran up the track. To his right he saw the helmets and faces of the auxiliaries as they whirled their slings overhead and released their missiles. To his left towered the earthworks protecting the enemy's gate. The sudden hail of shot, and the iron-headed bolts and fist-sized stones from the light ballistas had taken the enemy by surprise and they ducked down behind their palisade as the Romans' barrage smashed against the wooden posts. Macro knew the moment would quickly pass and the enemy would do all that they could to cut down the men making for the ram.

It was past midday and the heat had not abated. The air in the sheltered gap between the bastion and the fort was stifling. The weight of his armour and his exertions throughout the morning meant that sweat was streaming from his brow as Macro rushed towards the ram. Before him lay the bodies of the men who had fallen during Horatius's ill-fated attack earlier in the day. Not all of them were dead. Some still writhed and moaned. Others looked up hopefully as they caught sight of their comrades rushing up the track. One reached out to Macro and croaked, 'Water . . . For pity's sake, water . . .'

Macro swerved round him and ran on. He saw a head appear above the fort's palisade, dark against the bright sunlight, and heard the shout as the alarm was raised. Just ahead of him lay the ram, surrounded by bodies pierced by arrows and javelins, and more missiles lay on the ground about them. He reached the head of the ram, cut to an obtuse point to maximise its impact when it struck home. Ropes had been tied round the ram and provided the handles for its crew. Macro cast his ruined shield to one side and heaved aside a body lying across the roughly hewn wood. Then he grasped the handle nearest the front of the ram and glanced back as those legionaries following close behind discarded their shields and took position either side. As soon as there were enough men in place, Macro called out, 'On my command . . . lift!'

With strained grunts the men heaved the ram off the ground.

'Advance!'

They paced up the track as quickly as their burden allowed. An arrow shaft *shicked* into earth no more than a foot in front of Macro and he bellowed over his shoulder. 'Get some cover up here!'

Those men of the First Century who had caught up with their comrades carrying the ram hurried up the side facing the fort and raised their shields to protect themselves and their comrades carrying the ram. More arrows rained down, and stones, but the constant hail of missiles from the bastion forced the defenders to bob up and shoot without taking aim and they had little effect on the party moving steadily towards the gate. By contrast, the Romans in the bastion remained standing as they bombarded the wall of the fort opposite them. Ahead, Macro saw a ballista bolt smash into the top of the palisade, sending a burst of splinters into the air.

An enemy warrior, more foolhardy than courageous, rose up in full view and thrust his sword out towards Macro, exhorting his comrades to shoot the legionaries down. Then he was struck in the chest by a stone and was swept away by the impact, as if snatched from this life by an invisible giant hand.

Then there was cry just behind Macro and he felt the rope handle lurch in his grip. He hissed a curse as he was forced to a stop and turned to look back with a furious expression. One of his men had been struck on the helmet by a rock and had fallen back against the man behind him, causing them both to release their hold on the ram. Macro nodded to the nearest man carrying a shield.

'Take his place!'

The legionary obeyed at once, tossing his shield aside and stepping over the fallen man to grasp the rope handle. As soon as he had taken up the strain, Macro gave the order to continue the advance. They slowly climbed the last remaining stretch of track and approached the ditch in front of the gate. Eight feet across, as near as Macro could estimate it. The bridge had been drawn up and hung a small distance from the gatehouse. Macro gave the order to lower the ram and ordered the nearest three men to follow him. They scrambled down into the ditch and hauled their armoured bodies up the rear scarp, pausing at the top to catch their breath. Macro pointed to the taut lengths of rope bound to the end of the drawbridge.

'We have to cut those! Two men to each. Go!'

While the other legionaries scurried across to the other side, Macro nodded to the third man. 'Back against the wall and make a step.'

The man did as he was told and cupped his hands. Macro placed his boot on the soldier's hands and grasped his shoulders as he heaved himself up. 'Lift!'

The man heaved with a groan of exertion and Macro pressed himself against the wooden timbers of the gatehouse as he felt for the man's shoulder with his other foot. When both were in place, the legionary grasped Macro's calves to steady him while the officer went to work. The exposed rope was a short distance above his head and Macro drew his dagger and reached up. With his left hand clutching the edge of the bridge, he began to saw away at the thick weave of cords, the strands steadily parting beneath the well-honed edge of the blade. All the while Acer's men in the bastion did their best to force the enemy to keep their heads down.

Then there was a shout from behind the gate and Macro glanced down to see the dim form of a man looking up at him from the shade beneath the gatehouse.

'They're on to us!' Macro called across to the men cutting the other length of rope. 'Get moving!'

He continued cutting away furiously at the rope, his muscles aching and burning from the effort as he cursed the rope and willed it to part. Through the gap he could see several men moving towards the gate, and the dull gleam of the head of a spear. The spear point thrust towards him through the gap and glinted in the sun. Macro threw his weight to the side as much as he could while remaining steady on the shoulders of the man straining to hold him up. He just managed to maintain his balance and continue cutting. Only a slender strand remained, taut under the load it carried, which made it easier to work at. With a deep resonating twang the rope parted and the corner of the bridge lurched out, dislodging Macro from his perch on the legionary's shoulders. He fell sideways, scrabbling for purchase on the coarse wooden post beside the gate. The ground came up and Macro landed heavily on his side, the air driven from his lungs with a pained grunt. The legionary stumbled and fell beside him, just as the head of the spear stabbed out of the gap, missing the man by inches. On the other side of the gate the other men were still struggling to cut through the rope.

Macro tried to warn them but was too winded to utter a cry. The legionary with the knife shuddered and gasped as he was stabbed by an enemy warrior but clung on and continued severing the rope. A moment later it parted and the drawbridge swung down and the far end crashed on the lip of the ditch, sending an explosion of dust into the air. The legionary slid off his comrade and fell into the ditch, blood coursing from the spear wound in his groin. But Macro could pay him no attention as he struggled to his feet, still fighting for breath, and saw the enemy warriors retreating into the shadows. Before the Romans on the far side of the ditch could react, the gate swung shut and the locking bar thudded into place. Macro ran back across the drawbridge to the ram with the two surviving legionaries and they took up their rope handles.

Macro grunted an order to his men to lift the ram and it swayed up from the ground. The party moved over the drawbridge and stopped a short distance from the sturdy-looking gates. Each side of them their comrades again raised their shields to protect them all against the men above the gate and on the towering earthworks on each flank. Lining the head of the ram up with the narrow gap between the two gates, Macro yelled over his shoulder, 'Three swings then strike! One . . .'

The men braced their boots on the wooden boards of the draw-bridge and swung the heavy tree trunk back, then let it wing forward as far as its momentum would carry it before swinging it back, harder this time, as Macro called out, 'Two . . . three!'

The men swung the ram forward with all their might and the point crashed against the gates, dislodging more dust that shimmered from the seams.

'Again!'

Macro took up the weight and repeated the process and each time the ram crashed home, more dust and debris showered down on his helmet and shoulders. Then he saw a faint sliver of light between the timbers.

'The gates are starting to give, lads!' he shouted to his men. 'Keep going!'

The next blow drove in one of the thick boards of the gate and light poured through the jagged gap. The Romans let out a spontaneous cry of delight and pounded again, enlarging the opening. Now Macro could see glimpses of the men and weapons waiting for them on the other side. He felt his heartbeat quicken at the prospect of getting to them, avenging the men of the Seventh Cohort and putting an end to the rebellion before it could spread beyond Isurium. There was a deep crack as the locking bar gave way and the gates shuddered inwards a few inches.

'Any moment,' Macro warned his men as they swung the ram back again. Sweat gleamed on their faces but their eyes were bright with excitement. It took several more swings before the bar split in two and the gates leaped back on their hinges.

'Down ram!' Macro ordered. 'Up swords and at 'em!'

His comrades released their rope grips and the ram dropped on to the bridge. Macro turned to one of the men protecting their flanks and thrust out his hand. 'Give me your shield!'

The legionary hesitated for an instant, loathe to give up his personal property as well as his protection. Then discipline re-asserted itself and he handed the shield to Macro.

'Find yourself another back on the track and get stuck in,' Macro ordered as he adjusted his grip and then turned to the gate, drawing his sword. 'Follow me!'

He rushed forward, just as the enemy recovered and began to push back against the gates, forcing them to close. The horn sounded twice from the bastion and began to repeat as the men of the Eighth Cohort let out a roar and charged down the steps to join the attack. Pushing hard against the inside of his shield, Macro braced it against the gates and thrust with all his strength. His men piled in on either side and then behind their comrades, straining to keep the gates from closing. Slowly they stopped moving and the two sides struggled to hold their ground.

'Move aside there!' a voice boomed behind Macro. 'Make way!'

Then he felt someone push him roughly aside as Centurion Lebauscus, big and powerful, threw his weight into the contest. The

340

Romans began to gain ground at once, inch by inch forcing the gates back and opening a gap between them to reveal the dense ranks of the Brigantian rebels beyond, desperately trying to hold their ground.

'Hispania!' Lebauscus bellowed the name of the Ninth Legion. 'Hispania!'

The men of his cohort took up the cry as they added their weight to the struggle. The gates steadily parted until there was room for Lebauscus to fight the men in front of him. He let out a savage snarl and punched his shield into the first of the enemy, battering his body with the bronze boss before he stuck his sword in. The rebel grunted and tried to back away but there was nowhere to go and he was caught between the men behind and the ferocious Roman centurion in front of him, driving his short sword again and again into his vitals. Lebauscus eased back to let the body slip down, then stepped over it and engaged the next man.

At his side Macro pushed into the widening gap and pressed forward, stabbing through the gap between the edge of his borrowed shield and that of Lebauscus. The rebels were shoving their weight behind their own shields and the point of Macro's sword could not find a way through, so he drew it back and pushed. The shouting of war cries died in their throats as Roman strained against tribesman, separated only by the thickness of their shields, and there was no clash of weapons, just the strained grunting, hissed curses and the dull scrape of shield on shield. Each step forward was bought at the cost of immense effort but slowly the Romans edged forward into the shade of the gatehouse.

Macro knew what the next danger would be and shouted an order over his shoulder. 'Rear ranks! Shields up!'

The forward motion slowed and stopped as the legionaries gave themselves enough space to cover their heads with shields overlapping the man ahead of them. Once the men were ready, Macro gave the command to advance and they pressed on into the enemy again. As he expected, the rebels above the gate were standing ready to shoot arrows directly down at the Romans as they emerged into the fort. Some hurled down stones, but the shields kept them out. On the far side of the gatehouse the earth ramparts drew back like a funnel and the legionaries began to spill out on either side as they forced the enemy warriors back.

Macro turned to Lebauscus. 'Take some of your men and clear the gatehouse.'

Lebauscus nodded and forced his way back into the tightly packed ranks behind Macro and edged towards the wooden steps leading up to the tower above the gate. His deep voice sounded over the struggle.

'First Century, Eighth Cohort! Follow me!'

He strode up the steps leading to the rampart, his men running to keep up. A moment later Macro heard the clash of blades and the centurion's voice bellowing a war cry as he threw himself on the rebels manning the tower.

Macro led the rest of the men forward, noting that the enemy were giving ground far more easily now. He slowed his pace and allowed a gap to open up between the two sides.

'Dress the line!'

The men on either side took stock of the position of their neighbours, and the wall of shields shifted a small distance to and fro before the legionaries presented an even front to the rebels. Macro eased his sword forward so that six inches projected beyond the trim of his shield and then he gave the trim a sharp rap. The men followed suit and a sharp unsettling rhythm echoed across the interior of the fort.

'Forward!'

The two sides closed on each other again, but this was the kind of fight the legionaries were trained for, and excelled at. Using their shields as protection and to batter their foes, they stabbed only when the enemy exposed their bodies. The Brigantians, more used to a free-flowing melee, could not easily wield their longer swords and long-hafted axes or spears and began to fall beneath the grinding advance of the heavily armoured men assaulting the fort. Lebauscus's men were fighting their way along the ramparts either side of the gatehouse, steadily forcing their opponents back. Across in the bastion their comrades ceased their bombardment as they caught sight of the legionaries on the wall of the hill fort.

Then Macro saw a gap opening in front of him as the rebels backed away and aside, to reveal several warriors in mail armour with kite shields and gleaming helmets. He recognised their leader at once. Venutius.

CHAPTER THIRTY-FIVE

Venutius had joined the fight to steady the failing nerve of his followers. He had seen Macro's crest and made straight for him. With lips curled back from his clenched teeth, he surged forward and swung his sword in an arc at the crest of the centurion's helmet. Macro threw his shield up and went down on one knee just before the blow landed. He allowed the shield to give as he absorbed some of the numbing impact. At once he rose and threw his weight forward in a bid to throw Venutius off balance as the latter recovered his sword. He was rewarded with an impact against the warrior's shield and Venutius was forced back half a pace.

Then, with surprising speed, the Brigantian punched his shield forward, stopping Macro in his tracks. He slashed at the Roman shield, driving it into Macro's shoulder. At the same time Macro curled his own sword round in a sharp arc and the point tore through the sleeve of Venutius's tunic and struck his elbow. Ripping the sword back, Macro presented his shield and growled, 'First blood to me . . .'

Venutius paused and shifted his shield to test the joint, then came on again, slamming his shield forward and then pulling it back to counterbalance the vicious cut from his sword. This time Macro tilted the shield to deflect the blow and not block it. The blade gave a shrill clang as it glanced off the boss and slid over the curve of the shield and down towards the ground. Macro thrust the shield out to drive his opponent's arm out wide and then hacked at the exposed flesh in a brutally unorthodox move. The edge cut deeply and the force of the blow caused Venutius's muscles to leap and his fingers extended involuntarily and his sword dropped to the ground. His face screwed up in surprise as he snatched his wounded arm back.

Macro charged into him, hitting him again with the shield, and hooking his boot solidly behind his opponent's leg before he thrust again and Venutius tumbled on to his back. Macro sprang forward, sword point lowered, and thrust the tip towards the warrior's throat, stopping less than an inch from where his throat pulsed nervously. The fall of their leader stunned those close by and they fell back, aghast, leaving the immediate ground to Macro as he stood over the body of Venutius. Every instinct in his body told him to strike, kill his enemy, and move on. But then he recalled Cato's order. Spare all who could be spared.

'Surrender!' he shouted at the man beneath him.

Venutius stared back but did not answer.

'Surrender, you big barbarian bastard!' Macro flicked his sword hand and let the point graze the side of Venutius's neck. 'I won't tell you again.'

Venutius grasped the meaning of Macro's words, and the deadly intent behind them. He licked his lips and called out to his followers. They did not seem to respond at first and Macro feared that their leader had ordered them to fight on and sell their lives dearly. But then the first of them edged back from the Roman line. Then another, more quickly, until the Brigantians were a safe distance from the Roman shield wall. The men who had accompanied Venutius into the fight stood their ground a short distance behind where he lay on the ground at the mercy of the centurion, then one threw his sword down, followed by his shield. After a tense pause, the others followed suit and then rest of the rebels began to do the same.

Macro cleared his throat to shout to his men. 'Hold!'

The legionaries stood still, swords poised, but made no attempt to advance or strike at their enemy. A stillness filtered out across the area around the gate as the fighting stopped and the enemy threw down their weapons.

'Round them up!' Macro ordered, breaking the spell. 'Get 'em away from the gate but don't harm the buggers.'

As his men edged forward again, indicating with their swords that the Brigantians should move aside, Macro withdrew his sword and gestured to Venutius's followers to help him up. Once he was on his feet Venutius clasped a hand over his wounded arm and looked down in shame, refusing to meet Macro's gaze.

'Macro!'

He turned and saw Cato striding through the gatehouse, the men of the follow-up centuries of the Eighth Cohort moving aside to let him through. Vellocatus followed at his heels. The prefect was smiling with relief as he approached his friend. 'Thank the gods! You've done it, Centurion Macro. Fine work, my friend.' Then Cato saw Venutius and he grinned. 'Fine work indeed!'

He scanned the faces of the men around the rebel leader. 'But no sign of Caratacus. Ask him where Caratacus is.'

Vellocatus spoke hurriedly and Venutius looked up with a sneer as he recognised the voice but made no reply. Vellocatus asked again, more insistently, and still there was no reply. Instead Venutius spat on the ground in front of his shield-bearer.

'We must find him and make sure that the queen is safe. Come on!' Cato led the way past the defeated warrior with Macro, Vellocatus and a body of legionaries following on behind. The Brigantians parted before them, like whipped dogs. Passing beyond the ranks of the enemy, Cato and the others hurried between the huts until they emerged on the open stretch of ground in front of the great hall of the tribe's ruler. Some women and children saw them and ran for the cover of the huts. Outside the hall, guarding the entrances, were several men armed with spears. They hefted their weapons when they caught sight of the approaching Romans.

'Tell them Venutius has surrendered. Tell them the rebellion is over and they're to throw down their arms.'

Vellocatus called out to his compatriots as they approached. There was only the briefest of hesitation before the men saw the legionaries emerging from between the huts and accepted the truth of the shield-bearer's words and laid down their weapons.

'Macro, see to them,' Cato ordered as he continued to the entrance of the hall. He stepped warily across the threshold into the gloomy interior and it took a moment for his eyes to adjust. Then he saw that the benches and tables had been cleared to the side and over a hundred people were sitting on the floor, faces turned towards him, relieved to see the Roman officer and knowing what his entrance meant. Cato had no time for them but looked to the far end of the hall. Queen Cartimandua was standing in front of her throne. Beside her stood

Caratacus, one hand clamped tightly round her wrist. Cato approached them steadily, the sound of his nailed boots on the flagstones loud in the stillness.

'The fort has fallen and Venutius has surrendered,' he said clearly. 'The rebellion has been crushed. Now you too must surrender.'

'Liar!' Caratacus called back. 'Venutius would never surrender.'

'He did, and now he's our prisoner. As you are. It's over, Caratacus.'

'No! I shall never be your prisoner.'

There was an intensity to his words that alarmed Cato and he slowed to a stop, ten paces from the Catuvellaunian. He feared the man might mean to end his life rather than be captive once again, to be sent to Rome and his fate decided by the Emperor. As if in answer to Cato's thoughts, Caratacus suddenly drew the dagger from his belt. Then, with a violent jerk, he pulled Cartimandua in front of him, locked his left arm round her throat and pressed the tip of the blade against her breast, directly over the heart. Cartimandua's mouth opened in surprise and she gave a strangled gasp of terror.

'You'll let me go,' Caratacus said, 'if you want her to live.'

Cato drew a deep breath and shook his head. 'You're not going anywhere. Not any longer. Your war against Rome is over. It's finished.'

'That's what you think. I'll find another tribe. Other warriors with more courage than Venutius demonstrated. The war will go on.'

'No. It won't. I can't let you leave here.'

'If you don't, she dies. Do you really want to be responsible for the death of an ally of your Emperor? He'll have your head for letting it happen.'

Cato shrugged. 'He might. But until then, I think your capture is more important than the queen's death. If you surrender now, you may live. If you harm the queen, then I will kill you by my own hand. I swear this on my honour.'

'Kill me? Do you think you could defeat me in a fight? Man to man?'

More footsteps sounded as Macro and a section of legionaries entered the hall and approached the confrontation. Cato smiled and jerked his thumb over his shoulder.

'Not just me, it seems.'

Caratacus glared bitterly at the Romans as Macro came forward and stood beside Cato, shield in one hand and bloodied sword in the other.

'Let her go,' Cato said gently. 'Let her go and surrender.'

Caratacus jerked his head, more of a nervous tic than a refusal, as if he could not even contemplate the thought of surrender.

'Think it over,' Cato urged. 'If you kill this woman in cold blood, then the name of Caratacus will be reviled the length and breadth of Britannia. Is that what you want? Would you not rather be remembered for being the most indomitable of the Britons? You still have your honour. You have fought until the last. That is something no one can ever take from you . . . If you release her and surrender now.'

Caratacus's jaw set hard and he looked to be in agony. A low keening groan sounded in his throat. Then he slowly lowered his arms and gently pushed Cartimandua aside. She backed away swiftly and jumped down from the dais and hurried towards the protection of her Roman allies. Cato kept his eyes on the man standing alone and forlorn, then his gaze fell down to the dull gleam of the blade.

'Don't do it, sir. I beg you. You still have your life, and your family. They wait for you at Viroconium.'

Caratacus stood still and looked at him fixedly, an expression of pure desolation and grief etched into his face. Then he gave a deep sigh and sheathed his dagger. Cato approached him cautiously and held out his hand. 'I'll take that. If you don't mind.'

Caratacus thought for a moment and then pulled the blade out again and offered the handle to Cato.

'Thank you, sir.' He breathed a soft sigh of relief and turned to the nearest of the legionaries. 'Take King Caratacus to join the other prisoners.'

The soldier saluted and approached the enemy leader, watching him closely. Caratacus climbed down and allowed the man to take his arm and steer him down the length of the hall towards the light streaming in through the entrance.

Cato turned to the queen. 'Are you all right, your majesty?'

She smiled nervously. 'I am now, thank you.'

'And these people?' Cato indicated the prisoners who were stirring now that the drama was over.

'We were treated well enough. No one was harmed.' She nodded towards the entrance. 'If you don't mind, we've been cooped up in here since yesterday. Some fresh air would be welcome.'

For the first time since entering the hall, Cato realised how hot it was inside and he nodded. 'By all means. The rebels have been disarmed. Your people here might want to take their weapons.'

Cartimandua looked at him suspiciously. 'Your men would permit that?'

'Of course, your majesty. You are the queen of the Brigantes once more. I will leave a unit of my men here while you restore order and decide the fate of the rebels. Send my men back to the camp the moment you feel they have served their purpose.'

She looked at him shrewdly. 'I am in your debt, Prefect Cato. Or at least in the debt of your tribune, Otho. Where is he?'

Macro suppressed a smile as Cato stroked his chin before he replied. 'The tribune felt it best to entrust the capture of the fort to professional soldiers, your majesty. He will resume command of the column now that we have carried out our task.'

'I understand. Thank you, Prefect, and you too, Centurion.'

Cato bowed his head and Macro followed his lead.

The queen dipped her head in acknowledgement and was about to turn towards her people when Cato spoke again. 'There is one further matter, if I may?'

'Yes?'

'You might show some leniency to the rebels. Now that we have Caratacus, there will be no figurehead to lead those who would wage war against Rome. Except Venutius of course.'

Cartimandua's expression darkened. 'He will pay the price for his treachery. There are ways a man can die that make every instant of the process an unbearable torment.'

'I'm sure that's true. But he's a spent force now. The rebellion has been crushed at the outset. If you execute him, I fear it will only fuel the resentment of those who followed him.'

Cartimandua fixed her penetrating gaze on Cato. 'As you pointed out, I am the queen. The fates of Venutius and all those foolish enough to listen to him are mine to decide.'

'Of course. I only meant to offer my advice. Nothing more.'

'And I thank you for it.' She turned away dismissively and strode towards those who had remained loyal to her. As they made their way out of the hall, Macro shook his head.

'Could have been more grateful, given the blood that our men have shed to save her skin.'

'True. But we're here to serve Rome, and right now, putting her back on the throne is what is in Rome's best interest. Take some satisfaction from that.'

'Seems like I'll have to, given that we're not even going to get any loot out of it.'

At mention of the word, Cato glanced round the hall and saw that the legionaries were poking around curiously. 'I want these men out of here. Make sure they haven't lifted anything first.'

'Sir!' one of the legionaries called out and the two officers turned to see the man standing in the doorway leading through to the chamber at the rear of the hall. 'You should see this.'

They hurried over as the soldier ducked back inside. The room was lit by a hole far above a small fireplace and a single beam of light shone down at an angle. The legionary was standing next to an open chest at the side of the room. Part of the beam lay across the chest and reflected off the contents on to the inside the lid. Cato and Macro crossed the room to join the soldier and saw that the chest was filled with silver coins. All three stared at the hoard in silence for a moment.

'That explains a lot,' said Macro. 'Now we know how Venutius persuaded so many to back his cause.'

'Indeed,' said Cato.

Macro coughed. 'So what do we do with it, now that it's ours? Spoils of war?'

The legionary looked up hopefully.

Cato shook his head. 'No. It stays here. The queen will need it to buy off any remaining troublemakers.'

Macro looked horrified. 'But, sir—'

'It stays here, Macro. And we don't touch it. Those are my orders.' He turned to the legionary. 'You're to remain here and guard it until further notice. And don't even think about helping yourself to so much as one coin. Understand?'

'Yes, sir.'

Macro was still looking longingly at the silver. He reached down and picked up a handful and held them up. 'A hundred or so wouldn't be missed.'

'Macro . . .'

'A pity,' the centurion replied. 'A fistful of freshly minted denarians would be a nice little souvenir of our visit to Isurium.'

Cato frowned and muttered, 'Freshly minted?'

He reached down and picked up a coin. Sure enough, it was as Macro said. Barely a scratch on it, and he recognised the imprint well enough from the year before when he and Macro had been in Rome and the coins had just come into circulation, depicting the Emperor visiting his troops. A sudden thought struck him and he lifted the coin to his nose and sniffed.

'Good enough to eat, eh?' Macro grinned, clearly hoping that avarice had worked its merry way with his superior.

'Not eat . . .' Cato replied with a cold, calculating expression. He closed his hand round the coin and shut the lid of the chest. 'There's one final matter to be resolved before we return to Viroconium.'

CHAPTER THIRTY-SIX

'A fine result, Prefect Cato.' Otho beamed as he sat at his table in the headquarters tent with Cato. Outside, dusk was slowly swallowing the daylight. As the day had been sweltering so the evening was warm and close, and the insects were swarming to feed on the blood of the men who had been sweating in heavy armour throughout the day.

Following the defeat of the rebels and the release of Queen Cartimandua, Cato had ordered the auxiliary troops to remain in the fort at the disposal of the queen. The legionaries had cleared the fort, bastion and slopes of the hill of the dead and wounded. The former had been brought back to the camp and laid in long lines outside the main gate, while funeral pyres were built for the following day. The wounded were brought back in carts and wagons to be treated by the surgeons assigned to the column. Once the wound to his hand had been cleaned and dressed, Cato had a brief conversation with Macro before sending him on an errand, then made his way to headquarters.

'We have Caratacus in the bag, and we've stamped down on the anti-Roman sentiment amongst the Brigantes. The Druid's body was found amongst the dead and Queen Cartimandua owes us a considerable debt, and she knows it. As I said, a fine result all round.'

Cato suppressed a grim smile at the tribune's use of 'we'. Otho had spent the day safe in the camp and had merely acted as a spectator of the grim struggle to take the fort. He had not felt the heat, the exhaustion and the naked fear of battle. He had not fought the enemy, nor incurred any injury, and yet he was already taking credit for the result. It was not hard to guess how the final report of the mission to Isurium submitted by Otho to Legate Quintatus would bear only a passing resemblance to the actuality.

'We have concluded the task we were sent here to carry out,' Cato agreed. 'Although our success has come at a cost.' He paused to recall the details of the butcher's bill that Macro had brought him shortly before they had left Isurium to return to the camp. 'Besides the death of Prefect Horatius and Centurion Statillus, the Seventh Cohort lost sixty-eight men killed, and another ninety-two were injured. Including two centurions and an optio. The First Century of Macro's cohort lost twenty-one dead, and fourteen wounded. The other units got off lightly. The Eighth Cohort, six dead and eighteen wounded, and the auxiliaries ten dead and fifteen wounded. Only one of the Blood Crows was wounded. Knocked from his saddle while chasing down one of the fugitives from the fort.'

Otho nodded soberly. 'A sad loss of life, I'm sure. But sometimes one cannot cook an omelette without first breaking a few eggs, nay?'

'Eggs? I am not sure that I find that comparison easy to accept, sir.'

'A figure of speech, Prefect. Of course, our dead will be honoured and Rome will be saddened by the news, and grateful that they were prepared to make the supreme sacrifice for the good of the empire.'

'Yes, sir.'

There was a pause before Otho cleared his throat and continued. 'Now that the military operation is over, there is no reason why command of the column cannot revert to me.'

'That is true, sir,' Cato conceded. 'In accordance with the orders of Legate Quintatus, I hereby return command of the column to you.'

Otho breathed a quick sigh of relief. 'I thank you, Cato. Be sure that I will give you full credit for the role you played in our victory today.'

Cato bowed his head slightly.

'Then it only remains to prepare the column to break camp and march back to Viroconium,' Otho said cheerfully. 'I confess, I won't be sorry to return to the civilised comforts afforded by the army's base, such as they are.' He gestured to Cato's soiled uniform and the dressing tied round his hand. 'You could use a good wash, Prefect, and a change of clothes. I dare say you're exhausted as well. I suggest you look to yourself for the next few hours now that I have lifted the burden of responsibility from your shoulders.'

'Thank you, sir. I will do that. But first there is one final matter that must be dealt with.' Cato felt a tremor of anxiety as he broached the subject. 'One that touches on the rebellion at Isurium, as well as the escape of Caratacus from our custody at Viroconium.'

'You must not let the fact that you were responsible for his escape weigh on your conscience,' said Otho graciously. 'After all, your deeds before then, and certainly since, have more than made up for it.'

'I was not responsible for the escape, sir. That was the responsibility of another person.'

'Who then?'

Cato did not want to identify the culprit before he could justify his accusation. 'Sir, you will recall that the men guarding Caratacus were killed before they could react to their assailant.'

'Yes, so?'

'So it is my belief that they either knew their attacker, or that they had no reason to fear they were in danger.'

'I suppose so. What of it?'

'Then there is the question of who told Venutius that General Ostorius had died. That helped to provoke the deposing of Queen Cartimandua. Only a handful of us knew about the general's death last night and we had agreed to keep it from the Brigantes until they had handed Caratacus over to us.'

Otho nodded thoughtfully. 'You, me and Centurion Macro, besides my wife. I take it you do not suspect me? And if not me, and obviously not you, that leaves Centurion Macro.' He paused. 'I understood you are close friends. You've served together for many years. Surely you do not suspect Macro?'

'No, sir. I trust Centurion Macro with my life. I would never suspect him of betrayal.'

'Then it must have been someone else. The soldier who brought us the message. I'll have him questioned.'

'It wasn't him. He left the fort soon afterwards. It had to be someone else.'

All trace of his earlier good mood drained from the tribune's face as he grasped Cato's point.

'What are you saying, Prefect? Are you accusing me? How dare—'

'Not you, sir.'

353

'What?' Otho looked confused. 'Then . . . My wife? Poppaea? Are you quite mad?'

'No, sir. Just disappointed in myself for not realising it sooner.'

The tribune's expression darkened. 'If this is some kind of a joke, I am not amused.'

'Where is your wife at the moment?'

'Resting in my personal tent, not that it's any concern of yours.'

'Sir, a moment.' Cato stood up and walked stiffly to the tent flaps and looked outside. Macro was waiting a short distance away with Septimus and Centurion Lebauscus, just as Cato had arranged with Macro a while earlier. Both were admiring the new mail vest he'd taken as a trophy from the bastion. Cato beckoned to them and the three men joined him in the tent.

Otho looked up suspiciously. 'What is the meaning of this?'

'That's what I was wondering,' said Septimus as he glanced at Cato and cocked an eyebrow. 'Is it, perhaps, that you good gentlemen wish to order a stock of wine to celebrate your glorious victory?'

Cato let out an impatient sigh. 'It's time to put an end to your act.'

'I'm sure I don't know what you mean, honoured Prefect.'

'What in blazes is going on here?' Otho demanded. 'Why have you brought the wine trader in here?'

'He is no wine trader, sir. His name is not Hipparchus, it's Septimus, and he's an imperial agent, sent by Narcissus to uncover a plot against the Emperor. Specifically, he was tasked with identifying a traitor, namely, your wife, sent to Britannia to undermine our efforts to bring peace to the province. Not only that, but she was to ensure that myself and Centurion Macro were disposed of. Isn't that right, Septimus?'

For a moment the imperial agent was silent, his expression a blank mask. Then he nodded. Otho stared at him in surprise.

'An imperial agent, sent here to spy on my wife? Is that it? It's a bloody outrage. Poppaea is innocent. It's absurd to suggest otherwise.'

'Is it, though?' asked Cato. 'Perhaps that's how it appears. Who would suspect a high-born woman, the wife of a senior tribune? Certainly not the two men who were killed in order to release Caratacus. Certainly not me, not even after the battle when I now believe she tried to pass poisoned wine to me in the mess tent. Most important of all, not you, her husband, who was more than happy to permit her to accompany him on a crucial mission to the capital of the Brigantes, where she revealed the death of Ostorius to our enemies. Which reminds me, did you ask her to come, or did Poppaea insist? For that matter, whose idea was it really for her to accompany you to Britannia?'

The tribune's jaw sagged as he listened to Cato's words, then he shook his head. 'It's not true. It can't be. Not Poppaea. Where is your evidence!'

'She has been adept at covering her tracks. Except for the matter of passing on the news about Ostorius. There she took a risk, but she needed to in order to provide Venutius with a weapon to undermine the queen. Who else could have done it, sir? You? Me? Centurion Macro?'

'Why not you, or your friend?'

'Because we know where our loyalties lie. We took an oath to serve the Emperor. We're soldiers, not secret agents. That's why.'

'Bloody right we're not,' Macro added emphatically.

Tribune Otho shot him an angry glance, then turned his gaze back to Cato. 'I repeat, where's your evidence? Without hard evidence why should I believe you?'

Cato scratched the stubble lining his jaw. 'I don't doubt that Poppaea would play the innocent, and play the part well. After all, she has been very convincing as the pampered wife of an aristocrat. I should have suspected her earlier. There's nothing I can do about it now, other than report this back to Narcissus. I dare say he will be most keen to question her when he gets the chance. And if it turns out that Poppaea confesses that she has been working for Pallas, she will be in grave danger, as will any person closely associated with her.'

The blood drained from Otho's face. 'You wouldn't . . .'

Cato thought a moment and then shook his head. 'Perhaps I wouldn't, but he most definitely would.' He gestured at Septimus. 'Isn't that right?'

The imperial agent gave a thin, humourless smile. 'Yes, Tribune. It's my duty to protect the Emperor and nothing stands in the way of that.'

'Nothing,' Cato repeated. 'You see, Otho, your wife is playing a very dangerous game. Not only is she risking her own life, she's risking yours as well. There are men in Rome, like Septimus here, who are adept at quietly doing away with the Emperor's enemies. Believe me, you don't ever want to be there on the day when they knock at your door.'

The tribune slumped down on his chair and lowered his head into his hands, muttering, 'It can't be true . . . Not my Poppaea.'

'It is true,' Cato insisted. 'The question is, what is to be done about the situation? Clearly, she cannot be permitted to remain with the army. Poppaea must be sent back to Rome. If she was my wife I would make sure that she understood that this must all stop. Before it led to anything fatal.' Cato paused a moment. 'Sir, if you love your wife, then for her sake, you must make her abandon her secret life.'

Otho was silent for a moment, hunched over his desk as he stared down at the ground in numbed horror at the revelations about his wife. 'I can't believe it.'

'Trust me, all that I say is true. If you want her to live, you must ensure that she gives up working for Pallas and abandons her scheming for ever. Do you understand?'

Otho looked up, a faint expression of hope on his face. 'You'd let her live?'

'Only on the condition that she does as I ask. If not, then others will make the decision about her fate.'

'Now wait a minute!' Septimus interrupted. 'She's a traitor. There will be no mercy shown to her. My father wouldn't stand for it.'

'Your father is not here,' Cato said flatly.

'No, but he'll hear about this. Then you'll be in deep trouble yourself, Prefect Cato.'

'Shut up,' Cato responded wearily. 'Just shut your mouth.'

'What?' Septimus stepped forward. 'You dare to challenge my father, or me? What do you think Narcissus will say when he finds out that you have let her go? Your life will be forfeit. Better to let me take Poppaea back to Rome for questioning.'

'I don't think so,' Cato replied. 'Besides, I doubt that you would take her to Narcissus at all. Far more likely you would turn her over to Pallas.'

Septimus gaped at Cato before he asked softly, 'What do you mean by that?'

'That will become clear in a moment.'

Otho rose from his chair and made to leave the tent.

'Wait!' Cato blocked his way. 'There's something more.'

'What more could there be?' Otho replied coldly. 'You've said enough.'

'Not quite enough. Sit down.'

Otho hesitated, but then returned to his chair and slumped on to it. 'Well?'

'You should know that your wife was not acting alone. She had an accomplice. Someone who was sent to Britannia after her, to reveal himself and aid her in her schemes.'

'And who would that be?'

Cato stepped aside and gestured towards Septimus. 'Him.'

'Me?' The imperial agent started. 'What bollocks is this?'

Cato stepped up to him and stared him in the eye. 'You are working for Pallas, are you not?'

Septimus's brow crinkled and he laughed nervously. 'You're joking. You know I work for Narcissus. You know it.'

'That was true, until recently. Until you realised which way things were going in the power struggle between Pallas and Narcissus. You saw that Narcissus was losing influence over the Emperor. And once Claudius has gone and his wife, Agrippina, ensures that her son becomes Emperor then Narcissus is as good as dead, and his followers along with him. You decided that it was time to switch your allegiance to his enemy, Pallas. So when Narcissus sent you here to foil the plot, he never suspected that you would in fact be doing your best to ensure its success. Mind you, I should have guessed earlier myself.'

'Lies!' Septimus snorted. 'This is insane. Narcissus is my father. You think I would betray my own father? My flesh and blood?'

Macro glowered at him. 'Narcissus is a scheming snake. I'd place good money on the odds that his offspring has inherited the same characteristics.'

'Pfft!' Septimus rounded on Cato and jabbed a finger at him. 'Where's the evidence? You couldn't lay any at the door of Poppaea and it's the same for me. You can't prove a thing.'

Cato smiled thinly. 'That's where you're wrong, Septimus. You've covered your tracks fairly well. Except for one thing. We knew that

Venutius needed treasure to buy support for his rebellion. Without it, he was helpless. And then, suddenly, he had access to a fortune. We found a chest of recently minted coins up in the fort. Coins just like this.' He fished the silver denarius he had kept earlier and held it up for the others to see. 'Roman. You gave it to him. From the small hoard of silver you brought with you from Rome to buy the services of anyone who could help your true master's cause. You gave Caratacus a small fortune in silver in the hope that it would allow him to buy off Venutius and his followers and sabotage our efforts to bring peace to Britannia.'

'More lies,' Septimus scoffed. 'He obviously got the silver somewhere else. From Poppaea most like, given that we know she's a traitor.'

'Yes, that's what I thought at first,' Cato admitted. 'But then I asked myself how she could have delivered the silver into the hands of Venutius. I couldn't see how it was possible.' He handed the coin to Tribune Otho. 'There, sir. Examine it closely.'

Otho frowned, wrenching his thoughts away from his wife's treachery. He lifted the coin and scrutinised it in the dim light of the oil lamp. He shrugged. 'It's a denarius, like any other.'

'Not quite like any other,' Cato responded. 'Smell it.'

Otho hesitated and then sniffed cautiously. 'It smells of . . . slightly . . . of vinegar?'

'Not vinegar, cheap wine. Septimus has been storing the coins in his wine jars. The same jars I saw him handing over to Venutius's men yesterday.'

The tribune sniffed again and then lowered the coin as he stared at Septimus. 'Is this true?'

'Of course not! It could smell that way for any reason. He's lying.'

Macro delivered a sudden, hard, blow to Septimus's stomach, winding the man. 'Don't you ever dare accuse the prefect of lying, your treacherous cunt.'

Septimus slumped on to the ground, on all fours, gasping for breath. The others regarded him silently for a moment before Cato spoke. 'I should have seen it all much earlier. From the moment Caratacus escaped. Someone had to put the two guards at ease so that he, or she, could get close enough to kill them quickly. A moment's work for anyone trained to use a knife. That would be you, or Poppaea. Most likely she claimed to want to have another look at the prisoner, with you at her side, offering them a sample of your wines. As soon as you were close you went in with the knife. Between the two of you it was over in an instant. After you had got Caratacus out of the pen you planned to get him out of the camp in your cart. Of course, you had to make it look like he had beaten you senseless and run off with your cart and mules. Hence the blow to your head, and before that the deliberate planting of your purse in my tent, just so that you would have a good reason to be passing by when Caratacus escaped, and could make up the story about being knocked out and your cart taken.'

'But I *was* knocked out.'

'It had to look convincing. But the blow was light enough. That's what the surgeon said at the infirmary.' Cato weighed him up and shook his head sadly. 'There's no longer any doubt in my mind, Septimus. You were working for Pallas from before the time you left Rome. You murdered two of Macro's men, you helped Caratacus to escape and you provided the silver that destabilised the Brigantian nation. The question is, what do we do with you now?'

'So what are we going to do with him?' asked Macro.

Cato cleared his throat and answered in a flat voice. 'He's going to disappear. Just like his victims back in Rome. I'll tell Narcissus that he was killed during the fight with Venutius. There's nothing to be gained from telling the truth about his son.'

'Why not tell him?' asked Macro. 'He deserves to know what kind of creature he's fathered.'

Cato shook his head. 'Narcissus has no future. He's doomed. I see no reason to add to what he is bound to suffer at the hands of his enemies.'

'Really?' Macro sniffed. 'Then you're a better man than I am.'

'No. I don't think so, my friend. Besides, Narcissus's influence may be on the wane but he's still powerful enough to come after us to avenge his son.'

'So what now?' Lebauscus interrupted. He gave Septimus a kick that sent him sprawling. 'What do we do with this piece of shit?'

Cato answered without hesitation. 'He dies. He dies now. Macro, get him up on his feet.'

Septimus's eyes widened in terror and he tried to crawl towards the entrance to the tent. But Macro was on him in an instant and wrestled him to his feet before pinning his arms behind his back.

'Lebauscus . . .' Cato nodded. 'Kill him.'

'My pleasure,' the centurion growled. He drew his sword and approached the squirming spy. Leaning forward he snarled, 'This is for the lads who died today.'

'Wait!' Septimus gasped desperately. 'You can't—'

Lebauscus held his sword low and angled the point up sharply. Then he thrust the blade through the cloth of Septimus's tunic, through his stomach and up under his ribcage. Septimus threw his head back against Macro's shoulder and his mouth gaped in a pained gasp. Lebauscus gritted his teeth as he withdrew the blade and thrust again, working it around inside the man's vitals for good measure. Otho looked on in horror at the execution.

'No . . .' Septimus gasped softly, as if his protest could save him. 'No.'

Lebauscus wrenched his sword back and stepped away from his victim. The front of Septimus's tunic was already drenched with blood and as Macro released his grip, he fell to the ground and rolled on to his side, struggling to breathe. His lungs had filled with blood and it spurted from his lips as he convulsed for a while and then, at last, lay still. Lebauscus leaned down to use the dead man's tunic to wipe the blood off his blade.

'What now?' asked Macro. 'Get rid of him?'

Cato shook his head. 'No. Leave him here. I think the tribune here needs to be reminded of the dangers of plotting against the Emperor. This time it's Septimus. The next time it could well be his wife, and anyone close to her . . . Let's go.'

Cato was turning to leave when they all heard the sound of a challenge from close by and then a figure appeared at the entrance to the tent.

'Tribune Otho?'

'Yes.' Otho tired to recover his composure. 'That's me.'

'Message from Legate Quintatus, sir.' The man entered the tent and now Cato could see that he was covered in dust and grime from several days on the road from Viroconium. He stopped as he saw the body and glanced at the officers. When no one reacted he reached inside his sidebag and brought out a leather tube bearing the legate's seal. He handed it to the tribune and stood back from the table.

Otho held the tube in his hand and looked over the new arrival as he tried to recover his composure. 'You could do with some refreshment. Have one of my clerks see to your needs.'

'Yes, sir.' The soldier saluted and, with one last glance at the body, he strode out of the tent.

Otho continued to hold the message in his hands as he regarded the corpse. The others stood silently until at length Cato coughed. 'Aren't you going to read it, sir?'

'What? Oh . . .' Otho shook his head. 'No. Not yet. There's something I have to do first. Before I can take command of the column. You're in charge, Cato. Until I'm ready to resume command . . . You read it.' He rose abruptly from his chair and moved round the desk, thrusting the leather tube at Cato. 'Read it, and act on it as you see fit. If you need anything, I will be with my wife.'

Cato nodded. 'Yes, sir. I understand. I'll take care of it.'

Otho nodded. 'Thank you. You're a good man. I can see that.'

He stepped carefully over the body and hurried away, brushing through the tent flaps, leaving them swaying in his wake. Cato turned to Lebauscus. 'I think we've made our point. Have the body removed. Take it out of the camp and have it buried. Leave no trace, though. As if the earth swallowed him. Understand?'

'Yes, sir.' Lebauscus saluted. 'I'll see to it.'

He left and Cato took the tribune's chair and broke the seal on the tube. He took out the roll of papyrus inside and flattened it out on the table to read the contents. At length he looked up and met Macro's expectant gaze.

'Well?'

'The legate wants us back at Viroconium as fast as we can march. There's trouble amongst the Ordovices. The Druids have stirred them up again. They are raiding along the entire frontier. Quintatus needs every man to hold them back.'

Macro shrugged. 'No rest for us then.'

'Seems not. We'll break camp tomorrow, after the men have rested. They've earned it.'

361

'And so have we, my lad. So have we.' Macro smiled. 'As it happens, I know of a small cache of wine that needs drinking up. One previous owner. Want to join me?'

Cato stood up. 'Yes . . . Yes I do. I need a drink.'

'That's the spirit. Come on then.' Macro steered him gently towards the tent flaps. Outside, the last band of light stretched along the horizon and the first stars pricked out of the velvet night sky. Some birds called out in the darkness, clearly audible above the quiet hubbub of the familiar noises of the camp. They strode away from the headquarters tent and Macro chuckled.

'And who knows, if we're lucky, we might just come across a few coins that he's missed along the way. It's not just clouds that have a silver lining.'

A BRIEF INTRODUCTION
TO THE ROMAN ARMY

The Fourteenth Legion, like all legions, comprised five and a half thousand men. The basic unit was the *century* of eighty men commanded by a *centurion*. The century was divided into eight-man sections which shared a room together in barracks and a tent when on campaign. Six centuries made up a cohort, and ten cohorts made up a legion, with the first cohort being double size. Each legion was accompanied by a cavalry contingent of 120 men, divided into four squadrons, who served as scouts and messengers. In descending order, the main ranks were as follows:

The *Legate* was a man from an aristocratic background. Typically in his mid-thirties, the legate commanded the legion for up to five years and hoped to make something of a name for himself in order to enhance his subsequent political career.

The *Camp Prefect* would be a grizzled veteran who would previously have been the chief centurion of the legion and was at the summit of a professional soldier's career. He was armed with vast experience and integrity, and to him would fall the command of the legion should the legate be absent or *hors de combat*.

Six *tribunes* served as staff officers. These would be men in their early twenties serving in the army for the first time to gain administrative experience before taking up junior posts in civil administration. The senior tribune was different. He was destined for high political office and eventual command of a legion.

Sixty centurions provided the disciplinary and training backbone of the legion. They were handpicked for their command qualities and a willingness to fight to the death. Accordingly, their casualty rate far exceeded other ranks'. The most senior centurion commanded the first century of the first cohort and was a highly decorated and respected individual.

The four *decurions* of the legion commanded the cavalry squadrons, although there is some debate whether there was a centurion in overall command of the legion's mounted contingent.

Each centurion was assisted by an optio who would act as an orderly, with minor command duties. Optios would be waiting for a vacancy in the centurionate.

Below the optios were the legionaries, men who had signed on for twenty-five years. In theory, a man had to be a Roman citizen to qualify for enlistment, but recruits were increasingly drawn from local populations and given Roman citizenship upon joining the legions. Legionaries were well paid and could expect handsome bonuses from the emperor from time to time (when he felt their loyalty needed bolstering!).

Lower in status than the legionaries were the men of the auxiliary cohorts. These were recruited from the provinces and provided the Roman Empire with its cavalry, light infantry, and other specialist skills. Roman citizenship was awarded upon completion of twenty-five years of service. Cavalry units, such as the Second Thracian Cohort, were either approximately five hundred or a thousand men in size, the latter being reserved for highly experienced and capable commanders. There were also mixed cohorts with a proportion of one third mounted to two thirds infantry that were used to police the surrounding territory.

AVAILABLE THIS AUTUMN ON MOBILES AND TABLETS

THE CATO AND MACRO BATTLE GAME WILL BE AVAILABLE TO DOWNLOAD THIS AUTUMN ON MOBILE PHONES AND TABLETS.

IMMERSE YOURSELF IN A FAST-PACED, FUN AND ADDICTIVE GAME FEATURING THE ROMANS VERSUS THE BARBARIANS. UNLOCK EXTRA CONTENT, WIN PRIZES, AND PROVE YOURSELF ON THE BATTLEFIELD.

ROMA INVICTA!

CATO
AND
MACRO

THE GAME

AVAILABLE THIS AUTUMN

CATO AND MACRO
THE GAME